THE THINGS THAT FLY IN THE NIGHT

The Things That Fly in the Night

Female Vampires in Literature of the
Circum-Caribbean and African Diaspora

GISELLE LIZA ANATOL

Rutgers University Press
NEW BRUNSWICK, NEW JERSEY, AND LONDON

LIBRARY OF CONGRESS CATALOGING-IN-PUBLICATION DATA

Anatol, Giselle Liza, 1970– author.

The things that fly in the night : female vampires in literature of the Circum-Caribbean and African diaspora / Giselle Liza Anatol.

pages cm. — (Critical Caribbean studies) (American literatures initiative)
Includes bibliographical references and index.

ISBN 978-0-8135-6574-3 (hardback)

ISBN (invalid) 978-0-8135-6573-6 (pbk.)

ISBN 978-0-8135-6575-0 (e-book)

1. Caribbean literature—History and criticism. 2. Literature—Black authors—History and criticism. 3. Vampires in literature. 4. Tales—Caribbean Area. 5. African diaspora. I. Title.

PN849.C3A54 2015

809'.89729—dc 3

2014017496

A British Cataloging-in-Publication record for this book is available from the British Library.

Visit our website: http://rutgerspress.rutgers.edu

Manufactured in the United States of America

THE
AMERICAN
LITERATURES
INITIATIVE

A book in the American Literatures Initiative (ALI), a collaborative publishing project of NYU Press, Fordham University Press, Rutgers University Press, Temple University Press, and the University of Virginia Press. The Initiative is supported by The Andrew W. Mellon Foundation. For more information, please visit www.americanliteratures.org.

To Dee, who keeps me grounded but also pushes me to fly

Contents

Preface

I grew up in suburban New Jersey, but my dreams were haunted by the *soucouyant*. According to the stories shared by my Trinidadian aunts, mother, and grandmothers, the soucouyant seemed to be an ordinary old woman by day. Each night, however, she shed her skin, transformed herself into a ball of fire, flew about the community, and sucked the blood of her unsuspecting neighbors. Afterward, she would return home and slip back into her skin, and the repeated practice made her human form unusually wrinkled. She would not be able to re-don her outer membrane, however, if someone had discovered its secret hiding place and salted or peppered it; this would cause the soucouyant to perish in a frenzy of itching and burning. She could also be destroyed by scattering salt or rice on the doorsteps and windowsills of one's house: she might be able to enter the premises to satisfy her bloodlust, but she was obligated to count each grain before leaving. At dawn, if neighbors caught her in the midst of her task, they would beat her to death or drop her into a vat of boiling tar or oil; some storytellers alleged that the rising sun would destroy the skinless incarnation of the creature. (In one instance—the version found in Edgar Mittelhölzer's novel *A Morning in Trinidad*—the soucouyant has to bend down so low, for so long, to pick up every grain of rice, that she breaks her back and dies.) In any case, the phrase "soucouyant gon' come for you" has chilled the blood of Trinidadian children for generations—and not just those who misbehaved: *anyone's* blood could lure the soucouyant into their home.

As I traveled and met people from other Caribbean countries, I learned that skin-shedding, bloodsucking creatures could be found in a variety of cultures: Jamaicans and Guyanese might call her Old Hige or simply a hag; in Suriname, one could be drained by an *asema*; Haitians sometimes refer to *volant* or *loogaroo*; a St. Lucian might tell you about *gens-gagée*. What I found fascinating was that in most communities, the folk figure was exclusively female. As an undergraduate with an emerging feminist consciousness and then as a doctoral student focusing on Caribbean women's literature, my curiosity about the soucouyant stories intensified. What did it mean that this fearsome creature of the night was consistently female? How did a "neutral," if not sought-after, characteristic such as longevity come to be the source of suspicion and stigma for women? This tendency is not exclusive to the Caribbean, of course—stories of wicked old hags and witches can be found in cultures around the world. But in the case of my own cultural heritage, I began to wonder what other messages were conveyed by the story. Were the tales meant to train young girls to be content with staying at home instead of roaming their communities like men? Did they teach young boys to expect and demand this domestic containment from their mothers, sisters, wives, and daughters? Was the fear generated by the soucouyant's preying on her neighbors focused on the act of drinking blood, anxieties about having one's blood unknowingly and involuntarily taken, the fact that the creature was unrecognizable while traveling abroad as a ball of flame, or something else altogether? And what was to be made of the removable skin?

When I first embarked upon my study, the trend of recovering folktales was still prevalent in Caribbean scholarship. Collections such as Roger Abrahams's *Afro-American Folktales: Stories from Black Traditions in the New World* (1985), Gérard Besson's *Folklore and Legends of Trinidad & Tobago* (1989), Daryl Cumber Dance's *Folklore from Contemporary Jamaicans* (1985), Velma Pollard's *Anansesem: A Collection of Caribbean Folk Tales, Legends, and Poems for Juniors* (1985), Diane Wolkstein's *The Magic Orange Tree and Other Haitian Folktales* (1978), and Michael Anthony's *Folk Tales and Fantasies* (1976), as well as the work of Richard Dorson, Alan Dundes, Christine Barrow, Melville Herskovits and Frances Herskovits, Martha Warren Beckwith, and Elsie Clews Parsons, among others, proved to be valuable sources. However, these texts concentrate on the transcription and preservation of folktales rather than analytical interrogation. The more recent *Sacred Possessions: Vodou, Santería, Obeah, and the Caribbean* (1997) is one collection that moves away from this practice, combining descriptions of folk traditions with extensive analysis of the significance of various practices and representations. Editors Margarite Fernández Olmos and Lizabeth Paravisini-Gebert argue that African-derived religions and systems of belief have been vilified by mainstream culture, often in response to a real or perceived threat to European cultural and political dominance. As I will demonstrate throughout this book, the Black female vampire occupies a similar vilified space. However, rather than only serving to malign ethnic, cultural, and racial practices and traits, she also indicates society's negative attitudes toward women who appear as threats to patriarchal structures and gender norms. Much like traditional renderings of Lilith in the Jewish tradition, the messages embedded within the soucouyant tales mandate identification with community and family rather than a solitary life, maternity and nurturing rather than sexual fulfillment, and being "grounded" in the reality of the homespace. In short, they deter women's independence and their physical as well as imaginative mobility.

In the 1990s, more and more Caribbean authors—particularly women writers—began to employ the figure of the soucouyant in their fiction. Sometimes the depictions were conventional, but more often than not the skin-shedding, vampiric character was rendered in positive ways. These writers participate in a type of intellectual "voyage in" as described by postcolonial theorist Edward Said: they engage in a "conscious effort to enter into the discourse of Europe and the West, to mix with it, transform it, to make it acknowledge marginalized or suppressed or forgotten histories" (*Culture and Imperialism* 216). Similarly, while several contemporary African American writers might employ the figure of the vampire more conventionally—that is, without the skin-shedding feature—they, too, address concerns about exclusion from mainstream visions of society: their novels also attempt to wrestle with and complicate a Eurocentric patriarchal discourse. *The Things That Fly in the Night* explores the range of Black female vampires in literature of the African diaspora, particularly throughout the Americas. It begins by considering the intersecting gender and race messages conveyed by the traditional legends, takes a brief detour to explore narratives by White British writers from the nineteenth century—an era that generated the principal figure of the Vampire—and then moves on to consider how people of the Caribbean and Caribbean and African diasporas have appropriated these stories to suit their artistic, social, and political goals.

Acknowledgments

I am extremely grateful to the many, many people who contributed to the writing of this book; it is by no means an individual effort. I would, however, like to acknowledge several people in particular.

For my initial inspiration, I thank Professor Inés Salazar, whose spring 1995 class on African American and Latina feminisms spawned the first version of this work in the form of a graduate seminar paper. My English 774 classes from fall 2007 and spring 2011 helped me think and rethink ideas for the book as it was in its developmental stages. Members of the "KU in KC" writing group—Tamara Falicov, Kim Warren, Ann Rowland, and Nicole Hodges-Persley—gave me invaluable advice on various parts of the manuscript. Members of the University of Kansas (KU) English Department Gender & Sexualities writing group—Dorice Elliott, Dick Eversole, Doreen Fowler, Joe Harrington, Mary Klayder, and Misty Schieberle—also provided many insightful comments on the project. Participants of KU's Latin American & Caribbean Studies Merienda Series and the African & African American Studies Brownbag Lunch Series enthusiastically listened to preliminary talks on the project. Hannah Harris at the Spencer Museum of Art went above and beyond in helping me garner the proper rights and permissions for the fabulous cover illustration. Gerry Besson was wonderfully generous with his time, visual materials, and additional stories, many of which I lament could not make it into the book. My KU graduate research assistants, DaMaris Hill, T. Renee Harris, and Kristen Lillvis, served as super-sleuths, looking up missing page numbers and lyrics, tracking down additional sources, and serving as discerning readers of the manuscript.

Special thanks to experts in other fields who pointed out connections between medical conditions and vampirism (especially Dr. Kenneth Sonnenschein) and vampirism in different animal species (especially Professor Ray Pierotti). I have great appreciation for librarians everywhere, but I particularly thank Glenroy Taitt and the University of the West Indies Libraries Special Collections staff, as well as the Schomburg Center for Research in Black Culture staff, particularly Diana Lachatanere, former director of Collections and Services, Steven Fullwood in Manuscripts, Archives, and Rare Books, Alison Quammie in the Recorded Sound Division, and research assistant Naomi Bland. I also extend thanks to Colin Palmer, the former director of the Schomburg Scholars-in-Residence Program, and the spring 2012 scholars for their enthusiasm about the project and perceptive critiques.

Parts of my investigation were supported by the University of Kansas General Research Fund (FY 2007 and FY 2006) and a 2013–14 Shirley Cundiff Haines & Jordan L. Haines Faculty Research Fellowship. At Rutgers University Press, Katie Keeran was remarkably prompt and efficient but also encouraging and kind; Michelle Stephens's careful reading of my drafts and excellent suggestions of additional texts helped me further articulate my argument.

On a more personal note, but no less important, Sandra Pouchet Paquet, Daryl Cumber Dance, and Maryemma Graham have pushed me forward in my career for over a decade now, and I am grateful for all their words and acts of mentorship. I am deeply obliged, as always, to loving family and friends. Brenda Campbell and Camille Campbell Busby drove me back and forth to the UWI campus and were incredibly patient when I lost track of time in the stacks; Simone Anatol hunted down the 1982 folklore series of stamps from the Trinidad & Tobago Philatelist Society; my mother, Ann Anatol, fed me the fabulous foods of my childhood and refused to let me do dishes or grocery shopping when I stayed with her during my residency at the Schomburg. MJ and Miles Skyped and called to cheer me up when I got homesick in New York and good-naturedly waited for lunches, dinners, trips to the park, and trips to the mall while I wrote "one more line" or read "one more page." And D. allowed me to leave her with the kids for three whole months while I gallivanted around New York City's libraries. And reinvigorated me with endless words of confidence and inspiration. And snuck me the occasional Oreos, peanut M&Ms, and Snickers bar at 11:00 at night.

Finally, thanks to all of the people who shared their renditions of the soucouyant story with me but especially Auntie Yolande and Auntie Joan. I remember their stories the best.

Introduction

[E]very age "discovers" what in a work of art relates most to its own needs and desires, even if the artist himself was not consciously aware of all he created.
—LESTER FRIEDMAN

Soucouyant. Ol' Suck. Old Hige. Volant. Loogaroo. Gens-gagée. These words bring terror to the minds of children raised on Caribbean folktales about the elderly woman who keeps to herself, often chasing people from her yard or sleeping the day away, and then emerges from her skin at night, becomes a ball of flame, and plagues her community by drinking people's blood—sometimes straight from their hearts. For adults as well as children, the word "soucouyant" and its equivalents conjure images of frightening old age; alarmingly bloody, skinless creatures; terrifying invasions of the home; and nightmarish penetrations of the body. This book takes a closer look at the legend and the ways contemporary authors of the circum-Caribbean and other parts of the African diaspora have incorporated the lore into their writing. We have all heard the phrase "Sticks and stones can break your bones / But words can never hurt you," but what exactly lies beneath the words and tales that have been transmitted over many generations? Words can obscure ideas of much greater substance—a framework or symbolic skeleton that guides our social existence. As the novelist Tessa McWatt attests in *Out of My Skin*, which is explored in Chapter 5, "some words hide truth just like fat hides bone" (82). *The Things That Fly in the Night* attempts to strip away the "fat" and reveal the "bone" beneath traditional and reappropriated renderings of vampiric women in African diasporic—and particularly circum-Caribbean—narratives. A good many scholars have interrogated the connections between sexuality, gender, violence, and "respectability" in African diasporic popular culture forms; however, most of them focus on the media of music and dance (Cooper; Davis; Mohammed; Paquet, Saunders, and Stuempfle; Rohlehr; Sheller; etc.). I delve into the neglected form of folk narratives—both traditional textual transcriptions of folktales and literary adaptations in folk collections, novels, short stories, and poetry, as well as in calypso lyrics and visual art. Like Mimi Sheller, who attempts to illuminate a "theory of freedom" through her work on political structures that "legislate, govern, and police particular embodiments and sexualities" in the Caribbean ("Work That Body" 345), I unveil and hope to loosen the constraints to female empowerment and mobility that are inherent in most "vampire" tales—texts that are grounded in the notion of bodily encounters that occur in intimate, private spaces because a monstrous figure has transgressed numerous borders.

After interrogating a series of conventional narratives, I then turn to recent fictional treatments of the Black female vampire figure—a burgeoning genre since the 1990s—to explore how some contemporary writers propose to shift the power dynamics and urge for private *and public* erotic agency for women of the African diaspora. While Donna Haraway's 1985 "cyborg manifesto" argued for a blending of categories, especially given that "[t]he boundary-maintaining images of base and superstructure, public and private, or material and ideal never seemed more feeble" ("Manifesto" 207), the perimeters for many African Americas women (and with "African Americas" I resist the limiting U.S. scope of the term "African American") were increasingly reified and policed during this time period. The writers tackled in *The Things That Fly in the Night* battle "the privatization of violence, abuse, and terror within the household, the workplace, or the closed community" (Sheller, "Work That Body" 357) by bringing certain bodily encounters out of the dark, so to speak—out of the realm of the soucouyant's secretive nighttime flights,[1] out of the realm of the demonic, out of the obscurity of metaphorical associations—and into more explicit depictions of women's bodily sovereignty.

Furthermore, by following Irad Malkin's discussion of network theory but expanding it to include neglected references to writings from the Black Atlantic, I posit that the vampire narratives under investigation here establish a "small world" out of a discontiguous group of populations throughout the Caribbean and its diasporas as well as other communities—both African and non-African—in North America, Europe, and Africa. Caribbean literature and theory have long embraced this notion: the poet Kamau Brathwaite, for example, has asserted since 1974 that instead of "archipelago: fragments," it is more productive to contemplate that Caribbean "unity is submarine." The historical and cultural links between far-flung descendants of the Middle Passage are also well documented. However, the soucouyant stories, unlike a singular "Caribbean" identity, or a fixed moment in history and one-way passage from one continent to another, provide multiregistered, multidirectional, repeatable (if not repeating) ties between various geographical nodes, enhancing a sense of connectivity. Because the stories emerge from different geographical spaces, different local contexts, *and* different historical moments, highlighting "diffusion rather than concentration, [. . .] divergence rather than convergence" (Malkin 8), individuals familiar with soucouyant tales are revealed to share a collective identity that exists alongside other collective identities and can interact with those identities in a multitude of ways. One might, for instance, make a map indicating all locations to which Africans were transported during the slave trade, superimpose upon it a map of all places where soucouyant stories have been recorded, and superimpose upon *that* a map with lines marking where Caribbean sugarcane workers migrated during the nineteenth and twentieth centuries, followed by a map illustrating all known festivals, dedications, and rituals involving the goddess Erzulie. The soucouyant network will not lie directly upon any of the others but can overlap and work "with" *or* "against" the others. A soucouyant "network"—one in which physical space, lived experience, *and* "the space of the collective imagination" come together (Malkin 12)—plays a dynamic and creative role in shaping its members and their societies. And moving outside the realm *and* concept of a fixed, geographical space is something at which the soucouyant excels.

Metaphors of Vampirism in Political Discourse

The British Romantics claimed the vampire as a figure of mystery and rebellion against the social order, while early twenty-first-century interpretations of the vampire in mainstream North American and British culture cover a tremendous range, including metaphors for disease and contagion, rampant (often "perverse") sexuality, superheroic control and stoicism, and divinity. In 2011, Tomislav Longinović published *Vampire Nation: Violence as Cultural Imaginary*, an analysis of the late twentieth-century rhetoric used to establish Serbs as the metaphorical vampires of Eastern Europe, a violent and parasitical people associated with spillage of blood, dirt, and soil. This highly politicized trope of the vampire has been used for decades in the Caribbean and throughout the African diaspora to comment on the exploitation of colonized people and landscapes. In Langston Hughes's "Columbia," first published in 1933, one finds the lines

You're getting a little too old,
Columbia,
To be so naive, and so coy.
Being one of the world's big vampires,
Why don't you come out and say so
Like Japan, and England, and France,
And all the other nymphomaniacs of power (ll. 21–27)

The poem's speaker refers to the United States by the first popular moniker for America—"Columbia," the feminine derivative of Christopher Columbus's name—masking an explicit reference to the nation in the same way that the vampire's dangerous presence to its community is masked by its human appearance. Notably, Hughes's symbolic vampire does not prey on all human beings but rather "all the little brown fellows / In loin cloths and cotton trousers" (ll.10–11), pointing to racial and class predation unlimited by the geographical borders of the United States.

In 1955, the poet and postcolonial theorist Aimé Césaire published *Discours sur le colonialism*, or *Discourse on Colonialism*, a text that also implicitly addressed the vampiric nature of the colonial enterprise. Charging Western "civilization" with hypocrisy, *Discourse* describes the "appetite" of capitalists such as the "merchant," the "adventurer and the pirate" (10), whose greed—a type of vampiric thirst—exported all items of value from the colonies, sucking the land dry of raw materials and the laborers dry of their physical efforts, energy, and wealth. Césaire also aligned later colonizers' actions with the vampire: apparently invoking the European literary tradition, the Martinican writer referred to "these Gothic invasions, this steaming blood" (19) of brute military force, as well as a sort of vampiric conversion or transformation of the colonized since, rather than truly educating their subjects, colonizers were involved in the "hasty manufacture of [. . .] subordinate functionaries" (21). Like Frederick Engels, who a century before had explicitly named the propertied members of British society as the "vampire property-holding" class, and Karl Marx, who similarly described the French bourgeoisie as a metaphorical vampire, draining the life-blood from peasants and laborers by using Capital—"dead" products and commodities—Césaire spoke about class and politics. Each of these writers, however, failed to address the gender dynamics inherent to the equation.

Literary critic H. L. Malchow provides several other examples from England, where the image of the vampire was used to demonize capitalists, particularly those who crossed national borders for economic exploitation. A 1733 pamphlet, for example, accused Dutch financiers of sapping Britain's financial strength: "These are the *Vampires* of the Publick, and Riflers of the Kingdom" (quoted in Malchow 159). In the nineteenth century, when Jews were still associated with blood libel—the literal stealing of Christians' blood—and deceitful business practices, they were also configured as metaphorical vampires: "unscrupulous company promoters and (often Jewish) stock-jobbers were 'vampires,' [and] 'bloodsuckers'" (160). But members of the English upper class were also cast in this light since they figuratively "devoured the world" (74). English landowner Lord John Manners complained that members of the Anti-Corn Law League referred to him and others of his class as "vampires, Bloodsuckers" (269n115).

In more recent work, Mimi Sheller uses the language of vampiric drainage in *Consuming the Caribbean: From Arawaks to Zombies* (2003), taking women into greater consideration. The consumption of her title ranges from the symbolic "evisceration" of the Caribbean from Western conceptions of the world and notions of modernity—despite the archipelago's critical role in Europe's rise to economic, political, and cultural dominance (1)—to Europeans' rapacious desires for Caribbean delicacies and stimulants (sugar, rum, tobacco, medicinal plants, etc.)—desires that contributed to exploitation, death, and destruction in their colonies—to the exploitation of Caribbean women's bodies in the contemporary sex tourist industry. Like Césaire, Sheller posits Europe as a metaphorical vampire that has sucked the life out of the region, devouring "the natural environment, commodities, human bodies, and cultures" for over five centuries (3). Her research, however, is sociological. I propose to examine how these ideas filter into the literary and other artistic forms produced by the subjects at hand, very much parallel to Gina Wisker's reading of Erna Brodber's novel *Myal* (1988), which she argues uses the figure of the zombie to delve into the ways that colonizers "disempowered, deenergized, disenfranchised, and silenced colonized and enslaved people, taking from them their identities, histories, languages, and their right to imagine and to speak" (417–18). One poignant example of the figurative European bloodsucker in contemporary fiction can be found in the Jamaican writer Olive Senior's short story "Lily, Lily" (1989). In it, one of the narrators links England's political and economic practices in its West Indian colonies to vampiric monstrosity: "This country for centuries has been drained of its lifeblood to build up Mother England and the white people there" (141). The narrative plot, however, focuses on the everyday lives of a small community, where girls and women are exploited by local men as well as foreign men, Black as well as White. Senior's critique of conventional gender roles and her relegation of superficially "good men" to the realm of the monstrous come sharply into view.

The Power of Blood

In many of the texts explored in this book, the idea of consumption can be seen in a variety of ways: as political, economic, or social metaphor, as the spiritual draining of souls, and, more literally, as the ingestion of blood and accompanying depletion of the victim's bodily strength. For my purposes here, however, notions of cannibalism do not function in nearly as compelling ways as the concept of a vampiric satiation of thirst with blood. Sensuality and pleasure get lost in allusions to the cannibal, who might consume out of hunger, for strength, in a militaristic practice, or in sacred ritual. Vampirism more adequately conveys the carnal satisfaction associated with the act of imbibing another person's blood—whether this act is construed as demonic in early texts or extolled in the later ones. Thus, while there is certainly fear involved, fear is not the only emotion at stake. As Anne McClintock explains in *Imperial Leather*, explorers often voiced their terror—of getting lost, or swallowed up by the landscape, of death, of monsters, of monstrous women with their dreaded *vagina dentata*—by projecting images of the self onto the cannibal: "[The Americas as] riotously violent and cannibalistic represents a doubling within the conqueror, disavowed and displaced [onto the conquered landscape. . . .] [T]he fear of being engulfed by the unknown is projected onto colonized peoples as *their* determination to devour the intruder whole" (27).[2] The perspective is one-sided, eradicating the viewpoint of the Other but also erasing scenes of physical delight, emotional contentment, and the seduction involved when blood is taken.

Sheller, too, relies on the framework of cannibalism more than that of vampirism in her work, and granted, the taboo against cannibalism is a potent one in the Caribbean, stemming from Christopher Columbus's journals about the peaceful Arawaks versus the fearsome, flesh-eating Caribs and William Shakespeare's anagramic transcription of Caliban for the Can[n]ibal in *The Tempest*. Sheller provides examples of early ethical debates over the bodies of Amerindian, African, and Asian laborers who were diseased, viciously whipped, and otherwise mutilated during the production of "comestible commodities" (*Consuming the Caribbean*

74). However, in many cases, the drinking of another's blood was an equally potent signifier. In 1791, William Fox published his "Address to the People of Great Britain, on the Propriety of Abstaining from West India Sugar and Rum." It proclaimed that although the government might force sugar (and other products manufactured by enslaved people) "to our lips, steeped in the blood of our fellow-creatures; [...] they cannot compel us to accept the loathsome portion" (quoted in Sheller, *Consuming the Caribbean* 89). Likewise, a French writer of the time observed that he could not "look upon a piece of Sugar without conceiving it stained with spots of human blood" (quoted in Sheller, *Consuming the Caribbean* 88). Quaker abolitionists of the eighteenth and nineteenth centuries employed illustrated leaflets in a visual campaign targeting U.S. American and British women—the purchasers of many of the food items produced by slavery, such as sugar, molasses, and coffee, which were represented as "soaked in African blood" (73). And poet Robert Southey echoed this vampiric imagery when he identified sugared tea as a "blood-sweetened beverage" (Hochschild n.p.).

One should not overlook the powerful taboos against miscegenation that might also have influenced this discourse: revulsion over the idea of ingesting blood can be linked to the anxiety over what happens to that blood when it is taken into another's body, mixing in the digestive system and in the veins. As I discuss in Chapter 6, aversion to having one's blood ingested by others is easily relatable to the abhorrence of "contaminated" blood and "mixed" subjects—people who threaten the ostensible purity and separation of the races when the boundaries of sexual propriety are crossed. According to *Dracula* scholar John Allen Stevenson: "Blood means many things in [Stoker's novel]; it is food, it is semen, it is a rather ghastly parody of the Eucharist, the blood of Christ that guarantees life eternal. But its meaning also depends on the way humanity has made blood a crucial metaphor for what it thinks of as racial identity. Blood is the essence that somehow determines all those other features—physical and cultural—that distinguish one race from another" (144). As might be expected in these cases, the language and suggestiveness of blood are much more potent than those of cannibalism.

The draining of one's blood versus the consumption of one's body must be considered from the perspective of the African diasporic subject and not only from the conventional Western point of view. African slaves often longed for death during the brutality of slavery; being swallowed whole might have been seen as a gift rather than a fate to be avoided. I contend that the slow and tortuous draining of their literal blood through punishing beatings or the depletion of their "life-blood," or essence, through the agonizing and humiliating existence of slavery would have been perceived as much more horrific than the prospect of death and thus more readily incorporated into certain folktales such as the soucouyant stories.

In *Haiti, History, and the Gods* (1995) Joan (now Colin) Dayan details Haitian folklore about vampiric creatures such as *soucriants* (blood-suckers), *lougawou* (vampires), and *bizango*, which "are known by their hunger for humans, usually children" (258). The mixed and fluid terminology of oral tales becomes apparent here: in many stories, *lougawou* (also spelled *loogaroo*) are blood-drinking vampire figures, while in others—such as the Trinidadian *lagahoo* tales—the creatures more closely resemble European werewolves and the relationship to the French term *loup garou* is clearer. Either way, Dayan, too, interprets these creatures as "remnants" of the institution of slavery. Rather than viewing the monsters as representations of the people draining the life force out of their enslaved victims, however, she posits that the stories represent how slavery "turned humans into things, beasts, or mongrels" (258). Dayan identifies skin-shedding as the trait of yet another monstrous being: the *san pwèl* or *san po* ("without skin"). She asserts that these folktales are abstracted recollections of enslavement on the island of Hispañola, when slaves had their skins flayed and applied with "pepper, salt, lemon, and ashes." Her argument finds coherence with the early twentieth-century story "The Oranges," collected by Suzanne Comhaire-Sylvain in "Creole Tales from Haiti" and published in the *Journal of American Folklore* in 1937: a boy's wicked stepmother threatens to "take all the skin off his body" for eating her oranges, which causes intense fear (230). When a different informant relates a similar tale, the stepmother simply threatens, "I will kill you" (234), but later in the story the sibling protagonists sing, "Our stepmother said / She would skin us, my orange!" (235).

Dayan's claim that "Phantoms of domination and scenes of the past return, transmogrified and reinvested with new meanings" (265) also resonates in the work of the Guyanese novelist Roy Heath, who similarly argues for recognizing the connection between the myths that many dismiss as frivolous superstitions and the very real, though "puzzling[,] reflections of our fretful bitter past" (88). Although Heath clearly connects the Afro-Guyanese folk figure "Coolie Jumbee" to the "anxiety of the freed African slave[. . . .] in the face of the newly arrived indentured [East Indian] labourer" (86–87), and he identifies the Old Higue as one of the three most widely known folklore characters in Guyana, he never specifies what traumatic past or present experience the female skin-shedder might be associated with. Thomas Glave, too, links soucouyants, jumbies, and duppies to the legacies of slavery that haunt contemporary Jamaicans and other peoples of the African diaspora but does not distinguish between the figures (44). I propose a focus on the female figure as well as a more specifically articulated interpretation of her meaning—one that goes beyond the "monstrous" demon who merely "confounds the natural order of things" (Dayan, *Haiti, History, and the Gods* 265): as the soucouyant story gets retold and reworked by storytellers from generations further and further away from slavery, the fright associated with the peeling of the skin as well as the drawing of blood from another person remains, but a distinct shift occurs so that the action evokes a sense of agency and power. In other words, the soucouyant is no longer frightening as an objectified "thing" or "beast" whose skin has been removed by a separate brutalizing force, and neither is she the subjugated being whose blood oozes because of the viciousness of the master's whip. Instead, she is horrifying because she can strip off her own skin and penetrate the skins of others; she is also the one who draws blood, not leaks it. She is a powerful actor, not acted upon.[3]

Prohibitions against the spilling of blood and, even more commanding, anxieties over female menses have ensured that the association between blood and women remains gruesome. In cultures on every continent of the world, blood has long been viewed as a taboo substance. For the Kaguru of western Tanzania, "any spilled human blood is considered dangerous" to the natural order and "polluting" to the environment (Renne and van de Walle xxv). In the Middle Ages (although not exclusively then), Jews in Europe were accused of blood libel—sacrificing Christian babies and using their blood to make matzoh. The crime was not simply murdering "innocents" but consuming the stolen human blood. It might be argued that allegations of monstrous bloodsucking are rare in Africa prior to the arrival of Europeans because the consumption of blood was not considered as taboo as it is in the Judeo-Christian tradition, but it should be noted that in pre- and post-contact African societies, the blood consumed was typically from animals, not humans. In the Mandingo culture of present-day Mali and Guinea, for example, blood offerings are made to the divinities at weddings, the construction and consecration of new houses, harvest time, and the birth of a child (through the burial of the placenta). Throughout Africa, one can find the belief that the blood of animal sacrifices "purif[ies] the world, washing away corruption and recreating life" (Lainé 10). In stark contrast, the consumption of human blood was—is—typically looked upon with hor-ror. Furthermore, the consistent fear of *pilfered* blood reveals that the anxiety over vampiric women is partially generated by a belief that blood is a precious commodity—one that must be protected. Thus, whether seen as abject and corrupting or purifying and life-giving, blood that transgresses the boundary of the physical body has had, and continues to have, great potency and significance—power that must be kept out of Black women's hands.

Making the situation more complex, one must also acknowledge that women's monthly blood has an especially fraught history, cross-cultur-ally. Since biblical times, allusions to menstruating women as sources of debasement have existed (Leviticus 15:19). In 1878, the *British Medical Journal* declared as an "undoubted fact" that an actively menstruating woman who touched meat could make it turn rancid (Mulvey-Roberts 142). In contemporary Mali, traditionalists among the Bamana people deem that sexual intercourse with a woman during her menses can cause the man to get sick: one woman asserted that a "child conceived during menses will turn out to be a leper"; others stated that the child would be "sexually deformed" (Madhavan and Diarra 175). Time-honored Ashanti practice relegates women to special houses during their menses and prohibits them from entering men's homes. In Niger, Tuareg women clandestinely wash their menstrual cloths out at night to keep their blood from being stolen by witches and sorcerers: "a victim's menstrual cloth, permeated with life-giving fluid, may be used [. . .] to 'seize' men-struation, stop its flow," or cause an abortion (Renne and van de Walle xxviii). Among the Quechua people of southern Bolivia, actively men-struating women are forbidden from going too close to newly sprout-ing fields: Patricia Hammer's interviews in Coroco revealed a belief that actively menstruating women sustained a "hot" condition that could dry up fields and wither plants. "[T]he fecund, desiring state of menstruat-ing women may dangerously lure wet and inseminating natural forces away from the propagation of delicate crops and toward the women's bodies" (247). The construction of the "dangerous" woman's body as hot, dry, and destructive bears a striking resemblance to the soucouyant's manifestation as a ball of fire, suggesting yet another network that can be layered over the web of soucouyant stories.

Gender studies scholars in the United States also cite the feelings of "contamination and concealment," "shame and fear of discovery" that plagued most twentieth-century women when they first began menstru-ating (Lee and Sasser-Coen 5). Many late twentieth-century and early twenty-first-century women are encouraged by their mothers to think about their cycles as empowering, but they still associate their monthly blood with dirtiness, humiliation, and hypervisibility. These notions are integrally tied to the soucouyant tales and others condemning the vampiric female. By making her victim bleed, she distinctly feminizes the sleeping body and thus, in male-dominated societies, renders it powerless. The imagery is strikingly similar to Lee and Sasser-Coen's delineation of the ways in which many of the women they interviewed associate menarche with the loss or negative transformation of female power (85) as well as the "loss of authority and integrity" (103). Thus, like menstrual blood, the blood seeping from the vampire's victim does not leave the body arbitrarily or accidentally; it also makes the target exposed to the shame typically scripted onto women's bleeding bodies. And in the same way that the cultural narratives of embarrassment surrounding women and blood serve to inhibit certain female behaviors and attitudes, conventional soucouyant stories serve a distinctly restrictive cultural purpose wherever they are found.

Vampires in African-Diaspora Folklore

Folk legends, like other types of literature, set out behavioral rules and standards of acceptability. Therefore, while listeners expect to be "surprised and delighted" by a folk story's plot events, they do *not* "want novel and unconventional situations" introduced to the narrative (Abrahams, *Afro-American Folktales* xviii); resistance to changes along these lines confirms my argument that traditional soucouyant tales can be read as a rather uniform group and not as isolated attempts to curtail female mobility.

As the prominent Caribbean folklorist J. D. Elder emphasized in his mid-twentieth-century studies of song-games from Trinidad and Tobago, and Cynthia James echoed in her more recent exploration of West Indian orature, folklore contains a "hidden curriculum" (James n.p.) that plays a crucial role in childhood "indoctrination" (Elder, *Song Games* 14). Likewise, Alan Dundes, Paulo de Carvalho-Neto, and Lawrence Levine describe how, while folktales can entertain and educate audiences of all ages and validate traditions, they also encourage behavioral conformity. They can lay out valued personality traits, cultural expectations, and questions of national identity; they can prepare the child listener for difficult concepts like death, competition, or violence in society. But because they convey the ideals of behavior needed for a community to develop "unhampered by internal upheavals," they often encourage strict homogeneity (Elder, *Song Games* 17). "If I do not submit to the conventions of society, if [. . .] I do not conform to the customs observed in my country and in my class, the ridicule I provoke, the social isolation in which I am kept, produce, although in an attenuated form, the same effects as a punishment in the strict sense of the word" (Carvalho-Neto 20, quoting Emile Durkheim).

Elder, like fellow Caribbean musicologists Andrew Pearse, Alan Lomax, and Mitto Sampson, further links artistic creativity to history, local and national politics, and social stress (*From Congo Drum* 18). Looking at these political, economic, and social stresses will be a crucial element of *The Things That Fly in the Night*. Women's bodies often receive the greatest amount of policing and the brunt of the violence believed necessary to ensure the entire community's compliance.

Folklorists the world over repeatedly assert that folk culture must not be relegated to the "nonsense" of childhood. Much of Elder's work demonstrates "how song-games function in [. . .] society including both those games played predominantly by children *as well as those performed by adults*" (*Song Games* 7, emphasis added). These "performances" include moments of teaching children, where the implications differ for each participant: the lyrics under examination, like the stories under scrutiny in this volume, hold nuances for adults that often far exceed children's comprehension. Adult performances might also include instances where immigrants and other newcomers to a community are introduced to the values of an unfamiliar home.

While Roy Heath discussed a fixed "system of morals and lore, evolved to protect a whole community," he complicated the formula by describing how folklore could be used "to forge a morality for the protection of a class" (90). Class warfare was often at the root of the suppression of folk cultures by the emergent middle class and elites of African Americas society; it was not until the Independence movements of the 1960s that many Caribbean states recognized popular music and other folk forms as a part of the national culture, raising the status of these traditional genres and alleviating some of the antagonisms between the social and economic strata (Elder, *From Congo Drum* 12, 20). For over a century, however, folk narratives like the soucouyant tale easily transgressed rigid class boundaries, most often through domestic servants such as maids, cooks, nurses, and other childcare providers. These stories have been as slippery as the soucouyant's salted skin, ensuring a legacy in contemporary times.

Virginia Hamilton lays out the principle of social and cultural incul-
cation for younger audiences in her introduction to *The Dark Way: Stories from the Spirit World*, an international array of supernatural tales:

Tales out of darkness are frightful fun and have satisfied an ancient
need in humans to make order out of disorder and to control their
environment. Since the time of the first community, humans have
set moral boundaries beyond which they travel at their peril. [These
stories reveal some of the] limitations imposed by a commonality of
rules for right conduct [. . .]—what will happen to me if I do what
I want and not what they say is allowed? What might be my punishment? (xii)

Some scholars have questioned if and when the flights of fancy depicted
in folktales and the trickster element praised in much African diasporic
lore can also allow the tales to function as "a mechanism of resistance,
vital to retaining one's individual being and identity" (Bébel-Gisler
237n4). While trickster and "signifying" stories might be paradigms
for how *not* to behave, they are typically recounted in ways that relay
such uproarious tumult and so many acts of social disruption "that the
audience can only shake its collective head in wonder while laughing at
the audacity" of the characters (Abrahams, *Afro-American Folktales* 9).
It should also be noted that most soucouyant tales do not fall into this
category; in conventional tellings the figure is consistently demonized as
a model of antagonism and not a source of amusement.[4]

Contemporary audiences encountering the remnants of folktales in
popular literature therefore have much more to consider than entertainment value. Even though many stories in their earliest forms have
been lost and forgotten, the basic lessons and implications still linger
when they fit the contemporary situation. One should not lose sight of
the meaning of the tales during debates over the precise site and time
of origin: as folklorists such as Abrahams, Elder, Herskovits and Herskovits, Sidney Mintz, and Richard Price and Sally Price have discussed,
versions of lore from the African Americas can sometimes be found in
sub-Saharan Africa, but what remains more often is an African aesthetic, style, or essence of improvisation. The soucouyant tales under
consideration in this book are distinctly of the Americas; one might find
elements of the stories in West African renditions, but the meanings of
these details—and often the philosophical and political motives—shift
in the so-called New World. The vexations, sorrows, and powerlessness
of people of African descent in the Americas get embedded in these

stories, as do rebelliousness and hope: "It is both the continuities and the changes that occur in these stories as they are transmitted that allow us to regard them as useful devices for understanding the dynamic of the life of Afro-Americans in this alien environment" (Abrahams, *Afro-American Folktales* 15).

Despite incessant changes, however, a constant struggle for cultural preservation—one often tied to a nationalistic sense of racial pride throughout the African diaspora—suggests that future generations might be exposed to and reintegrate the stories and codes that have almost slipped away. Attempts to ensure the old stories were not forgotten seemed to occur every ten years or so in Independence-era Trinidad. Alfredo Antonio Codallo, a staff artist (1935–52) for the *Trinidad Guardian* newspaper, created visualizations of six popular folk figures for the public library in the 1950s; his 1958 painting *Trinidad Folklore* now hangs in the art gallery of the National Museum. In 1972, Al Ramsawack wrote a folklore series for the *Sunday Magazine*. And in November 1982, Trinidad and Tobago released a series of stamps with illustrations of figures from local folklore. (See figure 1.)

In the post-Independence moment when a surge in the publication of folktale collections occurred in many parts of the Caribbean (corresponding to a swell in publications of African folktales in the United States), the blatant code was cultural pride, interwoven with racial pride. Celebrating the stories of the long-denigrated folk culture served, in many ways, as an anti-European, anticolonial move. In this distinctly masculinist era, the soucouyant might have operated for some storytellers and writers as the colonial monster—a feminized creature of great power but one who could be defeated and destroyed by local residents. What is fascinating about the soucouyant, like many other creatures in horror narratives, is that layers upon layers of signification and ambivalence appear: the skin-shedding, bloodsucking female can be interpreted as an image of cultural resistance to colonial ideology, but she can also be read as shoring up colonial notions of propriety and respectability.

For a child, hearing the soucouyant story typically encourages obedience: threats of the soucouyant, la diablesse, long bubby, jumbie, duppy, the Bones, and the "Bogeyman" have long been used to instill good behavior in diaspora households. Again, such tales are typically meant to not only entertain but also promote submission in their young listeners through fear. Trinidadian author Elizabeth Nunez conveys as much in her novel *Prospero's Daughter* (2006). The protagonist is too old to believe in legends, but he knows why they've been shared with him:

Trinidad & Tobago 65c

FIGURE 1. The Trinidad and Tobago postal system released a sequence of local folklore stamps in 1982; the figures represented in the series included the soucouyant, la diablesse, Papa Bois, Mama D'Lo, and the douen.

> Lucinda had told me stories about the soucouyant[. . .] . I knew
> She wanted to scare me, to keep me within her boundaries. I didn't
> believe there was a soucouyant under the tree outside our yard, an
> old woman who shed her skin at night and turned into a ball of fire.
> And Lucinda couldn't make me go to bed when I was not sleepy by
> frightening me with her tales. (195)

"Good" children are to be rewarded by spiritual protection from the fate of the soucouyant's unlucky victims; "bad" children are vulnerable to all kinds of punishments, from parental to supernatural. Even children beyond the age of believing are reminded of the social parameters: Nunez's character Carlos might resist going to bed, but he knows he is expected to be there. For older listeners, therefore, tales serve as moral reinforcement but also the framework for much more complex, symbolic lessons.

In a preindustrial era when the distinctions between children and adults were much more obscure and entire communities enjoyed oral tales, soucouyant stories could induce behavioral orthodoxy as well as ensure social and cultural cohesion. This emphasis on the communal, however, was often at the expense of individual women's agency. In A. D. Russell's ballad "The Soucouyen of Sodor," for example, listeners/ readers are expected to privilege the safety of the larger community over the individual (female) citizen's life. The soucouyant in the poem is not immediately identified as male or female: it is simply "an evil Sprite" and "a gruesome ghost" referred to with the ungendered pronoun "it" (Besson, 1989, 28). However, the physical body that the creature inhabits by day is that of a woman from Sodor Town: "*She* slept away the blessed day, at night *she* lay for dead" (l. 12, emphasis added). As there appears to be no way to kill the soucouyant without killing the woman, the townspeople are represented as righteous and vindicated when they viciously torture the woman's bodily form: they "put fire to her toes" (l. 13), "racked her here, they racked her there, her blood was all a-froth" (l. 16). When the soucouyant returns from its nightly travels and flies into the woman's mouth, *she* begins to "roar" and sob for mercy (l. 18). Ostensibly this crying is the demon's sly attempt to bargain for its life and not meant to encourage sympathy for the possessed woman. The people are not fooled by the wailing and drown the "miscreant" in the sea (l. 19). The audience is thus expected to ignore—or recognize as justified—the brutality enacted on the bodies of women.

One purpose of the tales was thus to reify particular gender norms in a community; they also might have surfaced in attempts to calm adult anxieties over seemingly inexplicable events. During scientifically underdeveloped times, for example, conventional vampire myths might have explained conditions like cutaneous porphyria—an illness with symptoms including extreme photosensitivity, decay of gum tissue (resulting in the appearance of elongated, fang-like teeth), blisters and corrosion of the skin, and an increased growth of hair, sometimes on the face and forehead—and acute intermittent porphyria, which involves episodes of intense abdominal pain, the inability to tolerate food, hysteria, cortical blindness, and paralysis or coma. The sallowness, clamminess, aggression, and biting associated with human contractions of rabies might be linked to the lore; similarly, severe anemia—which all women can contract during pregnancy and can lead to both unusual pallor and cravings to eat dirt—might have found its way into tales about "abnormal" women consuming the taboo substance of blood. As Nalo Hopkinson hypothesizes in her collection of fabulist tales, *Skin Folk* (2001), female vampire myths might have been used in generations past to explicate mysterious deaths, especially those of babies. Women have long had lengthier life spans than men (when they didn't die in childbirth), and in a period when all life expectancies were significantly shorter, old women might have been believed to extend their lives through sinister, mystical means, including stealing the life forces of the young—those perceived to be the most vibrant members of the community.

Luise White's book *Speaking with Vampires: Rumor and History in Colonial Africa* (2000) provides interesting insights into the communal function of witch and vampire stories on the African continent, although her study focuses on select communities in East Africa and not on any of the West African societies along the former "Slave Coast"— the populations that would have been most likely to carry soucouyant tales to the Americas. White asserts that witches and vampires occupy distinct places in most African cultures. Most commonly, the accusation of witchcraft is reserved for people *within* the community who have wronged others, while vampires are associated with foreignness (typically European colonizers or their agents) and an outsider position. "[W]itchcraft is an idiom of intimacy" (20) and not, as is more frequent in European cultures, one of gender disparagement. One of the things I find compelling in the vampire tales of the diaspora is that the fear of the clearly determined outsider/Other gets lost. The soucouyant figure, an old woman who often lives just outside of town and refuses to mingle with her neighbors, is both insider *and* outsider. She is the figure of abjection, hovering in that liminal space, that border between "us" and "them," and also between life and death. A cohesive and contained community is definitively privileged over the singular desires of the individual who chooses not to belong.

Another striking difference between the East African stories that White discusses and most of the diaspora versions interrogated here is that the "vampire" allegations she recorded were leveled at both men and women. Whereas witches in several other African contexts are identified with women—in the Transkei province, for instance, "it is nearly always a woman" who is accused of witchcraft (Lainé 144), and Elizabeth Isichei describes a disturbing revival of witchcraft allegations against elderly women during the AIDS era in South Africa—vampirism is attributed to both men and women. (See figure 2.) Meredith Gadsby's brief discussion of the beliefs of the Vai people of Liberia concurs, as does the African vampire myth reported by collector Dudley Wright (despite its lack of cultural specificity): he records the story of the night-flying *obayifo* who discards its body, emits a phosphorescent light, and imbibes the blood of children. Wright refers to "men *and* women possessed of this power" (173, emphasis added). In a more culturally rooted analysis dealing with obeah traditions in the Americas, Margarite Fernández Olmos and Lizabeth Paravisini-Gebert define the *obayifo* as the Ashanti (and related Gold Coast tribes, such as the Akan) term for a witch *or* a wizard.[5] Again, the figure is not limited to women only. Certain U.S. African American versions of the folktale also feature "hags" who can be male or female: in Nancy Rhyme's collection, for instance—*Slave Ghost Stories: Tales of Hags, Hants, Ghosts, & Diamondback Rattlers*—Matthew Grant describes hags as people who have simply "learn[ed] the trade of slipping out of their skin" in order to facilitate their bloodsucking activity (3). He reports a tale involving a whole family of hags—mother, father, daughters, and son. And in *Folk-Tales of Andros Island, Bahamas* (1918), Elsie Clews Parsons collects a series of "Witch Spouse" tales, which feature men and women married to people who can turn into birds, and aligns them with stories of the skin-dropping vampires of the Caribbean and United States. While she notes that in the Leeward Islands "vampire-*women*" are the ones who "divest themselves of their skins at night" (41, emphasis added), on Andros Island both men and women can peel away their outer coverings. It cannot be stated with certainty, however, that the stories of male and female soucouyants are more *directly* descended from the "original" African sources. The complex variations make exact, causal links between African versions of the tale and their African-diasporic counterparts difficult to prove.

In the same way, although there are examples of shape-shifting vampiric females in several Asian cultures, one cannot assume that the folktale represents a direct link to Asia. Ursula Raymond's folklore collection cites the case of an East Indian woman named Ma Balgobin who was suspected of being a soucouyant (Besson, 1989, 32). Is her presence a case derived independently of African Caribbean culture, discretely passed on to the descendants of indentured servants who migrated to the Caribbean after Emancipation and brought their own stories with them? Indo-Trinidadian author Samuel Selvon creates a narrator in the short story "Johnson and the Cascadura," who, as the Indian overseer of a cocoa estate on which mostly Indian Trinidadian villagers work, regales a young English folklore researcher with a soucouyant story. The tale is corroborated by an aged watchman whose racial identity is also marked as Indian, dispelling the belief that these stories belong exclusively to African Trinidadians. One might point to the Malaysian Pěnanggalan or Filipino Aswang—creatures who are typically women by day but gain the

FIGURE 2. The "vampire sun" from Jan Carew's picture book, *The Third Gift* (1974), by Leo and Diane Dillon.

power of flight by night when their heads and intestines fly off to drink the blood of women in labor. Like the soucouyant, who must verbally coax her skin back on when she returns home at dawn, the Pěnanggalan must soak her intestines in vinegar to reduce their swelling or they will not fit back in her body. The Asian creatures are portrayed as "shining at night like fireflies" (Masters 61), echoing the image of the soucouyant's ball of fire.

Rather than a direct inheritance model, I believe that the paradigm that works best is the cultural contact model, which incorporates ideas of retention as well as reinterpretation and demonstrates a certain amount of cultural fluidity as well as generational conflict. Brinda Mehta argues as much in *Diasporic (Dis)locations: Indo-Caribbean Women Writers Negotiate the "Kala Pani"* (2004), as does anthropologist Aisha Khan, whose ethnographies of South Asian populations in Trinidad feature soucouyant stories that incorporate the scattering of salt around a house's entrances and "sleeping with both a Quran and a pouch with (undisclosed) protective items under [the] pillow" (113). What I intend to accomplish in *The Things That Fly in the Night*, instead of a direct tracing of the soucouyant myth to any "original" source, is an analysis of a multitude of soucouyant stories from the African diaspora—this is, in a way, the generation of a type of archive—that exposes a complicated web of relations and interactions between diasporic communities. At the epicenter of these communities stands a distinctly, powerfully, *female* figure—not a geographical location or physical space.

Elizabeth Isichei, who, as mentioned earlier, identifies African stories of vampires with colonial oppression and anxieties about the outsider, suggests that one "fit" between European and African vampire stories is foreignness. For Isichei, foreignness seems most evident in one's outlook, economic and social resources, and tangible capital: in the "profoundly egalitarian" ideology of many sub-Saharan African communities, such as Zaire's Bobangi, because "there was a fixed amount of wealth in the world [. . . and] one person's gain was another's loss" (11), any form of excessive consumption would be condemned as depraved. This strong sense of communal focus and disgust at (in)conspicuous consumption definitely comes through in the soucouyant stories. However, she also notes that the allegations of vampirism are gendered—they are lodged against unknown men much more often than at women. This trend speaks not only to the accumulation of wealth but also to the physical mobility that men have and women lack in cultures worldwide. Analysis of the lore is far from easy or unified.

But again, *The Things That Fly in the Night* does not attempt to identify the earliest historical, cultural, or literary source of the Black female vampire. Even stating that the figure hails from "African" culture is so broad as to be meaningless: to use Trinidad and Tobago as an example, research reveals that the Black population during the slave era comprised people from myriad regions and ethnic groups: Sierra Leone, Ivory Coast, the Guinea coast, the Mande Empire (Senegalese, Bambara, and Quimbara peoples); the Hausa Empire; the Yoruba Empire (Nago, Fon, Ibo); the Congo Empire (Lemba, Bomba, Kanga/Congo); and the Dahomean Empire (Arada, Fanti, Mine). There were waves of mass migration between the islands, further muddying the waters. In 1783, for instance, approximately 33,000 enslaved people of African descent accompanied 1,500 French planters and merchants from France, the French West Indies, and Canada to Spanish-held Trinidad as a part of a plan to increase the island's agricultural labor force. Beginning in 1792, the Revolutionary Wars of France led hundreds of African subjects from the francophone Caribbean islands to disparate locations throughout the Antilles; large numbers of people also fled from one island to another in the wake of hurricanes, massive fires, and volcanic eruptions. In the mid-twentieth century, the temporary establishment of Trinidad as the capital of the Federated West Indies generated an immense movement of foreign laborers to seek employment in the cane and oil fields, as well as the immigration of politicians and their families and servants to the island.

Furthermore, imagining Africa as the point of origin for the soucouyant tradition re-creates a problematic dynamic in light of recent conceptualizations of networks. According to postcolonial thought, refocusing
on Africa after years of idealizing European (and, later, North American)
metropoles as superior centers of political, cultural, and social power
shifted the ideological identification of postcolonial subjects, allowing
the validation of the Black self. However, this shift in many ways reiterates the traditional colonial network with a centralized, hierarchical
structure and outlook on relationships: people travel physically in only
one direction from the source and so do cultural elements. Aligning
myself with contemporary conceptualizations of the distributed network, I propose no "center"; instead, I focus on the cultural flows, back
and forth, between many different nodes: "multidirectional, decentralized, nonhierarchal, boundless and proliferating, accessible, expansive,
and interactive" (Malkin 25). (See figures 3–5.) The acts of imagining
and reimagining the soucouyant become *virtual* focal points instead of
concentrating on a fixed place of origin or locales where the stories are
most prevalent.

In other words, rather than trying to pinpoint the exact cultural
location from which the soucouyant tales come, this book focuses
instead on the conceptual paths they have taken. The change in
the gendering of the vampire, for instance—from male *or* female
to exclusively female—indicates a major ideological swing between
various populations of Africa and the diaspora. To state it more
plainly: rather than engage in a problematic search for *roots*, I am
more inclined to interrogate *routes*, examining a character generated
out of colonial and postcolonial spaces, where European, West African, and "New World" cultures (among others) come together in a
complicated mix. As Joseph Roach proposes in his book on circum-
Atlantic performance, "the relentless search for the purity of origins
is a voyage not of discovery but of erasure" (6). Because legends grow
and morph with contributions from various sources, "the notion of a
master-text becomes irrelevant"; rather, myth has a sort of "cumulative power" (Waltje 82).[6]

The female vampire myths of the African diaspora—both past and
present—serve as a method of tackling the problems with which members of the diaspora wrestle. The underlying *meanings* of the tale—a narrative that tries to comprehend dualisms such as life and death, edible
and noxious, earth and sky, and possibly even definitions of "man" and
"woman"—and not the *origins* are what concern us here.

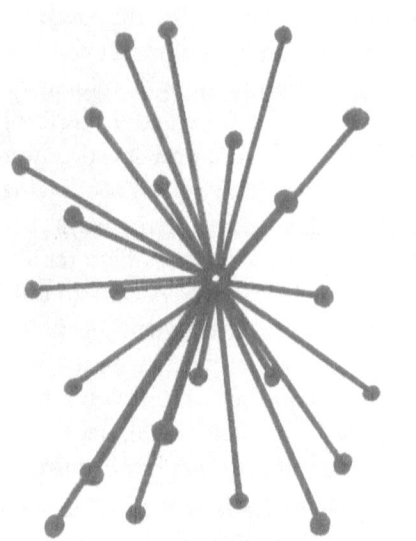

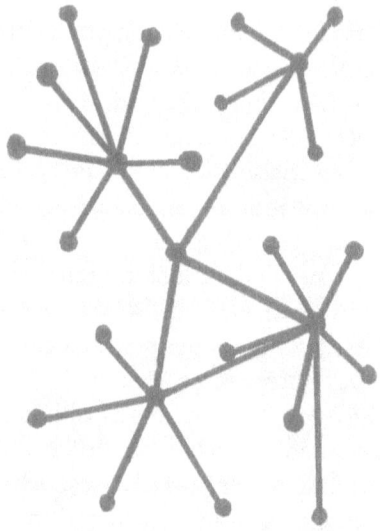

FIGURE 3. A centralized network: vectors from one large central dot to many smaller dots.

FIGURE 4. A decentralized network: vectors emanating from a small number of dispersed dots.

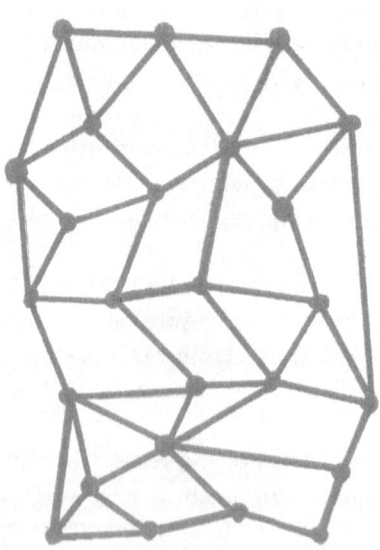

FIGURE 5. A distributed network: interconnected dots.

Theoretical Implications of the Soucouyant

As I have laid forth, in an overwhelming number of Caribbean folk-tales about vampire figures, and in some of the closely related African American hag stories, the creature is exclusively female. The *soucouy-ant/soucriant* from Trinidad, Dominica, and Barbados; *Old Suck* from parts of Jamaica; *Old Higue/Ol' Hig/Old Hag* (and, amusingly, the "hog" in a few 1880s recordings by cultural outsiders who might have misrec-ognized the term because of unfamiliar Caribbean accents) feared in Jamaica, Bahamas, St. Vincent, Guyana, and parts of the U.S. South; and sometimes the *volant* or *loogaroo* from Haiti and Guadeloupe are all women who cast off their skin at night and stealthily attack members of their communities, sating themselves on neighbors' blood before return-ing home to reenter their slippery outer coverings. In parts of Jamaica, folktales about the kin-oul, or kin-owl, predominate. Rather than taking flight as a ball of flame, the kin-oul sheds her human carapace and dons an owl's skin to fly about her community and drink people's vital fluids. Despite this fact, the *Dictionary of Jamaican English* identifies the crea-ture as a "witch" instead of a vampire (Cassidy and Le Page 346)—per-haps because of cultural pressures to associate witchcraft with women and vampirism with men. Salt and pepper are recommended for the empty, temporarily discarded skin, just as in soucouyant tales. Although I have not pursued the kin-oul in the current study because of time and space constraints, she clearly provides another cogent example of the old-time Jamaican proverb "The woman is like a shadow; the man is like an arrow"—women are mysterious and associated with darkness and thus often aligned with evil.

Because the soucouyant is typically characterized as a malign force, stories about her effectively socialize women to obey patriarchal man-dates and socialize men to expect them to do so. Unlike the "good" woman who marries, is faithful, bears and nurtures children, and anchors the domestic space, the soucouyant of conventional renderings is a woman who occupies a space completely outside of the phallic order. Thus when the speaker of the earlier described "Soucouyen of Sodor" claims, in the middle of the description of the torture, "Oh, Soucouyen of Sodor, 'tis time to be at home!" (l. 15), it becomes clear that containment and the domestication of women's bodies are central to the ballad's—and larger genre's—philosophical stance.

The African Caribbean folk figures of long bubbies and la diablesse also fit into this highly gendered moral imperative. Long bubbies are said to be the menacing spirits of dead women. Like the soucouyant, they appear late in the evening: they attack those who are out, threatening to flog them with their elongated breasts. According to the Reverend Charles Dance's 1881 *Chapters from a Guianese Log-Book*, "They are the scavengers of the night, terrifying or chastising according to the require-ment of the case" (quoted in Abrahams and Szwed 149). La diablesse (pronounced <lah-jah-BLESS>) are strikingly beautiful women with one human leg and one animal leg—typically the cloven foot of a goat or cow—underneath long petticoats. They flirt with men and lure them to insanity or to their deaths, often off of steep cliffs.

Because the overt sexuality of la diablesse is coupled with notions of danger and repulsion, it might be argued that this monstrous female folk figure provides a much closer parallel to the vampire than to the soucouy-ant: conventional vampires and traditional configurations of la diablesse are threatening outsiders who simultaneously represent repressed sexual desire, and the allure of both characters is often described as utterly irre-sistible. Caribbean scholar Gordon Rohlehr argued early in the 1990s for more thorough explorations of the "most powerfully anti-feminist" diablesse figure (171). More compelling for my argument here, however, is the liminal, boundary-crossing position of the soucouyant. Although she resides on the outskirts of an established community, the soucouy-ant is known to her neighbors and regularly penetrates their inner sanc-tums, both by invading bedrooms and by piercing their skins to drink their blood. La diablesse, in contrast, is clearly an unfamiliar presence to those who encounter her; she is always a stranger. And while la diablesse is formidable, her power manifests itself in highly conventional terms: she must rely on her heterosexual female body in a way that pleasures men, rendering that body a commodity.

Furthermore, la diablesse entices with a physical beauty that rein-scribes Western standards of attractiveness: she is usually described as a "mulatta" dressed in the clothes of a long-ago era. The problem is one addressed in Sylvia Wynter's afterword to the groundbreaking essay collection *Out of the Kumbla: Caribbean Women and Literature* (1990). The novelist and critic argues that the most significant absence in Shakespeare's *The Tempest* is not of Caliban's "legitimate" father, as proposed by Aimé Césaire, or of his mother, Sycorax, as discussed by Clarisse Zimra, but rather of "Caliban's Woman, [. . . his] physiognomi-cally complementary mate. For nowhere in Shakespeare's play, and in its system of image-making, one which would be foundational to the emer-gence of the first form of a secular world system, our present Western world system, does Caliban's mate appear as an alternative sexual-erotic model of desire; as an alternative source of an alternative system of meanings" (360). While Wynter's assessment of the ways this absence idealizes the White European woman (Miranda) and "canonizes" her as the "'rational' object of desire" is compelling, it also privileges heterosexuality and women's reproductive function. I propose that Sycorax, as the mother of a child who has reached adulthood, and the soucouyant, whose old age becomes associated with alienation and terror instead of infirmity and feebleness, allow the possibility of diasporic women's sensuality and erotic fulfillment uncoupled from marriage and socially mandated maternity. They serve as a new model for postcolonial subjectivity: one distinct from the mid-twentieth-century appropriations of Caliban, who has commonly served as the model of Caribbean resistance, independence, and reclaimed visibility; one distinct from celebrations of Miranda's ostensibly "universal" female voice.[7]

It should be noted here, too, that la diablesse is not associated with "night flying," a trait that aligns the soucouyant and other vampire figures with the taboo mobility and autonomy sought by Black feminists and womanists throughout the diaspora. The issue, then, is not simply *being* a woman but being a powerful woman who continually crosses and recrosses the boundaries of acceptability. In her book on witchcraft superstitions in Bermuda from the seventeenth to the twentieth centuries, Terry Tucker associates the earliest accusations of witchcraft with weakness. She (rather condescendingly) alleges that only "an adult of *weak* mentality, arrested development, or little education"—or deluded by mass hysteria—would believe in the world of magic and myths that young children ordinarily inhabit (136, emphasis added); similarly, "the old, as *the weakest*, the *least able to resist*, and perhaps the least necessary to the community" would have been the first targets to be accused (10, emphasis added). She further posits that "to look lonely, badly fed, senile and wool-gathering, was to invite the abject alarm of the neighborhood and the whispered craven comment: 'Witch!'" (134–35). What I will explore in the following pages is an inverse of this principle: how "evil" magic comes to be attributed to those whom society fears for their hidden strength and power—particularly *feminine* strength and power— and not their weakness.

Instead of using her body to be what feminist critic Sidonie Smith identifies as "the locus of patrilineal preservation, [...] contracted out to male authority to serve as the carrier of legitimate sons and order of those sons perpetuate" (153), the soucouyant figure not only satiates her individual physical needs and the associated sexual desires through bloodsucking, but she partially abandons her physical body when she temporarily discards her skin.[8] Like Drucilla Cornell's "wild woman," she is at once present *and* absent, everywhere *and* nowhere, and almost always a devouring figure. She does not merely represent the "bad" woman who is a "*potential* source of disruption and disintegration in the community" through her illicit associations with strangers, thereby possibly introducing illegitimate offspring and "an alternative genealogy" to the Order (Smith 153, emphasis added)—she is an active agent in society's destruction.

Her involvement in society's ruin might also be related to her position as the woman who lives alone but sleeps the day away: not only is she apparently lazy, but she resides on land that is not being worked to its full potential. If one looks to the Salem witch trials as a possible guide, recent discoveries of the accused witches' conflicts with neighbors over land rights and contested property provide a clue to why certain Caribbean and other African-diasporic women might have been charged with being vampiric skin-shedders. The desire for acreage and the indictment of the independent woman come together. Notably in the diasporic context, the impoverished woman gets aligned with evil just as readily as the wealthy landowning one who is aligned with colonial power. As a student of mine once inquired about the act of spreading rice at the crossroads or around one's bed or on windowsills and doorsills to stop the soucouyant: Wouldn't poor women rush to pick up free rice? The soucouyant who must stay to count the grains of rice, or salt, or pepper gets caught in the policing gaze of her neighbors and then by the hands of "justice."[9] In her study of twentieth-century British cinema, Lola Young poses that "[a]nxieties about power, control, virility and dependence may be identified whereby, protected by his power to define, to look, to control and to demystify through continual and intimate examination, the white middle class male characterized the troubling, confusing and unruly elements of his unconscious, as black, as working class or as female" (53). The soucouyant represents all three—Black, working class, *and* female—but the anxiety is not just that of the White, middle-class male: it is reflected by all members of the community who aspire to the norms of "respectability."

If the terror and revulsion that accompany the abject (those who, according to Julia Kristeva's theories, mark the radical margins of civilized society) serve to safeguard civilization and preserve patriarchal law, soucouyants—like other female vampires—are abject figures par excellence. They represent the horror associated with that which "cannot be assimilated" (Kristeva 1)—the female body-out-of-control—even as they reveal the necessary role such figures play in the preservation of a normative society. However, unlike conventional vampires, the soucouyant is not abject because she elicits the paradoxical sense of loathing *and* temptation generated by things that occupy the fragile border between living and dead, refusing to respect boundaries in an "interspace" that threatens the desired integrity of the independent Self (Kristeva 48). She instead arouses the ambivalent repulsion and fascination associated with the "unnatural" border crossings of her repeated transformations: her capacity to peel off her skin and her ability to slip it back on and take on the appearance of an everyday woman, both of which hint at her traversing the boundary between corporeal body and intangible spirit; her talent for turning into a ball of flame, not once, but night after night; her adeptness at inhabiting both the day and the night; and the transgressive sexuality implied by her nocturnal journeys. Like Kara Keeling's Black femme in *The Witch's Flight*, she "exists on the edge line, that is, the shoreline between the visible and the invisible, the thought and the unthought" (2). In this way, the soucouyant operates conversely to the African Americas trickster figures described by numerous folklorists:

[African Americas] tales betray an aesthetic fascination [. . .] with the transformative possibilities that can occur where the bush and human habitation abut, and where figures like [. . . the Trickster] are able to operate in the margins, playing the role of in-betweener[. . . . They] live between nature and culture and thus are able to see through the mask and costume of others. These figures break down all boundaries by roaming between the various worlds. (Abrahams, *Afro-American Folktales* 23)

In a striking divergence, the transformations and border-identity of the soucouyant are admonished, if not harshly penalized. While some might assert that this disparity reflects a greater incorporation of European moral codes where it comes to "right" (rewarded) and "wrong" (punished), I argue that the male gendering of the vast majority of tricksters and the female gendering of soucouyant figures is key to this difference.

Black Female Vampires in Contemporary Diasporic Literature

In sharp contrast to tellers and collectors of traditional folkstories who portray the soucouyant and other primarily female vampire figures as destructive in order to perpetuate patriarchal mandates, the contemporary writers whose work I explore in this book—authors of what Gina Wisker and David Punter might call the postcolonial Gothic— typically adopt the vampiric she-demon in an attempt to critique women's prescribed roles and the ways that these can bind and restrict one's "flight," much like the skin of the soucouyant. Jana Evans Braziel labels this shift in perspective on the soucouyant and celebration of transfor- mative, border-traversing figures as a "transaesthetic" (54). Because of her reliance on Jamaica Kincaid's *At the Bottom of the River* as her pri- mary text, Braziel collapses the soucouyant with "jablesse" (la diablesse), who, she claims, "takes many forms and incarnations," including those of animals. My research suggests that this figure is in fact the lagahoo, a type of shapeshifting werewolf. Regardless, the critic concurs in her analysis of folk figures in contemporary literature as insubordinate, with "insurrectional, anticolonial potential to disrupt the metaphysical para- digms and rhetorical parameters of colonialist discourse" (55).

Where Carvalho-Neto proposes "that the creator conceives the essence and form of the [folkloric] act, while the bearer transmits and modifies it" (27), one might classify the contemporary authors exam- ined in *The Things That Fly in the Night* as bearers of traditional, ancient stories, keeping them alive through their inscription in written text, but definitely making them their own, to suit their needs and the perceived needs of their communities. As such, they participate in a process by which "[c]ulture undergoes continuous transformation in order to bet- ter discharge its functions, to serve better, to satisfy in a better way" (Carvalho-Neto 35). Carvalho-Neto would likely assert that the writers explored here engage in acts of "aesthetic projection" rather than folk- lore. However, although the issues of whether the authors exploit their material, how they stylize and embellish the tales, and whether their ren- derings are elitist and condescending to the communities from which the tales are taken, or empty of any substance aside from providing amuse- ment, are important ones, they are not at the forefront of my concern. By taking up a maligned folk figure specifically from circum-Caribbean and African-diasporic culture and attempting to recuperate her, pres- ent-day artists urge for an interpretation that takes race and historical legacies into account. Their fiction points to the complex relationships that can exist between colonizers and colonized, White and Black, men and women. As illustrated by theorists such as Homi Bhabha and Robert Young—who use the idea of ambivalence to argue against troublesome binaries such as civilized "center" versus primitive "periphery," abusive versus nurturing colonizer, submissive versus rebellious slave, complicit versus resistant colonized subject, intense attraction versus pure repulsion—postcolonial writing, like that surveyed in *The Things That Fly in the Night*, reveals that the clear-cut, easily definable categories posed by racist and imperial discourse, patriarchal systems, and heteronormative ideology are as elusive as the soucouyant.

Rather than abide by notions of female mobility, female penetration, the mixing of blood, and non-Christian spirituality as demonic, various African diaspora writers attempt to convey the value of such traits and/ or the diasporic heritage out of which the soucouyant tales come. The work of these writers comes from a very different set of social pressures and historical circumstances than those experienced by European and Euro-American authors such as Heinrich Ossenfelder, Johann Wolfgang von Goethe, Lord Byron, Samuel Taylor Coleridge, John Keats, John Polidori, Alexandre Dumas, J. Sheridan Le Fanu, Bram Stoker, Anne Rice, Chelsea Quinn Yarbro, and Stephenie Meyer.[10] While some of the writers discussed in the following chapters can indeed be found guilty of romantic nationalism, or perpetuating conventional gender expectations, or invoking problematic aspects of class conflicts, they all consider the ramifications of the "original" vampiric tales and alter the stories to address pressing social concerns of their time.

A Note on Terminology

Outside the Caribbean cultural landscape, the notion of Black vampires from a longstanding tradition—much longer than the recent incarnations of the *Blade* comic books or the film adaptation of Anne Rice's *Queen of the Damned*—is practically unheard of. Contemporary U.S. cinema and young adult fiction seem to have cornered the market on the image of the vampire, and for most of the world, the vampire may appear young or old, European or American, creepy or seductive, but he is typically male and almost exclusively White. When, in casual conversations over the past few years, I mentioned my research project as work on Black female vampires, the statement I heard most often was "I didn't really know there were any!" And several 2008 postings on Gothic.net disparaged Black vampires in general. Comments included "You can go ahead and say I'm being racist but black people just don't make good vampires" and "The black vampire fucks up everything by infecting people."[11] These observations, despite their protestations, reinforce a racist hierarchy in which authority is granted only to White subjects. This book explores the interstices—opens the symbolic coffin—into which these figures of color have been relegated.

I have also been asked by numerous African Studies scholars: "Why are you using the word 'vampire'? Isn't that a European tradition?" Bloodsucking figures are rare in African societies before initial contact with Europeans, and in most U.S. "hag" stories, the skin-shedding figure drains the physical strength and energy of her victim but not literally the blood. These scholars admire the project but wish to claim the skin-shedding, bloodsucking figure as a part of unique culture that has been "untainted" by Western colonial influences and resists appropriation by these same influences. I would argue, however, that failing to use the word "vampire" consigns the African Americas' traditions to a marginal status, perpetuating the idea among majority populations that the only "true" vampires—the only "real" vampires—are White/European.[12] Because of this prevailing notion, even a collection like Otto Penzler's *The Vampire Archives* (2009), which claims to be "the most complete volume of vampire tales ever published," fails to incorporate a single story by an author of color. Furthermore, because the figure in the African diasporas takes on so many different names, with features and traits varying by culture and storyteller, the term "vampire" allows me to discuss a large body of work and access communities of readers who might not otherwise recognize their interest in the subject.

Luise White makes a similar point while discussing her terminology in *Speaking with Vampires*. Like me, White is less concerned with the origins of stories about bloodsucking figures in eastern Africa than with the persistence of the tales in various communities and what they reveal about specific anxieties, perceptions, and negotiations of power. She argues that unlike any other concept, "vampire" "conveys the mobility, the internationalism, and the economics of these colonial bloodsuckers. No other term depicts the ease with which bloodsucking beings cross boundaries, violate space, capture vulnerable men and women, and extract a precious bodily fluid from them" (9). White does distinguish between the numerous words for blood drinkers discovered during her interviews in Nairobi in the 1970s, the western Siaya district of Kenya in 1986, and Kampala in 1990: *mumiani,* who allegedly stole African blood in hospitals and other medical facilities to make medicines for White people; *wazimamoto* and *bazimamoto,* which literally translate as "firefighters"; *banyama,* or "game rangers"; *batumbula,* which means "lion from Europe." Unlike the majority of the North American and British literary criticism that explores the continually exploding genre of vampire literature but completely fails to acknowledge gender, sociopolitical and economic class, *and* race as key intersecting elements of the writers' and characters' identities and experiences, White demonstrates how "vampire stories [...] reveal the world of power and uncertainty in which Africans have lived" in the twentieth century (43), identifying the narratives as a distinctly colonial genre (89). I attempt to do the same, bringing overlapping trajectories to the discussion of the vampiric figure in African diaspora literature.

The Chapters

The first few chapters of *The Things That Fly in the Night* tackle the conventions of diasporic vampire lore. Chapter 1 surveys the traditional incarnations of the soucouyant figure in popular culture forms such as folk collections, calypso, and children's literature. While the soucouyant figure is often used in Caribbean literature as rhetorical flourish, or a quick way to ground the narrative in a Caribbean cultural space, I investigate texts where the character plays a larger part and serves a more subtle purpose.[13] My readings demonstrate how the soucouyant has been used to demonize female "drive"—whether this might be independence, ambition, the determination to escape the constrictive borders of the domestic space, or sexual enthusiasm.

For most people around the world, the term "vampire" and the name "Dracula" are interchangeable: "Huge though the corpus of vampire tales is, the character of Dracula dominates. His is probably the only vampire's name most people know. [...] Dracula is the vampire *par excellence*" (Dyer 8). However, images of vampirism surrounding the Black (and specifically Caribbean) woman predate Bram Stoker's 1897 novel. Chapter 2 investigates much of this imagery from the nineteenth century. I demonstrate how many of the selected works prescribe models of female chastity and sexual submission through representations of the hypersexual African woman. Although the sexual ideals teased out in this chapter were carried to the Caribbean by colonial literature and the colonizers themselves, they later seeped into the moral codes of the postcolonial middle class and continued to be perpetuated in much later twentieth-century literature.

The remainder of the book looks at how feminist and race-conscious interpretations of soucouyant and other female vampire tales can reclaim this folkloric figure as a paragon of agency for women of the African diaspora. Chapter 3 examines the ways that authors such as Nalo Hopkinson and Edwidge Danticat employ the figure of the soucouyant to discuss motherhood and maternal imperatives. The soucouyant provides an alternative to the route of motherhood for all women: her solitary

lifestyle represents an option other than the prescribed role of the dedicated, "naturally" nurturing mother. In Chapter 4, I consider the other
side of the heteropatriarchal "Virgin (Mother) versus Whore" paradigm
by interrogating the ways that three African Americas women writers—Octavia Butler and Jewelle Gomez of the United States and Shani
Mootoo of Trinidad/Canada—employ the figure of the soucouyant to
challenge the conventional myths of bloodsucking vampire as evil sexualized demon and same-sex desire as perverse.

Chapter 5 investigates fiction by Caribbean Canadian writers David
Chariandy and Tessa McWatt as well as Nigerian British writer Helen
Oyeyemi to consider the question of postcolonial nationalism: specifically, how these writers of color living in the "metropole" use the soucouyant figure to challenge White, nativist versions of the national
subject in the countries in which they reside. Chapter 6 continues this
discussion of national identity through considerations of race and ethnicity. As critic Sue-Ellen Case theorizes, the connection between vampires and racial anxiety is clear, not only in the xenophobia embedded in
European narratives of foreign invasion, like *Dracula*, but also in the terror surrounding the ingestion and subsequent mixing of blood. "Blood
[. . .] is geneaology, the blood right to money; and blood/money is the
realm of racial purity" (385). Chapter 6 examines narratives that portray
blood-sharing in a positive light, as well as those that expose the contradictions in conventional blood quantum ideology.

Chapter 6 also deals with issues of race in terms of complexion and the
social and cultural meanings of dark skin. In the works of writers such
as Lorene Cary and Jamaica Kincaid, the soucouyant's removable skin
can be read as a metaphor for a cocoon: the constrictive outer layers are
peeled away and left behind, and a transformed being emerges, endowed
with the freedom of mobility. Rather than suggest that the soucouyant
be feared for her ability to transform herself and fly beyond the domestic
space, these writers pose that the vampiric folk figure should be viewed
as a valuable model. One must also consider, however, what the desire to
abandon one's skin might reveal about the authors' conceptualizations
of race.

Some readers might argue that a radical feminist agenda demanding
complete liberation for women stands in direct opposition to a sense
of roots and a strong community. Caribbean Canadian author Dionne
Brand—a contemporary writer who employs the image of the soucouyant in several pieces of her work—warns against the potential alienation
that comes with flight. In the poem "no language is neutral," she makes

numerous references to women's desires for escape. In one example, a Caribbean woman has a premonition of freedom:

This time Liney done see vision in this green guava
season, fly skinless and turn into river fish, dream
sheself, praise god, without sex and womb when sex
is hell and womb is she to pay. (25, ll. 1–4)

Another subject sees her own flight as "only running away from something that breaks the / heart open" (28, ll. 3–4). I would counter that the two arenas are not necessarily exclusive; indeed, flight and freedom conjoined with isolation or, stated another way, stasis and imprisonment tied to social affinity *must not* be the only choices. Definitions must be enlarged and made more fluid to account for the simultaneous expression of multiple, seemingly contradictory ideas. Following Isabel Hoving's postulations about representations of the Home in Caribbean migrant women's writing, we must avoid constrictive binaries and allow for the concept of "bound motion" (15). So, too, in our reconfigurations of the soucouyant, we should look toward freedom and movement that can take place without the necessity of physical flight. Like Brand's speaker, we must strive to make that "flight to ourselves [which] is wide and like another world" (33, l. 19). This project seeks to illuminate the ways it might be possible to take up this goal.

1 / Conventional Versions: The Soucouyant Story in Folktales, Fiction, and Calypso

For it was indeed all about fear that this old man, as others had done before him, thought it his duty to teach the adolescent I was so that the adult I would later become would continue to carry it within him and use it in his turn against other adults and other children.
—YANICK LAHENS, "THE SURVIVORS"

The soucouyant story is quite old; there are a number of references to these diabolical creatures in narratives by eighteenth- and nineteenth-century English and French plantation owners and visitors to the region who penned tales that had been repeated to them by African Caribbean locals. However, traditional African cultures were oral, and the prohibition against literacy for enslaved peoples compounds the problem of having a lack of early primary materials with which to work that were recorded by the same group who generated them. Caribbean musicologist J. D. Elder notes that many U.S. and British folklorists showed interest in African Caribbean lore from the period 1895 to 1930, but their efforts concentrated on collecting Anansi (trickster spider) stories, proverbs, riddles, and children's rhymes and games, including a few song-games. And as Roger Abrahams observes, tale gathering was typically performed by outsiders to the community who recorded according to their own projects and/or only the items that locals allowed them to hear. Not only was there an obvious racial boundary that might have influenced storytellers throughout the African diaspora, but the fact that the collectors did not actually live in the communities that maintained the tales might have caused details to shift. (In *Afro-American Folktales*, Abrahams cites Zora Neale Hurston's *Mules and Men* as an important exception to this trend.) Despite these factors, the figure of the soucouyant (or whatever name she is called, depending on the region)[1]—the frightening old hag, skin-shedder, bloodsucker, fly-by-night—remained persistent in the cultural imagination. The renaissance of folk literature

that occurred in the years following the wave of Caribbean Independence movements in the 1950s and 1960s meant that many renditions
of the "original" stories—those heard at Granny's or Tantie's knee, or
"down the road" at Sonny's shop, or from the old men liming on the gallery—were recorded only in the last quarter of the twentieth century. No
claims can be made for the authority or authenticity of any of the tales,
but what remains consistent, and what will be explored in the next few
chapters, is the representation of vampiric evil as a woman of the African
diaspora—a woman, following the scholarship of Nicole Fleetwood, who
is perceived as suffering from excess body and excess flesh, and, typically,
excess sexuality, although the latter is not generally acknowledged in the
mainstream imagination. Thus, although it is true that the nineteenth-
century (and earlier) belief in Black women's innate degeneracy and sexual rapaciousness—especially when those women left the domestic space
to occupy the public sphere—largely got inverted in the late twentieth
century, a change Belinda Edmondson attributes to "modernity and
cultural progress [. . . being] linked to respectable women moving into
the public sphere" ("Public Spectacles" 2), attitudes about Black women's
dangerous, lascivious, and pathological nature continue to be rein-
scribed with the preservation of certain cultural forms. Daphne Brooks
describes how "black women's bodies continue to bear the gross insult
and burden of spectacular (representational) exploitation in transatlantic culture. Systematically overdetermined *and mythically configured*,
the iconography of the black female body remains the central ur-text of
alienation in transatlantic culture" (7, emphasis added). While her text
focuses on the plethora of images produced between 1850 and 1910, her
argument that the ideology continues to haunt contemporary women
coheres well with my work. It comes as no surprise that although the
eighteenth- and nineteenth-century critiques of Black women's behavior
in circum-Caribbean cultures were specifically taken from observations
of peasant women, the images ended up defining Black women of all
social and economic classes and restricting behaviors across borders of
caste, complexion, and time.

Yanick Lahens's short story, from which the epigraph is taken, is not
specifically about demonic vampire figures or even about folklore; rather,
the Haitian author details how different types of fear can paralyze people
and the effects these fears can have on social and political movements. The
quotation works well to set the stage for this chapter in that the narratives
considered here—whether in the form of carefully transcribed folktales,
modern adaptations of these "original" tales, or stories incorporated into

contemporary novels, short fiction, or song—all demonstrate how conventional portraits of the soucouyant figure are employed for various purposes: to entertain, to continue a Caribbean cultural tradition, to establish a strong sense of ethnic community, to curtail certain behaviors. Most important for this project is how these traditionally rendered depictions of the soucouyant and similar figures work to instill a dread of women's power and agency in young listeners and to remind older listeners of this threat and their duty to extinguish it.

An excellent example can be found in Joseph Zobel's renowned novel *Black Shack Alley* (first released in English in 1974; originally published in 1950 under the title *La rue cases-nègres*). This fictionalized autobiography is set between World War I and World War II, a time when Martinique's loyalty to the French empire and the dominance of colonial ideology go largely unquestioned by the book's characters; however, it is grounded in a particular historical moment, with the Négritude Movement spurring many intellectuals from around the Antilles to oppose— or at least expose—notions of European superiority and the suppression of folk culture. By incorporating Caribbean lore, mid-twentieth-century authors asserted a type of racial authenticity, reminded readers of their cultural roots, created and validated "home," and often celebrated a pan-Africanist ethic.

In the passage under examination here, found about halfway through Zobel's narrative, young José hears about *bâtons-volants* from his friend and classmate, Vireil: they are creatures "in the form of sticks with wings who at night flew over the countryside with a noise of wind that seemed to talk and spread sickness, misfortune and death" (84). Heavy Catholic influence is evident in this tale: a wooden cross erected on one's roof is not one of but the *only* weapon against the contagion-spreading monsters. Vireil goes on to relate one particular story of a motherless boy named Polo who lived with his godmother "[i]n the country, of course"— a detail that attempts to distance the content of the folktale from the middle-class village lives of students like Vireil, José, and their peers. Although José is from the country, his guardian, M'man Tine, has sent him away to school to ensure his upward mobility, which is linked to the urban setting, and, more disturbingly, to a European colonial locale for postsecondary schooling.[2]

The godmother character in *Black Shack Alley* parallels the wicked stepmother of European fairy tales: she is identified as "a wicked, wicked woman" who beats her ward (84). Besides vilifying her for her cruelty, the storyteller mentions that the woman was without a husband, making her social and financial independence a distinctly negative attribute. Vireil states that she secretly peeled off her outer membrane each night and hid it behind the bedroom door. After her flight and "diabolical expeditions" (86), she returned and re-donned it "the way you put on a jacket and a pair of trousers" (85).

Following a particularly harsh whipping and being sponged with a brine solution, Polo dips his godmother's skin in this same salty water to punish his guardian. His motherless status serves to generate sympathy for him; the story's conclusion rouses Vireil's schoolboy listeners to let out a cry filled "with vengeful horror and in a laugh of triumph" (86). For these children, the overt moral of the tale is that an oppressed youth can win out over a malicious adult: the defeat of the parental authority figure holds great sway for Vireil and his audience, all hemmed in by parents, neighbors, and a severe schoolmistress. Readers should note, however, that all of the listeners are boys—they are forbidden to play with the girls during recess, revealing a culture of starkly separated gender roles. When the godmother is unable to get her burning skin back on, she perishes in the sunlight of dawning day. "Since she had a fine shack and a large property, Polo inherited them. He bought a beautiful horse and married an adorable woman" (86). This happily-ever-after scenario eradicates the powerful female, celebrates the male character who has killed and displaced her, and rewards him with wealth, a legacy of property, and a "proper" woman—one who is valued principally for her physical looks and an unthreatening, childlike disposition, as suggested by the adjective "adorable."

Joseph Zobel seems to display an unconscious awareness of how these gender dynamics work themselves out as the stories and their themes are absorbed by their listeners: he follows Vireil's tale with a note about how the boys, not allowed to mix socially with the girls in school, "play jokes on them, tease them and call them all sorts of ugly names" (86). Desire turns into verbal aggression and the rest of the novel supports stereotypical notions of womanhood: José's grandmother and guardian, M'man Tine, and even his comparatively absent birth mother, Delia, represent the embodiment of maternal self-sacrifice; in later years, the women of his best friend Carmen's stories are chiefly the objects of seduction. For the reader, these images reinforce notions of Caribbean and other African diasporic women as aggressive and wicked, passive and sexualized, or motherly and eternally sacrificing.

The prolific Guyanese novelist Edgar Mittelhölzer also published a novel referring to the soucouyant tradition in 1950. In *A Morning in*

Trinidad, a minor character, Rafael Lopez, views superstitions as "the bane of the family." He tells his parents, who are of Spanish heritage, "You make me ashamed. Supposed to be intelligent people and devout Catholics, and believing in *obeah* and *soucougnant*" (230–31). His sister Josephine stops speaking to their mother when the older woman insists that the younger one sprinkle rice on the shelves and ledges of her new home to protect it from invasions by soucouyant. Josephine attributes her mother's traditional beliefs not only to a lack of formal schooling but also to a dearth of social refinement and urbanity: "apart from being well educated, [Josephine] was rising in society (she had married a Spanish creole of wealth and real, not sham, gentility)" (232).

Mittelhölzer's primary focus in this work is to call attention to bourgeois colonial values, the racism between ethnic groups in Trinidad despite the society's cultural multiplicity (the English, "French creoles" [locally born Whites], Spanish creoles [distinct from Venezuelans], "black" people [dark skinned, of African descent], "coloureds" [mixed-race, "olive"-skinned people], East Indians, Chinese, Portuguese, Syrians), and how the characters negotiate these boundaries. His "soucougnant" is clearly identified as a "vampire *woman*" (232, emphasis added), but her gender is not a pronounced part of the traits he attributes to her. In fact, the author alludes to a metaphorical skin-shedding potential with one of his White male characters and not with any of his female characters of color. Englishman Everard Murrain is described on numerous occasions as chafing in his own skin. At one point, self-conscious about how he is being perceived by his subordinates, "Murrain could feel that trapped-in-the-skin shudder creeping through him" (159). And recognizing, yet often distressed by, a sexual attraction for one of his mixed-race, Trinidadian office staff, he feels "trapped—trapped in his skin" (204). Unlike the female soucouyant, however, and the women who come to represent her—the old, the isolated, the impoverished, the sexually uncontrollable—Murrain is able to escape the symbolic identity when he meets another (male) character who changes his outlook on the world, his own past, and his sense of self: "Mr. Murrain regarded the scar on his forearm, and [. . .] [t]he trapped-in-the-skin shudders did not come on" (236).

Four decades later, folklorist Gérard Besson's primary focus in *Folklore and Legends of Trinidad & Tobago* (1989) is cultural preservation: his published pieces are more accurately described as "local color," taking certain liberties with the re-creation of the tales and taking more interest in cultural conservancy than the precise reproduction of voice, speech pattern, vocabulary, and order of the stories. Notably, however, even though certain rhetorical changes might have been made, many of the same stereotypes of the demonic Black vampiric woman get replicated in Besson's illustrated collection and continue to persevere since the book has been revised and reprinted, adapted into calendars, and consulted by numerous scholars, public storytellers, fiction writers, and lay readers.

In the 1989 version of *Folklore and Legends*, Besson describes the sou-couyant as an elderly woman who has the ability to cast away her skin, fly about in the form of a ball of flame, and invade the homes of her neighbors to drain them of their "life-blood" (32). When a soucouyant is caught, punishment involves dropping her into "a drum of boiling tar" (32). Brutality toward the female body is equally justified in the instruc-tion to rub the soucouyant's empty casing, if found, with salt to make its reapplication impossible and cause a sensation that "burns like fire" (31).

Besson's collection also features an early twentieth-century poem, "The Soucouyen of Sodor," discussed in the introduction, and the related tale of Gang-Gang Sara, an "African witch" (34) who was blown across the Atlantic Ocean to Tobago, where she was able to be reunited with her family, who had previously been "transported" there. The forced migration of slavery is implied, but not explicitly stated, in this passive construction of phrase. The same is true of Besson's wording of Sara's newfound employment: "She became the trusted house keeper"—not the captured slave—of "Grandfather"—not Master—Peter, who owned three plantations (34). Interestingly, the character of Sara, who has the ability to fly like a soucouyant, is portrayed as a benevolent figure: "She lived to a great age and is remembered for her wisdom and kindness" (34). Her positive status seems inherently tied to the ways she fits patri-archal models. She does not actively fly across the sea seeking adventure, nor does she intentionally leave the domestic space: instead, "she was blown from her home in Africa" by a storm. When she arrives in Tobago, she searches for family, eventually gets married to a childhood friend from Africa, and is further reintegrated into the domestic space by her employment as a "trusted house keeper."

At the end of the tale, after her husband Tom's death, Sara wishes to return to the land of her birth but has lost the "art of flight" because of the consumption of salt. Her fate resembles the Trinidadian story of the three "Congo men" who wouldn't eat salt during their forced resi-dence in the Caribbean: "They start fly to go back to Africa. Two stay up, one drop. Try again, again. He couldn't stay up. Say, 'Man, you eat salt.' Other two fly away, go back to Guinea" (Herskovits, *Trinidad Field*

Trip, 1939 field notes, Box 16, Folder 93). This anchoring of the body to the earth because of the ingestion of salt appears congruent to the use of sprinkled salt to keep the soucouyant from entering or leaving a house: she must count each grain before flying away. While some scholars have interpreted these tales as revealing "the myth of return to the native land, or read differently, a search for the root of tradition" (Mohammed, "Morality" 65), one should note that the obliteration of the character's ability to fly, signifying a distinct lack of mobility, is not rendered tragic but rather romantic in the case of Gang-Gang Sara: by dying in Tobago she is able to be buried next to her husband. "To this day the names of Tom and Sara can be seen inscribed upon the head stones of their graves where they have lain side by side for close upon two hundred years" (34). Despite being initially cast as a "witch"—quite a loaded term in the English language—Sara is the "good woman" who stands in stark contrast to the soucouyant figure.

In his 2001 expanded edition of the book, Besson expresses greater sensitivity to the gendered messages of the regional lore. He includes "A Note on Witch Tales," pointing to some of the realities of women's lives that might have led to their communities' accusations against them: inequalities between men and women resulted in many widows being exiled from their communities; poverty led old women to be seen as burdens to their neighbors or "just another mouth to feed" instead of respected for their life experiences and sagacity; women with land and possessions but without husbands or sons to protect them sometimes found themselves indicted for being soucouyants and then murdered, with their goods shared among the villagers (47). Interestingly, while conventional soucouyant tales tend to engender apprehension in the listeners, this short historical explanation—while definitely steering readers to sympathize with the accused women and turn away from stigmatizing the old—completely disempowers everyday women. They might live long lives, but without men to shield and defend them, they lie at the mercy of village politics and economic disaster. Their choices seem to be marriage and childbirth or death.

Besson's inclusion of several, new, short accounts of local soucouyants also seems designed to balance the gruesome representations of demonic vampire-women from the 1989 publication. The humorous tale of "old Mrs. Molay of Mayaro," for example, depicts a soucouyant who lives in peace with her neighbors: "She didn't trouble the village, and the village didn't trouble her" (22). As she gets older, however, she loses her sense of direction and winds up in unexpected places. One morning she retrieves her hidden skin from atop the police station water tank but cannot remember how to get down: she is discovered naked when the villagers awaken, to the apparent amusement of all (but her). The humor actually dampens the potency of the soucouyant figure in this story; she becomes a laughingstock, someone to be cared for, someone who cannot continue an independent life. Even when two mediums attempt to exorcise the soucouyant spirit from her body, the woman is represented as weak next to the demonic inner force, which possesses the true strength: "Although Mrs. Molay was old and frail, the soucouyant was strong. In the end, Mlle. Barth [one of the mediums] was savaged and subsequently died. She had been bitten and sucked by the creature on the sole of her foot" (22). Notably, Mrs. Molay is not the one represented as active in the attack; the passive sentence construction suits the passive portrait of the elderly woman. One again sees a pattern in which women who aren't demonized are deemed weak. Thus, despite Besson's attempts to express gender sensitivity, his collection ultimately conforms to gender and racial stereotypes by reinscribing conventional depictions of soucouyant figures as wicked, greedy, and frightening.

The anxieties engendered by the soucouyant figure in cases from all around the African diaspora can be attributed to numerous sources: discomfort with those who are advanced in age and perceived to be on the brink of death; the thought of an unwelcome visitor entering the private property of one's home; this uninvited figure breaching the sanctity of the sleeping quarters, where one is often in an exposed state of undress or in intimate apparel; being caught completely unaware and defenseless, in the vulnerable state of slumber; having one's body penetrated, whether by physical fangs or intangible powers; not knowing whether part of oneself—the blood or "life-blood," ostensibly the soul—has been stolen by another person. The notion of transgressed borders—whether those are the boundaries of one's property or of one's physical, corporeal body when its fluids are drained—seems to be one of the key factors in the distress caused by the folktales about vampiric characters.

And because men have long been associated with travel and crossing physical spaces to provide for their families, the concept of female mobility—another type of boundary transgression—holds some stigma, even in Caribbean societies where women have also participated extensively in work outside the home. In many traditional West African societies, men traveled for the hunt while women stayed closer to home for agricultural and child-rearing duties. Slavery in the Americas would not have allowed this distinction to continue, as both men and women were sent out into the fields to work and perform other acts of manual labor, but the influence of European colonialism and middle-class patriarchal models would have ensured that the "proper" place for women aspiring for the bourgeoisie after Emancipation would have been in the Home. Many African Caribbean women worked (and continue to work) as higglers, but again, this extra-domestic sales work was associated with the lower classes.

Additionally problematic, following Katherine McKittrick's scholarship on alternative geographies, is the fact that in African-diasporic history, travel, "voyaging, and rationality meet violence and enslavement," while White, European male explorations are tied to conquest, "colonization and domination: the profitable erasure and objectification of subaltern subjectivies, stories, and lands" (x). The soucouyant's repeated nightly journeys thus represent multiple layers of threatening and terrifying behavior.

The main soucouyant illustration in the 1989 edition of Besson's book, reprinted in the 2001 text, provides supplementary details that work to further demonize the folk figure and link this demonization to womanhood. (See figure 6.) For example, as the soucouyant squeezes her detached outer covering into a mortar, the prevalence of red hues emphasizes the sense of blood and gore, as well as the fiery ball the she-demon is about to become. Furthermore, the figure hovers menacingly above the ground, suggesting greater power and strength than that of the viewer, who must look "up" at her. The wrinkles on her face are eerily emphasized in contrast to the smoothness of her apparently skinless chest and bony arms; her face appears contorted, in that the bulging eyes, prominent brow line, and large nose with flared nostrils suggest something at once animal and human. Strikingly, her lower regions are obscured by wisps of smoke and the circling flames of her transformation, suggesting something treacherously indescribable about her sex. The absence conjures up the primitive alarm over the vagina dentata; the vampiric mouth that menaces the (male) body; sexuality out of domestic control; the region that exudes blood during a woman's monthly cycle; and the taboos that decree this blood dirty and contaminating.

Other textual details that Besson includes further cast the soucouyant as a fiend and specifically attribute her evil nature to her gender. She "lives alone at the end of the village road" (1989 version, 31), which, in many traditional Caribbean cultures would be unusual for both men and women, as a communal spirit commonly dictates that the elderly are taken care of by younger family members, but is more suspicious for

FIGURE 6. Illustration by Avril Turner, first published in Gérard Besson's *Folklore and Legends of Trinidad & Tobago* (1989) and then in *Folklore and Legends of Trinidad and Tobago* (2001). The soucouyant pours her skin in a mortar and is surrounded by swirls of smoke and fire. The image is superimposed on what looks like a diary entry. (Courtesy of Paria Publishing Co., Ltd.)

women. Her home on the edge of the geographical limits of her community therefore parallels her position on the cusp of society. She disobeys social mores by remaining single and refusing to live with her parents or husband (or male lover), or she declines remarriage (legally or common-law) after widowhood, simultaneously refusing to live with her children or other family members. Distrust is further enhanced by the specific reference to her economic status—she lives in a "miserable shack" (31)—and poverty is thus demonized as well. The soucouyant occupies a literal *and* metaphorical space outside the accepted boundaries; the woman is made monstrous by her repudiation of social norms. By emerging from her skin and flying in the night sky, she accentuates her flouting of the acceptable spaces for women to inhabit: she travels outside the domestic sphere as well as the physical landscape occupied by ordinary humans.

The details mentioned so far are common to almost all soucouyant stories. I am also interested in the specific editorial choices Besson makes—ones perhaps unique to his perspective but also telling about how hegemony works. When describing the soucouyant's pursuit of a victim from whom "she would suck *his* 'life-blood' [. . .] clean" (32, emphasis added), Besson's use of male pronouns might simply represent the once-conventional employment of "he" for an allegedly universal subject. One should not ignore, however, that specifically *male* anxiety is revealed and soothed by the fact that it is the "village *boys and men*" (32, emphasis added) who pour salt into the soucouyant's skin and "come and get her" with the vat of tar. Far from the woman-centered reinterpretations of the tales proposed by many late twentieth- and early twenty-first-century African Americas writers, Besson reveals how the soucouyant has historically and rhetorically been used as a trope to play on fears of women's mobility and power.

As I noted previously, however, Besson's inclusion of a few additional accounts of "real," individual soucouyants in the 2001 version of *Folklore and Legends* seems intent upon counteracting the purely grisly and repugnant visions of vampiric she-demons from the first edition. In addition to providing a more positively empowering portrait of the female folk figure, one of the tales in particular also seems to embody an anticolonial perspective. In a brief passage, the soucouyant Désirée from Paramin is represented as a gambling woman, suggesting that she has interactions with others in her community and is not completely alienated. Taking a bet, she flies to London to steal a gold spoon from Queen Victoria. Besides highlighting Désirée's strength and speed—she traverses the Atlantic Ocean in one night—and completely eliding any reference to a bloodsucking and predatory nature, the story suggests a challenge to colonial authority in its plot element of procuring gold from the British Empire and bringing it back to the Americas, from whence it was likely stolen in the first place. The gold spoon does not make any single person wealthy or famous back in Trinidad; rather, Désirée accidentally drops it on a rock in the middle of the First Bocas, where "to this day it lies" (22)—a part of the Americas landscape.

This sort of empowerment and positive vision of the soucouyant, however, is rare in documents that allege to hold true to traditional values. In Kwadwo Kamau's 1996 novel *Flickering Shadows*, the arrival of a missionary coincides with a violent hurricane, and one of the main characters, Cephus, is driven to the Brethren church where he has a premonition of a bulldozer shoveling up bloody, mangled limbs and a White man tossing scraps of flesh about. Kamau's alignment of the missionary with violence and the destruction of the local community clearly suggests his anticolonial perspective. Strikingly, though, it is the sighting of a soucouyant that motivates Cephus's initial attendance at the church: "the ball of light, he know is a hag—the obeah woman that live up the hill by herself and who does leave her skin and travel around the village at night" (85). The author does not focus on gender issues here, but the fear inspired by the local creature parallels the fear inspired by the foreign invader: the soucouyant thus gets linked to European religion and government corruption. Like the theologian Monica Coleman, who attributes diasporic fiction writers' incorporation of spirits from a variety of islands, "no matter which European power colonized them, or which African nation their ancestors were taken from," as a way of establishing a single circum-Caribbean identity (Pollard, "The World of Spirits" 33), I attribute Kamau's use of the soucouyant as a political process as well as an act of cultural preservation. At the same time, the gendered implications of the figure should not be overlooked. The connection between European male missionary and African Caribbean demonic female replicates notions of the sexually traitorous Black woman sometimes evoked by early Black nationalist movements throughout the Americas.

Even in *Leonora: The Buried Story of Guadeloupe*, an autobiographical narrative told to Dany Bébel-Gisler in the latter half of the twentieth century by a middle-aged, working-class woman who lives on her own and asserts her rights and independence, the soucouyant story retains its traditional features. Leonora, who calls marriage "[a] barrel full of broken glass in which the wife is trapped and injures herself at every turn" (148), initially appears invested in providing overt social critique. She likens husbands in Guadeloupe to vampiric figures who drain their wives of all vitality: "Must a wife endure everything, accept it all without fighting back? That's how men 'devour' women. They consume your will, your pride, turn you into a baby. Then they're happy, they're the masters" (149). The gender implications of this vampiric sapping of the woman's life force are layered with a racial dynamic and anticolonial overtones: the reference to "masters" and slavery also invokes Guadeloupe's status as an overseas department of France. Leonora demands to be treated with love and respect by her husband, claiming, "I'm a free woman who cherishes her freedom, and no one will keep me from being free. For me it's a question of honor" (149).

Despite her gendered social commentary, however, Leonora lapses into nostalgia while recalling moonlit storytelling sessions from childhood when "[e]veryone, old and young, parents and children, [...] roosters, chickens, pigs, dogs" were called together, instructed to be silent, and listened to the exploits of "Persillette, the brave little girl" (13). Unwittingly demonstrating the inherently coercive social nature of folktales (see Abrahams, Carvalho-Neto, Dundes, Elder, Levine, et al.), the book's speaker does not question the constrictions on female empowerment and mobility inherent in the treasured folk story.

The length and detail of the tale within the larger life-story show its place of privilege in Leonora's life and worldview—one that Bébel-Gisler establishes as both unique (especially the older woman's feistiness) and yet emblematic of many impoverished Guadeloupeans of the late twentieth century. Leonora notes that the story being recounted for the memoir was originally told to the villagers by Monsieur Fistibal. He began with an account reminiscent of the European "Rapunzel," in which a young girl is taken away from her birth parents by a nameless sorceress in conventional wicked-old-hag form who calls herself the girl's godmother. Fistibal transforms the tale, however, into one about a "valiant little *black* girl" (22, emphasis added) who outsmarts and withstands the physical and psychological tortures of an evil *soukounyan*. The old woman "never went out, never visited anyone, no one came to see her, and no one knew her name" (13), highlighting her social alienation. After she drinks an ominously red potion each night and recites secret words, her skin separates from her body, and she transforms into a ball of fire, flying off "to suck blood, bite people" (18). When Persillette comes into her care, she feeds the child a foul mixture of rat and bat meat and leftovers from her pig's supper, demonstrating a lack of the nurturing spirit typically associated with "good" women; even more sinister, however, are her plans to sacrifice the girl: she has signed a contract with the Devil to sustain her extraworldly powers in exchange for a child's heart. A woman staying within her home during the day but traveling outside her home at night is represented as a definitive threat; interestingly, however, she is still beholden to a male figure.

The social imperative for a woman's rootedness in the home, with a family, can be seen as manifesting itself in Leonora's own life when she describes the separation from her husband. She has informed him that as a self-respecting woman, she won't have affairs to revenge the trysts she knows that he has had: "It's not because of you that *I don't go running around*. I could have done *whatever I liked with my body*" (151, emphasis added). She is the body at rest, the body in control—the complete opposite of the soucouyant in her story.[3] Leonora describes feeling incredible sorrow and emotional pain when Joseph leaves her alone at night, but she refuses to leave her home and children: "at my wits' end, I thought about packing my bags, leaving, finding a place where I could live. But where? [...] Before walking out, you must think carefully about it" (157). She concludes, "Today when I take a bitter look back over my life, I find I did the right thing by not giving in to that desire to leave" (158). She cannot flee her current socioeconomic circumstances or relationship woes; she *will* not leave her children behind. One might be tempted to read her as the embodiment of Isabel Hoving's "bound motion"—liberty and movement without physical flight.

However, it is important to recognize that the image of females entrenched in the domestic space is also reinforced in Fistibal's soukounyan story through the fate of Persillette. As a girl away from her parents—and away from her home space—she is perpetually in danger: she unthinkingly retrieves a golden box from a hole in the forest floor until a friend urges her to drop it; her life is constantly at risk in the soukounyan's house; when she eventually runs away into the woods and employs the spell of repeating the creature's own magic words while planting a knife in a cross traced in the earth, she experiences tremendous physical pain. This last incident stresses passive endurance—a trait often stereotypically associated with the female body—rather than active courage:

Persillette resisted. Her whole body hurt more and more. [...]
Persillette was thrown into an abyss. She fell, head over heels; over and over she turned. "Lord God Virgin Mary!"
She couldn't stand it any longer. Again she moved her hand toward the knife [to remove it]. Her head stopped turning. Persillette responded:
"Nothing doing, *soukounyan*. You won't get me!"
[....] The forest crawled with devils, [...] Persillette was burned, stung, pinched, bitten; she was suffocating, her eyes ran,

her body felt as if it was being rubbed with hot pepper. . . . all the
time she heard: "Pull out the knife! Pull out the knife!"
 She dug in her heels. (22)

Thus, although she does leave the domestic space at several times in the
story, effecting great advantage for herself and the community, the protagonist is rewarded for defeating the soukounyan by being able to return
to her parents' home—a site of love but also containment—"And well she
deserved it" (22). This lesson has clearly been transmitted to Leonora, and
she conveys it to others in her retelling of this story from her youth. It gets
communicated locally, in her village, and then diffused to an international
array of readers through the published narrative. We see here a soucouyant
network that crosses space, culture, language, and time.

 Persillette clearly functions as a figure of resistance in the story but not
to gender norms. In this contest of "good" versus "evil" and young versus
old, "goodness" and youth triumph. Persillette is uneducated—she must
dash through the woods at night with the satanic contract to have her
father (a male savior) read it for her—but she is clever: she remembers the
process necessary to destroy a soukounyan as well as the tricky words
needed to recite the spell at the crossroads. As a member of the Black
peasant class she defeats a creature infinitely more powerful than she;
she also succeeds in obliterating the Devil's lair in the woods. The story is
one of empowerment; Persillette achieves a significant amount of agency,
but it must be acquired over the body of the female antagonist and with
the assistance of a man.

 One might identify C. R. Ottley's 1977 rendition of the soucouyant
tale as more individually generated and interpreted and less a part of a
communal oral/aural structure than Leonora's/Fistibal's: Ottley's collection, like Leonora's account, consists of versions of folktales he remembered from his childhood, but there are fictionalized and highly stylized
elements of the writing, making his work an example of "local color" and
not professional folklore collection. Despite this distinction, however,
and despite the political and social moves made during nationalist and
Independence movements of the 1960s and 1970s to bring women into
the public sphere, the lessons conveyed about women's "proper" place in
society stay intact in Ottley's compilation. His version of the soucouyant tale employs almost all of the familiar details and reinforces ideas of
limited mobility for women in circum-Caribbean culture.

 Ottley's soucouyant does not live alone; instead, the narrative is told
from the point of view of Mr. Jonesy, who has unknowingly been married

to a soucouyant for a score of years. He finds his wife's skin behind the door one night and fills it with salt, but once she returns and realizes that she has been discovered, Jonesy has a change of heart and washes the skin so that his wife can put it back on before sunrise. He receives no thank you from her, signaling her utter ingratitude, regardless of the fact that he has just saved her life. Jonesy therefore beats her with "a licking such as only the low-class Negroes in the village gave their spouses" (33), shocking the entire community. They conclude that either she has committed some grievous error or he has lost his grip on reality and gone insane. Because the reader/listener has just learned of the true reason for the abuse, however, he or she experiences a distinct *lack* of surprise and is placed in a position to feel comforted by the domestic violence. According to the ideology the audience is expected to absorb, this woman is not merely evil for her bloodlust and vampiric activity; she is the epitome of coldness and selfishness, so greedy for blood that she cannot commit to a loving husband, no matter how devoted to her he might be. She is thus rightfully punished for being self-seeking, ungrateful, and too independent.

The trope of husbands who kill their wayward supernatural wives is not uncommon. In addition to the tales of skin-shedding "witch-people" that she collects from informants in North Carolina and Georgia, Elsie Clews Parsons records several Bahamian "Witch Spouse" tales in which the skin-shedding wife is shot by her husband when he discovers her real identity. The true nature of the wife who casts off her human form and turns into a gaulding, or egret, is typically revealed by her own son, suggesting complicity between males in the family that surpasses the mother-son or wife-husband bond. The woman who "would pile [her skin] in the corner before she went out into the night" (*Folk-Tales of Andros Islands, Bahamas* 41n1) gets her skin salted and peppered by her husband before he kills her. And in the francophone context, Bertrand Velbrun, an informant for George Eaton Simpson, who published lore from northern Haiti in the *Journal of American Folklore* in 1942, relays the story of a man who sees his wife escape through the roof one night and so "spice[s]" her skin "with salt, red peppers, and lemons." She cannot put her skin back on and is found dead the next morning (quoted in Dayan, *Haiti, History, and the Gods* 265).

These same traditional gender roles are prescribed in Rosaliene Bacchus's short story "The Ole Higue"—even with its 2008 publication date. The skin-shedding, vampiric folk figure is brought into the twenty-first century with references to a Playstation2, social networking, and the

Transformers movie, which was originally released in 2007. Zina, the sixteen-year-old protagonist, reports that her neighbor, Mrs. Withers, is rumored to be an Ole Higue. She warns her brother Sammy: "She suck her husband 'til he dead. She going to suck you too." Although, as in Ottley's version, the old woman has fulfilled social imperatives by marrying, as well as by having children and living with her grandson—a potential patriarch—she is viewed as a threat to the community, and males in particular, from her deceased husband to the seven-year-old Sammy, who is preyed upon in the course of the story, to the male dog Cocoa, whose corpse is left on the family's doorstep as a grim warning to the children at the end of the tale. She is even, in a way, a menace to the children's father: "Dad can't enjoy his Saturday-night barbecues with his friends. She calls the police to complain about the noise."

Zina is the story's female hero, like Persillette from Leonora's narrative. Zina, however, is even more consistently depicted in relation to men. She vows to defend her brother despite typical sibling friction, but the empowerment that this dedication initially suggests is severely diminished by various textual details. First, she is constructed as a maternal figure, intimating that her protective behavior comes from an instinctive nurturing response, not any other type of bravery or sense of justice. "Sammy snuggles up under my left arm like he did when he was a baby. I hug him to my chest. Tonight, no Ole Higue is going to suck my brother's blood." Zina, not the siblings' mother, is responsible for making sure that Sammy bathes, brushes his teeth, eats his meals, and does his homework. Bacchus also painstakingly establishes and reestablishes the narrator's heterosexuality, whether to set her in direct opposition to Ole Higue, who preys on males instead of courting them, or to counter the stereotype that powerful women must be man-haters or lesbians: near the beginning of the narrative, Sammy teases his sister about kissing "that smiley-face tall boy," and her response is not to deny the accusation but to demand whether he has been spying on her. Later, Zina praises the *Transformers* film for being "non-stop action" but also for the attractive actor playing the central role. And, in an online conversation, she remarks, "The boys in my class are too childish and boring." In all of these details, the protagonist gets inscribed as responsive to men and not as independent.

Furthermore, instead of consulting her grandmother, as her brother suggests—and accessing the female, ancestral wisdom that the older woman represents—for advice on how to defeat the Ole Higue, Zina decides to turn to the Internet—a technological source symbolic of "progress," antithetical to the "old ways" of past generations. She finds several tidbits of information, including the idea of gaining protection by placing chalk marks on the stairs, hanging cubes of blueing over doorways, and scattering rice around the bedposts. Conspicuously, both she and her brother envision their father as the prototypical male rescuer, even though he does not believe in the Ole Higue myth. Zina proposes, "While she counting the rice, we can sneak out of bed and call Dad," to which Sammy responds: "Then Daddy can beat she with the pointerbroom." Physical violence against women is once again justified in the name of safeguarding one's family and community.

The gender roles are not presented in such a dichotomous way in Anson Gonzalez's contemporary poem "Tabiz," but opposition to the soucouyant is clear (as it is to the other folk figures mentioned); all seem to fly in the face of religion, making them distinctly "evil" characters:

> we'll chant the aves the halleluias
> the hosannas the alaikums and oms
> we'll bring the greater glory
> to your assistance and you will
> rise and soar
>
> or make it a stole of blue
> draping your possessed shoulders
> making all your ancestral contacts
> give you great strength
>
> encircled by the indigoed words
> you will bravely step through
> legs of phantoms
> put salt on soucouyants' skins (ll. 34–46)

Only the protected addressee of the poem is allowed to "rise and soar" (l. 38); the soucouyant is to be quelled by prayers and chants from Christian, Muslim, and Buddhist belief systems, as well as the words of the poem, which serve as their own charm, and the practices of Caribbean traditionalists who celebrate the ancestors and use the color blue to ward off malevolent spirits.

Hags in the U.S. South

Soucouyant tales might have arrived to U.S. shores independently of those that reached the English- and French-speaking Caribbean; they might have traveled north with slaves who were initially "broken" in the

Caribbean or with independent migrants; they might first have traveled south with runaways, rebellious slaves sent to have their will shattered, or U.S. African American soldiers. Regardless, one finds a complicated network of stories about skin-shedding, blood- or soul-sucking creatures throughout the Americas. Old hags in the U.S. southern folk tradition can be rendered as either male or female; however, the most commonly told and retold tales appear to focus on the figure of the suspicious old woman.

Zora Neale Hurston, for example, collected and recorded the tale of "De Witch Woman" in the 1920s from A. D. Frazier of Georgia. This molting figure "ride[s] people she didn't like," including her ex-lover, who "slipped in" to her house and salted and peppered her skin (63). Tellingly, his invasion of the woman's space is not condemned, while her infiltration of her neighbors' homes definitively is. The story turns on the image of the male punisher and the female figure disciplined for her nightly, extradomestic roamings, her vanity (she enjoys looking at her reflection in a large mirror while standing naked in front of it), and her alienated presence in opposition to a larger community.

In conjunction with this jilted lover, the married soucouyant figure found in both Ottley's and Bacchus's stories reappears in U.S. folklore, such as in the tales in Nancy Rhyme's compilation, *Slave Ghost Stories: Tales of Hags, Hants, Ghosts, & Diamondback Rattlers*, which features tales gathered between 1935 and 1943 from the Works Project Administration (WPA) narratives of former slaves from Georgia and the Carolinas. It should be noted here that most of the interviewers were White and untrained and had difficulty transcribing the heavy accents of their elderly, uneducated subjects, which led to some of the inconsistencies in the narratives. Folklore collector James Haskins also observes that while some subjects might have been serious about their beliefs in the supernatural, others might have made up details to satisfy their excited interviewers, and others might have purposely exaggerated their tales in mockery of the WPA representatives. For my purposes here, though, analysis will not consider the intent of the storyteller but rather the effects of the large number of stories with strikingly similar features.

In a narrative told to interviewer Maude Barragan by Rachel McCoy, the seventy-four-year-old African American woman recalls that "[a]ll the slaves [from her childhood . . .] knew about the woman who had a habit of going out every night. Her husband couldn't guess where she was gone. He didn't know she was a hag" (50). Each night, this woman does "the hag dance, shaking her hips till her skin got loose," at which point she sings a song to make her skin slide off, hides it in a gourd, and flies out the window. One again notices the impropriety associated with the woman leaving the domestic space every night, unescorted. The hip-shaking "hag dance" further suggests revelry and symbolic sexual "looseness." It would appear that even worse than the husband's inability to control his wife's movement is his complete ignorance of what is going on in his household. When he discovers her true identity and wonders, "What could he do to stop her from hagging?" it remains unclear whether his motivation is to protect his community, control his wife, or punish her behaviors. He salts and peppers her skin, which causes it to "bite" and "fight" her attempts to put it back on. She eventually flees, skinless, and never returns, though her skin—disloyal to her but apparently faithful to her husband—remains in the bed under the covers.

Although no explicit bloodsucking accompanies many of these tales, the draining of the victims' life force is clearly vampiric: hags commonly suck the physical and mental health of the people they "ride." South Carolinian Maulsey Stoney, born in the 1850s, informed her WPA interviewer that "hags can slip out of their skin at night and fly" (Rhyme 74), going about "tormenting people they know" (2); Stoney claimed to have been ridden for thirty-three nights during her adolescence before her mother defeated the wicked creature. She reported becoming "skin and bone" (72), unable to sleep, having strange thoughts and peculiar dreams, and suffering from a pain that "ractified my body" (73). The hag also has the ability to drain her victim of the power of voice: when Stoney's mother asks her what's wrong, the girl feels like "[s]omething locked my jaw" and later confesses "swallow[ing . . .] words [. . .] 'cause I was too scared to speak" (73).

Stoney suspected being targeted because of another girl's jealousy—a very ordinary reason. In other words, the attack is not a matter of divine ill will, fate or bad luck but rather bad feelings within one's own community. In this case, the vampiric evil does not signify a colonial or racially exploitative power: a stark contrast to the East and West African lore cited in the introduction, where vampires are typically associated with strangers and outsiders. The soucouyant tales of the Americas clearly have a different focus and source of anxiety, one that, here at the very least, centers more on femininity and womanhood.

Stoney's hag fits the model of the suspicious old female—one with lower economic status than the family being preyed upon: she appears in the narration as an elderly woman begging for salt (74). She is eventually "fixed" by a younger woman, suggesting a succession of generations as well as the eradication of a possible financial drain to the community: Stoney's mother possesses the knowledge to defeat the supernatural demon and "how to fix him so he stays fixed" (73), and she eventually shares the information once her daughter is grown. The empowerment of the *human* female is thus passed from generation to generation, but it comes at the expense of the *supernatural* female whose frightening power is crushed. It should be noted, however, that unlike the Caribbean-based stories where the soucouyant is almost always destroyed, the hag plaguing Stoney is merely trapped in a bottle.

Similar dynamics are divulged in Rebecca Fletcher's rendition of a "witch" story, collected by members of the Louisiana Writers' Program for the WPA.

> My Grandma told me about a witch what went into a good woman's house when that woman was in bed. That woman knowed she was a witch, so she told her to go into the other room. Ole witch went out and lef' her skin layin' on the floor, and the woman jumped out of bed and sprinkled it wit' salt and pepper. Ole witch come back put on her skin. She start hollerin' and jumpin' up and down like she was crazy. [. . .] Ole witch hollered, "Skin, don't you know me?" She said this three times, but the salt and pepper keep bitin'. The woman took a broomstick and shooed that ole witch right out, and she disappeared in the air. (Saxon, Dreyer, and Tallant 250)

This version of the story contrasts the "good" woman—the one who is found at home, in bed—with the wicked woman, who not only wanders outside her own domestic space but is a sloppy housekeeper who leaves her belongings (her skin) strewn on someone else's floor. The mortal woman again prevails over the supernatural figure, but the hag is not destroyed; she simply disappears.

To return to Stoney's story momentarily, I would like to comment on the abundance of male pronouns, which sometimes confuse contemporary North American readers: the narrative begins with the woman recalling how, when the hag entered her room, she "caught sight of *him*" and "light shone out *his* eye" (72, my emphasis). While U.S. hags can be either male or female, it should be noted that the stories were transcribed by the original interviewer, who might have misunderstood elements of the dialect, and some of the tales were also altered by Rhyme, who admits in her prologue to not recording all of the tales verbatim. More significant, however, is the fact that in many African-based language systems, "he" and "him" (sometimes "'e" or "'em") can refer to male or female subjects. The most convincing marker of the hag's gender, then, is Stoney's specific reference to the "old woman," reinforcing the notion of demonic women. For contemporary readers, however, the gender ambiguity might contribute even further to the notion of abjection.

Lynn Joseph's *A Wave in Her Pocket* serves as a corresponding Caribbean example. The narrator claims: "Anyone who had far to walk had to close up his stall early. [. . .] If [the soucouyant] found anyone [walking alone], she'd fly down and cover him up with fire, then suck de blood clean out of him" (3). Most of the people in the market would have been women—higglers were primarily female and the domestic task of shopping would have been relegated to women—but male pronouns are used, giving the illusion of female attacks on male bodies and heightening anxieties about uncontrolled women's bodies and desires. Similarly, when Virginia Hamilton adapts Stoney's account of the soucouyant figure in "Macie and Boo Hag," in her collection for children titled *Her Stories*, she eliminates the gender ambiguity by referring to the hag as a "she-thing" (51). This definitive gendering of the hag furthers the suspicion lurking around other women—not only the jealous young woman who might "put the hag on" a peer (51) but older women in the community, such as the one who, as in Rhyme's version, wants to borrow salt.

In addition to being either male or female in the WPA narratives, hags are sometimes represented as possessing a sought-after skill rather than exclusively in terms of terror. Matthew Grant relates a tale where, upon going courting, a young man witnesses the girl's father, mother, sister, and brother rub a mysterious liquid on their arms to make their clothes and skin slip off. They then fly up the chimney and into the clouds until just before dawn, when they must return to their skins. Twice the young man says, "I didn't know you was hags"—apparently without surprise or dread (Rhyme 12, 13). In this instance, the folk figure is clearly not malevolent; instead, the story hints at a revision of conventional ideology, which criminalizes and ostracizes subjects with dark skin as readily as women who discard their outer casings. The idea of a productive talent as opposed to a set of fiendish traits gets emphasized when the storyteller notes that "Hagging was their trade" (13). The young man decides to try some of the liquid, which allows him, too, to slough off his outer trappings and fly. The line "[he] learned to fly quick" (13) underscores the beings' activities—especially flight—as desirable rather than purely demonic. More revisionist narratives of this type will be explored in the latter part of this book.

The Soucouyant Figure as a Racial Metaphor

Interestingly, after an altercation with the father, the young man in Grant's account tells the slave master about the hags, which leads to their destruction: "Maussa killed out that family—all that race of people. [. . .] Put them in a barrel of tar and burned them up" (13). The excruciating deaths of the hags significantly occur at the hands of the White master, not the Black community in which they live. The tale serves as more of a commentary on the master's brutality—and, with the reference to a whole "race of people," to the physical and cultural genocide committed by European and American slave society—than as a horror story about the skin-shedding, life-draining flying hags of southern folklore.

This version of the tale, however, is rare. Conventional soucouyant narratives unmistakably mark flight as a motivating factor in the community's punishment of the figure. The anxiety over flight is attributable, perhaps, to the fact that the transatlantic slave trade ensured that people from various parts of the African continent were dispersed through North, Central, and South America against their will: flight, mobility, and journeys would have been rendered as something dire rather than positive, even if freedom of movement was later embraced.

During Mimi Sheller's examination of Caribbean travel books in *Consuming the Caribbean*, she notes that European and Anglo-American writers prided themselves on their ability to move throughout the region. They did not stay in one location but "travelled by boat 'through' the islands, as many of their titles indicate, and on arrival at each port they also described their journeys across or around particular islands" (136). Reading their "practices of mobility [and] border-crossing" through the scholarship of Sara Ahmed, Sheller argues that "boundaries [were] enforced rather than undone." In other words, by constantly moving, the tourists established themselves as distinctly different from the "backward," non-mobile islanders; they were subjects of dynamic, modern "progress" rather than primitive "stasis." The travel guides "become crucial to efforts to 'fix' others both in space and in time" (141). What better way for Caribbean peoples and other members of the African diaspora to challenge this "fixing" than by relegating stasis to the privileged position and mobility to a demonic act associated with invasion and theft. Even so, however, the gendering of the soucouyant as female accomplishes the racial commentary by relegating women to a subordinate social position.

In Jamaica, Herbert de Lisser's historical novel *The White Witch of Rosehall* (1929) aligns White womanhood with evil in the character of Annie Palmer. The narrative voice of work switches back and forth between White European characters and those of African descent; in this way, patronizing attitudes of White colonial settlers and visitors to the island—whether the characters are distasteful or heroic—get called into question. Thus, when Robert, the young Englishman temporarily staying on Annie's plantation, refuses to believe in the legend of the sou-couyant, or Old Hige, his proclamation comes across as violently racist and arrogant, despite his role as the central love interest and protagonist of the narrative:

> "Why do you people believe such horrible things?" A gust of anger (born of fear and a sense of helplessness) swept through him. [. . .] "[T]here is nothing clean and healthy about your minds. Your souls are blacker than ever your skins could be. [. . .] By God, if I had the power I would flog half to death any man that talked nonsense about Old Higes and the rest in the presence of children! Look before you now and see what your teaching has done!" (151–52)

Interestingly, the author displaces the demonic identity on the White female body as well as the Black woman's body in his novel. Three times a widow in pre-Emancipation Jamaica, Annie Palmer is rumored to have been born in England or Ireland of Irish parents, taken to Haiti as a child, and nursed by a "voodoo priestess" or apprenticed to a Vodun priest to develop supernatural powers before murdering each of her husbands. In fact, in Haiti her parents encouraged a relationship between Annie and "the Baroness," a childless Black "woman of position and property [. . .] who had marched with the armies of Dessalines and Christophe when these set out to free Haiti from the French domination" (137). She is a figure of power and rebellion against French European authority, but she is also a vampiric force who drains Haiti of its national potential and social health. The woman "hated the white race, whom she regarded as the natural oppressors of her people," but loved Annie, bestowed her with material gifts, and taught her the secrets of the spiritual world. In this way, she is cast as a distinct threat to Annie's normative nuclear family, displacing both of the girl's parents in her proper upbringing. She possesses more influence over Annie than does the girl's own biological mother, who is barely mentioned in the novel. Although nurturing to Annie—proper for an African diasporic woman during the slave era— the Baroness is the site of frightening excess: her power notably includes supernatural ties as well as strength in the financial, political, and social realms. She is thus made monstrous in the narrative: in the end, she is a "sturdy, coal-black female fanatic, and sometimes (it must be added) female fiend" (138). The Black woman's power is definitively denigrated, just as Annie's is by the conclusion of the novel.

Aside from the title and numerous textual references to her identity as a witch, Annie Palmer is configured as a soucouyant in Lisser's narrative. Jealous of a young biracial woman who threatens her sexual command over the wealthy young Robert, Annie uses her occult powers to threaten Millicent's life. At one point, she is identified as "the only living creature moving about at that moment" of the night (140), although she rides a horse rather than flying in the form of a ball of fire. Upon finding Millicent's residence, Annie is at first described as seeming about to "pierce with her vision through the solid wood" (140–41); here Lisser hints at the soucouyant's ability to penetrate rather than explicitly referencing the breaching of the home and then the victim's skin. Likewise, when Annie becomes almost "cataleptic" (141), knowledgeable readers can infer that she has cast off her outer carapace and that her conscious mind and soul have left her physical body (141).

When Robert approaches the site of the attack on Millicent, the soucouyant connection is made even more unequivocal. Millicent recounts "something" in her locked-up room—specifically "a woman" whose touch prevented her from crying out or struggling. When the creature bit her, "she suck me; I don't know how long. [. . .] it was an Old Hige, an' now nothing can save me" (148). Millicent can't see the visage of her attacker; she only perceives that "the face was all like a white cloud" (149). It is the White woman whom Lisser persists in depicting as demonic, and in the end she is punished by being strangled to death by formerly and currently enslaved, pro-Emancipation men. Their active measures to attain their liberty significantly correspond to the perceived roles of Black males during the economic, political, and social turmoil of the first part of the twentieth century, an era that saw the fomentation of the Jamaican labor movement as well as the Négritude Movement in the francophone world. The privileging of male points of view also seems at issue when the narrator remarks on the ironic justice of Annie being killed in the same way that she arranged for one of her husbands to be murdered: "Annie died as one of her husbands had, in the same way and by the same hand" (253). Thus, as in many of the formerly described literary and folkloric cases, the soucouyant figure is aligned with women and transgressions against patriarchal authority, but here it shifts away from conventional Eurocentric associations between blackness and evil and instead vilifies Whiteness.

The connection between the vampiric skin-shedders and Europeans might also be at stake in the story "Lonna and Cat Woman," collected in the Mississippi River levee country about forty miles south of New Orleans in the late nineteenth century. In several incarnations of the U.S. hag tales, hags can transform into cats; Hamilton notes that cats were common figures in African American tellers' "woman/witch" stories. "Witches became cats and vice versa. They shed their skins and flew away" (*Her Stories* 27). In "Lonna and Cat Woman," Cat Woman's nails "sheathe and unsheathe like a cat's claws" (*Her Stories* 57), she possesses "pointed cat's teeth," and she appears to purr as she sucks her victims' blood (58). Hamilton conjectures that this African American tale with its explicit reference to vampirism "may be the only one of its kind. For bloodsuckers—man, woman, or child—are rare in African American stories" (60). She focuses instead on Cat Woman's role as a conjure woman—a typical figure in lore from this part of the States—and makes connections to Vodun, "A religion derived from Africa" (60). While this link to Africa provides valuable historical and cultural context for the young U.S. readers of the collection, it fails to capture the richness of the diasporic web of vampire beliefs and stories.

In "Lonna," Pretty Polly and Lonna vie over Samuel. To get rid of her competition, Lonna decides to visit Cat Woman, a wealthy, powerful conjure woman and the source of terror in the community. Lonna's payment is to let Cat Woman suck blood from her neck. When Polly becomes ill, Samuel, too, goes to Cat Woman for a spell to heal his lover. He, too, must submit to the bloodsucking but on multiple occasions to make the magic stronger. In a scene quite different from any of the other soucouyant, volant, and hag stories, Samuel describes Cat Woman as an albino in a white turban, white gown, and with a face "covered in rice powder, to hide its foul-smelling rot" (57). All of these details accentuate her Whiteness, perhaps serving to align the creature's malicious nature with Europeans. Her financial status is also antithetical to the details of most soucouyant stories, suggesting yet another connection to the perceived wealth of the White community in poorer Black communities.

Significantly, at the end of Hamilton's version of the tale, Pretty Polly heals while Cat Woman almost kills Lonna for being disrespectful. The jealous younger woman—who almost gets dumped in a canal—gets well and learns her lesson: "she never tried any more nonsense over pretty Polly" (60). This conclusion rejects the moral code of European fairy tales where justice is starkly set forth in terms of "right" and "wrong," "good" and "evil." Here, the "bad girl" is not forced to dance to death in red-hot iron shoes, be driven around the village in a barrel studded with nails, or have her eyes pecked out by birds.[4] Instead, she is reintegrated into the community. At the same time, the "good girl" and true love appear to be rewarded. Pretty Polly's integrity is emphasized by the final description of her: she continues "courting her Samuel, and baking cakes and pies with her mama, and roasting turkey and hog. Goodness" (60). The word "goodness" functions as a vernacular interjection as well as the adjective for Polly's behavior: according to social dictates, she remains faithful to the man who saved her life through his physical sacrifice and maintains nuclear family ties and her place in the domestic space, cooking in the kitchen with her mother. In these "White soucouyant" stories, although vampiric evil might not be associated with African diasporic women, the same moral lessons about goodness and the traits that make females valuable remain foregrounded.

Interestingly, after Cat Woman shakes Lonna so hard as to make her faint, this powerful female is rendered as a typical damsel in distress: she panics and "sen[ds] for the him-vampire" (58). As the two attempt to discard the body, Cat Woman gets captured by police (her male partner in crime manages to escape). Without bail money and no way to get blood, she dies in jail. She is in the hands of the justice system but dies a death of passive neglect rather than active retribution for her "sins." This final detail might be read as a more African concept of justice at the hands of providence instead of human beings; it also suggests an African American take on the unfairness of institutions of Law and Order in the United States.

Flight in a Positive Context: The Flying Africans

Cat Woman is not permitted the power of flight to escape the police, her prison cell, or her earthly body; she is grounded, and thus neutralized, in this rendition of the skin-shedding vampire story. It should be noted here that although often terrifyingly associated with the soucouyant, the motif of flight has powerfully affirmative resonance in many folktales from around the African Americas. In his recollections of folk practices from his childhood, J. D. Elder describes his grandmother's "slavery stories," especially "Story after story after story about Congo Brown—the wizard who saw freedom coming and went from plantation to plantation telling the slaves the good news. Congo Brown—the slave who rose up in the air and flew back to Africa—is the great legend of Tobago" (Lomax, Elder, and Hawes, *Brown Girl* 185). The tale explicitly links the legal freedoms of emancipation to the physical autonomy of independent travel and to the cultural sovereignty associated with Africa. Lawrence Levine identifies the power of flight as a distinctly African ability—although teachable to American-born slaves—when he comments on the flying Africans stories being some of the most commonly recorded in WPA collections. He maintains that these African Americas folk beliefs—the "sacred world" of the enslaved—established a space between subjugated people and their owners as a technique to thwart legal slavery from becoming "spiritual slavery" (80). While belief in the power of flight definitely works in this way and simultaneously serves to encourage literal mobility, it typically occurs in the folklore under the leadership of a male—not a female—figure.

In "All God's Chillen Had Wings," for example, a U.S. folktale collected by Langston Hughes and Arna Bontemps (1958), an old man with a forked beard is labeled by the slave drivers as a "devil" but truly represents his enslaved community's salvation, helping them fly away—perhaps to be taken literally but also emblematic of escape to freedom in the North, and possibly to death and the proverbial "better place." Whether the purpose of the tale was to inspire runaways, give hope during the brutality of enslavement, flatter "good" slave owners, or provide the groundwork for change, the story situates the old man and all the flying slaves in an optimistic light—much the antithesis of the flying soucouyant figures.[5]

In contemporary literature, Guadeloupean writer Maryse Condé alludes to the flying Africans tradition in her novel *I, Tituba, Black Witch of Salem* (1992), when Tituba's adoptive father, Yao, whispers to her: "One day we shall be free and we shall fly back to the country we came from" (6). Published in the same year, Patricia McKissack's *The Dark-Thirty*, a collection of supernatural stories rooted in African American history and folklore, opens with a legend that features African Americans transforming into birds. Henri and Charlemae are forced to run away from their slave master in order to avoid the separation of their family. Immediately after they choose to leap with their infant into a raging waterfall rather than succumb to slave dealers and trackers, their owner sees "a large beautiful bird rise out of the mists. [. . .] Another bird, a female, joined her mate. Screeching loudly, a fledgling flapped frantically to stay in flight. [. . .] Once the three were airborne, the birds circled, then flew north" (13–14). Like the enslaved Yao, who eventually swallows his tongue rather than suffer the further indignities of slavery, the characters in "The Legend of Pin Oak" choose death over lives of enslavement. Toni Morrison's Sethe is an even more apt example of this choice since flight imagery pervades the scene in which she runs to the shed to kill her children before slave catchers can take them back to Sweet Home plantation:

[W]hen she saw them coming and recognized schoolteacher's hat, she heard wings. Little hummingbirds stuck their needle beaks right through her headcloth into her hair and beat their wings. And if she thought anything, it was No. No. Nono. Nonono. Simple. *She just flew.* Collected every bit of life she had made, all the parts of her that were precious and fine and beautiful, and carried, pushed, dragged them through the veil, out, away, over there where no one could hurt them. [...] And the hummingbird wings beat on. (*Beloved* 163, emphasis added)

In the same way that the flight of the birds intimates freedom and escape more than death, and Beloved's mysterious appearance and memories suggest the impermanence of death, McKissack's mystical twist allows Henri's family to achieve liberty through flight—further emphasized by the birds' movement north to the free states and Canada.

Set in contemporary England, Barbara Burford's "Dreaming the Sky Down" (1988) features a young Afro-British girl whose newfound ability to fly serves as a sign of rebellion not only to the racism of her White teachers, who assume she is foreign-born but also to their fat-phobia and mockery of her size and clumsiness. While the editors of an anthology of feminist supernatural fiction characterize Donna's flight as "a common desire of childhood, and a common experience of dreams [... ; the] perfect symbol of freedom, of specialness, of beauty unrecognized by others," they fail to recognize its place as a powerful trope of resistance in literature of the African diaspora. Noteworthy in this instance is the relief the protagonist feels when she sees her reflection in a mirror and realizes she is not a vampire. Difference is tolerable, but only to a certain extent. The vampire is not redeemed or seen as having any potential for creating an anticolonial, feminist, antiracist stance.

In children's literature, the protagonist in Faith Ringgold's illustrated children's book *Tar Beach* (1991) flies above her New York City apartment building in the 1930s. Here, flying is not associated with the legal and political freedom desired by the characters in the other texts; rather, it provides the little girl with a sense of geosocial authority that will lead to economic power and the fulfillment of dreams. Cassie asserts that flying allows her to stake a claim in the city: "All I had to do was fly over it for it to be mine forever." She states that flying over one of the buildings on which her father works construction will allow her to "give it to him. Then it won't matter that he's not in their old union, or whether he's colored or a half-breed Indian, like they say." The folk tradition becomes intertwined with the contemporary struggles of African Americans, making the myth of the flying Africans a story of relevance. Significantly, flying is a skill that ensures freedom for the community, not just the individual, in that Cassie can pass it on to others, like her little brother: "I have told him it's very easy, anyone can fly. All you need is somewhere to go that you can't get to any other way." Ringgold's use of the flying Africans tradition to create a heroic female character perhaps most closely resembles the project of contemporary writers who revision the soucouyant figure—those whose works will be explored in more detail in subsequent chapters.

Toni Morrison's *Song of Solomon* (1977) is likely the best-known contemporary rendition of the flying Africans myth. Milkman Dead learns to fly after reconnecting with the African American community in general and his own personal family heritage in particular: he is the descendant of the enslaved Solomon, who heroically flew away to freedom but left his wife and children behind. What readers typically fail to notice, however, is the reference to Pilate as a rumored soucouyant figure. Morrison's fictional town of Mercy is located on the shores of Lake Superior, but its African American citizens—people who have migrated from "Louisiana, Virginia, Alabama, and Georgia" (4)—know stories of supernatural women who can discard their skins and control fire. Community members describe Pilate as one "who never bothered anybody, was helpful to everybody, but who also was believed to have the power to step out of her skin, set a bush afire from fifty yards, and turn a man into a ripe rutabaga—all on account of the fact that she had no navel" (94). Displaced from their sites of origin, and placed in the hands of an author whose works consistently challenge patriarchal and Eurocentric norms, Pilate's soucouyant-like features do not generate fear—laughter is a more likely response to the line about the rutabaga—but rather inspire awe and warrant the respect of the local townspeople. Part of the characters' and the readers' absence of distress comes from the lack of vampiric element; Pilate draws blood from the man who abuses Reba, but she does not ingest it and commits this act selflessly. In this way she is an empowered and a positive character like the flying Africans but does not violate the conventional gender boundaries that mandate maternity and self-sacrifice for women. Traditional soucouyant tales and other vampire stories, on the other hand, focus on the sensuality, the physicality of—and often the sexuality implied in—permeating the skin and consuming blood.

Women's Sexuality

Because bloodsucking—with its penetration of a supine body and exchange of bodily fluids that typically occurs in the intimate space of the bedroom—has been read as a symbolic consummation of sex, the soucouyant can further be interpreted as a woman censured specifically for sexual voracity.[6] The female body in Western discourse is typically read as passive, vulnerable, and penetrable and, as Kara Keeling puts it, governed by "receptivity to sensations from the outside or in the sense of being an object of desire" (64). According to some modes of thinking, this female body is always haunted by ideas of vampiric danger because intercourse with women is said to drain men of their physical strength and athletic prowess. (In Mittelhölzer's previously mentioned *A Morning in Trinidad*, for instance, Rafael Lopez "believe[s] in rigorous abstinence as a means to first-class performance on the cricket field" [237].)

In contrast, the soucouyant is the instigator of the interaction; she is the active penetrator instead of the passively penetrated; she engages in this behavior with as many people as it takes to satisfy her cravings. Reading vampirism according to this sexual metaphor, we see the soucouyants in tales such as Ottley's and McCoy's can be interpreted as women condemned for being too sexually promiscuous to be committed to one man. Furthermore, when Ottley refers to the soucouyant as a "licensed practitioner," able to be hired out, his story resonates with references to prostitution. This she-demon, to be damned for her sexuality, renders chastity among women a social imperative.

Because of the colonial stereotype of women of African descent as hypersexualized, soucouyant lore incurs specific racial implications when transferred from pre-contact continental African communities into the colonial (and postcolonial) Americas. The myth of the African "jezebel" became prevalent during slavery when slave owners were determined to exploit women's bodies for both physical field labor and reproductive labor; they could be "mated" and "bred" like animals without concern for moral injury. Furthermore, White men were relieved of responsibility for their sexual desire for Black women—desire that would subvert theories of European superiority and African primitivism. The concept of the rape of African women was also effectively eradicated by the prevalent notion that they constantly sought out sexual partners. Abolitionists sometimes perpetuated the stereotype as well, arguing for the need to curtail the depravity that slavery caused among Africans, particularly African women. Keeling cites Frantz Fanon's observation that "the Negro is the genital" in the colonial racist mind; thus, from all sides, African women were approached in the same way: in terms of sex. This image has followed women of African descent down across the decades and into the present and is one of the ideas with which the contemporary women writers discussed in this book, such as Octavia Butler and Maria-Elena John, grapple in their novels and short fiction.

The case is somewhat different in the hag stories from the United States, where the flayed creatures can be male or female. Sexuality seems to be less at stake than control over another human being's body, as was the situation during enslavement. The notion of dangerous female sexuality does creep to the surface in several of the tales, however, such as Penny Williams's account in Nancy Rhyme's collection, in which the informant claims to have deflected assault by sleeping with a knife under her pillow. Strikingly, the weapon succeeds in warding off evil simply by its presence in the bed, suggesting phallic power. Williams's description of the attack clearly suggests sexual violation: "One night a hag tried her best to ride me. I was in the bed, and she thought I was asleep. That no-skin hag came flying through the window. I felt her when she crawled up on my left leg. It felt like a jellyfish—like jelly or rubber, sticky like. [. . .] Before the hag got up to my neck to suck the blood, I got up" (87). The location of the assault—in the bedroom, in the bed—plus Williams's emphasis on physical sensations and touch are compelling when read next to her insistence that the act was not consummated—the hag only "tried her best" to ride her, and the penetration of skin and exchange of fluids did not occur. The story might be one with homophobic underpinnings, but this is difficult to assert forcefully without knowledge of the characters involved. More likely it is a comment on enslaved subjects' lack of choice in sexual companionship. The tale immediately follows Williams's description of how her slave master tied cowbells to the enslaved men's necks to prevent them from crossing his property line to court women on other plantations. When Williams fights off the hag and "ain't [had] no more trouble with hags" ever since (87), she resists a forced "riding" that parallels forced matings, preserving her sexual, as well as her reproductive, agency.

Women's "Selfishness"

According to conventional dictates, the epitome of the "good" woman is the selfless woman, and this trait is typically associated with motherhood. M'man Tine from Zobel's *Black Shack Alley* stands as a prime example: she goes without food so that José will not be hungry, labors in the fields, "all the more to death," to make money for José's school clothes (77), and moves to Petit-Bourg—away from all of her friends and the people she knows—to help further the protagonist's education. The soucouyant of traditional tales is uncompromisingly anti-communal, in keeping with her choice to live in isolation, away from the rest of her neighbors, and antimaternal in the sense of consistently taking life instead of giving it.

In his linguistic study of British Black English, David Sutcliffe recounts a soucouyant story told by "Dorita." The tale traveled from the West Indies to England, but the gender principles remained unchanged.

> [My cousin's] friend was a sukunyah. She used to deal (i.e., in magic). So one day everybody tellin' him that how your friend deals and he didn't believe them—because his friend wouldn't do him nothing but she will suck other people and take away their blood inside them. And one day this woman, she was ever so wicked to people that deal, so she was ever so angry because the sukunyah suckin' every baby that she have, and killin' all her animals. So one day she *grind* pepper and she *mash* up pepper and salt[. . . .] She mash them up and everybody help her with . . . everybody have things with . . . Everybody start punging (pounding) with a martel, mortar 'tick. Everybody pung it. And all the sukunyah, when she *take* out her skin, and she *went* out, they take the pepper and they spread it right over her skin. And as she go to put her skin burn she and she bawl: "skin, skin, don't hurt me, don't hurt me skin, skin, skin!" (36)

Sutcliffe uses the story to discuss oral tales that have been transmitted from generation to generation, crossing national boundaries with their emigrating tellers. For him, the tales demonstrate skillful impromptu uses of language, serving as both static forms in their use of traditional material and dynamic forms in their employment of creative language choices. The symbolic details of the story, however, are equally as telling. For instance, the narrative clearly privileges the community over the individual—"everybody" helps pound the spices to spread in the soucouyant's skin.

In this account, a woman, and not a man, leads the people to the soucouyant's defeat. However, that woman is described as "wicked" in her behavior toward practitioners of magic—she is not cast as "powerful," or "devout," or even "persistent" in her battles against perceived evil-doers, lessening, in a way, her positive influence. Strikingly, she is motivated by maternal instinct—the soucouyant has sucked all of her children and possibly killed them (the reference to animals might be metaphorical) and is thus an ambiguously "evil" woman as a taker *and* a giver of life. The heroine can also be read as equally concerned with her children, her property, and her profits (if the animals are to be interpreted literally, as domestic farm animals raised for personal consumption or for sale); the soucouyant identity serves to place her outside of the role of the conventional "good" woman.

Ironically, in her fictionalized revisionist history of Tituba, the Barbadian woman from the Salem witch trials who was popularized in Arthur Miller's *The Crucible*, Maryse Condé divests witchcraft and the Caribbean spiritual practice of Vodun from their traditional Satanic associations, but she does not do the same for the soucouyant. Tituba's investment is in healing and curing, not harming the people around her. She explains: "Mama Yaya taught me the prayers, the rites, and the propitiatory gestures. She taught me how to change myself into a bird on a branch into an insect in the dry grass or a frog croaking in the mud of the River Ormond whenever I was tired of the shape I had been given at birth" (10). The abjection associated with the soucouyant's transgressing of fixed boundaries is completely removed: Tituba's ability to cross over into the animal world in the form of a bird and move from land creature to air creature, or from mammal to insect or reptile, is configured in the affirmative; the transformation reads as ordinary and natural, as empowering rather than troubling. Similarly, when Mama Yaya dies, Tituba does not mourn: "I did not cry when I buried her. I knew I was not alone and that three spirits were now watching over me" (10). Condé blurs the boundary between life and death but not to create horror; the fear of the "undead" is replaced in the Vodun framework by a belief that the two worlds are not so starkly separated and that deceased ancestors and the loa can interact with the living.

When it comes to the soucouyant, however, Condé preserves the image of a folkloric figure imbued with the power to generate terror. Tituba's mother, an Ashanti woman purchased by a Barbadian plantation owner, tells the planter's wife stories that her own mother had related in the African village where she was born: "She would conjure up all the forces of nature at their bedside in order to appease the darkness and to prevent the vampires from draining them white before dawn" (4). Here, vampires appear as Caribbean demons, countered by the fortifying Ashanti stories. Later, Tituba tells Elizabeth and Betsey Parris, wife and daughter of another master, stories of "people who had made a pact with the devil, zombies, *soukougnans*, and the hag who rides along on her three-legged horse" (42). Condé thus challenges stereotypical notions of "voodoo," obeah, and witches but does not extend the ideological inversion to the demonic characters of Caribbean lore.

The Soucouyant in Calypso

> *Suck meh, soucouyant!*
> *Suck meh, soucouyant!*
> *Suck meh, soucouyant!*
> *Oi! Oi! Oi! Oi!*   —CRAZY

In 1985, I am a teenager, listening to calypso on Saturday morning radio as I help my mother dust and vacuum. I am old enough to realize that when Trinidadian calypsonian Crazy begins "bawling" for the soucouyant to suck him, he is not really begging for his blood to be drained by an evil old vampiric woman. I snicker. In another room, my mother murmurs, "These calypsonians en't playing they're vulgar, yes?"

Starting in the 1980s, quite a few Caribbean musicians attempted to contribute to this project. Their titles and lyrics harkened back to the fantastical spirits from traditional lore; in Trinidad, for example, Scrunter's calypso "Suck Meh Soucouyant" (1985) spoke of how the title character "rulin' the highway," as well as referencing "the douen and Papa Bois / Them true mischief-maker," the Phantom, and "a La Diablesse in she long dress."[7] In Guadeloupe, the zouk band Kassav' included the song "Soucougnan" on numerous albums: tracks 5 and 9 on *Kassav' No. 3* (1981, Wotre Records); track 2 on Disc 1 of *La Légende* (August 1995, Alex Records); and track 11 on *Inoubliables* (November 1998, Arcade Music). In Martinique, as Triple Kay urged his audience to "Fly! (fly away, fly away) / Come on and fly! (fly away, fly away) / [. . . .] To the sky!" he simultaneously distinguished this empowering flight from the "evil" of the soucouyant:

soucouyant stay away!
Them evil thing,
me don't like dem doing[8]

And in Dominica, calypsonian Grammacks begged listeners to "watch out for that soucouyant":

Dominica, Dominica!

Watch out for that soucouyant!
Guadeloupe, Guadeloupe!
Watch out for those soucouyant! [...]

Lisette, Lisette!
Watch out for them soucouyant! [...]

Brooklyn! Miami!
Watch out for that soucouyant!
Port au Prince! Port of Spain!
Watch out for that soucouyant![9]

By incorporating English and Antillean patois, and mentioning places in the English-, French-, and Spanish-speaking Caribbean as well as "abroad," the singer is able to appeal to a wide-ranging cultural and geographical audience of several generations. All learn that the soucouyant represents danger, regardless of how much of the patois description of the creature they are able to interpret. Many of the calypsos also participate in what Cynthia James identifies as "cross cultural fusions" by placing folk figures into music that uses synthesizers—a form of the "fast-paced electronic [...] orality of modern Western culture"—to create a spooky but also distinctly cutting-edge quality in some of the instrumental interludes. This hybridity might be responsible for enticing younger listeners and helping garner larger audiences.

What is most noticeable and compelling for this project is the way that several of these songs ostensibly provide women with sexual agency and power. Feminist scholar Patricia Mohammed attributes "incredible versatility as a social instrument" to calypsos, which have often been employed to mock those in positions of authority, rally against racist and/or classist persecution, and "always mirrored gender relations in the society" ("Reflections" 33). She cites the period of 1970–90 as a time when calypso lyrics reveal a shift in gender relations, particularly more positive attitudes about women's independence and an increasing condemnation of domestic violence. Mohammed calls special attention to Scrunter's 1980 calypso "Take a Number," which followed the mounting number of reports of rape in the media and cast woman as "victim rather than as promiscuous female temptress" (34).

Upon closer examination of many calypsos, however, one sees that the lyrics often preserve the demonization of the sexualized soucouyant figure while also reestablishing the male singer and men in general as in control of their own bodies. These men remain outside the supernatural and seductive realm of power of the skin-shedding vampires. The threat of the female, but also her authority, is extinguished through the expression of male sexual desire, as well as through humor.

Scrunter's "Soucouyant" begins by celebrating the knowledge and culture of native Trinidadians, trumping the ignorance of tourists from the "First World," or Global North—those who were once viewed as possessing superior knowledge *and* culture:

She en't know 'bout Buccoo Reef—she's a tourist
She say there's something in we culture
Make she leave Australia
And fly for ten thousand miles to be suck by a soucouyant[10]

It is significant that the individual representing the tourist in the passage is a woman. More important for this project, the soucouyant serves as the crux of the Caribbean's preeminence, but she is also rendered perverse in the implied homosexual/lesbian activity of her sucking—as perverse as the stereotypical sex tourists (like the woman in the song) who leave Australia, Great Britain, Canada, the United States, and so forth and visit the islands to relax—a condition typically associated with the loss of all inhibitions.

The calypso's persona, in contrast, is established as unmistakably heterosexual. When he describes meeting up with la diablesse, who is "supposed to miss me"—and perhaps convey how much so by showering him with sexual attention, which is this folk figure's traditional role—he claims instead: "meh likely done with that; / I'm following soucouyant." He is the typical woman-trailing, if not woman-chasing, male. The lines reinscribe the soucouyant as a heteronormative female, and the chorus reinforces this notion as the singer urges and gives permission to the soucouyant's actions, rhetorically putting him in control:

Suck meh, soucouyant, suck meh!
You can fly in straight from Antigua
Suck meh, soucouyant, suck meh!
And mi partner here from Africa

The last line of the excerpt is especially telling: the soucouyant becomes shared between two men: the persona demanding "suck meh!" and his "partner," a term that traditionally carries the meaning of a close male friend. Thus the calypso suggests a pan-Caribbean and pan-African spirit through its references to Antigua, Venezuela, and Africa, but this is only accomplished over and through the sexualized bodies of African-descended women.

And as Gordon Rohlehr has noted, the ideology of male dominance under the guise of female authority becomes all the more apparent at Carnival time. Although women appear to be in full control of their shouting, gyrating, partially clothed bodies and their sexuality, "[they are] herd[ed] into a collective space where under the illusion of empowerment they move to the shouted commands of the soca men. And just as soca invites women to unmask their sexuality, it also represents the male as predator and voyeur" (quoted in Barnes 89). Natasha Barnes takes up this argument in *Cultural Conundrums: Gender, Race, Nation, and the Making of Caribbean Cultural Politics*: "because Carnival is a period that is licensed for the reversal of social order, women's subversion and appropriation of male-identified forms of sexual display may actually serve to reinforce the patriarchal structures that it otherwise critiques" (88). A great deal of ambivalence exists; it is unclear whether these women are mocking and rejecting, appropriating and revising, or reciting and repeating notions that render them as either good or bad, angel or demon, whorish soucouyant or virgin/mother.

Crazy's "(Suck Me) Soucouyant," released in 1985 on the album *Here I Am*, is perhaps the most well-known song of this genre. Rather than aggressively assert defiance of the soucouyant's authority, the piece goes back and forth between the "commands" for the creature to "suck meh"—a veiled sexual reference—but also a mild panic over waking *without* any pajamas but *with* "unusual marks" on his body, and a resignation to his fate as Sarah the Soucouyant's victim:

> I scaring myself all day
> I missing work
> Every week I getting half pay
> My wife think I going loco
> As soon as I hear the cock crow
> And straight in my bedroom I just go

In a "straight" reading of the lyrics, the singer appears to be without agency: some unknown force has removed his nightclothes and bruised his body, suggesting great physical strength. The singer's neighbor identifies the culprit as "Sarah, / That notorious bandit soucouyant," relegating the folk figure to the traditional position of demonic presence, and then suggests rice and garlic to keep the creature at bay. The persona, however, cannot resist her—she "leave me with nose open"—a phrase meaning he is completely captivated by her sexual prowess and suggestive of a bull being led by the nose ring. When the late-night hour approaches, he voluntarily retreats to the bedroom, completely compliant to her powers.

Crazy's tone is important here, however; the singer is not merely acquiescent; he is actually quite cheerful when succumbing to the nightly sucking. As the days wear on, he states that he goes "Just to be nice" and "Just to be sweet"; however, the first stanza reveals how physically pleasurable the experience is for him: before realizing that he is victim to a soucouyant, he sings: "I feelin' nice, nice, nice, nice, nice" and "I feelin' sweet, sweet, sweet, sweet, ʂweet"—word repetition being essential for emphasis in Trinidadian orature—and these lines recur in the next chorus. The sexual implications of fellatio are particularly clear when the singer professes to ignore everyone, including his wife, "As long as Sarah would bite me / Especially after I cross my knees!"

Barnes wonders whether, by "chanting the lyrics of Crazy's calypso [while singing along . . .], women consent to, rather than critique, their own subjugation" (88). On the one hand, the woman of the calypso narrative appears as the sexual aggressor. Second, as noted by Roy Boyke, editor and publisher of *Trinidad Carnival* (now out of print), by shouting "Suck me, soucouyant! Suck me!" along with the calypsonian, women in Trinidad and throughout the diaspora in 1985 were "reversing one of the most pervasive and chauvinistic [sexual] demands, using Crazy's words to taunt, torment, and quite likely, terrify a lot of men" (quoted in Barnes 86). Besides making demands of men, these women could also be viewed as expressing blatant lesbian desire—calling out to women, for woman—and rejecting the male presence in the sexual encounter. What remains striking to me, however, is that not once in the calypso do we hear the soucouyant's voice, words, or thoughts; she fades from view as the male persona's desires—and possibly the female revelers' demands—become the central point of the song. The character of the female neighbor provides yet another example of diminished agency. When the singer first awakens naked and bruised, he calls out to her: "Neighbor, neighbor! Neighbor come and see!" (And what exactly is she being summoned to see? His neck? His chest? His genitals? Is this a sexual invitation or another type of sexual assault?) The neighbor provides the information about what has happened, who is preying upon him, and what he should do, but although he admits knowing that "she wouldn't mislead me," her folk advice gets tossed aside. "I can't take she seriously," and the voice of the female and the folk—and possibly the elderly—is rendered silent once again.

Bringing in Younger Audiences

In her 2004 study of incorporations of the folk tradition in contemporary Trinidadian and Jamaican societies, Cynthia James asserts that despite some ambivalence toward the folk tradition, "the reality is that in Caribbean daily life, folk mores exist side by side with globalized Western norms." Ambivalence results from the remnants of decades of colonial conditioning: local oral tales were long seen as tawdry and inadequate when compared to the European literary canon, just as the folk themselves were believed to be inferior to Europeans. However, the pioneering work of folklorists such as Phillip Sherlock, Andrew Salkey, Paul Keens-Douglas, and Albert Ramsawack, beginning in the 1960s, and a growing awareness of the uses of oral forms for the teaching of print literacy, which led to an entrenchment of the folktale in primary school educational curricula, and sentimentality about "the old days" brought about a large number of folklore publications and performances for children from the post-Independence Era to the present. While the rootedness of folklore in the curriculum has the potential to reinscribe traditional gender, class, and race messages, reconsiderations of the tales have the potential for innovation. Rewritten soucouyant stories can provide new lessons and morals about Black women's roles in society—a subject to be addressed later in this book.

Al Ramsawack's *Flamme Belle* (1978) is a Caribbean version of the Cinderella story, replete with an island setting, flowering poui trees, and references to bush baths and obeah as positive forces. The protagonist's name, Flamme Belle, suggests a blending of the Cinderella tale and soucouyant lore: her skin metaphorically falls away when her foster father, an obeah man, cures her of the illness that makes her complexion "rough and spotty" (1). He then bestows her with the name that means "beautiful flame" in Creole, invoking the image of the soucouyant as a ball of fire. The author thus challenges the demonization of the soucouyant figure in several ways: Flamme Bell is not cast as a predator but as worthy of sympathy and a happy ending. As the title character, she becomes a model of identification for young readers. Her crime—that which makes the old man revoke his magical gift and Flamme Bell have to re-don her rough, spotty skin—is shame of her poor, country family. Once she repents of her vanity and unkindness, however, and "promise[s] to be good" (19), she is rewarded with an "even more beautiful" appearance and marriage to Prince Sunshine, who is also associated with a flaming ball through his name.

Quite conspicuously, however, the power of the "soucouyant" in Ramsawack's children's story is contained by the obeah man with whom Flamme Belle lives. The elderly man gets endowed with full patriarchal authority—he takes the young woman in and feeds her when she runs away from cruel neighbors; he cures her of her skin disorder, which allows her to attract the attention of not only Prince Sunshine but another wealthy man (the village store owner); he names her; in return for the cure (and a new dress, suggesting the old man's economic power), she vows: "From now on I shall call you father" and thereafter "cooked his food, swept the floor and washed his soiled clothes" (9). Flamme Belle's "fire" is symbolically extinguished by the end of the story: she obeys when the old man states, "you must have my permission before you are married or you shall suffer" (20), and she is passed into the hands of the young prince, who asks for her hand in marriage as soon as he sees her because she is the most beautiful woman he has ever seen. These modifications to the soucouyant tale do not lend respect or appreciation for the power of old women; a tale that features a young, physically beautiful, and vibrant woman only serves to bolster conventional fairy tale norms.

Lynn Joseph's previously mentioned *A Wave in Her Pocket: Stories from Trinidad* (1991), an illustrated collection of fiction based on local lore, attempts to introduce new audiences, both young and old, to Trinidadian folktales. It also serves to remind the adults who might be sharing these tales with listeners too young to read on their own of a cultural tradition that is in danger of being forgotten. Joseph initially appears to reinforce the conventional messages of the soucouyant tale, such as the emphasis on women's community involvement: Tantie, the great-aunt of the children in the framing narrative, teases them with the ghost story of "an old woman from this very family of ours [who] lived at de end of a village road. She never had any visitors and she didn't want any either" (3).[11] The scary soucouyant completely rejects the company of others, but Tantie, too, lives by herself "on a lonesome street" (13), away from the geographical heart of the village. Tantie, however, is recuperated according to traditional mores in that she is a distinctly maternal figure. Her child rearing and teaching the children the folk stories of their culture—including those that encourage panic over other women who don't meet the same dictates—make her "acceptable" according to conventional gender norms.

Joseph does complicate the story, however. The death of the soucouyant is much milder in her rendition of the tale, not only making it more appealing to modern-day parents who worry about violent influences but also suggesting that a gruesome death is not particularly *warranted* by the creature's behaviors. When the soucouyant's abandoned skin is salted in *Wave*, it keeps sliding off her body, and the rising sun slowly extinguishes her ball of flame. Rather than beating or boiling the woman to death and taking an active part in her destruction, the villagers merely celebrate with a big party.

Furthermore, in Joseph's version the soucouyant identity is brought within the intimate sphere of the family: the folk figure lives outside the physical community, but she is a relation "from this very family of ours" (3). The ambiguity of her current identity and Tantie's residence near the graveyard, in close proximity to death, suggests that the elder may very well be the soucouyant. This interpretation subverts the solely demonic status of the folk figure and potentially gives power to women. Joseph renders the soucouyant more like a phoenix than a monstrous vampiric spirit: "what those villagers didn't know is that every fifty years a new soucouyant rises up in this family of ours. Today is fifty years since de old woman sang her song, 'Skin kin kin, you na no me?'" (5). The soucouyant's presence and legacy become an undying, invincible force, passed between the generations.

Mind Me Good Now! (1997), illustrated by Marie Lafrance, was written by Lynette Comissiong, a specialist in Caribbean folklore and head librarian for the Trinidad Public Library System at the time of the book's printing, suggesting her investment in sharing information about folk cultures. The story features Dalby and Tina, children who get trapped by a cocoya—a close relative to the soucouyant—in her home for several days. The creature sings:

> Ball of fire, spin me round,
> I'm a Cocoya, put me down,
> Mama Zee, Mama Zee, is my name,
> My cousin Soucouyant has more fame,
> Little boys, mmm! They taste so nice,
> Boil them up with sugar and spice. (15)

Like the soucouyant, the cocoya must avoid daytime and the sunlight; she transforms from her human shape to a ball of flame in order to travel; from dusk to dawn she appears to be an elderly woman. Quite unlike the soucouyant, however, the cocoya preys on boys only. Tina recalls from stories she has heard that a cocoya "would do anything for little girls" (16), and so, with her quick wit, she manages to hold off the attack for several days until rescue comes from aunts, uncles, and other members of the community.

Strikingly different from the soucouyant, the cocoya welcomes people into her home, even if it is for the purpose of consuming naughty
little boys. She seems quite comfortable in the domestic space and with
domestic tasks. To lure the children in, she calls out, "Come in, come
in, children. You look hungry. Come, Mama Zee will give you food"
(10). She feeds them corn soup, offers them her "nice soft bed," and
tells them she will take them home early in the morning, hinting at a
benign, nurturing, maternal presence. She picks peas to make the dish
that Tina requests to eat; she rubs Tina with sweet oil to moisturize her
skin and soothe her before sleep; when Tina asks to bathe in river water,
Mama Zee runs to collect it so the bath can be properly prepared. While
definitely a threatening presence for Dalby—especially as she sharpens
her machete and lights fires under her cooking pot—she remains easily
under Tina's control, responding to her every whim but also too foolish
(or impulsive) to avoid being tricked. She never completes the peas and
rice dish because she can't figure out that the children are shelling the
peas too slowly to complete their task before sunrise; she takes a wicker
basket to the river for the bathwater and gets angry when it keeps leaking. And thus, as in Joseph's delivery of the soucouyant story, her death
does not occur at the hands of the villagers: because she is trying to fill
the wicker basket with water, she "pays no attention to the lightening
sky." The villagers arrive to her home and rescue the children at the same
time that a shriek is heard. Dalby shouts, "De sun got her, [. . .] de sun
shriveled Mama Zee!" (29), and no one ever sees her again.

In the United States, storytellers like Virginia Hamilton have fulfilled
the role of bringing traditional folktales to modern-day youth. Implicit
in many of her books is a call to young readers to remember the ways and
stories of the past: Macie of "Macie and Boo Hag," for example, laments
being ridden by a hag in her old age but not having any resources to get
rid of her: "Nowadays, this people generation don't know the tricks, and
lack knowing the way my mother knew" (*Her Stories* 55). Hamilton's "The
Witch's Skinny," an original story included in *The Dark Way* (1990) and
later expanded and transferred to picture-book format as *Wee Winnie
Witch's Skinny* (2004), again takes up the hag narrative. This hag preys
on a man in the community, and the author portrays the horror of an
adult male who is physically and psychologically controlled by a woman.
Big Henry becomes a voiceless beast of burden for the hag to "ride": she
puts a bridle on him and braids his hair into stirrups each night for over
a month: "Henry looking most like a horse [. . .] a-whinnying like he
about to die" (*Dark Way* 146). The strikingly sexual implications of being

ridden further put the victimized character in a passive, "female" position; when the witch brings Henry back to his house, "[s]he stretched him face down on the bed," promising that she'll be back the next night to take him again (146). He is drained of all traditional signs of masculinity: his large size, his courage, and proof of his virility; even his constant weeping makes him more like a woman or infant.

This position gets emphasized when Henry becomes the passive "female" object of all his neighbors' gazes rather than the active male perpetrator of the gaze. The narrator and other members of the community see claw marks and dried blood on Henry's shirt (143); they note "this mark in the corner of his mouth where that cat witch has put her bridle bit for to ride him" (144). His status as "feminized" victim becomes written on the body; he is at once racially invisible to the larger U.S. society—in the spirit of Ralph Ellison's *Invisible Man*—and gender invisible in a culture that privileges male bodies and agency, at the same time that he is made into a hypervisible subject. Furthermore, the hag's ability to completely control her prey and cause his association with animals has specific implications for people of the African diaspora—people once considered chattel. The hag in this case, like in Matthew Grant's version of the lore, denotes the slave-owning class, demonized for their treatment and perceptions of enslaved Africans, and African-diasporic men in particular.

Although no bloodsucking is revealed over the course of the story, the "witch" is clearly a symbolic vampire. She saps the robust Big Henry of his health, strength, and sanity: "he got lean and leaner till he so lean, he weren't Big Henry most at all. He was half-dead, stone-scared Henry. [. . .] And wild-eyed, moaning, and crying Henry" (*Dark Way* 144). The hag's nightly ridings also cause the man to lose his family—his wife and children run away in fright. In the end, her punishment is severe—Big Mama, Henry's mother-in-law, who possesses special powers, sprinkles an oil and red-pepper potion into the hag's skin, which she hung up before going out to ride. The treated skin burns and stings the hag when she puts it back on and eventually squeezes her to death. Neighbors find "cat fur all over the place and scraps of skin on the floor" (147), suggesting that the she-demon has imploded. It should be noted that an older woman—not a male rescuer—is the source of the hag's destruction. Female success can only achieved, however, by a woman who, unlike the soucouyant figure, has strong ties to the community, is known and respected primarily as a maternal figure ("Big Mama"), and triumphs at the expense of another female whose power is horrifying. The latter therefore must be exterminated.

When the story is transcribed for a contemporary children's audience, one witnesses that the adult male terror is replaced with a preadolescent male's bravery and awe. James Lee, the childhood narrator of the tale, gets grabbed from his room by the skinny and taken for a ride on Uncle Big Anthony (Big Henry in the original version). The sexual implications of the ride are eclipsed by present-day readers' sense of play; a "ride" now evokes carnivals, festivals, and amusement parks rather than sexual congress. James Lee calls out for help when first abducted, but his alarm quickly dissipates and he "wave[s] at everybody" from above the trees. After Mama Granny peppers the skin and destroys the hag, he tells "everybody about his night-air ride on the back of Uncle Big Anthony." He claims, "I don't ever want to see a skinny again, [. . .] But that night-air ride up to the twinkling stars? Whew-wheee!" Thus the child character and, by extension, child readers are empowered by the boy's adventure and lack of fright, displacing one's sense of the hag's power. Furthermore, *two* "respectable" women now achieve victory over the soucouyant figure: the grandmother, who physically annihilates her, and the mother, who names her—the diminutive appellation "Wee Winnie"—in a culture where the power of names and naming is significant.

Finally, although not coherent with conventional vampire tales, the idea of explicitly removable carapace can be found in African American folktales of the magic cat skin (sometimes a magic jackrabbit skin or a jackass skin) such as Hamilton's "Catskinella." In Hamilton's adaptation, the young protagonist's godmother gives her the advice needed to acquire the skin and escape an undesirable marriage. The membrane is alternately "skintight and all shimmery" and a "scary, skintight" outer casing that prevents people from seeing her as a real person (*Her Stories* 24) when she runs away from home; only the prince, who has fallen deeply in love with her, can see beyond the superficial covering.

"You mean, that girl with the catskin?" asks the queen.
"She's got the most beautiful face I ever saw," says the sick prince. Couldn't see nothing else; he was just love-blind. (26)

One might read the story as a racial metaphor: the prince sees beyond her skin, or her race, and notices her true beauty. However, what cannot be ignored is that he still focuses on her appearance—there is no mention of inner beauty, intelligence, or talents. When the prince chooses the cake she has baked and she tries on—and fits—the ring hidden inside, she is revealed to be the "true bride," much like Cinderella fitting the glass slipper. She shakes and shivers in her cat skin and it transforms:

"She glittered and glimmered in a dress of precious diamonds. They all had to cover their eyes. [. . .] Then they saw she was beautiful, in a fine gold-and-silver dress fit for a princess. [. . .] All that catskin vanished off her" (27). She matches his wealth with some of her own, making her a more "appropriate" marriage partner for royalty than her previous position as a chicken-maid wearing feline fur. And she has been physically beautiful all along, making the story conform to typical gender standards rather than overturning them: even though Catskinella is spunky and clever enough to resist the marriage that her father sets up for her, marriage—especially marrying "up"—is the desired result. Women are valued for their physical beauty and their domestic talents and must wait for the prince to bring about their rescue from drudgery.

This chapter provides myriad examples of the conventional soucouyant tale—nodes in a network that ranges up and down the Caribbean archipelago and North American continent as well as across the Atlantic. The soucouyant emerges not only from distinct geographical spaces and cultural contexts but from discrete eras in history and with a variety of different names. She makes one aware of the flexibility and diffusion of culture. Further, each tale appears to serve a separate primary purpose. Storytellers might overtly focus on entertainment; calypsonians provide satirical critiques of the societies in which they live; folklore transcribers like Elsie Clews Parsons, Zora Neale Hurston, J. D. Elder, and WPA interviewers seem intent on preserving the voices and words of actual people. Besson's folklore collections, like Ottley's and Joseph's short fiction, reveal embellishments that attempt to capture the spirit and individuality of the Caribbean setting and nostalgia for a particular moment in history—one distinctly anticolonial yet prior to the frenzy and technological developments of the present day. These writers engage in the cultural reeducation of their audiences, who have tended to stray away from the "old time stories."

In all of these cases, however, along with the plethora of novels and memoirs that feature references to the soucouyant figure—from Zobel's male-centered *Black Shack Alley* to Bébel-Gisler's woman-centered *Leonora*; from both of these francophone narratives to Lisser's British colonial *White Witch of Rosehall*; from Anson Gonzalez's poem "Tabiz" to the African American picture book *Wee Winnie Witch's Skinny* by Virginia Hamilton—certain traits remain constant: the soucouyant is a demonic antagonist. Stories featuring this figure might be conveyed

as conventional horror narratives, didactic warnings against particular behaviors, or with humor, but the skin-shedding, night-flying, and
typically vampiric female is almost always to be feared, contained, and
confined, if not destroyed. Her flight renders her frighteningly uncontrollable—it is not to be celebrated or emulated, as in the stories of the
flying Africans. And whether she rides her victims all night or penetrates
their skins to drain them of fluids, the soucouyant is easily aligned with
sexual activity and female greed, which evoke apprehension and shame
rather than pride, pleasure, or comfort.

To close this chapter, I want to discuss the incorporations of soucouyant folklore in two relatively recently published popular novels for adults
issued by Bootleg Press. Both introduce the vampiric figure in conventional ways, but she alarmingly serves an exoticizing purpose rather
than for cultural education or preservation. *Diamond Sky: A New Millennium Thriller* by Ken Douglas and Jack Stewart (2003) is the story of
illegal drug, gun, and diamond smuggling, with a contemporary triangle
trade set up between Trinidad, the United States, and West Africa.[12] The
narrative centers on Beth Shannon, a young American woman whose
dead husband's theft from a Russian organized crime ring leads to her
involvement in perilous situations, and Billy Wolfe, a California police
officer who is framed for related murders in the States and ends up coming to Beth's assistance in the Caribbean. Since much of the story takes
place on the ocean in Beth's boat and among various yachting communities, and the author builds tension by describing the difficult maneuvers
and dangers involved while at sea, the novel often reads like a sailing
manual coupled with action film script and romance novel.

On the surface, Douglas/Stewart attempts to create strong female
characters—Beth is determined to keep her boat after her husband's
death despite her lack of knowledge about sailing; her stepdaughter
Noelle is a capable medical student. Each woman is physically strong:
one breaks the neck of one of her assailants while the other breaks a
man's jaw and later grabs him by the throat and attempts to rip out his
windpipe with her fingers. There are repeated displays of outrage and
anger at being ogled or perceived as weak. When trying to rescue them,
Wolfe "sense[s] no fear" in either (290); "These women were tough" (292).

The writer also attempts to depict Trinidad and other islands in the
region with a bit of complexity, providing historical information on the
leper colony at Chacachacare, for example, as well as the reason for naming the December 26 holiday Boxing Day, facts about the geography of the
region, and allusions to the racial tensions on the island. The soucouyant

comes up in this vein: when Wolfe arrives in Trinidad, a local taxi driver mentions the vampiric folk figure. Beth explains to Wolfe that she is "an old woman that sheds her skin[. . . .] She flies out of her house and looks for human blood. When she finds it, she changes into an animal of some kind and sucks the blood away." Beth clarifies that the victim is "almost always a child or a young woman" since "[t]he soucouyant likes innocent fear" (110). Notably, however, it is Beth, the White American expatriate, and not the local taxi driver who explains the creature and the defense of putting rice outside one's door to keep her from entering. Further still, Beth calls the soucouyant a "local vampire type legend" as opposed to the Trinidadian cabbie's insistence that she is "Not a legend" (110). The soucouyant is never mentioned again; essentially the story is used for local flavor and serves to establish the African Trinidadian population as superstitious. Wolfe's perspective of the island night as "Spooky" (110) is related only to its pure darkness; the taxi driver, on the other hand, states, "You don't kid about the soucouyant" (111). Whereas Noelle's naïve comment about not thinking that people in Trinidad had guns (6) is quickly disproved through the course of the novel, as is the binary posed at the onset of the narrative that suggests Trinidadian lawlessness and government corruption stand in contradiction to the U.S. rule of law, the same is not accomplished with the folk beliefs.

Jack Priest's *Night Witch* (2003)—also penned by Ken Douglas under a pseudonym—appears to be a blend of disjointed myths and belief systems. Protagonist John Coffee, the hero of the novel, identifies an evil creature who preys on young women as "the old horror" (6) and "the old girl" (90), alluding to her aged status and female gender. He first encountered her in Trinidad, where he learned how to kill her: with briny seawater (270) or by filling her skin with rock salt and hot pepper (274). It seems clear that the "night witch" is a soucouyant. Near the conclusion of the story, when the demon reenters her salt-and-peppered skin, she emerges from the bushes as "an aging, screaming black woman" shrieking, "Skin, skin you no know me" (329).

The author's outsider perspective is also unmistakable, however. Whenever the old woman is mentioned, her identity as a person of African descent is highlighted through references to her black skin. One character notes: "A passerby [. . .] would pass their eyes over this old black woman and not see her" (143). When Coffee's eventual love interest, Sarah (who is also his daughter Carolina's teacher), first sees the old woman in the road, she glimpses the "weathered black face" (147). Later, she notices her peeping into a motel window: "It was the woman, the old black woman" (148). And when she reappears that evening: "The old black woman was standing in the center of the road. Impossible, but there she was" (156). The young boy Arty and Carolina discuss the old woman in the neighborhood who spies on people from behind her curtains: "You should see her skin, black as black" (19). Complexion is not simply another feature; it becomes a sign of the exotic and alien—that which does not belong. Ironically, on the back cover of the novel, the witch is a slim young White woman, naked and crouched on her knees. Her skin appears flawless; she is definitely not skinless or old. She has disheveled dark hair, but it is by no means "kinky"; the marketing eclipses all markers that reveal her identity as Trinidadian, as an African diasporic subject, as a member of a formerly colonized population.

In one battle with Coffee, the soucouyant is described as "sounding like a wounded animal. Her kinky hair caught fire and lit up her face. The black of her skin changed to a hot glowing white" (57). References to her dark complexion and course texture of hair closely follow the depiction of her howling, suggesting an integral connection between her race and her animalization. Later in the novel, the night witch is likened to "a charging bull" (56) and noted as having "gorilla power" (57). She transforms into a fiery ball when, injured in one clash, she needs to escape, but she also becomes a Rottweiler (6), a grizzly bear (213), a hyena (281), an enormous vulture (315), and, most often, a wolf with "glaring red eyes" (60, 129–30, 206, 324). Further, her laugh is described as "primitive" (281).

When Arty sees a wolf transform into an old woman, the reader familiar with soucouyant tales might infer a confusion of werewolf mythology with soucouyant legend—perhaps Priest has conflated the Trinidadian ligahoo/lagahoo with the soucouyant? This muddling of details continues, however, when the creature gets wounded by silver (97). Silver is revealed as "kind of like their Kryptonite," weakening them so that a wooden stake can be used (270). This is European and U.S. symbology, not particularly Caribbean. And although the Herskovitses' report on the soucouyant figure in Haiti also features red eyes—their "evil [. . .] nature is revealed by their red eyes, though some hold that they have a black spot in the corner of the eye" (*Life in a Haitian Valley* 239)—in the context of Priest's novel, the demon's "two glowing red eyes" (50) seem very Hollywood, as does the detail of her "stench," a rotten egg or sulfur odor that is attributed to the smell "of something long dead" (56).

In the same way, the children of the novel rely on the expertise of Harry Lightfoot for help with the "wolf lady" (167): "'He knows things.' Every kid in town knew about Harry and how he knew before anyone when it was going to rain, and when it was going to stop, and how he could walk in the forest and talk to the animals" (169). Harry is not perceived as the stereotypical Indian in perfect communion with the natural world simply because of the children's naiveté; the narrative itself reinforces these tropes. Harry fits the image of the silent, stoic Indian with the wisdom of the ages evident in his "wise brown eyes" (266). He advocates for "seeing without seeing" (228); he learns American Indian shape-changer tales from his grandfather. When he appears for the final confrontation with the soucouyant, "Harry stood firm, a wild Indian, long hair blazing in the wind, fringed buckskins flowing, and a lone feather stuck in a leather head band. The moon at his back covered him in a soft glow, his hair, whipping out from around the head band, picked up the moonglow, reflecting it away and forming a halo that surrounded his grinning face" (312). He is the Noble Savage and the Warrior Brave, softened by the Judeo-Christian angel imagery suggested in the halo surrounding his face. He sacrifices his life in an attempt to destroy the soucouyant and save his White charges, becoming a modern-day incarnation of the Last of the Mohicans. And the reader learns that he has encountered the soucouyant before: during a trip to Trinidad in his youth, he witnessed a wolf draining a young woman of her blood and then changing into a ball of fire (267–68). When Carolina asks how he knew it was not just a big dog, since wolves are not indigenous to the islands, he replies: "I'm an Indian. I know" (268), suggesting an "Indian" expertise in all things natural.

Coffee is being pursued by the soucouyant because he broke into her home "at the end of the road" (53)—a detail consistent with conventional tales—and stole her magical locket, which allows the soucouyant to avoid aging or dying (274). This last element, Priest's own creative addition, puts readers in a situation where they are encouraged to identify with a thief: someone who has invaded another person's private residence—the very thing for which the soucouyant is condemned—and taken an item that was not his. If we compare the locket to a victim's blood, we are again expected to excuse behavior from Coffee—a White American man and, in many ways, a hypermasculine "man's man"—for which the soucouyant, a Black Caribbean woman, would be punished.

Priest does make gestures toward the possible recuperation of the soucouyant figure. She kills several characters whose murders appear justified: Seymour Oxlade, for example—a heavy drinker who molests his daughters, beats his wife, and expresses pedophilic attraction toward young boys—and Bill Gibson, also abusive to his wife and child. When his own son, Arty, sees him dead, the boy "didn't care if his father lay across the sidewalk forever, till his skin rotted off, till buzzards ripped him apart, till his bones bleached in the sun, till hell froze over" (178). Therefore, when Arty's young friend Carolina expresses compassion for the soucouyant, stating, "It's kinda sad, she'll be gone and there won't be anybody to remember her," it is Arty's perspective that rings most true, since he has lost the most at the hands of the creature. He replies, "Nobody's gonna wanna remember her" (288). Even though Carolina at one point wonders, "what if it doesn't want to hurt anyone? Just because werewolves are bad in movies doesn't mean this one's bad" (168), the audience is not encouraged at any other moment in the novel to adopt this stance or ever question the night witch's motives. She is cast as purely demonic, objectified, and voiceless throughout the novel—the epitome of Spivak's subaltern.

2 / Nineteenth-Century Connections: European Vampire Stories and Configurations of the Demonic Black Woman

Some of the foolish customs out here [in then British Guiana] must have come originally from England or perhaps it may be vice versa.
—REVEREND J. S. SCOLES, 1885

This chapter considers a coexisting influence on the soucouyant myths that were rooted/routed in West African cultures—another set of sites for the network—and on the contemporary renditions of Black female vampires, both within the African diaspora and without: nineteenth-century British narratives. The colonial presence of the British in the Anglophone Caribbean ensured the exposure to, if not absorption of, canonical English literary texts, historical narratives, and social norms by the resident population. As folkorists of the African Americas such as Melville Herskovits and, later, Roger Abrahams and John Szwed argued, "Peoples cannot live side-by-side, even in the most extremely restricted situations, and not affect each other culturally" (Abrahams and Szwed 10–11). One must recognize, however, that cultural transmission is not a one-way process, a unidirectional flow from one node (the colonial "center") to another (the "periphery" of the colonized). Ingrid Thaler asserts as much in her study of Black Atlantic speculative fiction: "[There are] processes of constant (and often indirect) interaction through which tropes travel between black and white cultural contexts across the Atlantic. [. . . T]he boundaries of these cultural contexts are permeable and flexible instead of strictly separate. Therefore, cultural production takes place as communication, interplay, and exchange" (2). Thus, while soucouyant tales were already in existence among the African Caribbean population—most likely transferred from Africa by enslaved peoples[1]—these tales were not inviolable: Caribbean culture is a syncretic one. Some storytellers might have preserved "African sensibilities" and only "selectively adapted" European values to their needs as members of the African diaspora (Abrahams and Szwed 48), while others might have embraced European political, economic, and cultural dominance and persisted in repeating tales that most closely reflected European mores and beliefs. And just as some of the African renderings surely blended with European elements, some British stories certainly appropriated African Caribbean elements. "This was no one-way cultural inter-play[. . . .] Rather, it is the inevitable by-product of cultural fascination and renewal that occurs when different groups encounter each other. [. . .] From our earliest documents on the slave populations and their social ways, it is evident that Europeans were fascinated by the tremen-dous energies devoted to these [folkloric performances and] recreations by the slaves" (Abrahams and Szwed 37). Historian Lawrence Levine discusses how "difficult, often impossible" it is to date African Americas folklore: not only are the identities of creators and points of origin "lost in the obscurity of the past," but texts were filtered through many unre-liable sources. Narratives were "collected belatedly, frequently by men and women who had only a rudimentary knowledge of the culture from which they sprang, and little scruple about altering or suppressing them" (xii). Cultural studies scholar Joseph Roach further contributes to the complexity of the situation when he discusses transmission in transat-lantic cultural performances: "[T]he memories of some particular times and places have become embodied in and through performances. But [. . .] memories torture themselves into forgetting by disguising their collaborative interdependence across imaginary borders of race, nation, and origin" (xi). Therefore, rather than assume that stories of vampires in the Caribbean and other African Americas communities were taken wholesale from European folklore and literature, or even that the sto-ries can be traced directly back to Africa, one must look at the colonial Caribbean as a cultural crucible for the generation of a new form of the legend, one that addressed the dynamics of race and creolization—intri-cacies of *blood*—and the enactment of gender in very specific ways.

Mimi Sheller notes that after the abolition of slavery in the Carib-bean, emancipated subjects "at times had to (indeed wanted to) perform normative scripts of sexual citizenship such as the 'good mother,' [and] the 'respectable woman'" ("Work That Body" 352). Deborah Thomas's study of nationalism and cultural politics in twentieth-century Jamaica follows in the same vein: she demonstrates how middle-class discourses attempted to control "vulgar" performances of sexuality—whether these discourses were generated by the White British colonizers *or* by the "brown" middle-class Jamaicans who took on the project of post-Independence nation building. The latter legitimized their political and cultural roles by "reproducing the colonial value system," especially when it came to ideas of "respectability" (Thomas 57). While there clearly have been multiple modes of anticolonial resistance in the history of the Caribbean—from political rallies to folktales, musical forms, and dramatic expressions—one must be careful of making "'narratives of liberation' out of every gesture of the popular" (Barnes 87). In other words, not every tale generated by "the People" served to undermine hegemonic ideas and structures.

Some of the earliest recordings of soucouyant tales were taken down by English landowners and travel writers. Many of these men would have interpreted the lore and transcribed it, possibly *translating* it into the context of the British culture, including popular narratives and European vampire stories. For all of these reasons, it is essential to look at early European literary versions of the vampiric African/African-diasporic woman before interrogating twentieth- and twenty-first-century renditions. The writing explored in this chapter takes into account how twentieth-century "performances" of Black female vampires from diaspora sources as well as those generated outside the diaspora may have been correspondingly shaped and molded by pervasive European images from the late 1700s to the very early 1900s—a long nineteenth century. The chapter is not a survey of the history of vampire literature but rather a study of some of the antecedents that set the cultural milieu for this book's main project: an exploration of contemporary revisions of the demonic, Black female vampire.

One might use Alice Besson's twenty-first-century artwork as a visual example of the composite nature of soucouyant folklore. (See figure 7.) In this 2002 piece, Besson overlays a watercolor image of an African Caribbean woman, based upon a painting by Michel-Jean Cazabon (1813–88), onto an Alfredo Codallo woodcut, which was originally commissioned by Trinidad's Fernandes Distillery (acquired by Angostura in 1973) as an advertisement for Vat 19 rum. Cazabon, acclaimed as the first internationally known Trinidadian artist, was classically trained in Paris and Italy; his work, however, primarily focused on Caribbean nature scenes and portraits of mixed-race subjects. His journeys and heritage suggest a complex trail of cultural origins, as was also true of Codallo (1913–71). In Besson's work, both female figures stare out of the picture's frame, potentially unsettling the viewer: the past emerges to scrutinize the present, and while the Creole woman invites interaction, the soucouyant

FIGURE 7. Alice Besson's creation, superimposing a watercolor image of a Black woman in a headwrap onto a black-and-white woodcut image of a hideous soucouyant figure. (Courtesy of Paria Publishing Co., Ltd.)

looks out hungrily, ready to consume the object it regards. What is most significant for this chapter, however, is the way both figures conjure up notions of African women's sexuality. The younger woman's gaze appears especially bold given contemporary assumptions of Victorian propriety for women, and her right hand, somewhat obscured and somewhat suggestive, is either raising her skirts or emerging from beneath them. Her youthful beauty stands in striking contrast to the ways Codallo renders the soucouyant as ugly and horrific: not only is she peeling away her skin, but her eyes are asymmetrical, lending her a lizard-like air, and features like her broad shoulders, protruding nose, unruly hair, and disfigured teeth serve to masculinize her. However, she—and, by extension, the woman represented in the overlay—stands next to a bed. Their proximity to this object projects the notions of overabundant sexuality— simultaneously desirable and frightening—that have haunted African diasporic women over the past three hundred years.

Because many present-day readers are unfamiliar with the wide array of vampire novels and short stories that preceded *Dracula* (1897), as well as the myriad vampire tales from cultures outside of Europe, Bram Stoker typically receives the majority of credit for developing the paradigmatic bloodsucker: an aristocratic man who hails from Transylvania—a European but ethnically "Other" nation—possesses the ability to transform into a bat and shows vulnerability to garlic and crosses. Historian H. L. Malchow identifies Stoker's Dracula as *"the* defining fictional vampire" in popular culture (167), and vampire scholar Milly Williamson also comments on this trend: "[T]hroughout the twentieth century, Dracula (both Bram Stoker's novel and the many screen adaptations) [has] dominated critical interpretations of the vampire, eclipsing earlier incarnations of the vampire and their many progeny" (5). Ancient Greek literature features stories of vampiric threat: Philostratus's *Life of Apollonius of Tyana* depicts a foreign Phoenician woman as a *lamia*, a life-draining menace to philosophy student Menippus. The 1773 ballad "Leonore" by German poet Gottfried August Ossenfelder (translated into English by writers such as Sir Walter Scott and Dante Gabriel Rossetti) is credited as one of the primary sources for a fascination with the vampire that arose in Romantic literature, even though the term "vampire" is never explicitly used in the work. John Polidori, uncle to Dante and Christina Rossetti, published the novel *The Vampyre* in 1819; French author Alexandre Dumas, who penned often-translated adventure stories such as *The Three Musketeers* and *The Count of Monte Cristo*, released "The Pale Lady" in 1848; and the penny dreadful *Varney the Vampire, or, The*

Feast of Blood, by James Malcolm Rymer, was read by the British public in serialized form from 1845 to 1847.[2] In the Caribbean context, the Reverend Charles Dance, a British missionary to the West Indies, wrote in 1881 about local people's beliefs in the skin-shedding female vampire:

> The coast people [of Guyana] are also not without their firm faith in [. . . Old Hags]. These old women, by the recitation of some absurd lines, are said to be empowered to take off their skin, which they fold up and hide in a convenient place. They then anoint their skinless bodies, and assume superhuman powers. They fly through the air; they enter closed rooms, and suck the life-blood of infants. During the time that they remain without their skin, a lurid halo surrounds them. If the wrapped-up and hidden skin can be found and pickled while the owner of it is skimming the air high overhead, or, like a vampire bat, gorging and disgorging infant blood, it ceases to be of use when the hag attempts to replace it, for it burns the skinless body. (quoted in Abrahams and Szwed 150)

And seven years before the release of *Dracula*, Englishman Eden Phillpotts published *In Sugar-Cane Land*, in which he described

> Another Ethiopian [*sic*] monster, akin to the vampire or wer-wolf [*sic*], [called] the loup-garou. [. . .] They always take off their skins when at work, to be cooler no doubt, and they invariably hide these coverings at the root of a silk-cotton tree. If anybody finds a skin, he can put the loup-garou who owns it in an extremely awkward position; because, if not returned, the owner catches a chill and grows faint and poorly from exposure, and ultimately fades away altogether. (166–67)

Finally, in the same year that Stoker published *Dracula*, Florence Marryat published *The Blood of the Vampire*, a novel detailing the predatory nature of a beautiful young "psychic vampire" from Jamaica—one who drains the energy, health, and life essence—rather than the literal blood—of her victims.[3]

What remains strikingly absent from current scholarship is how British exploits in the Caribbean and Africa *as well as* cultural attitudes toward women—and Black women especially—affected portraits of vampiric figures in nineteenth-century literature and beyond. The representations of vampires in the body of texts explored here clearly reveal the writers' beliefs about evil and superstition. They also expose social anxieties about "aberrant" female behaviors, as has been investigated by numerous critics. Concerns about disease and the fears resulting from nationalist projects, such as foreigners' penetration of British geographical, racial, and cultural borders—ideas as threatening as the bite of the vampire itself—have also been addressed critically. The unease has typically been interpreted as concern about immigration from eastern Europe, and sometimes Ireland or India, but I concur with Teri Ann Doerksen, who is one of the few to posit that Africa also contributed to the social distress of the time:

> Vampire texts, which became increasingly popular as the images of the Dark Continent proliferated, provided an exploration of illicit sexuality shrouded first in the construction of metaphorical "creatures of darkness," to replace the inhabitants of Darkest Africa, and second in the displacement of the kind of penetration involved in literal sexuality into the metaphorical realm of a somewhat different kind of "penetration." (140)

For Doerksen, vampires and Africans are mythologized in the Victorian imagination as hideous figures of darkness and an uncivilized lack of bodily control. What remains unstated, however, is how the figure of the African and African-diasporic woman *in particular* came to function as this dangerous creature of unrepressed desire and social corruption.

In his work on images of race in nineteenth-century British Gothic fiction, H. L. Malchow discusses how "perverse" sexuality and race were typically portrayed as monstrous: "The racial fiend is often a sexual threat and the sexual 'pervert,' a racial (that is, eugenic) menace. [. . . Both are] in theory mastered by their lubricious and bestial natures" (148). The obsession with the animalized yet sexualized African was by no means exclusive to the British isles. In 1896, one year before the publication of *Dracula* and *The Blood of the Vampire*, a group of Ashantis was put on exhibition in Vienna. They were housed in the zoological gardens and often approached for sex. Critic Sander Gilman reads Austrian writer Peter Altenberg's *Ashantee* (1897) as both a condemnation of this exploitation and an example of the public's fantasizing about African women and their genitalia. (Edward Long's *History of Jamaica* [1774] had gone into circulation over a century earlier, disseminating notions that people of African descent were prone to lasciviousness and possessed extraordinarily sizable genitals.)

What is at stake in *The Things That Fly in the Night* is how concepts of racial menace and sexual perversion adhered to Black women. Nowhere was this more apparent than in the showcasing of Saartjie Baartman/

Sarah Bartmann, the southern African woman who, in the early 1800s, was paraded around Europe as a "half-woman/half-animal" (Doerksen 142) and came to be known as the Venus Hottentot. In the field of medicine, researchers asserted that the prominent buttocks of African women like Baartman were signs of their hypersexual nature. When she died at the age of twenty-five, her buttocks and external genitalia were excised and donated to Paris's Musée de l'Homme. In this way, the medical establishment "deployed pseudo-scientific and racist discourses to rationalise this projection of illicit desires onto an Other" (Williamson 20)—a specifically female Other at once enticing and grotesque (and thus a prime example of Kristeva's abject). U.S. gynecologist Robert T. Morris, for instance, furthered notions of African primitivism that centered on the female body by publishing an article in 1892 in the *American Journal of Obstetrics and Diseases of Women and Children*. In it, he argued that the more civilized the group, the smaller the clitoral glans: "In negresses the glans clitoridis is free [of the prepuce covering] . . . excepting a few individuals who probably possess a large admixture of white blood. . . . In highly domesticated animals the glans clitoridis is free" (quoted in Williamson 20).

   In comparison to Baartman, John Boby, a Jamaican man with vitiligo who was displayed at London's Bartholomew Fair in 1795, managed to maintain a modicum of masculine subjectivity—an 1803 etching notes that he "exhibits *himself*" (emphasis added). Notably, however, Boby's birth also raised the specter of female sexual perversity. Royal College of Physicians accounts report that his mother, frightened by the white blotches on her newborn's brown skin, did not fear the baby itself but rather that the pigmentation was a sign of her own sexual indiscretions: she was afraid she would be accused of adultery with a White man. Her fear was not unfounded, as African Jamaican women were often accused of licentiousness and sexual immorality.

   In his 1793 publication *The History, Civil and Commercial, of the British Colonies in the West Indies*, British-born Bryan Edwards, who inherited considerable property in Jamaica and made numerous observations of enslaved peoples and plantation owners during his years there, recorded a cultural practice that linked the consumption of blood to women of African descent and their allegedly uncontainable sexuality:

   Human blood, and earth taken from the grave of some near relation, are mixed with water, and given to the party to be sworn, who is compelled to drink the mixture, with a horrid imprecation, that it may cause the belly to burst, and the bones to rot, if the truth be not spoken. *This test is frequently administered to [the] wives, on the suspicion of infidelity.* (Abrahams and Szwed 69, emphasis added)

The issue that arises again and again in the literature of this time is anxiety over African women's sexuality, coupled with worries over racial purity. Apprehensions about miscegenation were as prevalent in realistic fiction of the era as in stories of the supernatural.[4]

Unlike scholars who explore how racial difference was imagined as frightening and sexually perverse in nineteenth-century Britain, or how gender and sexuality were configured as abject, this chapter deciphers how concepts of race *and* gender came together to create a narrative of the grotesque African woman. Decades later, the modernist writer Lawrence Durrell continued the same association between Black women's genitalia, White male fascination, and the threat of the vampiric bite in *The Black Book* (1938): the character Miss Smith is observed by the White narrator as possessing eyes that "incandense," "large languid tits rotating on their own axes[. . . .] African worlds of totem and trauma," laughter that significantly "gets in" and "penetrates" (145), and a mouth that suggestively resembles the vagina dentata: the "fanatical rictus of the dark face [. . . with its] long steady pissing noise under the lid of teeth" (146). The narrator continues: "The strange stream of sex [. . . a] vision of the warm African fissure"—and in this phrase, the corporeal/vaginal gets collapsed with the geographical—"opened as tenderly as surgery, a red-lipped coon grin . . . to swallow all the white races and their enervate creeds, their arks, their olive branches" (146). African women's sexuality is compared to dangerous crevices in the earth into which White men can fall; to surgery, suggesting its ability to excise parts of the White male Self; to destructive cyclones (146). And while Durrell claims in his 1959 preface that his writing is a poor approximation of reality—"only a savage charcoal sketch of spiritual and sexual etiolation" (8)—and that his primary focus is to articulate "the problems of the anglo-saxon psyche" (8), he does little to undercut his portrait of the Black female character as anything more than hollow image. He participates in adding to the larger trope of the hypersexualized Black woman—another kind of "savage charcoal sketch."

Thus this chapter considers how British texts from the long nineteenth century contribute to notions of Black womanhood—with a special focus on African Caribbean womanhood—as inherently vampiric. As is obvious in Durrell's text and myriad narratives that follow, this discourse prevails well into the twentieth century, and eventually into the twenty-first, serving as a means of curtailing its subjects' erotic agency, even within the private sphere. It should be noted that although British colonists around the world and the colonized subjects who were flooded with British cultural narratives would definitely have been influenced by European fiction like *Dracula*, Kipling's verse, and Marryat's novel, which accentuated the horrors of "deviant" women, other cultural traditions—particularly from the previously ignored regions of the Caribbean and African diaspora—might also have contributed to this ideology, attributing female sex and bloodsucking to a demonic figure. This back-and-forth movement of ideas conforms to Roach's description of the "collaborative interdependence" of certain cultural acts (xi).

Early Stories of Caribbean Bloodlust

Long before Stoker's novel was published, documents about vampirism, cannibalism, and bloodlust in the Caribbean were available in England. The above-mentioned Bryan Edwards, a wealthy White merchant and plantation owner, described the events of a 1760 slave revolt in Jamaica, which later came to be known as Tacky's Rebellion, in terms of the vampiric consumption of blood: "[The rebels] surrounded the overseer's house about four in the morning, in which eight or ten White people were in bed, every one of whom they butchered in the most savage manner, and literally drank their blood mixed with rum. At Esher, and other estates, they exhibited the same tragedy" (Edwards, *History* 2, 60). Haiti's Independence in 1804 was viewed by many Europeans—particularly the French and the English—as a key moment of degeneration in the Caribbean. Englishman James Anthony Froude connected Black rule by the majority populations throughout the British West Indies to the "child murder and cannibalism [that] have reappeared in Hayti" (207); he argued that British rule was necessary or "these beautiful countries will become like Hayti, with Obeah triumphant, and children offered to the devil and salted and eaten" (144). In 1865, George Gordon, the son of a Black slave and a White plantation owner in Jamaica, was hanged by Governor Edward John Eyre for instigating riots among Jamaican people of African descent. In this case, Malchow details how African Jamaicans' political and economic complaints were transposed by White British subjects to "a fantasized gothic realm of black rage and bestial lust" (212); the same can be said of many events of the long nineteenth century.

What is especially relevant to *The Things That Fly in the Night* is the way women of African descent were particularly implicated in this discourse of bloodthirstiness: the initial London *Times* account of the 1865 riots described how a group of women tore one man's body apart and dragged his innards out; days later, the paper reported that women grievously mutilated *several* bodies. Governor Eyre commented that Black women in Jamaica "were even more brutal and barbarous than the men" (Malchow 213). And the belief in African Caribbean women's threat to the White male establishment was not new in 1865. In 1825, when a statute prohibiting the flogging of women was proposed to the Grenada House of Assembly, plantation owners objected vigorously. They argued that such a ban, although intended to protect female modesty, would encourage enslaved women's defiance: Caribbean historian Cecilia Green cites documents claiming that the African Grenadian female slaves were "the worst subjects upon an Estate" (par. 76, n71: *Report of the Select Committee of the [Grenada] House of Assembly on the Despatch of Earl Bathurst etc*, printed in *The Chronicle* (Roseau, Dominica), April 6, 1825). An 1826 report from the House of Assembly in Barbados reported that female slaves "evince[d], at all times, a greater disregard to the authority of their owners than the male slaves" ("Report of the House of Assembly on the Subject of the Slave Laws," *Barbados Globe* [Bridgetown: December 4, 1826]). In Trinidad, William Burnley, the major slave owner on that island in the early nineteenth century, believed whipping female slaves to be essential to the efficient operation of slave society. In *Opinions on Slavery and Emancipation* (1833), he claimed: "If the power of corporal punishment over the female Slave is taken out of the hand of the Master, she will proceed in a career of vice injurious to herself, destructive to her progeny, and to the utter annihilation of the beneficent expectations of the British Legislature" (quoted in Cudjoe, Introduction 8).

This "vice," of course, was most often related to unabashed sexuality. In his 1871 travelogue, the English writer Charles Kingsley commented, "The Negresses [of Trinidad], I am sorry to say, forgot themselves, kicked up their legs, shouted to bystanders, and were altogether incondite" (quoted in Edmondson, "Public Spectacles" 4). Lamenting the participation of young Black women in Trinidad's yearly carnival, an 1884 issue of the *Port of Spain Gazette* published: "The obscenities, the bawdy language and the gestures of the women in the street have been pushed to a degree of wantonness which cannot be surpassed and which must not be tolerated" (quoted in Edmondson, "Public Spectacles" 1). And in 1899— two years after the publication of *Dracula* and *The Blood of the Vampire*—W. P. Livingstone, editor of the *Jamaica Gleaner*, wrote about the failed attempts of British colonizers to "civilize" Jamaican women over the years—particularly when it came to their uncontained and uncontrolled sexuality: "To be married was, to a woman, to become a slave, a stone's throw in the past. She preferred her freedom, and accepted its greater responsibilities with equanimity. It was this unconscious sensuality which proved the greatest obstacle to the development of their character" (quoted in Cudjoe, Introduction 16). At this point in history, "freedom" and its responsibilities are linked to self-destructive "sensuality" and the gratification of the flesh, and this slippage remains in place in a variety of narratives.

Froude continued the association between bloodlust and the Black Caribbean population for a readership that carried well into the 1890s. Known for his efforts to attract White English settlers to the British West Indies colonies, especially at a time when Africa was capturing the British imagination (to be discussed shortly), as well as to prove the necessity of White rule over those of African descent, Froude penned *The English in the West Indies; or, The Bow of Ulysses* (1888), in which he depicted Black islanders as innocent, amiable, and nonthreatening—both physically and morally. He wrote: "they are not licentious. I never saw an immodest look in one [of] their faces, and never heard of any venal profligacy[. . . .] There is sin, but it is the sin of animals, without shame, because there is no sense of doing wrong" (43). Froude was quick to assert, however, that the dangers of bloodlust—a state distinctly tied to African savagery— threatened to consume the region if it, like Haiti, was allowed to degenerate under Black legislature. Joan Dayan asserts that for Froude, Haiti was the emblem of "the dark and heady substratum of Africa, which for him meant a legacy of cannibalism, blood drinking, and lust" ("Vodoun, or the Voice of the Gods" 13).

Interestingly, after his first visit to Haiti, Froude observed that "Children were running about in thousands, not the least as if they were in fear of being sacrificed, and babies hung upon their mothers as if natural affection existed in Jacmel as much as in other places" (165). He seems to have achieved some understanding of the Eurocentric myths surrounding the society (even though this later gets dislodged: by the end of his second visit to the island, he is again promoting rumors of bloodthirsty savages who participate in "serpent worship, and the child sacrifice, and the cannibalism" [303]). More striking for the current argument, however, is the revelation that women—the mothers in the quotation just cited—are implied to be the ones preying upon their children.

The prominence of diabolical African and African Caribbean women in the British imaginary is also evidenced in a document published one year later: *Obeah: Witchcraft in the West Indies* (1889) by Sir Hesketh J. Bell, defines *loogaroos*—a Grenadian term for soucouyants—as old women (and occasionally men) who must drink human blood every night in exchange for occult powers from the devil (166). As a self-proposed example of European rational thinking, Bell dismisses "these ridiculous idea[s] and stories [that] are believed in most firmly by Quashie" (169), noting that fears of the loogaroo are typically exploited by thieves, who know that locals will remain in their homes while crops and horses are stolen. At the same time, the tale reinforces European anxieties about darkness and the collapse of meanings between darkness of night, darkness of the skin, and "darkness" of the soul. As Abrahams and Szwed note in their collection of Caribbean travel writings from the seventeenth, eighteenth, and nineteenth centuries: "Nothing troubled the plantocrats more than the association of their slaves with nighttime activities. This equation, of course, fits in well with the whole group of stereotype traits: nighttime, diablerie, hypersexuality, and so forth" (34).

Despite identifying the stories with supernatural elements as "ridiculous," Hesketh Bell recounts yet another such tale—this time from the African slave coast—that further contributes to the systemic establishment of African women as diabolical. Bell accounts for the story as one learned from a "very rare, valuable old work on the West Indies" (184–85), *Nouveaux voyages aux Isles d'Amerique*, by Père Jean-Baptiste Labat. The descriptions of the text as "rare," "valuable," "old," inscribed on the page, and European-authored all seem to lend additional weight to its contents. In it, Labat claims that all Africans from the Continent attained mysterious magical abilities once they reached maturity. The story he proceeds to relate concentrates the fear of these abilities in African women. The priest describes a vessel full of enslaved people, taken from Goree Fort in 1696 to be transported to the French West Indian islands. "Some black women much versed in the diabolical sciences" prevent the ship from progressing more than a few leagues from the shore for seven weeks, even though winds are favorable for sailing (185). Although all of the adults have the capability, it is the women who excel.

Correspondingly, in the United States, WPA narratives from Florida include several accounts of Old Julie, a "conjure woman" who wreaked so much havoc, death, and mutilation on her master's plantation that he sold her. After a day's journey to the Deep South aboard a steamboat, she used her preternatural powers to make it travel back to its port of origin so that her master was forced to retain her. Labat's report, the Old Julie stories, and soucouyant tales all suggest trepidation over women with the power to control their own movement and migrations. And as was illustrated in Chapter 1, this pervasive discourse of the demonic woman of African descent does not grow weaker as one progresses into the twentieth century; rather, it gets solidified in a multitude of later narratives featuring Black female vampires and only begins to shift to more positive representations in the 1980s and 1990s.

To conclude the reading of Father Labat's narrative: during their extended time on the ship, some of the slaves accuse one old woman of threatening "to eat their hearts out" (186). When they mysteriously perish and their bodies are opened to determine the cause, their hearts and livers are found drained of blood. When the surgeon-major of the ship brutally beats the old woman and she curses him, he, too, dies inexplicably, with organs "dry as parchment" (186). Fearing the rest of the slaves will revolt if he kills the old woman, the captain negotiates with her: if she will let the ship go, she and two or three friends can return to their country. Before leaving, she promises to show him more of her strength: he locks several watermelons in a box, and they are later discovered to be "entirely empty, and nothing but the skin remained, inflated like a balloon and dry as parchment" (187). In this way, the tale of the frightening, vampiric, African (but soon to be Caribbean) woman was transmitted to a European reading public—one eagerly awaiting tales from the exotic foreign colonies. As Margaret Hunt contends, travel documents and ethnographic texts such as the ones described here did not provide the initial lessons on racism, but they certainly buttressed already-held beliefs.

Black Vampires Invade Europe

In the early 1800s, the Polish count Jan Potocki published *Manuscrit trouvé à Saragosse*, or *The Saragossa Manuscript*—first in St. Petersburg (1804 and 1805) and then in Paris (1813 and 1814). This collection of short stories, told by various narrators (much in the style of Boccaccio's *Decameron*), is woven together around the premise of a young man's escapades in Spain. On the first day, in an attempt to prove his valor, Captain Alfonso van Worden of the Spanish Walloon Guard (and thus most likely of Gaul origins) stays overnight in a deserted and allegedly haunted inn. When the clock strikes midnight, "a beautiful negress, half naked" (24), enters and invites him to share supper with her mistresses. The dining room is filled with a number of other Black women, whose "ebony-colored skins" stand in sharp contrast to the "rose and lily complexions" of sisters Emina and Zibeddé Gomélez (25). The first servant woman leads Alfonso through an intricate maze of corridors, emblematic of the mental contortions he will go through over the course of the ten-day narrative and of her deceptive nature. The rest dance "with a liveliness that bordered on license" (26). Alfonso later wonders whether the events were real, a mysterious dream, or evil demons sent to tempt him; in any case, seductive Black women's bodies are integrally involved in setting the scene.

Similarly, although the two sisters are first marked by their fair complexions, described as "strikingly beautiful, [. . .] svelte, dazzling [. . .] appealing" (25), and rooted in Europe—they speak Castilian Spanish and claim family origins in Granada—they, too, become sexually seductive figures closely associated with the African continent and the Black female body. They identify themselves as devout Muslims raised in Tunis, and, like the Black servant women, they entice Alfonso with their dancing: he admires "the charm of those two *African* beauties whose grace was enhanced by their diaphanous draperies" (26, emphasis added). This description of their clothing seems to be a refined way of implying that the mistresses are "half naked," much like their servants. And even though they are members of the elite, after being rescued with Alfonso from members of the Inquisition, Emina, impressed with the fact that he has kept a promise not to admit knowing them or reveal their names, cries, "Alfonso, you are greater than all the heroes *of our race* and *we belong to you!*" (65, emphasis added). She pledges herself and her sister to him, like wives to husband but also—quite distinct because of their African heritage, their religion and "race," as referenced here—like slaves to master. Emina is repeatedly characterized by her race and ethnicity: she is "the beautiful Moor" (26, 27); one of "the two Moorish girls" (64); one of "the beautiful African girls" (60); and "the beautiful African" (75). In this way, the reader is continually reminded of the dangers of the blood lurking beneath the skin: despite their appearance as White women, Emina and Zibeddé are distinctly marked as sensual female *African* bodies, creatures of the night who cause a loss of control in the European subjects they corrupt.

The sisters have grown up in a seraglio and had no contact with men, but they have experienced "an unusual capacity" of passionate connection to each other (27) and practiced the love scenes read about in a forbidden copy of *The Loves of Medgenoun and Leillé*. This hyperemotional, hypersexual nature is stimulating for Alfonso but also somewhat frightening. After dining, he wonders if the sisters are "insidious succubae" (26), coupling demonic and sexually vampiric behavior with the African women. The fiendish aspect is reinforced after Alfonso experiences a night of "incredible marvels" with Emina and Zibeddé, in which "I knew I was dreaming and yet I was conscious that the form I held in my arms was not a dream" (34). He awakens under a set of gallows next to the rotting corpses of two brothers, who have been cast as a specifically Spanish "species of vampire," descending each night to torment the living (22). The homosexual and necrophilic implications for the narrator are the source of his distress and the reader's horror, and the African sisters initiate Alfonso's sexual desire and sexual transgressions, as well as his loss of "civilized" inhibitions, the ability to control the transport of his body from one location to another, and his memories of the actual deeds. They represent what Gilman identifies as the Black woman as "the embodiment of sexuality, her genitalia [. . . as] the sign of decay and destruction" (124–25).

The vampire connection is repeated later in the text when Alfonso believes he sees the sisters in the guise of Gypsies:

could it be possible that those two passionate and alluring creatures were really mischievous sprites, who make game of mortals by assuming various forms? Or were they perhaps sorceresses, *or, what would be more revolting, vampires* whom heaven has allowed to assume the hideous bodies of the men hanging in the valley? (119, emphasis added)

The repeated references to demons, vampires, beauty, and Africa create a strong cultural association between African (and African-diasporic) womanhood, sexuality, and evil.

The most renowned reference to Caribbean vampirism in Europe, though, is found in Charlotte Brontë's *Jane Eyre* (1847). This novel helps set the cultural milieu for interpreting the "Black" female body in mid-nineteenth-century England, reinforcing connections between this body and the demonic, life-draining vampire. As a "classic" of British literature, it continued to perform this task in the colonies as well as in the British isles, and as readily in the twentieth and twenty-first centuries as one hundred and sixty years before.

While scholars such as Raymond McNally and Carol Senf observe that Rochester's mad wife is compared by Jane to "the foul German spectre—the Vampyre" (Brontë 242), they fail to acknowledge that Bertha Rochester (née Mason) is a Caribbean woman—she hails from Spanish Town, Jamaica. Like Potocki's Gomélez sisters with their lily-colored skin, Bertha is also White: she is a creole, or Americas-born European subject. However, in the scene where Jane first sees her, she is described both in terms of a supernatural ghoul—"fearful and ghastly" with a "gaunt head" and "fiery eye"—and in terms of the primitive Other: "It was a discoloured face—it was a savage face. I wish I could forget the roll of the red eyes and the fearful blackened inflation of the lineaments" (242). Rochester responds that ghosts are typically pale, to which Jane replies, "This, sir, was purple: the lips were swelled and dark; the brow furrowed; the black eyebrows widely raised over the bloodshot eyes." The language here is strikingly similar to the caricatured images of the African savage, as well as the African American "sambo." In this way, the protagonist significantly racializes the "unnatural" figure the vampire. She has also established it as discernibly female in its nightclothes, although she makes the gender much more ambiguous with her choice of the pronoun "it."

The author herself might well have been relying on her British audience's anxieties regarding rebellion in the British West Indies, and Jamaica in particular. The Gordon "revolt" had not yet occurred when *Jane Eyre* was published, but Tacky's Rebellion of 1760, the Jamaica Maroon Wars of 1795–96, the failed British involvement in the conflicts in Saint Domingue/Santo Domingo (the present-day island of Hispañola), the 1816 slave revolt in Barbados, the 1823 insurrection in Demerara, and the Jamaica uprising of 1831 had heightened British worries over the Caribbean colonies and the roles women played in the violence. Significantly, the reported leader of the Jamaican maroons was a woman of African descent: "Nanny" rallied the forces and, according to legend, inspired fighters who watched the bullets of the British military bounce off of her in battle. Additionally, a literate, Caribbean-born Black woman named Nanny Grigg was identified as "the revolutionary ideologue" of the slaves involved in the 1816 Rebellion in Barbados (Beckles, *Natural Rebels* 171).

In English literature before 1760, Jamaica does not appear as such a site of menace. A key example would be Samuel Richardson's *Pamela; or, Virtue Rewarded* (1740). Pamela's pursuer-turned-husband confesses that in his past, he impregnated a young woman who escaped his influences and her weakness of resolve by fleeing to Jamaica with two female friends. There, she passed as a youthful widow and married both "happily" and "well." Rather than serving as a punishment to the impure or a site of further corruption, Jamaica is represented as a haven where one can socialize with other well-bred people, establish a fortune, and "preserve [one]self from further [sexual] Guiltiness" (443). And when Black Jamaica escapes its boundaries and enters the British isles, Richardson neutralizes the threat of contamination: the ten-year-old enslaved boy—his sex is significant here—who is sent as a "present" to the young woman's daughter dies of smallpox within a month of his arrival. Both aspects correspond to the messages embedded in *A New History of Jamaica*, the second edition of which Richardson printed in the same year that *Pamela* was published. That text encouraged increased immigration to the island from Britain while acknowledging the colony's reputation for "lawlessness, lack of schools, unhealthy conditions," and cruelty to the enslaved (573).

In *Jane Eyre*, the vampire imagery is repeated when Rochester takes Jane to view Bertha in her attic cell. On a previous occasion the Jamaican woman had drawn blood from her brother, Richard Mason; in the latter scene she springs at Rochester "and grappled his throat viciously, and laid her teeth to his cheek" (250). Her penetration of the men's skin holds distinct vampiric connotations. She is simultaneously animalized: Jane again refers to Bertha as "it," unable to distinguish whether she is animal or human: "it groveled, seemingly, on all fours; it snatched and growled like some strange wild animal: but it was covered with clothing; and a quantity of dark, grizzled hair, wild as a mane, hid its head and face" (250).

Senf also asserts that Bertha is likened to a vampire when she bites her brother on one of his visits ("Daughters of Lilith" 200). The critic employs the scene for a "feminist" reading of female rebellion against male authority: "Bertha Mason savagely attacks both her brother and her husband, the men responsible for her incarceration, but she does not harm Jane Eyre" (203). It should be noted that a simple gender binary does not account for the colonial nuances of the narrative, however: these men are colonial agents who steal her wealth. In a sense, they represent vampiric figures themselves: Rochester, the inheritance-less second son who must make his fortune in the Caribbean—which he accomplishes through marriage to Bertha—and Richard, who by "selling" his sister to a husband who will control not only her finances but her mobility, social life, and reputation, acquires a higher station in society.

Much of Rochester's angst in the novel is linked to Bertha's racial ambiguity: she is of European descent, but her close proximity to African Caribbean peoples and cultures and the stereotypical associations between the region of her birth, excessive sensuality, and the loss of inhibitions invoke the possibility of racial corruption. In "Women and

Vampires: *Dracula* as a Victorian Novel," for example, Judith Weissman claims that "The one violently sexual woman in a major Victorian novel is Bertha Rochester, an older woman [. . .] and a Creole, part black" (395). In nineteenth-century Europe, however, "Creole" meant "born in the Americas," not racially mixed. Weissman's allegation is emblematic of Rochester's *anxiety*, not the reality of Bertha's ancestry.

When he describes his first wife's monstrous appetites—"What a pigmy intellect she had—and what giant propensities! Bertha Mason [. . .] dragged me through all the hideous and degrading agonies which must attend a man bound to a wife at once intemperate and unchaste" (261)—it is clear that although Rochester finds her sexual hunger loathsome, he claims powerlessness in his attempts to resist it. The seductive powers of the African "jezebel"—one of the most potent and long-lasting stereotypes of women of the African Americas—are too great. At the same time, his statement holds hints of her vampiric nature, especially in that authors such as Stoker and Marryat later played with the trope of vampiric mesmerism and mental control over their victims. Marryat, for instance, aligns her vampire with snakes, which were often associated with the hypnosis of their prey. As victim Margaret Pullen "tried to disengage herself from the girl's clasp, [. . .] Harriet Brandt seemed to come after her, like a coiling snake, till she could stand it no longer" (21).

Rochester's description of Bertha's "most gross, impure, depraved" nature (261)—a stereotype perpetuated about people of African descent (among others, such as the poor, homosexuals, and the mentally ill), who were said to be hypersexual and immoral—coupled with his suggestion that she is just like her mother ("the true daughter of an infamous mother" [261]) hint at his belief that her bloodline is equally as impure as her character. Anxieties over the corruption of blood remain key to most European vampire narratives, a topic to which I will return in Chapter 6. It should be noted here, however, that Rochester's imprisonment of Bertha in his mansion's attic ensures that his pure blood cannot get tainted by hers (and the taint need only be real in his mind, not in actuality)—either through vampiric or sexual/reproductive acts—and neither can any other "pure" White *or Black* British subject. Because Jamaican Bertha represents the threat of miscegenation in the White British imagination—both her own and in the potential children she might bear for her husband—she must meet her doom by the end of the novel.[5]

Reference to a threatening Black woman can also be found in J. Sheridan Le Fanu's *Carmilla* (1872). Set in Styria—a region in central and southeast Austria (and the location in which Bram Stoker originally

intended to set *Dracula)*—the novel focuses on the isolated and uncivilized nature of the foreign landscape. The story is narrated by Laura, an
innocent young woman born of a Hungarian mother, now dead, and an
English father. A Swiss governess, Madame Perrodon, and Mademoiselle de Lafontaine, a finishing governess of French and German parentage, as well as a nurse and a nursery maid, have helped raise Laura
in what might be identified as typically English fashion: she calculates
distances in "English miles," for instance, and her father insists upon
having tea every evening. The ominous details of her physical surroundings, however, loom large at the start of the tale. In it, Laura's family
temporarily takes in a beautiful and charming young woman—Carmilla—who appears to be the same age as the protagonist. As time goes
by, young women start dying in neighboring villages, and Laura eventually becomes sickly herself. Carmilla is revealed to be a vampire who has
preyed upon the community for generations, although always appearing
to be the same age.

Irish literature scholar Margot Backus makes a compelling claim for
reading the protagonist's upbringing as emblematic of "the enclosed and
isolated childhood of an Anglo-Irish girl [. . . with] its ambivalent relationship to the culture that surrounds it, and its economic raison d'être"
(127). However, the dynamics also ring true of British colonial families
in the West Indies, India, and most other British colonies of the mid-
1800s. And Laura's emphasis on her home as a "primitive place" (244)
in the midst of essentially pathless woods and far from other people
seems to resonate most with British explorers' accounts of the wilds of
Africa, with its primitive people and need for the cultivation of the land,
resources, and pagan subjects. British narratives of the barbaric African
titillated European readers throughout the nineteenth century.[6] As Vic-
torianist Patrick Brantlinger argues, "such accounts of African exploration exerted an incalculable influence on British culture and the course
of modern history" (176).

The specter of the African woman as a ferocious yet enticing force
haunted several of these African travel narratives. Winwood Reade's *Savage Africa* (1863), for example, published about a decade before *Carmilla*,
characterizes the daughter of Congolese warrior queen Mussasa as "at
once voluptuous and bloodthirsty" (quoted in Malchow 91). A shadowy
Black woman also haunts Le Fanu's text. When the vampiric Carmilla
is first taken into the narrator's home, it is because of an alleged travel
accident: the carriage in which Carmilla and her mother are traveling
tips over, and the young woman is left to recover with Laura's family

while her mother continues on the journey. Madame Perrodon remarks that there was another woman in the carriage who did not get out when Carmilla and her mother emerged, although neither the narrator, her father, nor Governess de Lafontaine observed her: "[S]he described a hideous black woman, with a sort of coloured turban on her head, who was gazing all the time from the carriage window, nodding and grinning derisively towards the ladies, with gleaming eyes and large white eye-balls, and her teeth set as if in fury" (257). Le Fanu leaves the reality of the Black woman's existence ambiguous, suggesting the often-imagined horror generated by the female subject of color and the border-crossing nature of the soucouyant, who continually travels between physical body and intangible essence, the world of the living and the essence of death. And while editor Robert Tracy assumes that Carmilla's name for the woman—Matska, "a feminine diminutive"—suggests "a Czech or Polish servant" (345), I would argue that the name simply serves as evidence of the language that Carmilla speaks and the terms with which she, as a member of the eastern European upper class, refers to her retainers. It is unclear, too, whether the "hideousness" in the passage is attributed to the woman by Madame Perrodon or added by the narrator; regard-less, the obscured Black woman clearly generates fear. She is depicted in terms of savagery, with glinting white eyes and gnashing teeth, and in terms of racial otherness, as well as ethnic strangeness with her head-scarf. She also exits the narrative just as quickly and mysteriously as she enters. By not reappearing for the remainder of the story, she functions much in the way the so-called Dark Continent did—as a prop for the European imagination.

Backus asserts that the woman's turban and complexion suggest a dark-skinned East Indian figure who represents "the moral and geo-political alterity at the root of the creation and circulation of creatures such as [the vampiric] Carmilla" (130). The phrase "a sort of" that modi-fies "turban," however, intimates that the garment is not a true turban, only like one. Coupled with the description of the shadowy figure's black skin, it seems likely that she is specifically a Caribbean woman—one also figured in terms of "moral and geopolitical alterity" but more closely aligned to witchcraft and savagery in the nineteenth-century British imagination. During his 1887 travels to the Caribbean, Froude com-mented on similar hair accessories among the Black women of Trinidad, who "dress themselves with real taste. They hide their wool [hair] in red or yellow handkerchiefs, gracefully twisted" (69). He notes that the fash-ion extended back in time to Columbus's accounts of Carib women.

Teri Ann Doerksen reads the character of Carmilla as emblematic of the African continent: because she is "impervious to Laura's tentative explorations" about her family and past, "her nature remains unfathomable. She is a Dark Continent, but she is the Dark Continent of English nightmares: instead of waiting in one place to be explored and illuminated, she comes in search of civilization in order to corrupt it where it lives" (141). Even without this connection, Carmilla's primary moral and ethnic influence—the Black woman in the carriage who perhaps spends more time raising her than her cold and stately mother—is distinctly of African descent. In Europe, wet-nursing was practiced well into the nineteenth century, despite the exhortations of numerous preachers, moralists, and physicians; it was believed that children might "imbibe something of both the physical appearance and the character of the nurse along with her milk" (Thurer 199). In the British colonies, Black nannies often breastfed White children because elite White women often viewed the practice of nursing of their own children as "unseemly" (Beckles, *Centering* 69). The custom persisted despite arguments that White children could be tainted by Black women's blood. In *The History of Jamaica*, for example, Long commented: "[White mothers] give [their babies] up to a Negroe or Mulatto wet nurse, without reflecting that her blood may be corrupted, or considering the influence which the milk may have with respect to the disposition, as well as health, of their little ones" (quoted in Brathwaite, *Omens* 18).

Horror surrounding the idea of imbibing both milk and blood from a woman's breast is prominent in *Carmilla*: after Carmilla's arrival, Laura dreams of a large, feline, black animal menacingly pacing about her bedroom. When it eventually leaps onto the bed, the narrator suddenly feels "a stinging pain as if two large needles darted, an inch or two apart, deep into my breast" (Le Fanu 278). The scene parallels an event she remembers from when she was six years old: she awakened and saw a lovely young woman gazing at her from the bedside. (Readers later learn that this was Carmilla.) "She caressed me with her hands, and lay down beside me on the bed, and drew me towards her, smiling; I felt immediately delightfully soothed, and fell asleep again. I was wakened by a sensation as if two needles ran into my breast very deep at the same moment, and I cried loudly" (246).

The later mirroring between the characters of Laura and Carmilla becomes more closely tied to a blended identity caused by the corruption of blood. In the end, both women are revealed to be descendants of Mircalla, Countess Karnstein ("Carmilla" is an anagram of "Mircalla").

Laura's mother's bloodline as well as the homoerotic/breastfeeding vampiric penetration have ensured that tainted blood lurks in the young protagonist's veins, and nineteenth-century fears of miscegenation rear their hydra-like heads.

The tale of the vampire of Croglin Grange—popularized in Augustus Hare's *Story of My Life* (1896) as well as in orally conveyed legends—provides yet another example of invasion by a frightening brown-skinned vampire, although its gender remains ambiguous.[7] Hare reported that the family of a Captain Fischer of Cumberland, England—his informant—had rented the Grange out to two brothers and a sister. Looking out of her window one night, the sister witnessed two lights flickering among the trees and approaching the house. Just as she jumped up to alert her brothers, she saw a "hideous brown face with flaming eyes glaring in at her" (Masters 134). The creature eventually breaks open the window and bites her throat. When the family returns to the Grange after an extensive recuperative stay in Switzerland, the young woman is awakened by scratching on her window and "the same hideous brown shriveled face, with glaring eyes, looking in at her" (135). This time she is able to scream and her brothers fire upon and pursue the vampire. In a vault filled with desecrated coffins, they locate the creature: "brown, withered, shriveled, mummified, [. . .] hideous" (135). The repeatedly pronounced detail of the vampire's brown complexion suggests a heightened racial anxiety in the story—one as significant for understanding the social climate of the Hare's Victorian England as the late seventeenth-century period in which the story was supposedly set. A brown face could have conjured images of the desperately impoverished—as Laura Sagolla Croley notes: "Social reformers and journalists throughout the [nineteenth] century used the language of race to talk about the very poor" (173). However, the rhetorical move that invokes the race of the foreign Other as frightening and aggressive serves to reinforce ideas about the perversity of the Other and reestablish the legitimacy of White, bourgeois, male control.

In the Line of the Mother: Maternal Inheritance in *The Blood of the Vampire*

Marryat's 1897 novel, although published nearly thirty years later, continues to convey anxiety about ideas of blood purity—particularly the corruption of the British national subject by Black women—and the notion of taint passed down through the maternal line. Historian Erlene Stetson asserts that laws supporting the principle of *partus sequitur ventrem*, which dictated that children followed in the condition of the mother in the antebellum United States and much of the pre-abolition Caribbean, make the sexual exploitation of enslaved women transparent. These laws tacitly sanctioned sexual intercourse between White men and female slaves, suggesting that there was no threat of paternal responsibility or potential decrease of property to the man and his ostensibly legitimate children. Marryat's novel reveals that the ideology did not end with slavery.

The book did not attract much attention when published; at this point in Marryat's life, her reputation as a writer had begun to fade, and she was known more for her spiritualism. One reviewer supposes Stoker's *Dracula* to be the inspiration for *The Blood of the Vampire*, but given that both were published in the same year, it seems likely that Marryat had started the work independently. Catherine Pope, a Marryat scholar who maintains the author website www.florencemarrat.org, concurs: "[I]t was assumed that Marryat had simply cashed in on the vampire craze, but she must've been writing it before 'Dracula' was published. There's no evidence that she knew what Stoker was writing. Although they collaborated on 'The Fate of Fenella,' they wrote completely independently and had no need to correspond."[8] Either way, Marryat's references to the Caribbean and her creation of a mixed-race female vampiric character point to some of the social preoccupations of her era.

The narrative opens with a group of upper-class British tourists vacationing at a seaside resort in Heyst, Belgium. Harriet Brandt, a nineteen-year-old woman of independent means who has just left convent life in Jamaica, is revealed to be the central vampire of the tale. Over the course of the novel, readers learn of at least ten victims. There are two African Jamaican wet nurses from Harriet's infancy, one of whom falls ill, the other of whom dies, and Caroline, the daughter of a neighboring plantation owner. After spending a night with this friend of her youth, Harriet thinks, "Poor little Caroline! [. . .] So pale and thin and wan she was!" (199). Harriet unknowingly sapped her essence, or "life-blood," and this minor character dies as well. Sister Theodosia from the convent grows grievously ill after letting the six-year-old Harriet sit in her lap for extended periods of time; Olga Brimont, a fellow convent student, fares poorly on their sea journey to Europe, claiming, "I did not feel as if I could breathe there [in the cabin]—such a terrible oppression as though some one were sitting on my chest—and such a terrible feeling of emptiness" (27). In Heyst, when Harriet leans affectionately against Margaret Pullen, the older woman feels faint, as if she has been "scooped hollow" (21); Margaret's baby Ethel later starts sleeping excessively and "unnaturally" (49), and after a period of feverish exhaustion, She, too, perishes. Captain Ralph Pullen, affianced to Elinor Leyton, succumbs to his own lack of morals as well as Harriet's beauty and effervescent personality but escapes with his life; the inexperienced Bobby Bates, however, and the noble Anthony Pennell do not. Bobby grows "whiter and more languid every day" (179) in Harriet's presence, and upon his death, his mother, the Baroness Gobelli, cries out: "it's your poisonous breath that 'as sapped 'is! [. . .] She has the vampire's blood in 'er and she poisons everybody with whom she comes in contact" (187).

Although Brenda Hammack discusses Harriet as a "hypersensual" and "over-sexed female" who saps the vigor of her male partners and attributes this representation to late nineteenth-century views of women as "potential vampires" in all situations (xiv), it should be noted that only three of Harriet's ten victims are male. The lesbian subtext is raised explicitly in the novel: when Harriet looks at Margaret with a gaze of obvious yearning, the latter feels amused: "She had heard of cases, in which young unsophisticated girls had taken unaccountable affections for members of their own sex, and trusted she was not going to form the subject for some such experience on Miss Brandt's part" (27). Teri Ann Doerksen's analysis of the lesbian subtext of *Carmilla* can be applied in this instance as well; however, overall it seems that Harriet's choices are less dictated by a homoerotic or homosexual impulse than by mere greed and the availability of female victims to a young, unmarried, and unchaperoned woman.

Other aspects of the novel, however, ensure that Harriet Brandt's gender, sexual voracity, race, and vampiric nature are inextricable. The explicitly vampiric women of the narrative all hail from Jamaica, reestablishing the African Caribbean woman as an individual, racial, and national menace for British subjects. Protagonist Harriet Brandt, for example—a Jamaican woman who is white-complexioned enough to pass for White but possesses more than the requisite "one drop" of African blood that categorizes her as Black in mainstream discourse—nearly manages to seduce a British captain away from his aristocratic fiancée and eventually marries a wealthy English philanthropist. Miss Carey, Harriet's biracial mother, is maligned for her ferocious bloodlust as well as her carnal nature—she had sexual relations with Harriet's Swiss father for several years out of wedlock. And Harriet's grandmother, bitten by a vampire bat while pregnant with Miss Carey, was an unnamed slave involved with a White "Barbados judge" (16).

Hammack reads the narrative primarily through nineteenth-century theories of imaginationism: the "excessive emotion" experienced by a pregnant woman was believed to be impressed onto her fetus (x). Thus, whereas today's readers would likely focus on the idea that the vampire bat corrupted Harriet's grandmother's blood with some sort of poisonous element, Marryat and those of her era would have believed that a frightening encounter with a bat was traumatic enough to result in vampirism (xi). As a "psychic vampire" (Hammack v) who doesn't physically bite or drink the blood of any of her victims, Harriet drains strength, energy, and even the literal lives of several people in her purview. Hammack demonstrates that this "figurative blood lust," like her mother's more literal desire to shed blood, can be seen as "transmitted to the fetus in utero" (xi).

Hammack is completely accurate in her claim that, as a product of both imaginationism and miscegenation, Harriet "threatens the mainstream" (xv). I would push this argument further, however, linking the threat specifically to Harriet's—and her maternal relatives'—position as a Caribbean woman of African descent. Thus, while Hammack attributes Harriet's role as "as much victim as victimizer" (viii), comparable to Florence Marryat's position as a professional woman and public figure in an era when society frowned upon assertive women, I ascribe the ambiguous portrait to a conflicted view on race as well as gender norms. Marryat's vision of the vampiric African Caribbean woman definitively contributes to the plethora of later narratives that feature Black female vampires as compulsively promiscuous, frighteningly uncontained by death, men, domestic spaces, or their lands of origin—they are, in almost every way, abject bodies, out of control.

Interestingly, the source of guilt in many instances in Marryat's novel can be traced to the European males as readily as it would have been credited to the African Caribbean females in the author's time. While it is true that the vampire bat attack is overtly identified as the initial site of trauma in the narrative—one that gets mapped onto ensuing generations of female bodies—the grandmother's identity as a nameless Black slave warrants certain attention—at least as much as the fact that she is preyed upon by a vampire bat. Marryat leaves open the possibility that the grandmother's impregnation by the White slave owner—another type of vampiric assault in that he penetrates her sexually and, as a slave master, symbolically drains her of physical labor and freedom of choice—is equally as harrowing an experience. The lack of free will and the power discrepancy between master and slave imply a vampiric violation even if the female/enslaved partner is "willing"; thus the interaction between Harriet's grandmother and her owner serves as a scarring encounter that simultaneously leaves its impression on the fetus. The grandmother dies in childbirth—the result of this sexual ordeal (or, possibly, the literary "punishment" for challenging the taboos surrounding interracial sex).

Interestingly, as in her mother's case, Miss Carey was also "taken" as a mistress. The young age of the character—she goes to Henry Brandt when she is fourteen—would likely have been read by Marryat's metropolitan readers as a sign of *her* sexual vampirism—a promiscuity attributed to all people of African descent but especially to Black women draining the sexual strength and will to resist from their White male victims. It also hints, however, at Henry Brandt's sexual exploitation of a minor (more of an issue today, of course, than a century ago, when it might not have raised many eyebrows) and a member of the biracial "mulatto" caste: his actions can be considered vampiric in terms of the sexual penetration that occurs, the sapping of youthful innocence, and the predatory nature of choosing a girl who is ultimately powerless and voiceless because of inferior social standing.

In Miss Carey's case, certain characters intimate that she could not marry Henry Brandt because of her biracial identity (she is, rather, his mistress, and ostracized by Black and White communities, not considered fully either). Social laws would definitively have condemned her marriage to a White man. Cecilia Green notes that up until the "the eve of emancipation [1833], visitors to the Caribbean were still remarking on the absence or dearth of white women, married couples, and practiced religion" (par. 19). The scarcity of White women meant White men typically took on African Caribbean "concubines," but marriage was rare even between Black men and women. Although civil and religious authorities in England encouraged slave marriages—largely in order to uphold the "moral and civilizational integrity" of the British Empire (par. 1)—slave owners resisted this pressure as an assault on their rights as property holders (slaves being a type of property), a threat to property values, a violation of their rights to self-legislate, and an erosion of revered beliefs in the racial exclusivity and superiority of White people. As mentioned earlier, children in slave societies followed in the line of their mothers—not their fathers—ensuring the primogeniture of the "legitimate" (i.e., White) offspring (and the added benefit of the free reproduction of the labor force). This ideology continued after the abolition of slavery, guaranteeing that the perceived stigma of slave status and African blood could be traced through the maternal line.

Harriet, like Miss Carey, is ostracized by the British for being of mixed race. When her first British lover, Captain Ralph Pullen, learns of her "terrible parentage" (81), he says "it would be impossible for any man in my position to think of marrying her! One might get a piebald son and heir! Ha! ha! ha!" (173). Notably, it is *her* blood mixed with his that would cause the speckled appearance in their children, not his mixed with *hers*. And although the morally and physically superior Anthony Pennell *does* marry Harriet, their relationship ends tragically before the birth of any offspring. He falls victim to her vampiric nature, and she commits suicide to prevent the deaths of any other innocent people. Each female vampire in the novel thus follows "in the line of the mother" in terms of the fixed identity of the child and the traceability of the vampiric condition, a notion that harkens back to the slave codes where, if liaisons between an enslaved (typically Black female) person and a free (typically White male) person resulted in progeny, the child took on the legal status of its mother.

Paternal heritage and influence went unacknowledged during slavery because, as Hortense Spillers notes, "if 'kinship' were possible, the property relations would be undermined, since the offspring would then 'belong' to a mother and a father" (75). The conventions of slavery in the Americas—as rigid, Spillers claims, as grammatical rules—dictated that the child was legally *possessed* by the male owner although never *related* to him, thus preventing cross-racial claims "of bloodline, of a patronymic, of titles and entitlements, of real estate and the prerogatives of 'cold cash'" (74). A child could not "belong" to its biological father if the latter were enslaved, since he had no say over the child's welfare. Green notes that on plantations in the British West Indies, account books kept by owners and managers "routinely recorded domestic units as defined by a mother and her children, regardless of the (usually duly noted) presence of a co-resident male and his biological relationship to the children" (par. 92). Along the same lines, the child was *born* to the mother but could never "belong" to her, given her position as a woman in patriarchal society and as chattel in slave society. Spillers's argument that these rules—this early "grammar"—led to a misnaming of Black women's social and cultural power in the second half of the twentieth century applies to the current project as well: Black women in contemporary society become "a meeting ground of investments and privations in the national treasury of rhetorical wealth" (65); "markers [. . .] loaded with mythical prepossession" (65); distorted symbols enshrouded in "the semantic and iconic folds buried deep in the collective past" (69).

Dr. Phillips—a character granted great authority in *The Blood of the Vampire* by way of his age and experience, his career in the medical

establishment, his membership in the British upper class, and his identity as a White British male—consistently stresses maternal blood inheritance when discussing Harriet's monstrous nature. He depicts Harriet's
"terrible mother" as "a sensual, self-loving, crafty and bloodthirsty half-
caste" in order to stress that while "[Harriet] may seem harmless enough
at present, so does the tiger cub as it suckles its dam, but that which is
bred in her will come out sooner or later" (84). He continues: "if this girl
is anything like her mother, she must be an epitome of lust" (86). There is
no mention of her father's influence at this point; clearly, the inheritance
is a maternal one.

The vampire storyline competes with the racial one but never over-
shadows it. When Dr. Phillips describes Harriet's mother as "a revolting
creature," his language emphasizes her uncivilized, bestial nature. To
him, she is a

> fat, flabby half caste, who hardly ever moved out of her chair but sat
> eating all day long, until the power to move had almost left her! I
> can see her now, with her sensual mouth, her greedy eyes, her low
> forehead, and half-formed brain, and her lust for blood[. . . .]
> [S]he thirsted for blood, she loved the sight and smell of it, she
> would taste it on the tip of her finger when it came in her way. (83)

Miss Carey is cast as more animal than human—much like the product
of human and bat but also highly suggestive of the chattel slave. Her
physical taste for blood is transformed in her daughter into a craving for
life essences, but metaphors involving blood and the repeated accentua-
tion of Harriet's mouth continually remind the reader of the possibility
of the consumption of blood. When she turns to the young innocent
Bobby Bates, for instance, in an effort to try to forget Ralph Pullen, she is
compared to the "tigress deprived of blood, [who] will sometimes conde-
scend to milder food" (109). Margaret Pullen describes her as possessing
an "enormous mouth" (142). When Harriet discovers that Ralph has left
Heyst without leaving word for her, she takes a pillowcase in "her strong,
white teeth, shook it and bit it, as a terrier worries a rat!"(108), suggesting
the fanged vampire bite as well as her association with a dog.

Additionally, voracity remains pronounced in both mother and
daughter. Harriet is depicted as "greedy by nature" (118), not only at the
dining table—"she was always eating, either fruit or bonbons" (40)—but
even for words, compliments, attention, and stories: Madame Gobelli tit-
ters that the young girl "swallows everything you tell 'er" (46). This glut-
tony likely led Marryat's contemporaries to think of insatiable vampiric

thirst for blood as well as the bloodthirsty cannibalistic cravings attributed African and Caribbean "savages," such as were emphasized in Froude's allusions to Haiti.

Interestingly, Baroness Gobelli is also cast as a vampiric female in the novel because of her greed. The book opens with this characterization of her, and she is later described as "having devoured enough cake and bread and butter [at a tea] to feed an ordinary person for a day" (157). Additionally, when she repeatedly strikes her son with her walking stick in public, denies him food, and makes him cry, she symbolically drains him of masculinity. She does the same to her husband: making all decisions, helping run the shoe and boot factory, swearing at him in mixed company. She is White European, but she is poor—several denigrating remarks are made about her background and rise in social and economic class—suggesting the collapsing of two categories of alterity.

Reading Africa and the Caribbean in *Dracula*

Several scholars have read Dracula as the menacing figure of "the wandering Jew";[9] as Malchow notes, however, "one must remember that Jew, Asian, and Black shared a rhetorical opprobrium that although each possessed in the literature of prejudice uniquely repulsive elements, tied them together" (149). Joseph Valente makes an equally strong case for Dracula as the Irish "other," arguing that because Stoker's mixed ethnicity resulted in an uneasy identification with both cultures (his father was Anglo and his mother was Irish), the novel cannot be read as possessing a coherent framework. Valente posits that the Eastern threat could represent *both* Transylvania/eastern Europe (invading England) *and* England (invading Ireland); the invaded Western space would then relate both to England and to Ireland. This both/and argument is important to my interpretations as well, especially since, to date, *Dracula* scholars have not fully considered the implications of British imperial work in Africa and the Caribbean, where numbers of African and African-descended subjects overwhelmed White populations. Stephen Arata's influential writings focus primarily on the anxieties generated by England's colonial pursuits in eastern Europe, the "Orient," and Ireland, but what needs further analysis is the British attitudes toward the "South"—especially the West Indies and colonial Africa—during this era, which was the height of "the Race for Africa."

Dracula is a monstrous foreigner who will "batten on the helpless" (Stoker, *Dracula* 54) in attempts to conquer a new land. Arata lays out how his vampirism is "interwoven with his status as a conqueror and invader"

(463); Stoker links vampirism to anxieties precipitated by the workings of empire, especially its imminent collapse. British colonial expansion in the second half of the nineteenth century brought 4.5 million square miles to the empire; critic Geoffrey Wall notes that *Dracula* was published in 1897, the year that Lenin identified as imperialism's apex. What critics have failed to note, however, is how the author's innovative connection between Dracula and bats invokes fear of an ambiguously defined "South." The bite marks on victimized children's necks are initially attributed to a bat—not one of the "harmless ones," common to London, but rather "some wild specimen from the South of a more malignant species" that "some sailor may have brought [. . .] home" (174). Van Helsing is somewhat more specific when he mentions South American bats from the Pampas that "suck dry" the blood from cattle and horses (171) and bats from "some islands of the Western seas" that drain the blood of sailors (171–72). Although the link is not explicit, the centuries-long British preoccupation with the West Indies easily connects vampiric activity to the Caribbean. Like the foreign Dracula, foreign species get aligned with horror—a horror that has been introduced to England by British subjects returning "home." Unlike Marryat's novel, which overtly locates danger in the Black woman's body but intimates its cause as being the European man who has left the continent, Stoker's novel suggests that the threat to British civilization is not generated by the invasion of completely alien outsiders; instead, as Arata confirms, the bodies of Others massing inside England's boundaries are the result of the initial imperial move outward. *Dracula* implies that British expansion will lead to its own demise; it serves as a predictive rather than a cautionary tale.

One might compare these anxieties to those generated by Dumas's 1848 short story "The Pale Lady." Dumas—even though the grandson of a French marquis and an enslaved woman from Haiti—situates his Polish heroine Hedwig in the Carpathian Mountains, relegating the threat of her vampiric suitor to a distinctly eastern European space, outside France's borders and distant from political troubles in the Caribbean. The conflict is set out strictly in terms of East versus West: Hedwig proclaims western mountain ranges to be "civilised in comparison" to the eastern Carpathians (6); the vampiric Kostaki, who represents the East, is half-Greek and half-Moldavian, animalistic, "untamable" (15), and "unintelligible" in French (16), while Hedwig's beloved—Kostaki's half brother Gregoriska—denotes the West. He speaks refined French as well as Polish and has traveled through western Europe with a father who, raised in Vienna, "learnt to appreciate the advantages of civilisation" (14).

Given the dominance of Africa in the social and political discourse of the time, it is striking that Africa is never explicitly mentioned in Stoker's text as a source of disquiet and unease. The eerily knowledgeable Van Helsing says of the vampire: "he is known everywhere that men have been. In old Greece, in old Rome; he flourish [*sic*] in Germany all over, in France, in India, even in the Chersonese; and in China, so far from us in all ways, there even is he" (285–86). Not only is the passage entirely male focused, but the lack of acknowledgment of an African presence hints at something akin to repression. The omission is telling, but of what? I concur with Irish literature scholar Joseph Valente that as an Irish writer, Stoker had a complex relationship to empire. Valente asserts that Stoker's mixed Anglo-Irish parentage brought about a troubled identification with both a "conquering and a conquered race, a ruling and a subject people, an imperial and an occupied nation" (4); *Dracula* must therefore be read as encompassing "opposed yet overlapping ethnic significations, class associations, partisan connotations" (4).

Perhaps this is one reason that although the novel consistently frames its male protagonists as aligned with an imperialist agenda, Africa and the Caribbean—sites generating tremendous British wealth as well as the fame and glory of numerous British explorers—go unmentioned. Quincey identifies Jack Seward as an "old pal" from "the Korea" (62)—a contested imperial site in the 1890s, when Britain and the United States attempted to halt Japan's cornering of the market. Quincey, Jack, and Arthur have also shared adventures in the prairies—ostensibly in the States, during the period of Manifest Destiny—as well as in the Marquesas Islands in the South Pacific and on the shores of Lake Titicaca. At one point in the novel Jonathan attacks Dracula with "his great Kukri knife" (266), a weapon used by the Gurkhas of Nepal, who were allies of the British army in their conquest of India. Where Stoker represents North and South America, Asia and the South Pacific as training grounds for the heroes of his novel, Africa and the Caribbean seem to be more controversial locales for the writer—perhaps seen as spaces that were more likely to lead to the British subject's moral and physical corruption than the strengthening of their positive attributes.

Notably, in Stoker's *The Mystery of the Sea* , published in 1902, five years after *Dracula*, Africa and the Caribbean are more obviously present. When the character Don Bernardino—a member of the Spanish nobility—is observed at one point by the British hero, Archibald Hunter, the don's canine teeth began to show. [Bernardino] knew that what he had to tell was wrong; and being determined to brazen it out, the cruelty which lay behind his strength became manifest at once. Somehow at that moment the racial instinct manifested itself. Spain was once the possession of the Moors, and the noblest of the old families had some black blood in them. In Spain, such is not, as in the West, a taint. The old diabolism whence sprung fantee and hoo-doo seemed to gleam out in the grim smile of incarnate, rebellious purpose. (194)

The connection to *Dracula* seems clear: no actual vampires prowl about the text, but the references to the Spanish nobleman's canine teeth, cruelty, strength, aristocratic bloodline, and origins in a place that is "not [. . .] in the West" all conjure images of the Transylvanian count. Clearer here than in the earlier novel are allusions to Africa and the tainting "black blood" that is connected to devil worship, including "fantee" and "hoo-doo." Strikingly, "fantee" is not a religion but an African ethnic group: the Fante are one of the Akan peoples, residing primarily in southwestern Ghana. And while Hoodoo is an active religion in the southern United States, correlating to Vodun in Haiti, popular culture in the States and in Europe has traditionally denigrated it; in England in 1885, for instance, Robert Louis Stevenson and Fanny Van de Grift Stevenson, in their book *The Dynamiter*, described a sorceress practicing the "horrible rites" of Hoodoo among the enslaved people of Cuba.

Don Bernardino therefore brings the Caribbean and African American populations from the U.S. South into much sharper focus in *The Mystery of the Sea* than is the case in *Dracula*. And British anxieties generated by the Black body—in this instance, the Black male body— are further established through the character of Hunter when, later in the novel, he has a supernatural vision in which the heroine, a young American woman named Marjory, is kidnapped. He views all of the culprits "with complacency" except for one: "a huge coal-black negro, hideous, and of repulsive aspect" makes his "blood run cold" and fills him "at once with hate and fear" (252–53). The threat of rape is made explicit when Marjory sends Hunter a coded message, claiming that she will commit suicide rather than submit to the manifestation of her kidnappers' "frightful threats to give me to the negro" (235). When Hunter finally encounters his opponent, he thinks: "I would have killed this beast with less compunction than I would kill a rat or a snake. [. . .] In feature and expression there was every trace and potentiality of evil; and these superimposed on a racial brutality which made my gorge rise"

(259–60). The vicious African male stands in contrast to the beguiling African female, but both represent a distinct sexual threat to individual bodies and the larger body politic.

Along with the rhetoric of imminent sexual violence from men, images of White British subjects languishing in the African and Caribbean tropics—especially under the charms of women of African descent—were well established by the date of *Dracula*'s publication. John Stedman's 1796 narrative about his experiences in Suriname depicts how he only "nearly escaped" being "bewitched" by the vision of an enslaved woman he sees when he first arrives; he adds that male visitors to the land "do not always escape with impunity" (43). John Davis's 1803 publication provides statements about enslaved Africans whose brute strength could withstand tropical temperatures that would "enervate," and possibly even kill, Europeans (Malchow 19). In fiction, Bertha Mason's brother Richard from *Jane Eyre* is observed by the ostensibly objective Jane to be someone whose "features were regular, but *too relaxed*" after his residence in the Caribbean: his eyes further reveal that "the life looking out of [them] was a tame, *vacant* life" (Brontë 162, emphasis added). Rochester himself is subject to the contamination that the Caribbean air seems to breed. Because he is "physically influenced by the atmosphere and scene" of his Jamaican landscape (335), he is on the brink of "going native." He is about to be transformed, converted, *physically altered*, and only "a wind fresh from Europe" (263) brings him to his senses. This degenerative influence of the physical environment can be read into the opening of Marryat's novel as well: when Harriet Brandt arrives in Belgium and compares it to Jamaica, she exclaims, the weather is "so soft and warm, something like the Island, but so much fresher!" (11). And as mentioned during the discussion of *Carmilla*, British explorers traveling to Africa from the late 1850s onward provided compelling tales of African savagery for readers back in Great Britain. Henry Stanley's *In Darkest Africa*, for example, published seven years before Stoker's *Dracula*, sold more than 150,000 copies in English and was identified as "read more universally and with deeper interest than any other publication of [1890]" (Brantlinger 176, quoting M. E. Chamberlain's *The Scramble for Africa* [1974]). By the 1884 Berlin Conference and the European partitioning of Africa in the last decades of the 1800s, the British had cast Africa as a region "possessed by a demonic 'darkness' or barbarism, represented above all by slavery and cannibalism" (175). Similarly, the proclamation by a British government commission that Governor Eyre had acted justifiably following the 1865 Morant Bay Rebellion implied that African savagery must be met by European brutality in order to ensure order and peace in the colonies.

In Stoker's novel, the danger begins for Jonathan Harker when he crosses the border into Transylvania, a move resonating with that of the earlier explorers who perceived themselves to be at peril on the "imperial frontier," where they confronted the alien Other as well as being forced to acknowledge the alien Self. Like Sir Richard Francis Burton, who casts the African peoples he recounts in his 1861 *The Lake Regions of Central Africa* as childish, idle, morally deficient, and superstitious, Jonathan identifies Dracula's homeland as harboring "every known superstition in the world" (10); the population of Saxons, Wallachs, Magyars, and Szekelys are identified as "savages," with the Slovaks being "more barbarian than the rest" (11). The character tries to suppress fear that might arise out of his description of this last encounter: "They are, however, I am told, very harmless and rather wanting in natural self-assertion" (11). He intimates that these strange foreigners might be uncivilized, but they are no match for the superior British agent; Jonathan, with his imperialist eye, notes that this population would be easily conquerable by more "assertive" nations.

Within a short space of time, however, Jonathan has assimilated to his new environment: he feels increasingly grateful for the talismans given to him by the Catholic locals; he follows Dracula's nocturnal schedule, and he physically mimics the count in an eerie, lizard-like trek down the castle's outer walls: "why should not I imitate him, and go in by his window?" (49). He is also willing to submit to the vampiric women in the castle. Like the infamous Kurtz from Joseph Conrad's *Heart of Darkness*, Jonathan goes horrifically "native."

And again, as in Le Fanu's novel, published more than twenty-five years prior, it is the foreign woman and her abject appeal as both frightening demon and enticing seductress that link *Dracula* to many of the African travel narratives. Winwood Reade's *Savage Africa* (1863) casts the continent of Africa itself as a woman "[f]rom whose breasts stream milk and honey, mingled with poison and with blood" (quoted in Malchow 95). The image here is distinctly vampiric: Africa nurtures its subjects to be bloodthirsty blood drinkers; each generation is bred and conditioned to be as corrupt as the last. And in the fantasy literature, the perversion of the vampire is rendered as akin to the perversion of the African race—particularly the woman.

The sole reference to the Caribbean in *Dracula* appears to lie in Renfield's comment that Arthur's father was alleged to be "the inventor of a burnt rum punch" (215): it alludes to the sugar trade, sugarcane plantations, and the elder Lord Goldaming's time spent in the West Indian colonies, where many Englishmen amassed their fortunes. Significantly for the discourse of bloodsucking in *Dracula*, the production and consumption of sugar throughout the late eighteenth and early nineteenth centuries were connected to the ingestion of blood by abolitionists. They urged citizens to view the Caribbean commodity as fouled by the spilled blood of enslaved people. In 1791, William Fox published his "Address to the People of Great Britain, on the Propriety of Abstaining from West India Sugar and Rum," which described sugar as "steeped in the blood of our fellow-creatures" (quoted in Sheller, *Consuming the Caribbean* 89).

The drinking of human blood is definitively taboo, but Dracula's monstrosity does not simply lie in his consumption of his victims' blood; neither is it a matter of his attacking and killing his prey. Instead, he corrupts the blood of his victims, transforming them into vampiric beings like himself: Like Marryat's Harriet, who stands a figure of literal racial corruption, "Dracula imperils [. . . his victims'] cultural, political, and racial selves" (Arata 465), albeit in a more fantastical way. The tainting of "pure" White British blood was at stake in all places where the British came in contact with racial "Others."

White Women's Bodies in Narratives of Miscegenation

As early as the eighteenth century, a national effort was made to control White, middle-class British women and harness their reproductive potential in the service of the empire. To meet the rising social and political demands of colonization, including "a large, able-bodied citizenry" for trade, military service, and civic duties (Nussbaum 1), "proper," "respectable" women were encouraged to reproduce while those on the margins of British society were demonized for their sexual activity: "The idea of aggressive and excessive female sexuality was predominantly projected [. . .] onto black African women, Native American women (as well as poor women)" (Williamson 19). Nussbaum expands this list of the sexually Othered: "Androgynous, transgressive, 'monstrous,' lesbian, and working-class women—indigenous *and* colonizing women" were aligned as "bawdy women" and "located on the fringes of respectability akin to brute savagery" (10). As discussed earlier, White male colonists in the Americas repeatedly engaged in sexual relations with the African (and Amerindian) women to whom they felt entitled—both forcibly and through allegedly "consensual" sex—but the stereotype of the uncontrollable sexual desire of women of color allowed the culpability for desire, the sexual act itself, and sexually transmitted diseases to be placed squarely on the shoulders of Caribbean and African women, and not European men.

Returning to Stoker's novel, one sees the character of Lucy becoming horrific when her "purity" transforms into "voluptuous wantonness" (187)—a sexual and blood lust that Doerksen asserts make her representative of the African "savage": "Lucy represents a devolution, an active movement [. . .] toward the savage, the primitive, the sexual, the uncontrolled. Clearly the 'Darkness' has the potential to infect the 'Light'" (Doerksen 142). In addition to her potentially racialized manifestation of the sexual woman, however, Lucy's body represents a site of abject horror because of miscegenation anxieties. The fact that children follow in the line of the mother guarantees that her body functions as the origin of blood corruption and the eventual tainting of the entire race.

Part of the fright that Lucy inspires centers around her antimaternal sucking of children's blood as the "bloofer lady"; perhaps more significant is that she desires to suck blood from men. Her fangs allow her to pierce the skin, breaking the bodily boundary that is meant to contain, and she becomes the penetrator rather than the penetrated. A key part of why Lucy must die, however, is that "foreign" blood muddies the English blood in her veins. To cure her in her waning condition after she has been penetrated by Dracula, Dr. Van Helsing gives her blood transfusions from her fiancé, Arthur Holmwood, but also from Drs. Seward and himself, as well as from the American, Quincey Morris. The act, an exchange of vital fluids, has been extensively read as a symbolic manifestation of sexual intercourse.[10] And Stoker's word choice heightens the fear of miscegenation, rather than of impiety: the male protagonists must "sterilize" (213, 255), not "sanctify," the earth in Dracula's boxes. However, even though Van Helsing is Dutch and Quincey is from the United States, concern is quickly dispelled—all of the men who contribute blood for Lucy's transfusions are western European and male, and the fluid transfer is "proper" in that the blood is being injected into a female body.

But besides being "intimate" with Dracula, Lucy has expressed pity for Shakespeare's Desdemona—another woman who places herself in the position to create mixed-race babies: "I sympathize with poor Desdemona when she had such a dangerous stream poured in her ear, even by a black man" (59).[11] And as Hughes asserts in Beyond Dracula: Bram Stoker's Fiction and Its Cultural Context: "The use of 'blood' to signify race and ancestry is pointed" in Stoker's writings, especially since nineteenth-century eugenic fears heightened during British conflicts in southern Africa (103).[12] Lucy's staking, then—ostensibly an act of spiritual purification that allows her "holy calm" (192)—is doubly significant in that it can be read as purifying her ethnically tainted blood and stilling the life of a character who sympathizes with interracial couples. It is this acceptance that does not allow her to survive, whereas Mina can.

More than a preoccupation with "the aristocracy and their blood-lines" (Hughes and Smith 6, citing Clare Simmons), I would argue that the obsession over blood and vampirism in Marryat's *Blood of the Vampire* and Stoker's *Dracula* is a distinctly racial *and* gendered one. Harriet Brandt is explicitly a mixed-race subject, and Dracula himself might be interpreted as a figure of miscegenation, especially in light of his peculiar Whiteness. Jonathan notes that the count is not simply pale but rather "[t]he general effect was one of extraordinary pallor" (28). When he is spotted on the ship to England, he is described as being "ghastly pale" (106), and after his vampiric penetration of Lucy, the young woman becomes "ghastly, chalkily pale" with an "awful, waxen pallor" (163). Mina's complexion is also described as "ghastly" (337). These descriptions stand in stark contrast to the "natural" blanching and pallor associated with the non-vampires of the book—those whose blood has *not* been tainted: just as Van Helsing turns "ashen white," but in response to shock and fear (155), Arthur, in Lucy's tomb, is initially "very pale" but then blushes momentarily, bringing blood to his cheeks. Critic John Allen Stevenson also notes that "Color, [. . .] which is commonly used in attempts at racial classification, is a key element in Stoker's creation of Dracula's foreignness" (141).

Race clearly functions on the symbolic register in Stoker's novel, but there is something more tangible going on—something that lies at the heart of Marryat's narrative as well. Stevenson asserts that race is "a convenient metaphor to describe the undeniable human tendency to separate 'us' from 'them'" (140)—that Dracula represents someone of another race because he is "strange to those he encounters—strange in his habits, strange in his appearance, strange in his physiology" (140). Whereas Stevenson argues that Dracula provides his partners a "new racial identity" by taking their blood away (144), the antagonist's role as a contaminated and contaminating force is much more palpable, and this makes the connection to Harriet Brandt clear.

Valente argues that because the longstanding effects of Dracula's blood exchanges do not involve any permanent "adulteration of the blood or in any mongrelization of racial or species makeup" (81), Stoker's novel reads "less like the British fears of admixture than the British hope [. . .] that sexual commingling with the Irish might tend to their racial 'conversion'" (82). While this might be the case with the Irish or other groups whose members physically resemble the English, it was not so for those of different races and complexions. Similarly, although Harriet does not physically penetrate or contaminate the blood of her victims within the scope of the narrative, her draining the strength of healthy White British subjects means the weakening of the English race. Furthermore, her physical presence as a young, attractive, Black woman means the specter of mixed-race babies haunts each scene. According to the rhetoric of the "one-drop rule," once a bloodline is corrupted, it cannot be recuperated. Women are the focus of these narratives of contamination, rendering the control of their behavior essential for the nationalist project. I will continue the discussion of African-diasporic women's sexuality and relationship to motherhood and reproduction in the next two chapters.

3 / Draining Life Rather than Giving It: Maternal Legacies

[Lynda Barry's Filipina vampire] symbolizes her maternal history, the fractured female relationships in her family, and the replication of this troubling system through four generations: how grandmas, like the [vampire] herself, suck the life from their own daughters by bonding with and thus "stealing" their granddaughters' affection away from their own mothers.

—MELINDA DE JESÚS

In an ancient text from Kabbalistic Spain, there is a story detailing an encounter between Lilith, Adam's first wife who refused to succumb to his authority, and the prophet Elijah. When he asks where she is going, she replies: "My lord Elijah, I am on my way to the house of a woman in childbirth . . . to give her the sleep of death and to take her child which is being born to her, to suck its blood, and to suck the marrow of its bones, and to steal its flesh" (Patai 299). Children were perceived to be at special risk because Lilith and her demonic female offspring were supposed to plague newborns, sucking their blood and strangling them. While early twentieth-century Aramaic scholar James A. Montgomery attributes the source of the Lilith legends to "the morbid imagination" of "the barren or neurotic woman," pregnant mothers, and frightened children (quoted in Patai 298), I contend that the stories are just as illuminating about patriarchal anxieties and "neuroses": very much like the stories of the soucouyant and other female vampires, Lilith tales reveal disgust for—and punishment through the demonization of—the woman who refuses to be dominated by male authority or to abide by social dictates for the "naturally" maternal, nurturing, and demure female presence.

This chapter asserts that conventional soucouyant stories from the circum-Caribbean and other parts of the African diaspora are typically used to control women's behavior, especially when it comes to childbearing and child rearing. Although grandmothers, mothers, and daughters have often been complicit in maintaining this control and curtailing female independence by passing on the stories in similar ways as the rest of their communities, many contemporary women writers attempt to imbue their works with a narrative strain that undermines orthodox models of womanhood and motherhood. Like the authors that Gina Wisker identifies as employing the postcolonial Gothic, those under investigation here feel "the need to explore, reimagine, and record in literature the magical, the historical, and the still contemporary, everyday mythical that is frequently overlooked, denied, and invisible in culturally dominant forms of literary expression" (401). They simultaneously depict characters who refuse to use their bodies as "the locus of patrilineal preservation" (Smith 153) and instead thrive as single mothers, Other-Mothers, or women who privilege their own individual physical and sexual needs over and above others'—including their children's. Some writers juxtapose the demonic, bloodsucking female with ever-suckling "vampiric" children; some invoke practices from slavery in an effort to explain away damaging stereotypes, such as the apathetic Black mother, that have followed African-diasporic women into the twenty-first century. Some end up conveying a good deal of ambivalence in their re-visioning of the soucouyant figure and their representations of maternity, but all of the fiction encourages female readers to re-create heroic figures in their own images and to extend this new mythology into the future.

Using vampiric figures to contest maternal conventions falls in line with Donna Haraway's praise of the cyborg: "[O]rganismic, holistic politics depend on metaphors of rebirth and invariably call on the resources of reproductive sex. I would suggest that cyborgs [. . .] are suspicious of the reproductive matrix and of most birthing." Like cyborgs, vampires duplicate their condition in others, "requir[ing] regeneration, not rebirth"—a feat that is both "monstrous" and "potent" ("Manifesto" 223). Unlike Haraway's model, which turns to the future and new and innovative technologies, the African diasporic writers discussed here turn to folklore and the past. By reclaiming a cultural heritage long used to denigrate them as colonized peoples, they "restabilize the cultural imbalance of power," writing back "to Western scholarship that sees cultural motifs [. . .] as mythical, ironic, and often humorous 'insertions' in an otherwise static and petrified representation of Caribbean realities" (Mehta, "Shaman Woman" 234). At the same time, the writers reject a wholesale appropriation of the ideology embedded in this body of lore, refusing obeisance to the masculinist notions of what women should be and do.

Audre Lorde's *Zami: A New Spelling of My Name* (1982) provides an interesting case with which to begin. Lorde's choice of the term "biomythography" to describe her book suggests that entrenched within her collection of biographies of "each woman who shared any piece of the dreams/myths/histories that give this book shape" (v), there are myths to be celebrated and myths to be unraveled. One of these myths to which Lorde alludes early in the text is the story of the soucouyant. In doing so, she simultaneously conjures up the story of her all-powerful mother, rendered as a mystical figure:

[My mother] knew about mixing oils for bruises and rashes, and about disposing of all toenail clippings and hair from the comb. About burning candles before All Souls Day to keep the soucouyants away, lest they suck the blood of her babies. She knew about blessing the food and yourself before eating, and about saying prayers before going to sleep.
   She taught us one to the mother that I never learned in school. *Remember, oh most gracious Virgin Mary, that never was it known that anyone who fled to thy protection, implored thy help, or sought they intercession, was ever left unaided. Inspired by this confidence I fly unto thee now, oh my sweet mother, to thee I come.* (Lorde 10)

The soucouyant stands in striking contrast with the other female foci of the passage: Lorde's biological mother and her spiritual mother, the Virgin Mary. The harmful woman, distinctly antimaternal, looms, held back by the helpful women: the protective Virgin and Linda Lorde, who not only knows cures for physical ailments such as bruises and rashes but teaches Audre formal prayers, the proper way to bless food and people, and the protection to be gained from folk belief systems that lie outside of organized Catholic religion. In this passage we see the demonic woman juxtaposed with the sacred woman. The woman who sucks life is set against the woman who gave Audre her individual life and the woman who, according to Christian faith, gave life to the world's savior, Jesus Christ. And yet, throughout her memoir, Lorde challenges hegemonic forces by refusing to capitalize words like "america," "white," "catholic," and "god," while simultaneously capitalizing Grenada, Harlem, Black, and the Virgin Mary. Resisting the nationalistic, xenophobic, racist, classist, homophobic, sexist, and patriarchal systems of the United States is a large part of the author's goal, but the soucouyant appears to hover just beyond hope for redemption.
   The connection between Linda Lorde and sacred mothers highlighted in this passage gets established even earlier in the text, when Lorde describes DeLois, a heavyset Black woman who "moved like how

I thought god's mother must have moved, and my mother, once upon a time, and someday maybe me" (4). The author creates a distinct legacy of women of African descent who are, in a sense, more powerful than God. Her metaphor contests the idea that God is the source of all creation and decenters the patriarchal power of the male, fatherly force. Again, however, Lorde's revisionist project does not get applied to the soucouyant. The vampiric figure is a passing allusion—one that anchors the text in Caribbean culture and spiritual perspectives. Because she remains a she-demon and nothing else, however, she does not get reconfigured to allow for the positive empowerment of women who choose (or do not choose) to remain childless.

In contrast to Lorde's positioning of the soucouyant *against* Christian models, Nalo Hopkinson's work blends African Caribbean spirituality with folklore and speculative fiction. By doing so, she creates powerful narratives about the roles of women and people of the African diaspora in contemporary society. Hopkinson is quite conscious of the ways that she incorporates folklore in her fiction. She states:

> Science fiction and fantasy tend to . . . examine the results of humanity's efforts to understand, explain and manipulate our environments, whether through devising tools, machines, methods of enquiry or ritual codes of behaviour. Folklore is one such system. Folktales encode mores and archetypes in story so that they are easily taught and passed on by word of mouth. (Wolff 27)

Her intentions to acknowledge, present, examine, and defy these norms thus stand ripe for interrogation.

While Hopkinson is more conscious than most of the role of the soucouyant folk figure in shaping cultural norms, she ultimately falls short in her attempt to undermine conventional sexist representations of the character. Although she makes great strides in *humanizing* the female folk figures that have long been simply vilified, in the end, they are still "bad women" and certain archetypes—particularly those relating to the "good" mother—remain intact. *Brown Girl in the Ring*, for instance, tells the story of a Caribbean Canadian family of four generations—grandmother Gros-Jeanne, mother Mi-Jeanne, daughter Ti-Jeanne, and her unnamed infant son—who attempt to survive in a futuristic inner-city Toronto where the wealthy have fled and the remaining population must battle hunger, homelessness, drug lords, and a new plot for harvesting the healthy bodies of the dispossessed. Through the course of the novel, Ti-Jeanne comes to understand her place among her foremothers, the true significance of their traditional practices and beliefs, and her role in her community of residence. Folk figures like the soucouyant remind the novel's characters that the worlds of the slave past and the slave future have cultural as well as moral and ethical continuities—geographical nodes of the cultural web are simultaneously linked to a variety of historical and future moments.

The gender narrative of Hopkinson's first novel is productively analyzed in conjunction with issues of nationalism and the post-race, posthuman discourses typically associated with apocalyptic futurism. However, while scholarship on posthumanism explores the emphasis on the mind and transmission of information—"data made flesh" (Hayles 5)—as the locus of identity, extending the liberal humanist notion that the core of a subject lies in the consciousness and not the material body, Hopkinson proposes the essential connection between perception and corporeality in her work. There must be a careful balance between the two, especially since the racialized body has often been rendered as invisible *and* hypervisible myth rather than reality, and, as most obviously suggested by second-wave feminists and their pointed critiques, women's (potentially) gestating and lactating bodies have been a source of their "imprisonment" in male-dominated, Western societies.

Hopkinson takes her epigraph—"*Give the Devil a child for dinner, / One, two, three little children!*"—from the play *Ti-Jean and His Brothers* by Nobel Laureate Derek Walcott. Her numerous allusions to the dramatic work firmly insert the novel into a nationalist tradition of Caribbean literature that employs folklore to acknowledge and celebrate the regional culture, one that was long denigrated by proponents of European colonialism. Hopkinson's Ti-Jeanne, her mother, and her grandmother are the female namesakes of Walcott's three brothers, each of whom engages in a battle of wits against the Devil. Ti-Jean, the youngest and smallest of Walcott's three (he is compared to David, slayer of Goliath), manages to outsmart his opponent with instinct and common sense as well as patience. He also triumphs because of his esteem for the natural world and for creatures small as well as great; his deep respect for his mother and the old ways; his faith in God; and his reliance on communal efforts rather than individual strength—"Together they are strong, / Apart, they are all rotten" (Walcott 164)—coupled with his spirit of rebellion against unjust power-wielders and exploiters of the poor. *Brown Girl*'s Ti-Jeanne embraces a similar ideology; however, whereas Walcott's Devil is often represented as a plantation owner, and significantly white-skinned— "Powdery as leprosy, / Like the pock-marked moon" (89)—the "devil" whom Ti-Jeanne eventually defeats is the drug-dealing, power-greedy, capitalist Rudy Sheldon, a Caribbean man of African descent. The strict Black versus White, Caribbean versus European binaries of earlier Independence and Black nationalist movements do not apply to Hopkinson's futuristic Canadian landscape, and women's cultural, sexual, economic, and political roles become a greater focus.

While establishing Rudy as the "devil" in her novel, Hopkinson also constructs him as a vampiric figure. Indeed, although the obvious "vampire" of the novel is the duppy, a ravenous spirit who craves and drinks the blood that Rudy provides, it is Rudy who has created the bloodthirsty monster by trapping his daughter's spirit and forcing her "to do he dirty work" (160). Besides mystically increasing his social and political power, the blood-drinking spirit preserves his health and youth—very much in the tradition of conventional vampires. In one gruesome scene, Rudy bleeds a chemically zombified servant to death in order to feed the duppy. Resembling the mind control that Stoker suggests of his Dracula and Marryat attributes to Harriet Brandt, Rudy's power is demonstrated when he commands Melba not to scream while flaying her alive, and she obeys. He then instructs her to stretch out her neck, and as she complies, he slits her jugular vein. Rudy's socioeconomic status also resonates with Stoker's vision of the vampire. His tailored suits contrast sharply with the cheap, off-the-rack clothes of a man who comes to hire his services (1); in a community where almost all the residents have had to resort to bicycles and walking, Rudy rides in a "predatory" Bentley (23); his office is the penthouse of the tallest freestanding building in the world, evoking Dracula's castle stronghold, high in the mountains.

Hopkinson's dystopian narrative also suggests other vampiric figures who are infinitely more ominous than the duppy. Premier Uttley is willing to exploit all Canadian citizens for their votes, but more compelling is her search for a human heart donor: she and her agents target the dispossessed residents of Toronto. Uttley further belongs to the group of city natives who are wealthy enough to have fled the "doughnut hole" (10) for the gated-off communities of the suburbs. Having "lured" the immigrant population to the North American metropole—where the CN Tower seems to stand as a literal representation of this "pole"—whether through economic incentives or the colonial project that encouraged colonized peoples to identify with the "Mother Country," they now proceed to suck the city dry of its economic life force, health and sanitation services, the public transit system, law enforcement and justice system—its very means of survival.[1]

While the contemporary author's appropriation of traditional Caribbean folk characters seems at first to parallel Walcott's use of these figures (much like her subtle gestures toward Stoker's vision of vampire
myth), her novel reveals some resistance to her literary forefather's male-
centered representation of gender roles. In Walcott's play, the devil's
frightening troops include the diablesse, the werewolf (also known as the
loup garou, la garoup, lagahoo, ligahoo, legawu, and nigawu, depending
on the Caribbean nation in which the story is told), and the shrieking
bolom/foetus—the spirit of a baby who is considered "neither living nor
dead" (98). Hopkinson's Ti-Jeanne is similarly plagued by visions of the
predatory diablesse and other creatures that seem to be spawned in Hell.
Strikingly, however, the bolom/foetus reappears in her novel in the form
of the protagonist's own infant, simply called "Baby" but to whom she
sometimes refers as "Bolom." Hopkinson thus mirrors Walcott's narrative focus on often-forgotten characters from Caribbean legend, but she
revises the tradition to include commentaries on women's places in contemporary society—particularly women's roles as mothers and mother
figures.

Like her mother before her, Ti-Jeanne possesses a type of "second
sight." Haunted by visions of the gruesome, violent deaths of others,
she comes to hate the gift that few others have. Her insistence upon cat-
egorizing the ability in terms of dichotomies—all good or all bad, to be
loved or to be hated—ironically constitutes part of her symbolic blindness. Unable to embrace the numerous paradoxes that surround her, Ti-
Jeanne fails to see the complex whole of life. Another example of this
visual impairment occurs when she literally fails to recognize her biological mother, Mi-Jeanne, who ran away from home and became "Crazy
Betty," one of the many street people of urban Toronto. Adhering to the
theme of maternal legacy, Hopkinson makes Mi-Jeanne blind as well.
Her lack of sight is not figurative—her eyes have been physically dug
out—but it also works metaphorically, like her daughter's, in that she,
too, wanted to shield her eyes against the prophetic visions.[2]

One of the visions plaguing Ti-Jeanne early in the novel is that of the
soucouyant. In one nightmare, a soucouyant appears and expresses a
desire to devour Baby: "I hungry. I want to suck he eyeballs from he head
like chennette fruit. I want to drink the blood from out he veins, sweet
like red sorrel drink" (44). The she-demon is emblematic of the antimaternal woman: she brutalizes children rather than nurturing them;
she drains liquid (blood) rather than supplying it (milk). In a sense, the
skin she sheds is the role of motherhood, and the punishment for this

crime—her obvious refusal to mother but also, perhaps, representative of women's *inability* to biologically mother (as in "to father") once they reach old age—is to be cast brutally out of the community. She represents African American writer Jewelle Gomez's "bitch"—the woman who is denigrated for "mak[ing] her own existence the center of her life," as opposed to the womanist "hero," who "makes survival of the whole an extension of herself, the center of her being. Not financial security, not men, not approval" ("Lye Throwers" 125).

Ti-Jeanne notices that the jab-jab devil figure, who also appears in this early vision, scatters rice on the floor of her room and antagonizes the vampiric crone. Because of the protagonist's initial fear of the jab-jab—whose name invokes double devilment (diab-diab, as in "diablo," sounds like "jab-jab" in many Caribbean accents) but who turns out to be an incarnation of the Yoruba deity Eshu Legbara, the Prince of Cemetery, and Ti-Jeanne's personal spirit guide—she cannot initially comprehend his protection, not even when he helps her destroy the soucouyant by instructing her to pull back the curtains and let sunlight into the room. The gender implications of this scene are distressingly clear. First, the threatening force is female and cast in specifically witch-like terms: the soucouyant is "a[n] old, old woman, body twist-up and dry like a chew-up piece a sugar cane" (44). As in classical European fairy tales, women with power are evil, and evil women are typically depicted as aged and neglectful of children, if not virulently hostile to them. Feminist scholar Karen E. Rowe asserts: "Not designed to stimulate unilateral actions by aggressive, self-motivated women, . . . tales provide few alternative models for female behavior without criticizing their power. . . . [B]ad fairies and villainous stepmothers who exhibit manipulative power or cleverness. . . . [face] punishment through death, banishment, or disintegration" (356).

Second, Hopkinson's protagonist exhibits strength and courage in order to save her baby, not herself: "Terrified as she was, Ti-Jeanne stood firm beside the crib, planting her body between Baby and the hag. She would not let it have her child!" (*Brown Girl* 44) The notion of maternal sacrifice pervades societies worldwide, typically positing the mother's life as less valuable than that of her offspring.

Third, a male deity comes to the rescue of the female mortal and her child, replaying the traditional "damsel in distress" storyline. His physical abuse against the female antagonist—striking her repeatedly with a large stick while she attempts to collect the rice—is presented as justified. This detail resembles one from C. R. Ottley's version of the soucouyant story, described in Chapter 1: upon discovering his wife's soucouyant identity, the ordinarily compassionate Mr. Jonesy beats her with "a licking such as only the low-class Negroes in the village gave their spouses" (33). Both narratives are designed to elicit relief from witnessing justice meted out, not shock at the brutality of the act or any kind of reproach. As far as readers of *Brown Girl in the Ring* know, the novel's soucouyant has no loving husband at home, waiting to bring her back into line by means of a physical thrashing: anyone in the community is free to engage in this act of violence upon the female body that threatens the social order and the safety of its members.

As Ti-Jeanne describes a string of similarly fearful dreams to grandmother Gros-Jeanne—also called Mami, highlighting her maternal presence, knowledge, and authority—readers learn of an extremely tall woman with shark-like teeth, wearing an old-fashioned dress and headscarf, who haunts streets and alleyways and preys on unsuspecting children. When the protagonist mentions "one good foot and one hoof like a goat" (48), Mami identifies the figure as la diablesse, the devil woman portrayed on her tarot cards as an "arrogant-looking mulatto woman in traditional plantation dress and head-tie. Her smile was sinister, revealing sharpened fangs. Behind her ran a river, red like blood" (51–52). Again, although the male jab-jab figure is reclaimed as positive by the conclusion of Hopkinson's narrative, the female figures are not: in Ti-Jeanne's dream, la diablesse jumps on a young boy and "fasten she teeth in he throat. I could see blood running down he neck and he screaming, screaming" (52).

Whereas traditional accounts of la diablesse folklore concentrate on the threat of the overtly sexualized female, most stories refer only to the irresistible allure of the figure and her ability to induce madness in her victims or lure them to their apparently accidental deaths, falling off cliffs. Hopkinson's iteration is strikingly bloody and induces mental images of bodily penetration by a female force, suggesting a merging of soucouyant and diablesse traditions. For while la diablesse typically refuses to consummate the sexual act, the sexual metaphor implicit in the soucouyant's penetration of her victims suggests a forceful stealing—and mixing—of blood in addition to female sexual aggression. The specter of miscegenation is therefore raised. I will return to more extensive analysis of the racial discourse surrounding the skin-shedding, bloodsucking soucouyant and other vampire figures in Chapter 6 but for now simply note that the biracial identity of the diablesse character bolsters readings of racial mixing as menace. While an emphasis on the folk figure as "mulatto" seems consistently tied to her remarkable beauty in traditional tales, it simultaneously contests Eurocentric standards of beauty and social superiority. The reality of many Caribbean societies revealed that physical approximations of Whiteness corresponded to social mobility; however, the myth of la diablesse casts the woman of mixed race and blended features as extremely dangerous, not simply desirable and physically superior to those possessing more distinctly African characteristics. Promoting a type of African pride, the figure echoes established negative depictions of the Mulatta, who threatens to further corrupt "pure" bloodlines with her seductive behavior. As both evidence of miscegenation and the promise of future "taint," the biracial character occupies a condemned space in both White and Black communities.

At the same time that these racial considerations are contemplated, the gender implications of the myth should not be ignored. As I have already stated, race and gender intersect inextricably in Hopkinson's afro-futurist novel. Thus la diablesse's height in *Brown Girl* is striking but marked as more threatening than appealing, reminiscent of the terror inspired by the "vampiric" Bertha Mason's stature in Charlotte Brontë's *Jane Eyre*.[3] With the other traits described, she gets thrust outside the realm of the conventionally feminine—perhaps even into the purported realm of the masculine, echoing notions of African diasporic women as outside the category of "true womanhood."[4] Haunting public pathways, Hopkinson's diablesse, much like the soucouyant, strays from the interior domestic space. Akin to Dracula's "Bloofer Lady," she actively attacks children rather than fostering them; she kills rather than bearing life. In essence, the British novel and both sets of circum-Caribbean folk narratives lock "good" women into the role of the nurturing mother.

While the soucouyant and la diablesse in *Brown Girl in the Ring* clearly serve as paradigmatic antimaternal figures, it should be noted that Ti-Jeanne also fits the image of the apathetic, even antipathetic, mother throughout much of the novel. By constructing her character's affection toward her infant as wavering and largely learned, Hopkinson does, in fact, subvert the notion of the naturally nurturing, doting biological mother. When Baby screeches with hunger, the protagonist "[shakes] him a little, hoping to startle him into silence" (33). Later, as he cries in his crib, she raps on the side, again "to startle him into silence" (69). At yet another point, she considers spanking him into submission: "Her mother and grandmother had raised her with the strap; it was what she knew of discipline" (33). She is on the brink of striking him when, while nursing, he pulls on her hair: "Irritably, Ti-Jeanne pulled the plait away . . . and was about to slap the mischievous hand" (49). Perceived as tiresome and frustrating, Baby comes to represent an almost rancorous presence for Ti-Jeanne. She even briefly contemplates abandoning the child in order to carry out her larger mission unencumbered: "Leave him here alone, perhaps to starve to death, or take him with them? Baby looked at her, reached for her. Another life tied to her apron strings" (166). In many ways, the character of Baby brings the role of mother out of the realm of myth and into reality; he prompts the everyday irritations and frustrations of Ti-Jeanne's experience of motherhood.

For most of the novel, as the protagonist awaits the nine-week naming ceremony, she calls the infant "Baby"; however, as mentioned earlier, she also calls him Bolom and "my bolom baby" (33) on several occasions. Reading *Brown Girl in the Ring* in conjunction with *Ti-Jean and His Brothers*, one cannot fail to notice that Walcott's Bolom character is also constantly shrieking. Bolom frightens Ti-Jean and his family, wailing and screeching, jumping about the house and hiding in bowls, cups, and, most disturbingly, "Here, crawling up your [mother's] skirt!" (95). This last example might initially be read as sexually suggestive, given that the Bolom travels in the company of the devil and his ghouls. However, as one learns more about this character's desires to be reborn as a human being and live a life marked by pain and suffering as well as joy and contentment, one can interpret the passage as evidence of the spirit's desperation to crawl into a womb and experience birth. And just as tensions mount between Hopkinson's Ti-Jeanne and Baby, Walcott's Bolom reveals a troubled relationship with its biological mother—he claims to have been strangled by her: "a woman, / Who hated my birth, / Twisted [my body] out of shape, / Deformed past recognition" (97). Walcott's Bolom character is consequently seen not as evil but as worthy of compassion. Ti-Jean's mother, at first fearful of the creature, wishes peace upon it and welcomes it into her home: "Let a mother touch you, / For the sake of her kind" (96). The myth of the good woman gets powerfully reinforced in the play through these examples of the "good" and "bad" mother.

Ti-Jeanne by no means desires to murder her child, but when Mami instructs her granddaughter to be gentler with Baby, Ti-Jeanne ashamedly confesses that she never wanted the infant and sometimes longs to rid herself of the burden. Gros-Jeanne does not lambaste her but instead reassures her that these feelings are normal: "Don't feel no way, darling; children does catch you like that sometimes. It ain't easy, minding babies, but if you don't make the time to know you child, you and he will never live good together. I know" (*Brown Girl* 49). Some of the great advances that Hopkinson makes in her narrative are not only destabilizing the idea of the innately maternal woman but specifically debunking the contradictory European constructions of African-descended women as (a) hypermaternal mammies and (b) genetically apathetic, coldhearted, and emotionally distant mothers—stereotypes generated during the slave era and continuing into the present day in various forms.[5]

Ti-Jeanne's story of resisted, "apathetic" motherhood resonates with that of Abena in Guadeloupean novelist Maryse Condé's *I, Tituba, Black Witch of Salem* (1992). Abena relegates the caretaking of her biological daughter Tituba—the product of a brutal rape aboard a slave ship—to her husband Yao, who adopts Tituba as his own child. For years, he expresses more devotion to her than does the "natural" mother. Abena can become dedicated to Tituba only after her death: Condé suggests that the life her character leads in slavery, as a material, purely physical body—an ungendered-yet-highly-sexually-gendered body at the whim of a White master—does not allow her the luxury of "mother love." Examples of this antipathetic relationship to African-diasporic maternity can be found in U.S. African American literature as well. In Toni Morrison's *Beloved* (1987), Nan tells the young Sethe that the girl's mother was raped and impregnated many times during the Middle Passage but "threw them all away but you" (62). Lack of a maternal bond is carefully attributed to the profoundly traumatic circumstance of conception, not to the women themselves.

The maternal legacy in relationship to the history of slavery comes across in quite a different way in the previously mentioned soucouyant tale by C. R. Ottley, in Florence Marryat's *The Blood of the Vampire* (also discussed in Chapter 2), and in Hopkinson's short story "Greedy Choke Puppy," to which I will return in more detail later in the chapter. According to all three of these narratives, the bloodsucking creature inherits her traits and abilities from "a long line of ancestral soucouyants" (Ottley 31). The evil and corruption of vampirism is passed on through the mother, and only through the mother, because all soucouyants are established as female. The history of slavery in the Americas seems subtly referenced: much like children's status was determined by their mother's position during slavery, soucouyant children follow in the line of the mother. There are important cues for readers about the intertwinings of gender and colonialism here, but these prompts malign women's sexuality: the notion of women's general untrustworthiness becomes ingrained in the ideology of "mama's baby, papa's maybe." Within the confines of slavery, the Black male presence gets elided by the authoritarian presence of the slave master/Father, but that power gets displaced onto women of African descent, as Hortense Spillers so aptly describes in "Mama's Baby, Papa's Maybe: An American Grammar Book." Both inside and outside the institution of slavery, men's longstanding inability to determine whether the children produced are truly their own biological offspring represents a threat to the patrimonial system, which relies on property remaining exclusively in the male bloodline. Thus throughout these folkloric, fictional, and historical narratives where power gets passed from mother to daughter, readers witness trepidation over the inability to regulate female sexuality.

In Hopkinson's *Brown Girl*, the negative legacies of slavery are still very much a part of the characters' lives. The author reveals that the allegedly "post-racial" future is largely a social fiction. The character of Gros-Jeanne, for example, voices her recognition of the destructive behaviors and ideologies generated in the past that continue to harm present and future generations: "From since slavery days we [African] people get in the habit of hiding we business from we own children even, in case a child open he mouth and tell somebody story and get them in trouble. Secrecy was survival, oui. Is a hard habit to break" (50). Hopkinson critiques dangerous silences, the practice of withholding information from children, and other breaks in the relationship between mother and child. She makes it clear, though, that the legacy of slavery and a painful oppressive past are to be blamed, *not* the mother who raises her child and attempts to heal herself.

Ti-Jeanne ultimately develops into a powerful hero who is also a caring mother. She follows in the line of her own mother, who succumbs to the strains of mother-child relations but then reconciles with her daughter and continues the healing process. Mi-Jeanne is able to be redeemed only when she puts her daughter's needs above her own desires. Near the end of the narrative, Mi-Jeanne tearfully describes her prior resentment of her child: after Ti-Jeanne was born, her mother perceived her as "eat[ing] up my whole life" (242). Upon hearing this confession, the protagonist does not feel anger or regret but shame: the sentiment was a "bit too close to the bone. She knew what her mother had been feeling" (242). Hopkinson's specific description of the child who threatens to "eat up" her character's "whole life" provides the reader with even more insight into the role of the vampire figure in the narrative: babies are clearly configured as occupying a vampiric position, devouring not only mother's milk but all of her energy—her life force. The author hence encourages understanding for women who feel consumed and erased by their children's needs and society's expectations for the ever-giving mother.

However, while the needy Baby, depicted as a constantly sucking infant, is by no means portrayed as abhorrent, a constantly feeding woman definitely is. Mi-Jeanne "couldn't take" the physical, emotional, and psychological nourishment her child required and ran away (242); she is later transformed into a soucouyant-like duppy spirit who takes the lives of many people, including numerous children. The sympathy the reader feels for her unwanted, uncontrollable soucouyant-hunger is always tempered by disgust for her bloodsucking, if not judgment for her abandonment of her daughter.

Like Mi-Jeanne, Ti-Jeanne is presented as fully matured and developed only when she reconciles herself toward her expected role in her son's life. Notably, but partly as a matter of practicality, the protagonist's evolution into a powerful agent of the spirits and conqueror of the evil Rudy Baines can occur only when she has temporarily given Baby into the custody of Romni Jenny, a village elder. She must do battle alone. Hopkinson suggests that the actual physical caretaking of a child and heroism are incompatible, leaving intact the option for childless women as productive members of society. After her victory, Ti-Jeanne reconnects with her son and her affection increases. She "comes into her own" as a mother. The sight of Baby's fat cheeks "fill[s] her with glee" and she no longer handles him roughly. She "gently pull[s] his tam down to protect his ears from the cold" (247) and is ready to settle on a name for this permanent presence in her life. What remains: while creating more options for women, and African diasporic women in particular, the narrative ultimately promotes motherhood—complete with the birth of a male heir.

In *Skin Folk*, Hopkinson proposes to push the boundaries of acceptability much further by unequivocally appropriating the metaphor of the soucouyant. The author states:

> Throughout the Caribbean, under different names, you'll find stories about people who aren't what they seem. Skin gives these skin folk their human shape. When the skin comes off, their true selves emerge. They may be owls. They may be vampiric balls of fire. And always, whatever the burden their skins bear, once they remove them . . . they can fly. (1)

In a 2005 interview with Nancy Johnston, Hopkinson elaborated that while all "[f]iction is about taking a protagonist through some life-changing moments, and science fiction and fantasy can literalize that change into actual bodily transformations," the pieces in the *Skin Folk* collection are linked by

> something I'd found in a few African diasporic folk tales; when the soucouyant can't get back into her skin because someone has rubbed the inside of it with hot pepper, she says to the skin, "Kin-kin, you don't know me?" (something like, "skin of mine, don't you recognize me?"). [...] I liked the idea that people changed into different things by taking off their skins. Hence, *Skin Folk*. (John-ston 207)

As reviewer Denolyn Carroll observes, "Hopkinson deftly explores the twin themes of being bound and being free" (56). Carroll specifically references the story "Greedy Choke Puppy" as an example: she describes the three generations of soucouyants in the tale as experiencing the thrill of liberation when they shed their skins and glide through the night skies but still held captive by their bodies and the physical needs of nourishment: they must seek out the life-breath of infants in order to survive. In striking contrast, another pair of reviewers presents "Greedy Choke Puppy" as the tale of "a bitter woman [who] discards her skin at night and kills children for their life-force" (Zaleski and Canon). Their review in no way alludes to the conflicting states of freedom and imprisonment, and their description of the protagonist as "bitter" could be said to ignore the physical, domestic, and social constraints of women in patriarchal societies.

Hopkinson does indeed allow her readers to speculate about the *potential* freedom and empowerment of women through the soucouyant in this story. The soucouyant character identifies leaving her skin behind as an emancipating action: "Oh, God, I does be so free like this! ... I flying so high. I know how many people it have in each house, and who sleeping. I could feel them, skin-bag people, breathing out their life, one-one breath" (*Skin Folk* 177). She not only feels physically free from the restrictions of her body, but she commands a type of extrasensory knowledge. Furthermore, Carmen, a minor character, expresses not fear but longing for the possibilities that the soucouyant represents: "[The story] didn't really frighten me [as a child], though. I always wondered what it would be like to take your skin off, leave your worries behind, and fly so free" (172).

In spite of these allusions to radical mobility, the story's main sou-couyant is by no means a role model. She easily fits into the evil, anti-maternal category of vampires of old: she sucks the life-blood of her good friend's firstborn and only child, killing it five days after its birth. Hopkinson does incorporate a womanist message in her depiction of the soucouyant when the character spouts forth a sexist ideology that demands to be challenged. The soucouyant claims: "When your youth start to leave you, you have to steal more from somebody who still have plenty. . . . [I search] for a newborn baby" (170–71). She preys on children, not because this behavior is necessary for her survival, but out of vanity. She laments growing older, not because it brings her closer to death and a time when she will not be able to fly free but because she is no longer able to attract male attention: "[W]hen you pass you prime, and you ain't catch no man eye, nothing ain't left for you but to get old and dry-up like cane leaf in the fire" (170). She thus voices the socially sanctioned belief that women's worth is determined exclusively by male desire. Feeling "[l]ike something wither-up" (170) and trapped by her skin because "it getting old" and wrinkled (177)—again, not because it restricts her flight—she expresses disgust with her woman's body as it undergoes the natural aging process. Finally, by identifying herself as "some*thing*" rather than some*one*, the antagonist objectifies herself. Early in the story, remembering her body as once young and "sweet," she furthers this dehumanization: "Sweet like julie mango, with two ripe tot-tot on the front of my body and two ripe maami-apple behind. I only had was to walk down the street, twitching that maami-apple behind, and all the boys-them on the street corner would watch at me like them was starv-ing, and I was food" (170). Describing her form in terms of fruit, she sets herself up as a willing participant in her literal consumption by male gaze and sexual appetites. The story inherently critiques a society that grooms women to feel this way.

At the same time, however, the story's conclusion leaves no doubt in the reader's mind as to the vileness of the female folk figure. Despite the author's womanist message, her soucouyant figure still functions in traditional ways: to demonize women's agency. Jacky is a woman with intellectual ambition and talent: she is working toward her doctoral degree. Her aggressive flirtations with Terry in the library, in which she is depicted as "glowing" (173), suggest the fiery nature of her true soucouyant identity and are presented as unattractive. After only two weeks, he breaks up with her, unable to handle her pressure "to settle down" (176). Hopkinson casts both Jacky and her mother as too grasping for the things they desire, and, as the title informs readers, "greedy[ness will] choke [a] puppy." Before the revelation of their soucouyant identities, Jacky and Mummy demonstrate their rapaciousness when they gulp down food from scalding pots. Granny observes, "You mother did always taste straight from the hot stove, too. . . . You come in just like she, always in a hurry" (175–76). The lesson goes unheeded, however, and the women's avarice extends to babies. Granny asks Jacky: "That little child you drink, you don't hear it spirit . . . ? I try to tell you, like I try to tell you mother: Don't be greedy" (180).

While early in the narrative Jacky appears to be desperate for children and acts "scandalised" when Carmen complains about her pregnancy (171), the discovery of her penchant for sucking infants' blood leads the reader to question this initial desperation. Does she simply wish to have a child to feed off of it and maintain her youth? Is her desire for children further evidence of her uneasiness about being regarded as a "real" woman according to hegemonic standards? Is her initial concern for Carmen's baby's death the clever pretense of a vicious killer, or is her murderous behavior part of her unconscious, allowing the reader to feel sympathy? If this is the case, Jacky becomes even less empowered. The small bit of agency one might read into her desires and actions is effectively taken away if its manifestation is accidental.

As discussed previously, all three generations of women in Jacky's family are soucouyant, sharing in this maternal legacy, but Granny is revealed as the only "good" woman in that, as the epitome of female sacrifice, she destroys both of her children—her daughter and her granddaughter—in order to protect the larger community. She tells Jacky, the last in the ancestral line of vampiric women: "We blood hot: hot for life, hot for youth. Loving does cool we down. Making life does cool we down" (180). The older woman does not go so far as to state that unmarried women—those who are not "cooled" by the love of a "good man"—threaten the social order. Her broad definition of the loving that cools includes loving one's work, any of the "people close to you," and one's life (180). The dictate for "making life," however, suggests that women who do not biologically bear children cannot be integrated into a safe and healthy society. Motherhood— and specifically the physical acts of conception, pregnancy, and labor—resurface as requirements for "good" women, anchoring them to their corporeal bodies and the domestic space. The soucouyant plainly violates these roles. One might also observe that on the symbolic register, by making her victims bleed regularly—emblematic of the woman's monthly cycle—she prohibits her adult female victims from carrying out these tasks.

Whereas Jacky's research posits a Caribbean folklore in strict opposition to European literary forms, Hopkinson's story avoids easy associations between the greedy (White) foreign colonizer—one might think again of Stoker's Dracula here—and the (Black) Caribbean victim, whose life-blood is drained by this oppressive force. The conclusion of the piece continues to complicate the European-Caribbean binary by having Granny, a respected community elder, destroy Jacky, also a well-known member of the community.

In Toni Brown's short story "Immunity," found in *Night Bites: Vampire Stories by Women* (1996), the vampiric figure is a mother, but she has not given birth. The narrative ostensibly proposes to widen definitions of motherhood as well as to open up the "canon" of Eurocentric vampire fiction: Celeste originally hails from Africa, "south and far west of the Sudan" (77), although she currently resides in a small university town in the United States. She cares for her six-year-old daughter, Nia, as a single parent. When the child comes home from school worried about vampires and pressing for a cross for protection, the protagonist recognizes that "this was only the first of many misrepresentations of people, distortions of history that Nia would learn" (74). Author Toni Brown links horror stories about vampires to the ways that people of the African diaspora, as well as members of the LGBT community, have been made monstrous by the dominant culture. By setting her fiction in the Americas and creating a shape-shifting—albeit not literally skin-shedding—vampire of mixed European and African cultural heritage, she also establishes another node in the network of soucouyant tales.

With Celeste and Nia, Brown replicates a pattern described by Canadian Caribbean author Dionne Brand: an emphasis in the works of Caribbean women on relationships between mothers and daughters that labors to conceal, rather than reveal, when it comes to female sexuality—especially the typically unacknowledged sexuality of mothers. In the 2005 interview, Nalo Hopkinson conjectures that this suppression is the result of a long history of being associated with rapaciousness: "I think that we (Caribbean people) are so used to protecting our sexualities from prurient gaze that we've built up these huge taboos against many types of sexual expression" (Johnston 208). Black people—and Black women in particular—"are too often the victims of having white sexual fears projected onto our bodies, often in dangerous ways. So we can be cautious about making any room for that to happen. But I think there's a cost when black communities keep too opaque a veil over the fact that black people's desire and sexual inclinations are as varied and human as anyone else's" (211).

Brand similarly argues that confining the subject of Caribbean women's writing to dynamics between mothers and daughters allows only veiled discussions of "sex without the sexuality" (*Bread* 99). Consequently, by casting her protagonist as "an older single woman" living with her child and failing to mention any male (or female) lover or partner, Brown establishes a fully independent Black female, one not plagued by stereotypes of the hypersexual African-diasporic female but one so completely dissociated from any form of sexuality that she seems ensconced in a metaphorical landscape of frigidity and sterility. Nia comes to Celeste as the result of a predatory encounter gone awry, not biological reproduction; when she kidnapped the infant and prepared to consume it, Celeste "felt a conflict between the instinct to eat the sweet, warm-blooded creature and the urge to somehow suckle it" (78). She cannot pass down her transformative capabilities or elongated lifespan to her daughter, nor can she procreate in the future: she believes she is the last of her kind. In true horror story fashion, Brown's vampire narrative illustrates great power in its protagonist, albeit conventionally frightening power in Celeste's case, since she transmutes into a Medusa-like creature when she hunts, with writhing hair, the body of an enormous snake from the waist down, and a row of sharp teeth. This last detail appears designed for purely visual effect and not to evoke the horror of female penetration, since Celeste does not use fangs to lance or insert poison into her victims; instead, her formidable serpentine form constricts around and then stifles them. In this slippage, however, her potency is ultimately contained: it lacks the possibility of "contamination" or being spread to others—a threat that comes across as distinctly sexual in texts from Stoker's *Dracula* to Gomez's *Gilda Stories* and Butler's *Fledgling*, which I will discuss in greater detail in Chapter 4.

Furthermore, Celeste herself is not the product of a sexual union: she comes from the Awon Iya Wa Aje people—an all-female group of ethereal witches who have performed a mutual exchange of magic with the lamia, a bloodsucking supernatural people who journeyed to her original community in Africa from Greece. The two groups "become as one tribe," making an agreement "[t]o never hurt each other, to be as if sisters" (76). Notably the word "sisters" removes any allusion to sexuality

from the dynamics of creation of this new set of beings: ties are consan-
guineous and not generational.

Correspondingly, the "tiny sips of blood" that Celeste takes from Nia's
wrist (78) do not serve to mystically transform or biologically alter the
child but rather, apparently, to sustain and nourish the mother. This
inversion of the suckling child image might read as a compelling attempt
to broaden constrictive notions of motherhood, where the (birth) mother
is expected to sacrifice body and soul to the child. Here, we find a girl participating—although unwittingly—in an act that physically nurtures her
mother without harm to herself. Nia also provides emotional sustenance
to her mother, who feels intensely isolated: "Nia brought a focus to her
eternity, a consanguinity[. . . .] [A]t least for a time in this foreign place,
she would not be alone" (78). Nonetheless, the issue of choicelessness is
key to understanding the true dynamics of the piece. Nia has no option
in the matter of how her body is being employed since Celeste drains her
blood while she is sleeping. Accordingly, although the protagonist deeply
cares for her daughter's well-being, she still comes across as a menacing
force—especially in that the repeated, involuntary penetrations involve
a female body of African descent.

In striking contrast, Jamaica Kincaid's novel *Annie John* (1983) highlights the sexuality of the mother figure despite the daughter's attempts
to deny it. The young Annie is mortified by her mother's active participation in an intimate moment in bed with her husband, which, in the
preadolescent's mind, clearly displaces her as the primary object of her
mother's affection. The girl processes her mother's attempts to encourage
her maturing as abandonment; she feels a return to maternal protection
and nurturing only when Ma Chess, her mother's mother, appears to care
for her during a serious illness. Although Kincaid includes no references
to bloodsucking or skin-shedding in the novel, literary critic Helen Pyne
Timothy reads Annie "Senior's" mother not only as an obeah woman and
bush healer but also as evocative of "the mythological 'flying African' able
to cross the seas without a boat, and the flying 'soucouyant' (female witch)"
(241). In the spirit of much contemporary Caribbean women's literature,
Kincaid's soucouyant figure in *Annie John* is neither predatory nor self-
centered. Timothy defines her as "comforting and healing because of [her
worldview's] coherency, its validity, and its verity" (241).

Despite its contradictions, one of the important developments in
Toni Brown's short story is to erase notions of generational relationships
between Europeans and Africans, colonizers and colonized. Rather
than supporting the ideology of a one-way production and provision of

knowledge, medicine, religion, culture, and "civilization"—the unilateral flow of people, products, and information between the nodes of a transatlantic network—Brown asserts that each people has something to teach, something to learn, something to give, and something to take. At the same time, the conflicting imagery also makes the text read as an anxiety narrative about the bicultural, and possibly biracial, subject. It seems that the fully human, U.S.-born Nia is the strong Black female character with whom readers are meant to identify. When Celeste first abducts her, the vampiric woman seems captivated by the child's anger and spirit of resistance rather than her vulnerability and infant cuteness. The baby cries without tears, her hands "balled into hard fists," and shakes "with fury." Further female power is suggested by the fact that her ringlets "looked like tiny, shiny snakes" (78), evoking Medusa. She does not possess the Gorgon blood or fearsome proficiencies, however, and thus Brown leaves the myth of the demonic Black female vampire figure very much intact.

"Old Flesh Song" by Ibi Aanu Zoboi, from Sheree Thomas's speculative fiction collection *Dark Matter: Reading the Bones* (2004), also addresses the connections between women and the non-birth-related children in their care, as well as fraught relations between mothers and their biological children. Like many of the other pieces discussed in this chapter, it considers the dynamics between ever-suckling "vampiric" children and bloodsucking mothers, making successful in-roads toward breaking down stereotypes of Black womanhood—this time the "Mammy" figure—but also reinforcing particular ideas about demonic women of the circum-Caribbean.

In Zoboi's story, two soucouyants fight over the bodies and souls of a set of infants from wealthy New York City families. "Old Flesh" is one name of the story's antagonist; she is also known as "Lady Bag" and, in the past, as "Lorraine" when she existed as fully human. Because she totes three mismatched bags, resembling a homeless person, and "the odor of the underworld" reeks from her body (150), no one desires to approach her. She is the typical alienated soucouyant figure: despite *physically* occupying space on a crowded Manhattan sidewalk, she lies on the metaphorical margins of this Upper East Side community. Furthermore, she has become "an isolated sore" in her bitterness, and the beginning of the story suggests that Old Flesh's belief that she is the last "of her kind" only intensifies the problem (150).

Zoboi initially casts Old Flesh as the conventionally demonic—and particularly antimaternal—soucouyant character. She preys on babies, draining them of their blood and life. Luring them to her with a song, she encourages them to suckle from her milk-dry breasts, but as "Young Blood pulled, Old Flesh pulled harder—her desiccated breast suctioned for life, for blood. Young Blood's plump cheeks stiffened in the pull, Old Flesh's breast inflated. Not giving milk, but receiving fresh young blood for her old flesh" (154). And once she starts crooning the enchantment, the elderly woman "could not stop the command/spell" (157). This detail confirms conventional notions of the female vampire's uncontrollable greed and sensual desire.

However, as the narrative develops, rather than completely disparaging Old Flesh's lack of maternal impulses, the story indicts the racial and class structure of contemporary U.S. society—one specifically bound up in the practices and legacies of the slave era. Racial and class prejudice and vestiges of the Black Mammy trope become the true source of blame for maternal deficiencies in women of all races. Old Flesh is identified as a transported African: mud cloth is "the tapestry of her native home" (150). While she waits for victims on the sidewalk outside an upscale store, she notices that the White babies are "[a]lways in a stroller, never in a slingy or carried in enveloping arms," implying a lack of physical contact and affection. In addition, these strollers are always pushed by "temporary, rented parents"—all women of colors, "some [with faces] blue-black like hers and others in various shades of brown" (151)—instead of their own parents or other biological relatives. She actually appears to pity the first child she snatches—assuming he was "probably weaned at a too-young age" (154)—and as she holds the second stolen infant, she thinks, "She would fulfill its desire" (159). She comes across as kind and almost giving, rather than selfishly consumed with taking. This impression is reinforced by the method Zoboi creates for having the soucouyant drain her victims: rather than penetrate the skin and suck the blood of her prey, hunger and thirst are satiated by having the infants suckle her.

Readers come to learn that Old Flesh once labored as an exploited nanny. She "[f]ed, cleaned, healed them little sickly things 'til my breasts feel flat. Never had enough for my own" (159). While the imagery resonates with the practice of wet nursing during the U.S. antebellum period, when enslaved women could be forced to provide for their masters' children before their own, the distinction that Old Flesh's breasts "feel" flat instead of "are" flat (or have been "made" flat) suggests that she worked as a paid childcare giver, metaphorically being drained, rather than as a literal wet nurse. In any case, the ideological connection is clear: regardless of whether readers assume mid-eighteenth century or mid-twenty-first century, a particular paradox arises for women of African descent: "By nourishing well 'their' white children, [Black wet nurses] sowed the seeds of their own [possible] manumission, as well as strengthening the forces of oppression" (Beckles, *Centering* 68).

"Manumission" does not seem a likely possibility for the antagonist of Zoboi's text: once imprisoned by her job, she is now trapped by her bloodlust. Her existence as a soucouyant might be interpreted as retribution and vengeance against all wealthy White families who give their children over to nannies and demand their employees' very "souls." (Old Flesh does not possess a soul, although she steals and hordes the souls of the babies she kills.) She states that because her own children died while she was caring for her employers' babies, she is currently "[j]ust taking back what's owed to me, that's all" (158).

Her secondary justification of her actions is to free young nannies from enslavement to their jobs and being sucked dry by their charges. She looks at one young woman whom she identifies as "Starting out too early. Lured to leave home with the promise of food, shelter, and if lucky education, to be at the beck and call of nice folks—good families that take care of you, if you take care of them" (152). "Good" turns out to be wealthy and not necessarily kind; to "take care of" means solely financial support on one side and a disproportionate amount of emotional caretaking and physical nurturing on the other. Old Flesh mimics the employer's voice, "*Ms. Nanny, Baby hungry now. Can't eat until Baby is fed. Can't go home until Baby sleep*" (154), and imagines that stealing the baby will put the young woman in front of her "out [her] misery" by getting her fired. To Celia, the second nanny she encounters in this way, Old Flesh commands: "Give 'em [infant twins] to me and you can go back to your own children" (158).

The introduction of Celia complicates the narrative in some interesting yet disturbing ways. Celia, the second soucouyant featured in the story, is a "high-yellow" woman with long dark hair and a strong Spanish accent (156). If readers are tempted to read biographically, the fact that Ibi Zoboi was born in Port-au-Prince, together with these textual clues, might suggest that Lorraine represents the Haitian childcare worker while Celia hails from the Dominican Republic. Celia's claim that she *knows* Lorraine suggests an intimacy that can be read symbolically: even more than a past relationship between individuals, the *knowing* intimates the imbrications of their two nations. Both countries occupy one

Caribbean island and have been caught up in fraught yet inextricable ways over several centuries: military clashes and attempted political domination, economies and commerce, agricultural and domestic service, brutal massacres, unofficial families. In any event, Celia's accent, devotion to the deity Yemaya, and soucouyant identity (revealed later in the story) all locate her as a member of the African diaspora, simultaneously revealing the linguistic, phenotypic, and cultural diversity of the Caribbean and its diasporas.

Celia stands in striking contrast to Old Flesh. One is extremely light-complexioned; the other is "charcoal" dark (153). One sings the enchantment "sweetly" (160); the other's version is repeatedly described as "grating" (153, 161). One frees the imprisoned souls of the stolen babies; the other traps as many as she can. One is explicitly called "beautiful" (156); the other is rendered physically offensive by her stench. The racial connotations of this dichotomy are distressing, in that the adjective "beautiful" is textually surrounded by the details of Celia's complexion and hair length; the imagery confirms the perception in many African diasporic communities—not to mention European and North American cultures—that light skin and long, straight hair are more beautiful than African features and possess an inherent "goodness." On a more positive note, the text does not support a reading that equates this beauty with youth or conventional notions of femininity: Celia is "old and conditioned" (156), possessing the endurance, wisdom, and confidence that allow her to defeat Old Flesh. Her voice is commanding; her "[s]weet and tender" rendition of the song-charm is acknowledged as "[d]eadly and entrancing, nonetheless" (159).

Although Celia calls the twins in her care "mija" (my daughter) (156) and "mi hijo" (my son) as well as "my baby" (158), she carefully articulates a strong sense of self and separation from the all-encompassing mother-role, which Old Flesh distinctly lacks. Old Flesh believes that she is a soucouyant because she was cursed by Yemaya (her matron saint as well as Celia's) when her care for her employers' children coincided with the deaths of her own: "I mothered them babies like they my own. But they wasn't. Was supposed to be taking care of mine. Let them die instead. [Yemaya] cursed me" (159). Her vision of the events is distinctly disempowering; not only does she view her current existence and identity as an imposed fate rather than a choice, but she reinforces notions of maternal blame. She believes she was not the "right" type of mother and has been punished for it. Celia tells Old Flesh that the problem lies within her: "You no let them suck you dry like that. You come first. Feed you first" (159). In lines resonating with the conclusion of Morrison's *Beloved*, when Paul D tells Sethe that *she* is her own "best thing" (273), Zoboi asserts the right of women to possess multiple identities, not a wholly sacrificial maternal one.

Nevertheless, the message of empowerment appears severely undercut when, only a few words later, Celia claims, "You don't know there's enough love in those *tetás* to feed the whole world" (159). She reaffirms the concept of the ever-giving mother, the figure whose social and emotional identity is premised on her physical body's abilities to give birth and breastfeed. Furthermore, when she sings the spell to urge the stolen infant souls out of the bag, Celia prevails upon them to take sustenance from Old Flesh: "The smoke of weeping souls spiraled her breast, pulling life, *just as they were supposed to*" (161, emphasis added). The scene suggests not just that babies are "supposed to" feed from their mothers but that it is fine for them to drain their mothers' lives. The imagery reiterates the injustices of the slave era and the wrongs implied by Zoboi's opening critique of the contemporary "nanny trade": White babies come to peace and rest while the physical bodies of Black women are dissipated.

The ambivalent conclusion of "Old Flesh Song" leaves one further perplexed when considering Zoboi's revisions of the soucouyant figure, which initially seemed to assert a fluidity of roles for women of the Caribbean and African diasporas. Once Old Flesh disappears, Celia takes the "body-filled bag and licked her lips. There were enough bodies to feed on for a while" (161). What on one hand might be read as the author's dismantling of stereotypes of the light-skinned woman as good, pure, and beautiful on the other hand reads as the re-containment of poor and brown women's bodies by the U.S. racial and economic system that was critiqued in the story's early pages. Celia may be a soucouyant, draining her charges without killing them so her true identity is never suspected and her employers view her as the "perfect" nanny, but her position as a voiceless maternal caretaker continues. The last line of the piece ends with her "reach[ing] down into her pocket for her list" (161)—the instructions given to her by her employers, implying "*that they don't trust Ms. Nanny's taste, [. . . and] know just what Baby needs*" (151). In other words, her thirst and hunger get satisfied by her work, she privileges her own health and survival over anyone else's, and she strikes out against exploitative employers by feeding on their heirs; however, she is still perceived as a simple servant with no say, no choices, and no agency in the fulfillment of her daily tasks and her relationships to the children she raises.

In terms of its appropriation of the soucouyant myth, Edwidge Danticat's "Nineteen Thirty-Seven" from the collection *Krik? Krak!* (1996) is the most radical of these narratives that simultaneously address issues of motherhood. In this piece of short fiction, set in Haiti a few years after 1937, the young protagonist Josephine visits her mother in a prison for women convicted of being "lougarou": according to the local lore, such creatures are women by day but generate wings of flame at night in order to fly from house to house and steal children's breath and lives. The evidence against the inmates, who have all received life sentences, is that they have many wrinkles, believed to come from repeatedly removing and re-donning their skins. Apprehension grows as the women remain incarcerated: their skins sag as they literally starve to death, only serving to reinforce the guards' conviction that they are somehow escaping both their cells and their physical bodies each night. No explicit vampiric element accompanies Danticat's version, but the protagonist at one point observes that her mother's teeth are red, "as though caked with blood from the initial beating during her arrest" (37). The color clearly suggests the sucking of blood, demonizing Manman[6] by default, although readers, like Josephine, recognize that this appearance of monstrosity is accomplished through the physical brutalization of women's bodies.

Danticat opens the story: "My Madonna cried. A miniature teardrop traveled down her white porcelain face, like dew on the tip of early morning grass. When I saw the tear I thought, surely, that my mother had died" (33). As in Lorde's biomythography, Catholic faith and iconography and the possibility of miraculous occurrences are brought sharply into view. Josephine takes the figurine to visit her imprisoned mother, traveling barefoot even though the roads are strewn with sharp pebbles. Her journey, comparable to her mother's annual pilgrimages to the Massacre River before her incarceration, is one of willingly endured suffering, resembling a Catholic penance.

When the protagonist arrives at the prison, several institutions come under closer scrutiny. Josephine reveals that the statue was given to her "great-great-great-grandmother Défilé by a French man who had kept her as a slave" (34). The Madonna is worshiped and held in high regard by Manman in particular, possibly as much for its link to past and future generations of women as for its religious significance. She tells Josephine: "Keep the Madonna when I am gone[. . . .] When I am completely gone, maybe you will have someone to take my place. Maybe you will have a person[. . . .] But if you don't, you will always have the Madonna" (43). And while the original Jesuit missionaries to the island of Saint

Domingue (now Hispañola) might have been exiled for their radical views on education and insistence on teaching the enslaved population how to read, later Catholic presence in Haiti was associated with catering to the mulatto/a elites. In "Nineteen Thirty-Seven," Danticat subtly references a correlation between religion and enslavement—whether that be physical, intellectual, or economic oppression. The French man who controls the physical and sexual labor of Josephine's enslaved ancestor paradoxically bestows the gift of the *Virgin* Mother: she who brought Christ and the promise of freedom from sin and death into the world. The gift represents the height of irony when one considers that Europeans often portrayed African women (and men) as hypersexualized: what is one to assume of the relationship between a master and the enslaved woman on whom he bestows presents? Furthermore, the statue of the Madonna is made of white porcelain, reflecting the European complexions of traditional Christian iconography. If not for the physical, mental, and cultural brutality of slavery, people of African descent might have openly maintained the religious beliefs of their African continental ancestors, including worshiping the loa and spirits whose appearances reflected their own, perhaps eliminating the complexes of color to which I referred in the discussion of "Old Flesh Song." Finally, the great-grandmother's name holds a significant double meaning. As a form of *défiler*, to file past, it can be read as a parade or procession, suggesting the woman's position as a slave on the auction block. It also implies her role as the foremother whose image is paraded past her descendants; her story is a legacy as much as the inherited statue and provides bonds between the ensuing generations. Another meaning of *défiler*, however, is to defile, and the name thus simultaneously refers to the atrocious loss of options and identity in slavery, whether the defilement alludes to enduring sexual predation or to the violation of the cultural practices that were held before the Middle Passage. In this way, Danticat's story is one of the very few to bring the element of sexuality into the consideration of maternity and maternal legacies, rejecting the pattern of "sex without the sexuality" noted by Brand.

Lest the reader be tempted to lock the brutal practices against enslaved women exclusively in the far past, Danticat brings neocolonialism to light in her description of the jail. "The yellow prison building was like a fort, as large and strong as in the days when it was used by the American marines who had built it. The Americans taught us how to build prisons. By the end of the 1915 occupation, the police in the city really knew how to hold human beings trapped in cages, even women like Manman" (35).

The U.S. occupation of Haiti lasted nineteen years, from 1915 to 1934. Irony drips from the passage: the military force that arrived to protect the hemisphere from perceived threats of invasion during World War I ends up harming more than helping; the "enlightened" are more savage than they first appear; their lessons replicate a legacy of bondage for a people struggling to escape their history of slavery; "bone-thin" old women (35), weak from malnutrition and physical abuse, are viewed as the most virulent danger in the society.

Joan Dayan unites the Marine occupation with tales of soucouyants, lagahoos, and other demonic figures from Haitian folklore in *Haiti, History, and the Gods* (1995). She discusses U.S. publications of the era that disparaged the superstitions of the Haitian people: "What better way to justify the 'civilizing' presence of Marines in Haiti than to project the phantasm of barbarism? What might be dismissed as harmless but titillating tales of gore and spirits flapping in the night always have serious consequences" (14). In sharp contrast, we have Danticat's piece. Over the course of the story, the author works toward shifting the focus from a Eurocentric, male-empowering hierarchical religion and from a military-industrial complex to practices that have greater resonance in the lives of African Haitian women. This shift is accomplished through her use of soucouyant imagery.

Josephine describes trekking to the Massacre River "every year on the first of November" (41) with her mother and several other women. November 1, All Saints' Day, marks the celebration of God and all of his saints, both the known and unknown. This feast day was first established in the 600s when the Roman Pantheon was consecrated as the Church of the Blessed Virgin and All Martyrs. The original emphasis on the Virgin Mary correlates strongly with the Haitian women's ritual. Their purpose is not to praise God the Almighty or God the Father, or any formally canonized saints, but specifically to remember and celebrate the lives of the ordinary women who were lost in the 1937 Dominican massacre that gave the river its name. These dead women are framed, like Mary, as mothers. The survivors chant: "We were all daughters of that river, which had taken our mothers from us. Our mothers were the ashes and we were the light. Our mothers were the embers and we were the sparks. Our mothers were the flames and we were the blaze" (41). The imagery stresses a progression of strength from the older generation to the younger: from smoldering to blazing, dim to bright. The women who remain and remember are cast as heirs to great power. And in Danticat's story, there are no official Roman Catholic priests; all the celebrants are women. There is no official church structure; the women pray on the shores of the river. There is no baptismal font; the women sit "with our hands dipped in the water" (44).

Interestingly, by depicting this annual celebration of women whose lives were lost and concentrating on a family of women who participated in relocation to the Dominican Republic and the subsequent escape back across the border, Danticat subtly intimates a link between migration, gender, and social threat: Manman's "flight" away from the brutality in the DR and the ensuing local attack on her as *lougarou* might be tied together as a complex portrait of Haitian society's fear for their national sovereignty, as well as fear of threats to patriarchal norms. It should be noted that Manman does not kill just any babies but specifically Haitian babies. Manman, who had lived in the Dominican Republic long enough to make a life for herself, gets pregnant by relations with an unknown man—possibly another Haitian immigrant but potentially a Dominican subject—making her a threat to the concept of Haitian racial, linguistic, and cultural "purity." The text serves as a counterdiscourse to ongoing Dominican rhetoric that plays on fears of the African/Haitian corruption of "pure" Dominican bloodlines and national identity.

Danticat's piece also complicates simplistic formulations such as male oppressor versus female victim, Dominican (non-African) versus Haitian (Black). Josephine's mother is Haitian, but she is distinctly othered in her Haitian community as a Dominican exile, a *lougarou*, an outsider, a threat. She is female yet accused by another female villager; she is abused by the official guards and attacked by local townspeople as well. Via the soucouyant trope, Danticat holds up for critique the villagers' anxieties over women's local mobility as signified by their fear of the creature's flight into their homes at night. At the same time, the fear also stands as symbolic of Manman's larger geopolitical travels across the Haitian-Dominican border. The acclaimed author also comments on the denunciation of women who do not fulfill expected social roles— and motherhood in particular—as implied by the community's violent reaction to the supposedly antimaternal women said to drain away children's breath: Manman is viciously beaten with rocks, sticks, and fists because, while staying with a friend, the woman's colicky baby dies. Fear of the unknown—in this case a misunderstood illness coupled with an unfamiliar woman in the town—leads to socially sanctioned violence, and the mob of strangers nearly kills the protagonist's mother before the police arrive. When Josephine arrives at the prison, she notes: "[My mother's] face was swollen to three times the size that it had been. She had to drag herself across the clay floor on her belly. . . . She was like a snake, someone with no bones left in her body" (39). The allusion to the snake calls forth biblical imagery, linking serpents and women as in collusion against Man/Adam and God. Conventional tellings of the legend of the soucouyant, too, with her serpent-like skin-shedding, situate women as evil in the Garden of Eden.

At one point, as the young protagonist is leaving the prison, her mother says, "Let your flight be joyful." Rather than avoiding associations with the soucouyant's abilities and burying them in shame, she appears proud to pass on the legacy of flight. Josephine colludes in this reinforcement of the association between her mother and the soucouyant when she remembers stories of her mother's escape from the Dominican Republic in 1937. Rafael Trujillo, the dictator of the Dominican Republic (DR) since 1930, ordered the massacre of thousands of Haitian immigrants on the Dominican side of the border. Fomenting a racialized uneasiness under the guise of national interests, Trujillo labeled Haitian laborers in the DR as "the enemies of peace, who are also the enemies of work and prosperity, [. . .] keeping the nation in fear and menacing stability" (quoted in Danticat, *Farming* 97). Josephine's mother fled the Dominican soldiers and emerged safe on the Haitian side of the Massacre River. Bloody from the waters, which were discolored by the macheted bodies of those who did not make it across, she "glowed" red and appeared aflame. The protagonist proposes that the river thus gave her mother wings of fire. This allusion to fire further aligns the imprisoned woman with the soucouyant, who flies at night as a burning globe of light. The trait used by the majority of the people to condemn and scapegoat certain women thus becomes a symbol of empowering flight and escape to safety. In Danticat's hands, the image of the soucouyant is transformed and celebrated as desirable.

The imagery is replicated in Danticat's novel about the same moment in history, *The Farming of Bones* (1999). As the protagonist flees from her home in the Dominican Republic and attempts to reach the Haitian side of the border, she witnesses a gruesome event:

From the back of the cart fell a girl, seventeen or eighteen years old. [. . .] She was wearing an orange-yellow dress with a cloth of purple madras wrapped around her head. A machete had struck her at the temple and on both her shoulders.

Her face flapped open when she hit the ground, her right cheekbone glistening as the flesh parted from it. She rolled onto her back and for a moment faced the sky. (168)

The orange-yellow dress alludes to a body engulfed in flames just as the flesh parted from the bone suggests the shedding of skin. The pronoun "she" and active verb tense make it appear as if the girl is alive and purposefully rolling to face the sky, about to take flight. The truly monstrous figures are the men who commit these atrocities and the politicians who incite them, not the folkloric figures who inspire the author's work.

In a similar move, Danticat reverses the concept of demonic woman in "Nineteen Thirty-Seven." After her mother's death, Josephine notes that the fellow prisoners in the cell resemble "angels hiding their wings" (42, 47). Identifying these women as angels further recuperates them from their social construction as wicked and evil and reclaims them in the name of protective forces. Unfortunately, the time has not yet arrived when these women can display their wings—their inherent capabilities—before the rest of the society. In these ways, Danticat appropriates the soucouyant figure to establish a connection of strength and bonding between mother and daughter and a larger community of women and to revise notions of the "evil," alienated, and alienating woman in the Haitian society about which she writes. It is clear at the end of the tale, however, that much work needs to be done before the larger society will reach the same state of awareness and appreciation as the young protagonist. When readers learn that the prison guards burn the bodies and belongings of each woman who dies in jail in order "to prevent her spirit from wandering into any young innocent bodies" (36), we recognize their dread of the transfer of evil—but hopefully also see notions of succoring power—passed from one generation to the next. This idea is strengthened by Danticat's suggestion of a cyclical story arc: Josephine is born on the same day that her mother's mother dies. Manman repeatedly tells her: "At least I gave birth to my daughter on the night that my mother was taken from me[. . . .] At least you came out at the right moment to take my mother's place" (41). And because the story is projected in the past, Danticat evokes hope for the near future.

Danticat also alludes to the soucouyant figure in her first novel, *Breath, Eyes, Memory* (1994): during a short visit to the rural village of Dame Marie in Haiti, the protagonist, Sophie Caco, hears the men in the cane fields "singing about a woman who flew without her skin at night, and when she came back home, she found her skin peppered and could not put it back on. Her husband had done it to teach her a lesson. He ended up killing her" (150). The narrator's voice suggests a condemnation of the husband's brutality, but the prevalence of these violent folktales in the novel intimates the intense cultural presence of male aggression

toward women in the name of respectability. In another one of the stories, a wealthy man marries an impoverished young woman because of
her virginity and ends up killing her when he cuts her "to get some blood
to show" the townspeople. "The man had his honor and reputation to
defend. [. . .] The blood kept flowing like water out of the girl. It flowed
so much it wouldn't stop. Finally, drained of all her blood, the girl died"
(155). Danticat insinuates the doubled horror of the young woman's wed-
ding night: the sexual violence of the man's fervent attempts to penetrate
his virgin bride and draw blood from her come across as equally ruthless as his choice to slice her with a knife. Furthermore, the bridegroom
is not the only guilty party; the townspeople who monitor the sexual
activity of their neighbors and promote the rigid behavioral standards of
the community are also to blame. Both stand as symbolic vampires, the
monsters who "drained [the girl] of all her blood."

Both tales in *Breath, Eyes, Memory* reveal the coercive influence of
folklore as well as potential social stigma. Although one story is allegedly supernatural and the other is realistic, in essence both women die
from failing to adhere to social norms. Danticat's novel circles round
and round the constraints and often traumatizing effects of cultural
expectations for Haitian women. In another scene, Ifé, the protagonist's
grandmother, scolds Atie, one of her daughters, for taking nightly reading lessons from a friend: "The way you go about free in the night, one
would think you a devil" (107). Ifé's complaints are rooted in the idea
that women should stay home after dark, anchored to the domestic space.
Those who travel at night, like the soucouyant, volant, or loogarou, are
associated with evil and looked upon with suspicion. It is a matter of
safety but also of reputation: the novel concentrates on the extremes to
which mothers go to preserve their daughters' sexual purity. Because of
a cultural obsession with girls' chastity, the women in the Caco family perform the "testing"—a mother's insertion of her finger into her
daughter's vagina to check for an intact hymen—although it traumatizes
members of each generation. This monstrous penetration—akin, I would
argue, to conventional visions of the soucouyant—ostensibly serves to
protect young girls' purity and their family's honor. In truth, it exposes
another type of maternal legacy: women's complicity in a patriarchal system that conceives of females as goods—either "new" or "used," physically pure or "spoiled," "whole" or "broken"—to be preserved until they
can be handed over to their husbands. Sophie recalls how Tante Atie
taught her about the purpose for each of her ten fingers: "Mothering.
Boiling. Loving. Baking. Nursing. Frying. Healing. Washing. Ironing.

Scrubbing" (151). "Testing" is not explicitly stated but lies implicit in the "mothering."

Atie's refusal to obey certain gender norms and the resulting sugges-tion of the soucouyant is also implied when her niece asks her what will happen when her best friend succeeds in her attempts to immigrate to Miami. Atie responds: "I will miss her like my own skin" (145), referring to the pain of shedding the skin, an organ so necessary to life. Readers might attribute these same feelings, and thus the potential of the sou-couyant, to Louise as well. Whereas Atie suffers, staying in Dame Marie and caring for her mother out of duty even though she is miserable, Lou-ise provides a more liberated image in that she decides to take flight; she sheds her "skin"—Atie—in order to pursue her dreams of freedom and opportunity in the United States. She emblematizes the positive recu-peration of the soucouyant figure.

Martine, Atie's sister and Sophie's mother, is also associated with the vampiric folk figure. Readers can easily connect her mother's passion for red as her desire for a symbolic connection to the Haitian landscape, with its scarlet-tinged soil, "crimson *flamboyant* tree[s]" (97), and the "blood red hibiscus" (112). When Sophie first enters Martine's apartment in New York City, she notes that "[t]he tablecloth was shielded with a red plastic cover, the same blush red as the sofa in the living room" (44). Her next house is similarly decorated: "red, everything from the carpet to the plastic roses on the coffee table" (65). Even when she redecorates, the color scheme remains the same: "red everywhere, even the new sofa and love seat were a dark red velvet" (180). When Martine returns to Haiti for the first time, more than two decades after her original departure, she wears a cherry-red jumper and carries a red parasol (158–59). Conspicu-ously, she is described as "glowing" (159, 167), suggesting a body on fire. She has moved, in a way, from being the victim of a brutal rape to being a figure of power. The connection between Martine, flight, blood, and fire is made once again when one considers that Caco, the family's surname, is attributed to the name of a vibrantly colored redbird. Birds evoke flight, but more significantly, when the creature dies, "there is always a rush of blood that rises to its neck and the wings, they look so bright, you would think them on fire" (150). In the end, after Martine dies tragically by her own hand, she is buried in a red suit "the color of flames" (234). The author carefully undercuts the strict binaries that make soucouyants purely evil, women either "whole" or damaged, sexually pure or tainted, and red dresses the clothes of the Whore. Through each of these works, Danticat participates in a re-visioning of the soucouyant figure that functions to empower female readers, challenging the norms that make biological motherhood the imperative for all women but also inspiring listeners to remake mythology in their own ways and pass these new stories along to future generations. As I continue to explore in the next chapter, resistance must accompany a wrestling with notions of the African diasporic woman's aberrant corporeality. The texts to be explored in Chapter 4 attempt to establish women's sexual agency over their bodies without needing to reject those bodies' materiality.

4 / "Queering" the Norm: Vampirism and Women's Sexuality

> *My character, Gilda, is a lesbian because I'm a lesbian. Even though some lesbian-feminists have challenged my choice, suggesting it was too negative an idea to connect to lesbians, I feel I can remake mythology as well as anyone.*
>
> —JEWELLE GOMEZ

As innumerable feminist critics have stated, battles for patriarchal control have often been fought for and on women's bodies. The bodies of women of African descent are especially fraught sites, and the ideology surrounding these bodies is a legacy that must still be combated in the twenty-first century. Not only are there individual and state attempts to influence reproductive potential (as is the case with almost all women), but the experience of enslavement meant specifically racialized readings of the Black female body—one that was moved from place to place at the "master's" will, one ever-available for and allegedly ever-desirous of sex, one able to be manipulated for the reproduction of "property," and one, especially in the cases of circum-Caribbean women and women from the U.S. Deep South, often compelled to migrate to and from the "metropoles" to seek economic opportunities for supporting family "back home." Significantly, the soucouyant moves *herself.* Tracing the movements of this vampiric trope across time—stretching back to the incipient Americas colonies—and across space—both between the Caribbean islands and from them to continental American locations in the United States and Canada as well as in contemporary Europe—reveals a linked network of images, ideologies, and narratives that coalesce around a Black female subject at the center of discourse, not off in the margins as Caliban's mother, "woman," or daughter.

Numerous postcolonial writers, including authors of the African diaspora in the United States, have sometimes challenged colonial belief systems and the oppressive sexual history and legacy associated with colonial rule through depictions of homoeroticism and other expressions of transgressive, or "queer," sexual desire.[1] Carolyn Cooper notes in her often-cited study of Jamaican dancehall culture that "Slackness is potentially a politics of subversion. For Slackness is not mere sexual looseness—though it certainly is that. Slackness is metaphorical revolt against law and order; an undermining of consensual standards of decency. It is the antithesis of Culture" (141). One can apply this theory to earlier instances of female resistance in Caribbean society. Jamaica Kincaid, in *Annie John*, describes young Annie's insistence on playing marbles despite her very proper mother's mortification. Folklorist J. D. Elder strikes at the heart of the issue when he reminisces about his own childhood: "In Charlotteville [Tobago,] tops was a game for boys and for man. You had no right to a top if you were a girl, although we had some Congo people, some Amazon kind of folk, whose daughters used to play top like men. *We were afraid of them*" ("I Recall" 189, emphasis added).

In what I see as a parallel argument to the one presented in this particular chapter of *Things That Fly in the Night*—that the bodies of women of African descent are fraught sites throughout the African diaspora, especially when it comes to physical labor and sexual labor versus sexual pleasure—Margot Gayle Backus explores portraits of sexuality and family in a series of Anglo-Irish Gothic novels for themes of imperial resistance: "[These novels] depict colonialism as a pervasive historical system that appropriates the sexuality and lives of Anglo-Irish children. In [these texts], gender and sexual transgression, including lesbianism and reversals of historical patterns of sexual victimization, symbolize the overthrow of the colonial order" (8–9). Although in most traditional Gothic narratives, the anticolonial/sexually transgressive force is contained at the end of the story, making the text "a cautionary tale through its self-righteous expulsion of the monstrous" (72), Backus's framework is useful for analyzing African diasporic works that employ the soucouyant figure and other Black female vampires in a recuperative manner: as a representative of sexual freedom and erotic agency instead of gruesome perversity.

As many scholars of vampire literature have asserted (Bentley, Bosky, Craft, Dijkstra, Rose, Skal, and others), the vampire's bite is inherently sexual: the teeth, easily viewed as phallic symbols, penetrate the flesh of a prone body; the mouth, "engulfing yet penetrating," blurs male and female genitalia and identity in perverse ways (Bosky 228); bodily fluids are exchanged; encounters occur at night, in bedrooms, in dark alleys, or in other secluded spaces. Mainstream feminist critics such as Bonnie

Zimmerman have described how the myth of the "lesbian" vampire was often employed to explain away love between women by attributing it to lurid "elements of violence, compulsion, hypnosis, paralysis, and the supernatural"; at the same time, it was contained within "boundaries of sexual violence, to force it into a patriarchal model of sexuality. By showing the lesbian as a vampire-rapist who violates and destroys her victim, men alleviate their fears that lesbian love could create an alternate model" (3 of online essay).

The authors examined here challenge the conventional "cautionary tales" by attempting to "remake mythology," as Jewelle Gomez remarks in the epigraph. However, unlike White and/or male anticolonial writers, women authors of color carry an additional burden. Because the monstrous character in traditional Gothic texts is so often gendered female *and* racialized or made ethnic or exotic, artists face the difficult prospect of defying the stereotype of the hypersexual female Other or else leaving it firmly in place. And yet this sexualization of a racialized identity is often overlooked by mainstream critics. Bosky, for example, identifies "the urbane vampire" and the outcast vampire as the two main types in contemporary sexual vampire stories. The outcast breaks taboos and is thus "literally an outlaw, or culturally marginalized due to poverty, youth, or membership in a despised subculture" (222), but the critic does not include race or ethnicity as "subcultures"; rather, she specifies "the leather scene, open sex based on sadomasochism and/or dominance and submission; and the Goth scene" (230).

The authors in question in this chapter must contest myths of African hypersexuality, myths of the female bloodsucker as perverse because she inverts traditional conceptions of masculine penetration and feminine sexual passivity, *and* myths of same-sex desire as abomination. The soucouyant might at first seem like a poor choice for embracing the female body in that she abandons her skin in order to pursue her nightly bloodsucking. She also seems to fight against her corporeal self when she cries out, "Skin, kin, kin—you na know me? You na know me?"[2] However, her piercing the skin of her victims and her power over the shape and form of her body—old woman, skinless creature, ball of fire—all suggest agency that has long been denied women of African descent in mainstream Americas societies. As Nicole Fleetwood asserts of the Black women artists and cultural producers in *Troubling Vision*, this physical variability can be read as emblematic of the possibilities women of African descent have to "engage with [. . . the] reinscription of their corporeality" (105).

An early incarnation of the soucouyant in U.S. African Americas literature attests to this burdensome prospect. Zora Neale Hurston, well-known for her attempts to combat the confining strictures on Black women's behavior and attacks against their morality, includes a fascinating soucouyant metaphor in the novel *Jonah's Gourd Vine* (1934), one that jettisons the hypersexuality of the Old Hag figure away from her main female character but ends up erasing her bodily presence and simultaneously reinforcing notions of lasciviousness in her male protagonist. The Reverend John Pearson, the ever-philandering protagonist of the novel, has an emotional breakdown near the story's conclusion where he laments the death of his first wife, Lucy, and the suffering he has endured since her demise: "He sought Lucy thru all struggles of sleep, mewing and crying like a lost child, but she was not there. He was really searching for a lost self and crying like the old witch with her shed skin shrunken by red pepper and salt, 'Ole skin, doncher know me?' But the skin was never to fit her again" (183).

As poet Rita Dove observes in her foreword, Hurston constructs Lucy as the epitome of the conventional Good Woman before her tragic death. She is faithful and forbearing despite distress over John's numerous sexual transgressions; she is a doting wife and mother. Hurston removes any suggestion of excessive sexuality from Lucy at the same time that she gives her a sort of supernatural presence: she "haunts the novel" (xiv)—not as a demonic force but an angelic one— "and her absence is at least as compelling as John's suffering" (xiv). It is John, and not Lucy, who is associated with the soucouyant/witch and all of her implicit sexuality (removing her clothes *and* her skin, invading sleeping quarters, "riding" her victims). He is the one who cries and seeks comfort, like the witch seeking to re-don her skin. Hurston clearly identifies the typical witch as female, but by establishing a connection between John and the folk figure, she allows a space for African Americas women that lies outside the stereotypes prevalent in her early twentieth-century cultural context.

Maria-Elena John's *Unburnable* (2006) provides a more contemporary example of a book that battles conventional myths of the aberrant Black woman. Protagonist Lillian Baptiste is born and raised on the Caribbean island of Dominica but is sent away to the United States during her teenage years because of a series of family traumas and secrets, which lead to her mental collapse. John attributes the character's increasingly aggressive sexual behavior to her devolving psychological health, thus subverting the stereotype of the naturally "loose" Black woman, but most of the novel's characters, including Lillian's lover Teddy, are unable—and unwilling—to recognize the connection.

[T]he bright light [of morning] allowed Teddy to revise his memory of what had happened. [. . . In] his recollection of the kind of love they had made the previous night—love that held desperation; love that spoke of destruction—her spine had not bent backward over the [balcony] railing and down, her head had not hung suspended above the river's boulders, and her legs had not gone rigid, had not lost their grip around his waist.

    The memory of the panic, the terror he had felt [. . .] was all blotted out in the light of morning[. . . .]

    When the sun woke them up the next morning, Teddy just re-membered it as the fuck of his life. (257)

The passage complicates the demonization of women's sexual activity by revealing Teddy's engagement in an act of "disremembering": he significantly participates in rewriting herstory as history. Rather than acknowledging a Black woman's attempts at crossing over into death—evocative of the soucouyant's position as an abject being who penetrates the border between land and sky, inside and outside, blood and skin, life and death—he focuses on his physical pleasure and Lillian's role in satisfying his sexual needs.

John further complicates society's vilification of women's eroticism and sexual activity by identifying women's sexual "propriety" as a dis-tinctly middle-class construct, deeply influenced by the European colo-nial presence on the island. As M. Jacqui Alexander asserts:

Women's sexual agency, our sexual and our erotic autonomy have always been troublesome for the state. They pose a challenge to the ideological anchor of an originary nuclear family, a source of legiti-mation for the state, which perpetuates the fiction that the fam-ily is the cornerstone of society. Erotic autonomy signals danger to the heterosexual family and to the nation. And because loyalty to the nation as citizen is perennially colonized within reproduction and heterosexuality, erotic autonomy brings with it the potential of undoing the nation entirely, a possible charge of irresponsible citi-zenship or no citizenship at all. *Particularly for the neocolonial state it signals danger to respectability.* (64, emphasis added)

In markedly different depictions of city folk and rural islanders, John contrasts the "high-class town people" of Roseau with rural communities that are more understanding and flexible in their perception of women's nonmatrimonial, nonreproductive sexuality.

> [T]o the credit of the country people, islandwide, [. . .] none of them, woman or man, considered [Lillian's mother, Iris] to be a prostitute. The villagers [. . .] understood the practicality of what is today called [. . .] the sex industry. The women, in particular, [. . .] had a definite appreciation for Iris: she kept their men from bothering them when they were too occupied with raising their children to be concerned with the effort of sex; [. . .] she kept their young boys from experimenting on their young girls, thereby keeping down underage pregnancy. (2)

Iris plays a distinct and valued role in society. She is a type of soucouyant figure—"her skin was reputed to actually glow in the dark" (1); her passion, or innate fire, is renowned throughout the community and frightening to "fainthearted" men (1); she flies at the men who visit her, throwing "them onto their backs and attack[ing] them brutally," and yet they are largely "oblivious" to the anger of her assaults (2), much like the soucouyant's victims are often unaware of being preyed upon. Unlike in conventional renditions, however, John allows this soucouyant to be accepted by her neighbors and function as an integral part of the community.

At the end of the novel, Lillian drives toward a mountain from which she intends to jump—very much like the leap made by Milkman at the conclusion of Toni Morrison's *Song of Solomon*, which precludes a definitive inference of the character's life or death. Lillian's final thoughts embrace the notion of flight through reference to the soucouyant, but it is a journey of the soul, not one of the body. In light of her sexual encounters with Teddy, the association with the soucouyant also suggests a resolution of the shame attributed to women with intense sexual desires in the very Catholic culture of Dominica.

> Lillian had decided that it would be best to be the worst of the lot, a *soucouyant:* a woman who takes off her skin at night and flies around in search of victims whose blood she sucks. Yes, she would give them [*chanté mas* singers who spread rumor, news, and myth] that pleasure, and it made sense for her to go back to where the Maroons had jumped; she would fly through the air for her country people—and at the bottom there were enough trees and branches to tear off her skin, so that when they found her she would be exactly

what they wanted her to be: their nightmare come true, a *soucouy-ant*. (292)

Her suicide is meant to suggest women's choice and agency, since for much of the novel Lillian has *withstood* but not been able to *act*. Her demise is construed as rebellion against the constrictive middle-class and European social norms that led to the deaths of mother Iris and grandmother Matilda, in that John portrays the site and style of fatality as an imminent reunion with her Maroon ancestors—Maroons serving as the epitome of rebellion in Caribbean discourse. Lillian has heard their "calling to her, she had *felt* it, the sensation of a thousand pairs of wings, beating like butterflies all around her" (291). However, it should be mentioned that Lillian cannot achieve this freedom from pain, psychological distress, and social alienation in life because of her maternal heritage and past "sins"; this ending leaves little hope for true change among those still living in the Caribbean. Maria-Elena John posits that a complete healing and empowerment of the female protagonist and a full recuperation the soucouyant figure are not possible in contemporary society.

For Shani Mootoo, a Trinidadian author of Indian heritage, the soucouyant provides an emblem of womanhood outside the heteronormative paradigm: the folk figure lies on the physical margins of society and outside the domestic marriage plot. In Mootoo's first novel, *Cereus Blooms at Night* (1996), Nurse Tyler lies outside the conventional gender script as well. S/he chooses and changes gender identities like garments—or skin—to be taken on and off: during working hours he appears as the only male nurse on the island, but in Mala Ramchandin's hospital room one night he gathers enough courage to shed this persona and don the pantyhose, makeup, and dress that Mala has stolen for him. The "skin" into which Tyler was born feels more constrictive than natural, and his "true self" needs to escape: "I was certainly excited by the possibilities trembling inside me" (76). Mala is the conduit to this release: "She was not one to manacle nature, and I sensed that she was permitting mine its freedom" (77). By the end of the novel, Tyler puts on powder and a female nurse's uniform—the "skin" that fits. Similarly, Otoh Mohanty is born biologically female and named Ambrosia after her father but chooses to shed this identity and live life as a man. Mootoo also repeatedly refers to snails and their empty shells throughout the narrative; these creatures, too, take their outer "apparel" on and off. The same can be said of the soucouyant, who takes off her skin each night.

The soucouyant is referenced more specifically on several occasions. Before Mala enters Paradise Alms House, for instance, adults use stories of her to frighten local children into obedience:

According to their parents, she possessed the ability to leap her fence, track an offending child into its hiding place and tear out its mind. No one had experienced such a fate but the children feared it as if it were proven fact. Their parents used her legend to their advantage, as though she were a whipping cane. Should she suddenly appear while the children were walking along the road they would fall silent, conceal themselves behind the twelve-foot-high poinsettia shrubs, pray feverishly and make noble promises. They watched as the tall, upright, wire-thin woman with matted hair the colour of forgotten silver emerged from the bramble patches, carrying a silver bucket of snail shells. (113–14)[3]

Although the folk figure in traditional incarnations is not associated with ripping out victims' minds, violence and violation are key. Conventional soucouyants generate fear by penetrating the body; Mala is perceived as able to penetrate the mind—the site of the life force, not unlike blood. Like the conventional soucouyant, the silver-haired Mala is also aged, a single woman, and living in isolation from her community.

As a "madwoman," Mala refuses to follow the behavioral norms dictated by society; one prime example can be found in her vision of snails as beautiful, rather than generating disgust. She boils the shells she finds in her garden and is rejuvenated by the snails' scent, which she sharpens with "a pin prick of fresh blood[. . . .] It wove itself through Mala's hair and penetrated her pores," giving her "the impression of reversing decay" (115). This process, like the soucouyant's nightly activities, requires blood and repeals the decomposition associated with aging.

When Otoh first approaches the Ramchandin house at the bequest of his father, who is Mala's former lover, he wants "desperately to see her yet hop[ed] she would not show herself. He had grown up hearing all the rumours, even the ridiculous one that claimed she turned into a ball of fire and whipped across the sky at night. His skin tingled as he approached the gravel path" (117). Ironically, Otoh's skin prickles as if he is also a soucouyant with sheddable skin: "She had secrets and I had secrets. Somehow I wanted to go there and take all my clothes off and say 'Look! See? See all this? *I am different!* You can trust me'" (124). Besides symbolically shedding his skin as a transgender character and expressing the desire to shed another layer by "tak[ing] all my clothes off," Otoh experiences a sense of bonding with the alleged soucouyant: both are alienated, "queer" members of the community.

Mootoo further inverts the traditional soucouyant tale in developing Mala's traumatic incestuous relationship with her father, Chandin Ramchandin. Although it is "sightings [of Mala that] became the substance of frenetic dreamings at night" among neighborhood children (114), in reality, she is the persecuted, not the predator; she is the stalked and haunted, not a demonic creature, worrying the community. The narrative clearly configures her as hapless victim and her father as monstrous aggressor. One of Mootoo's goals, then, might be interpreted as shattering the ideal of the biological nuclear family with its innately protective patriarch—the counternarrative to the conventional soucouyant story.[4]

Mootoo further ascribes vampiric soucouyant imagery to Mala when she has the character bite her abusive father after he destroys a gramophone given to her by her timid young lover, Ambrose: "Mala's fury was so uncontrollable she didn't notice her hair being ripped out. She forced her face toward the hand holding the cleaver and sunk her teeth deep into Chandin's wrist. Chandin released his grip on her hair and curled his body in sudden agony. Mala had drawn blood" (227). In desperate jealousy, Chandin had attacked Ambrose; in fright, Ambrose fled, leaving the overwrought Mala behind. Even in this moment of rage and bloodletting, Mala is cast as the most sympathetic character of the three. When Ambrose hears Mala calling his name and pauses, he turns back and sees "an unrecognizable wild creature with a blood-stained face, frothing at the mouth and hacking uncontrollably at the furniture in the drawing room" (228). She begs him not to leave her, but, again panicked for his life, he runs. It is this abandonment that pushes Mala over the edge of her already tenuous existence into insanity. In his cowardice, Ambrose ironically represents a more monstrous presence in the novel than the blood-stained victim of rape, physical abuse, and maternal, sororeal, and community abandonment. In the same way that readers must reevaluate the community's ostracization of Mala, they should reconsider conventions that dictate that aged, isolated women be treated with suspicion—if not the literal label of soucouyant—rather than celebrated as wise, independent survivors.

As a Black, feminist, Trinidadian Canadian lesbian, Dionne Brand contests the colonial concept of "a white, middle-class 'centre'" that surpasses and subsumes "a constantly deferred Caribbean origin"

(Sturgess 214). She accomplishes this in the content of her fiction but also in her form, as she often incorporates "the discontinuities of a fractured, post-colonial imaginary" (214) into a fragmented writing style. Her tendencies to subvert conventions are evident in her 1997 novel, *In Another Place, Not Here*. By employing references to the soucouyant, the author challenges the norms that limit mobility—whether physical, economic, or social—and sexual freedom for Caribbean women of African descent. Her sympathetic treatment of a soucouyant whose power can be used for "selfish" ends destabilizes overly romanticized views of female bonding and belonging. The novel simultaneously writes back to prevailing Black nationalist narratives that attempt to "expunge femininity and genital sexuality from [the Worker's Movement's] revolutionary subject[s. . . .] The figure of the black lesbian femme is among those [. . .] render[ed . . . as] impossibilities within the project of Black Liberation and within the common-sense black nationalism that currently solidifies black belonging" (Keeling 8).[5]

Protagonist Elizete is first seen as an abandoned child, given away by impoverished parents. When the woman who has been caring for her dies, she is again passed along but this time to a man, Isaiah Ferdinand. Elizete resigns herself to her economic and sexual oppression: "Who is me to want anything big or small. Who is me to think I is something. I born to clean Isaiah' house and work cane since I was a child and say what you want Isaiah feed me and all I have to do is lay down under him in the night and work the cane in the day. It have plenty woman waiting their whole blessed life for that" (4). Eventually, however, resentment replaces acceptance. Elizete seeks escape not merely from her oppressive situation but, like the soucouyant, from her physical body: "What morning I running running, can't find no track, no sense in how, *no way out* [. . .] *of this body* what everybody use for leaving, for toting water, for beating and beating" (76, emphasis added). When she gathers the courage to run away, she is caught by Isaiah and literally whipped, reinforcing notions of the (domestic) enslavement of contemporary women. She succumbs to the brutality and stops trying to flee but fantasizes about absconding to Maracaibo, Suriname. Brand's imagery raises the specter of the soucouyant but this time in its bloodsucking incarnation: "I dream the vine, green and plump, blood running through it and me too running running, spilling blood. Vine like rope under my feet, vine strapping my legs and opening when I walk. Is like nowhere else. I destroying anything in my way. I want it to be peaceful there" (12).

Elizete craves to spill blood—a blood that is eroticized in the description of it coursing through vines "plump" like veins. The protagonist dreams of dominance and destruction, but her acts are generated out of a desire for peace and freedom instead of the standard vampiric desire to harm others. She continues on: "Fearless. I dream my eyes, black and steady in my black face and never close. I will wear a black skirt, shapely like a wing and down to my toes. I will fly to Maracaibo in it and you will see nothing of me but my black eyes in my black face and my black skirt swirling over thick living vine. I dream of flying in my skirt to Maracaibo" (12). No longer will she be fearful, but neither does she conceive of herself as predator. Rather, Elizete envisions the skirt as "shapely" and swirling. There is something distinctly feminine about the apparel she imagines, calling to mind the singularly female presence of the soucouyant figure. Elizete's emphasis on flight reveals a desire for self-empowerment and mobility, while the detail of eyes that never close suggest hypersensitive sight. She is a supernatural being, able to see "beyond." These eyes are repeatedly referred to as black; this detail, along with repeated references to her "black face," intimates positive connotations of blackness and an affirmative racial vision.

Soucouyant imagery is also elicited with Brand's depiction of her character's work in a sand quarry: "If I dig enough it cool me and take my mind off the junction [the site of the initially attempted getaway]. I feel my body full up and burst. All me skin split. Until I was so tired I could not run" (11). Again readers witness the desire for escape—for flight from her current circumstance—coupled with a splitting, or shedding, of the skin from which her body bursts.

Elizete eventually becomes romantically involved with Verlia, a Caribbean woman engaged in the Worker's Movement, who arrives from Toronto to try to convert the exploitative sugar plantation into a cooperative. Watching Verlia cut cane, Elizete thinks, "That is the first time I feel like licking she neck. She looked like the young in me, the not beaten down and bruised" (15). Brand casts Elizete as the traditional "old woman" of the soucouyant legend; she has not extended her life supernaturally through grisly bloodsucking, however. Instead, her body has suffered from emotional abandonment, poverty, and physical and sexual abuse. Her position as a subjugated member of society can be read in every wrinkle, every scar, every bruise.

Situating this scene in the cane fields is also crucial to the author's revisioning of traditional narratives. Omise'eke Natasha Tinsley cites Edouard Glissant's "Pleasure and Jouissance" for its intensely masculinist and heteronormative conceptions of the sexual legacies of slavery: Glissant posed Martinique's cane fields as sites of potential resistance, where "slaves' hidden sexual encounters—acts completed almost literally in flight, as male slaves grab and penetrate females while both move through the cane" (Tinsley 177)—rejected the European masters' complete domination over their physical bodies. Tinsley argues: "This leads [. . .] to a cultural understanding of the penetrating penis as a dangerous tool-cum-weapon, a redeployed machete that simultaneously steals the master's property and subjugates the penetrated partner to create a fleeting sense of power." Women's bodies are rendered simply as "the penetrated orifice [that] becomes an abject site of powerlessness and degradation, a sticky object of revulsion entered and exited as quickly as possible" (178). In the Black nationalist discourse that arose out of and after the colonial era, Tinsley sees a recurrence of this power play, with African Caribbean men

> charged with reclaiming that frustrated potency by using the penis to fight for access to phallic power, staking a claim to "real manhood" through their hyperperformance as masterful heterosexual lovers, husbands, and fathers. In turn, black females, like the slaves on their backs in the cane, are charged with opening their vaginas as vehicles through which black men stake a claim to phallic masculinity. (179)

In contrast, Keeling argues that according to Black nationalist ideology in the United States, the African Americas woman "actively must reject any attempt to constitute hers as a feminine, sexual body because [. . .] the constitution of the black body as feminine and sexual has been the work of colonization" (65). *In Another Place, Not Here* firmly rejects both of these heteropatriarchal models. Illustrating the relationship that develops between Verlia and Elizete, Brand does not hesitate to detail the erotic charge or physical particulars of the sexual encounters.

Not only are the accounts of the couple's sexual intimacies absent of the masculinist presence and gaze, but the dynamic is not glossed over by considerations of or references to mother-child dynamics or working toward the construction of an idealized, sacrificial mother, as is detailed in Chapter 3.

> I abandon everything for Verlia. I sink in Verlia and let she flesh swallow me up. I devour she. She open me up like any morning. Limp, limp and rain light, soft to the marrow. She make me wet.

She tongue scorching like hot sun. I love that shudder between her legs, love the plain wash and sea of her, the swell and bloom of her softness. (5)[6]

Elizete's frank description of lesbian sex lies in remarkable contrast to her description of heterosexual relations with Isaiah ("[I] lay down under him in the night"). Furthermore, both women are actively engaged in this convergence of their bodies. Both women are also aligned with the vampiric acts and the traits of the soucouyant: Elizete "devour[s]" Verlia, but Verlia's "flesh swallow[s] [Elizete] up." Elizete "sink[s] in Verlia," suggesting penetration, but it is Verlia who is connected here to the transformation into a ball of fire: her tongue is "scorching like hot sun." This image is repeated later on, when "You could see she burning bright" (9), and again when she "turn transparent and blue in the rain-damp dirt" (84). Furthermore, during the section of the novel depicting Verlia's childhood, the narrator conveys her soucouyant-like yearnings:

[S]he fears that any mortal self is heavy and persistent, full of pres-entness, which jostles the air and is unpleasant. She knows that drawing breath is the first mistake; it limits you to feeling your finite body, that empty box with nothing but a greed for air. She'd like to live, exist or be herself in some other place, less confining, less pinned down, less tortuous, less fleshy. (126–27)

In a series of repeated dreams, she sees "her mouth full of teeth, she's spent her whole dream pulling and pulling, trying to empty it. She's dreamt every-one turned into hummingbirds" (127). The passage goes on: "She is peerless in the competition of dreams[. . . .] then she dreamt lots and lots of blood" (128). These dreams of foreboding, blood, teeth, birds, and flight all reveal her unconscious connection to the vampiric figure from diasporic folktales.

During the 1973 Toronto march in which she partakes as an adult, Verlia reports

the crowd around her like sugar, sugar is what she recalled, shook down her back by her sister, sticky and grainy and wanting you to laugh, and the shock and strangeness of her skin shaking sugar. The crowd like sugar down her back, [. . .] So much goes through her when the chant pushes from her lips, she wants to cry and all of her feels like melting into it, sugar. (167)

The divergence from the conventional folklore is marked. Sugar, and not salt, is poured into the skin, shocking the system yet making her want to laugh, not cry out in pain. Here the rebellious female experiences acceptance from the community instead of a brutal attack; she is "melting into" the group rather than standing apart. Provocatively, Brand also relies on sugar's positive connotations in distinct variance from traditional renderings of sugar as the emblem of colonial exploitation.

This sense of belonging continues when Verlia returns to the Caribbean. When Elizete employs metaphors of flight to represent Verlia, it is significant that they are associated with her speech—her means of communicating with others: "This woman with her mouth flying[. . . .] Her mouth too fast, she tongue flying ahead of sheself" (13). Verlia is not the conventional alienated subject, the demonic predator, but rather the celebrated leader of the villagers. The cane workers make sweet bread and ice cream for her and envision her as rescuer (9) since the plantation owners are the true predators. Verlia carries the pain and sadness of those who died in the fields in her own body: "Vein does remember blood. The spirits call she and make their display in she" (84). In a sense, like a vampire, the blood of others flows in her veins; she has imbibed the trauma of the workers and seeks retribution. Similarly, when Vee describes people in the Toronto Worker's Movement, she claims: "Their skin is electrified Black, burning. It is as if they suddenly became aware of its power where they had only known its weakness" (166). This image shifts the site of horror to the burning of African diasporic victims of lynchings and away from the fireball-form of the soucouyant. Brand's soucouyant becomes revolutionary, not revolting, and clearly accepted by those around her.

Interestingly, when Elizete imagines Verlia's experiences in Canada, she envisions her as feeling lonesome at night "because Verlia could never sleep. And at four in the mornings she must have been most lonely and most awake" (100). The suggestion of the soucouyant, awake at night, is softened and emptied of its conventional association with predation. Later, Verlia specifies that her nights in Canada were sleepless because of her fear: "Always the door creaks, a dog barks, a frog's well throats inky, a curtain moves in a breath of wind, a tree yields to a breeze, the constant night flute of a *mot mot* hesitates and she thinks someone is out there. Nights pass in long, almond-shaded darkness, waiting" (121). She is made worthy of compassion and set up as a potential victim rather than a victimizer, and the symbolic skin she wishes to shed is her terror: "Although she could not remember the nightmare, it lay over her like a skin" (146).

At the same time, Brand does not flatten her character by making her noble and purely self-sacrificing. At several points in the novel, Verlia expresses the soucouyant's desire for solitude—an attitude often viewed as masculine and taboo for women in cultures that associate women with emotion, family, and communal nurturing. Feeling the pressures of intimacy from Elizete, Vee declares: "In the middle of everything Elizete asks me why I'm with her[. . . .] This is too much now. I don't want to be responsible like that for anyone. I can't stand the feeling of being attached" (223). At another point, yearning for physical seclusion, she writes in her diary: "Today I feel calm but I don't want anyone to touch me and I'm not turning the radio on. I'm not leaving this place" (227). She describes how, early in life, she had slept with men to appear "normal" to her community; now, embracing her lesbianism, she delights in the physical connection of sex but still remains on the margins in her rejection of what others might see as "domestic bliss." She longs for

the brush and ease of the skin [of women], the melt into the soft and swell of the body[. . . . But] nothing more. Not the bed that comes with it, not the kitchen, not the key to the door. She hates the sticky domesticity lurking behind them. [. . .] [J]ust the empty floor and sometimes a woman with her back to kiss, her company to keep all night. (204)

Verlia ostensibly commits suicide in the novel, but Elizete describes her final deed as active and intentional, very much like the protagonist's last act in *Unburnable*: "I like it how she leap. Run in the air without moving" (7). The other revolutionaries in the cemetery merely dream of flight:

One dreamed she multiplied into pieces and flew away, one dreamed his feet clawed and he flew away, one dreamed she feathered and flew away, one dreamed he sprang like a tree, one dreamed she blew into dust, one dreamed her dress dried into a stone, one dreamed he shrank from sight little by little, one dreamed his arms took flight. (243)

Verlia moves beyond passive dreaming and dynamically leaps off a cliff, avoiding a death at the hands of others when the U.S. forces invade. Elizete perceives

She is laughing and laughing and laughing[. . . .] She's flying out to sea and in the emerald she sees the sea, its eyes translucent, its back solid going to some place so old there's no memory of it. She's leaping. She's tasting her own tears and she is weightless and deadly. (246)

Like the soucouyant, Verlia is flying and lethal; she is one to be reckoned with. Like the ancestress Adela, she is not an angelic soul floating docilely up to Heaven but a potentially violent being who wills and wings her way to Guinea—not the literal continent of Africa but a more mystical landscape described in narratives from throughout the diaspora. Elizete continues: "She doesn't need air. She's in some other place already, less tortuous, less fleshy" (247). The novel ends on this note—a somewhat ambivalent conclusion for the contemporary reader who seeks a place of empowerment and freedom attainable by the living, but a positive revamping of the soucouyant myth as well as a healing re-memory of the event for Elizete and others who suffered through the U.S. invasion of Grenada in 1983 and are still dealing with the trauma.

Jewelle Gomez's *The Gilda Stories*, set predominantly in the United States, can be read not only as an expansion of the all-White peoplescape of conventional U.S. and European vampire literature but also as an explosion of the idea of vampirism aligned with contamination, infestation, and predation. In this way, it contributes significantly to unraveling the association between African diasporic women's bodies and corruption and perversion. While not explicitly a soucouyant narrative—Gilda never sheds her skin or transforms into a ball of flame—the novel is a productive extension of the trope simply because of its focus on a Black female vampire who embraces the previously abject space of the border. Gomez and her protagonist create room for the voices, concerns, imaginative spaces, and erotic corporeality of women of African descent—not merely their invisible yet hypervisible presence.

In Gomez's novel, vampiric immortality is a gift bestowed on the protagonist by the original Gilda. It is consistently affiliated with notions of freedom and enslavement rather than death, disease, and infection and thus provides a rich symbolic framework for discussing the experiences of African Americas subjects. The protagonist and her extended family of vampires kill "reluctantly and infrequently" (31) and perceive those who murder their blood donors as "rabid" (45). The language of contagion consequently comes to be linked to only a limited number of their kind. When the vampires who thrill off of leaving death and destruction in their wake are identified as "ghouls" by another vampire (67), they become the so-called monster's monsters.

In contrast, the "good" vampires maintain a "connection with life, not death" (45), embodying the soucouyant's occupation of the liminal space between the living and the dead; between land and sky; between the old and infirm and the ageless and highly mobile; and the allegedly inviolable integrity of each human body. Gilda identifies the taking of blood as a joyful exchange rather than a parasitic sapping of another being's vital fluids: "We draw life into ourselves, yet we give life as well. We give what's needed—energy, dreams, ideas" (45). Gomez's emphasis on the mind echoes Mootoo's reference to minds torn out of children in *Cereus Blooms at Night*; both writers link thought to one's essence—what might be called the soul. In addition to the physical aspect of the blood, these references break down the "mind/body dualism" (Brinks and Talley 166) so prevalent in Western societies; this is especially crucial in the soucouyant discourse, where authors make efforts to reject longstanding images of the hypercorporeal woman of color.

Gomez's protagonist, initially identified as the Girl, eventually inherits the name Gilda and becomes the novel's central character. At one point she observes that she can see her reflection in a mirror; it is "not banished to some soulless place" (56). Neither is she afraid of or completely vulnerable to the sun (110). Gomez thus challenges the conventions of the myth that connect vampires to evil and darkness—both physical and moral—and the racial denigration that is engendered by this association. Critic Caroline Rody has convincingly argued that the Girl—whose journey takes her from just having escaped enslavement in Mississippi in 1850 to Machu Picchu, Peru, in 2050—is a "vehicle for a transhistorical African American heroine, [. . . one] who embodies her people's past more fully than any other figure in this literature [of slavery fiction]" (79).[7] She is transhistorical, transatlantic, and the traverser of numerous boundaries. It is clear that she is also a figure of postcolonial defiance, especially since the sanctuary she chooses at the novel's conclusion is a *non*-contact site, undiscovered by Spanish explorers and later colonizers during the early (or middle) phases of conquest and colonization. Ingrid Thaler further argues that the sacred pre-Columbian location signifies "a refusal of technology and 'progress,' which [the novel] identifies as exclusively Western developments. [. . .] The vampire is thereby imagined as a figure outside of the destructive tendencies of the West" (67). Gomez's ending thus distances her novel from afro-futurist work, which typically addresses the correlations between race and technology in futuristic settings; rather, the conclusion aligns the narrative with soucouyant stories that harken *back* in time to folktales while simultaneously resisting the gender-constraining messages of those conventional tales.

Gomez renders the second Gilda's physical body—particularly her sexual and sexualized body as a woman of African descent—in ways that counter established Western tropes. The vampire trope highlights flexible relationships and social dynamics for both women and men; *The Gilda Stories* additionally functions to "explode the myth of the family romance" (Hall 395) that confines women to narrow roles as asexual mothers and heterosexual wives and men as paternal providers, as well as challenging the reinscription of state sovereignty that "most often occurs within black nationalist narratives of the black family" (Lubiano 236).

In terms of mere bodily strength, Gilda's physical power comes across as much more ominous than her bloodsucking; however, her acts of force are typically framed as self-preservation. As a runaway slave, she kills the bounty hunter who is about to rape her before taking her back into captivity. The overseer is animalized as a "beast from this other land" (11), transposing the historical categorization of Europeans as "civilized" and Africans as less-than-human savages. When he smiles at the prospect of "invading her" (11), Gomez invokes the idea of vampire as calculating, violent penetrator, making the Girl's attacker more of a "monster" than she will ever be, even once transformed.

Interestingly, when the Girl stabs the man, she reverses the penetration, foreshadowing her own conversion into a vampire. She feels "the blood draining from him, comfortably warm" on her skin (11), and likens the sensation to the first time her mother immersed her in a bath: "The intimacy of her mother's hands and the warmth of the water lulled the Girl into a trance of sensuality she never forgot. Now the blood washing slowly down her breastbone and soaking into the floor below was like that bath—a cleansing. She lay still, letting the life flow over her" (12). Gomez modifies typical representations of blood, making the negative a positive. Associated with the bath, blood becomes a "cleansing" substance rather than a tainting one. Linked to the Girl's mother, and to the Girl's past, it represents maternal bonds and ties to heritage and community. Tellingly, there is no sense of the abject here: the Girl "felt no disgust" (12).

The author continues to invert conformist narratives of race, gender, and monstrosity throughout *The Gilda Stories*. At one point, the Girl's mother swears that White slave owners are "not fully human" (10); at another she declares that White people are "just barely human. Maybe not even. They suck up the world, don't taste it" (11). These lines are spoken when the Girl asks why the nameless "they" can't distinguish butter from lard; her mother answers: "They ain't been here long 'nough.

They just barely human." Besides revising the vampire metaphor, Gomez reverses historical conceptions of Africans as less evolved than Europeans. The short length of time "here" suggests they are a newer species.

Slave owners don't just greedily "suck up the world"; they drain the life-blood of their slaves as they exploit them for their labor and concurrently refuse to treat them humanely. At one point, when Gilda breaks the neck of a racist attacker, he and his companion—a man who has joyfully drawn blood from multitudes of enslaved peoples with his whip—are cast as much more vampiric than Gilda (113–14). Additionally, others use up the land and its natural resources. Bird, the Native American character who helps transform the Girl into a vampire, maintains this correlation between European Americans, destruction, and monstrosity. After the transformation, she warns the Girl about turning toward terrorizing mortals and destroying life: "this lesson mustn't be forgotten. To ignore it, to wallow in death as the white man has done, can only bring bitterness" (110).[8]

One way that Gomez avoids the constant reference to the sexual desires of and "perverse" sexual penetrations by her African-diasporic protagonist is that Gilda and her chosen family are never depicted as actually *biting* their blood donors; instead, they cut the skin and then seal the gash after the "sharing." The first time readers witness the mutualistic exchange enacted, they learn that the original Gilda "extended [the sleeping stranger's] dream, making him king of the riders as she *took* her share of the blood. He smiled with triumph[. . . .] Her touch [. . .] sealed his wound cleanly" (33, emphasis added). Later, the second Gilda ("the Girl") is portrayed as participating in the same ritual: she "*took* the blood while listening for his thoughts[. . .] , seeking out one that might benefit from her aid" (91, emphasis added). Gomez stresses a "taking" rather than a drinking of blood, avoiding stimulating anxiety in the reader by leaving the issue of blood ingestion just beyond the reader's gaze.

As I have already stated, in the initial representation of the blood exchange, there is much more emphasis on the psychological piercing of the donor's thoughts than a physical boring into his body. Such an authorial move deemphasizes the sexual metaphor and the aggressive sexual nature of the prototypical vampire. The original Gilda is styled as "slipp[ing] inside" her donor's thoughts (33); later, the second Gilda is shown in similar terms: she "sliced the flesh on his neck and[. . . .] insinuated herself inside his preoccupations[. . . .] When she had slipped an idea of her own in among his, she felt the loosening of his unconscious,

Gilda closed the wound and leaned him gently against the gate" (91). Tellingly, while her *body* is not sexualized according to pervasive stereotypes, her *sexuality* is not utterly erased—she does suggestively penetrate her donor's mind—and she leaves something behind—a metaphorical "seed" that, depending on the blood donor, will gestate as hope, confidence, or pleasure.

Examples of metaphorical penetration abound in the text. Witnessing distress, the original Gilda "easily quieted the Girl's turmoil with the energy of her thoughts" (17). She drains away turmoil, penetrating the Girl's mind rather than her neck or any other part of her physical body. Later, the protagonist resists Eleanor's infiltration of her thoughts (89) because her discomfort is tied to her identity as a former slave: when on the plantation her mother often repeated, "We can keep our thoughts to ourselves and out of their hands" (89). Eleanor's sense of racial and class privilege links up with her obliviousness to the implications of insinuating herself into another person's thoughts.

In her initial contact with Julius, who will eventually become a part of her vampiric family, Gilda infiltrates the young man's fantasy about her: "she entered the dream" (178) and causes him to have an erection. She does not allow him to physically enter her, however; rather, she lies across him, "providing a comforting sensation" rather than a sexually arousing one. "As the moment approached when his mind provided the gratification his body hungered for, she sliced across the flesh of his neck with her fingernail and watched the blood ease slowly to the surface" (178). Clearly, blood, not semen, is the life-giving liquid in this women-centered narrative. As Gomez herself explains: "I chose to make my black woman hero a vampire because no one would understand the cycles of blood and life more than a woman" ("Black Women Heroes" 13).

At the end of the encounter, Gomez writes that Gilda "pressed her lips eagerly to the wound"—almost as if in a chaste kiss—"and drew the life from him as his body exploded with the joy of his imagination" (178). Once again there are no teeth or fangs involved in the act. As in the previous cases, the lack of description of an actual bite assuages the potentially stress-inducing image of the donor's corporeal body being pierced, and Gomez further quells the unease in readers who anticipate the abject—fleshly perimeters crossed, open wounds spilling blood, the feminization of the leaking body, the interior made exterior. The mystical healing of wounds likewise serves to suggest containment, and the phrase "lanc[ing] the flesh gently" (68) suggests medical expertise and curing rather than the spreading of infection.

The absence of biting starkly contrasts the actions of vampires who are depicted as antagonists to humans, such as Eleanor and Samuel. When being kissed by Eleanor, the protagonist experiences "the sharpness of Eleanor's teeth as she bit her lip and continued to press her mouth onto Gilda's, taking in her blood" (97). The emphasis on the White woman's sharp teeth and her decision to use them align Eleanor with "savagery" and cannibalism, again reversing the trope of the civilized European and the savage African (or American Indian). The same occurs when Samuel attempts to bite Gilda: "It was a moment before she realized Samuel was not trying to strangle her but to rip open her throat" (98). These two White vampires, rapaciously violent and violently greedy, allow conventional vampirism to be negatively associated with a European heritage and any grasping, exploitative, power-hungry outlook to be aligned with vampirism. As opposed to Gilda's "taking" of blood, Eleanor takes *in* the blood of the object of her desire, emphasizing consumption and calling the repulsive aspect of abjection into full view.

Besides depicting several lesbian and gay relationships throughout the novel and including a few transgender characters, Gomez portrays the experiences of her vampires as parallel in many ways to the experiences of "queer" subjects. When Bird tries to return to her Indian nation, she is rejected (34). In Yerba Buena, California, vampires—whose Otherness is not immediately visible as is the case for many LGBT people—mingle in Sorel's salon with the mortal townspeople "as if there were no difference between them" (56). Years later, in Rosebud, Missouri, when Gilda decides to leave Aurelia, she decides "to break silence with someone outside the family" (128). In a symbolic "coming out," she leaves a letter explaining her history to Aurelia. Gomez writes: "Her secret had been kept as a protection against others' fear" (128), again alluding to homophobia. The author calls specific attention, however, to the position of people of color within the larger nonheterosexual community: Gilda finds herself troubled by some of her fellow vampires' "inattention [. . .] to some mortal questions, like race[. . . .] She didn't believe a past could, or should, be so easily discarded. Her connection to the daylight world came from her blackness. The memories of her master's lash as well as her mother's face [. . .] all fueled her ambition" (180). The issue is an important one for women of the African diaspora and other communities of color, who, as Audre Lorde discussed, found themselves to be "sister-outsiders" in White lesbian circles.

More interesting to this chapter's discussion of sexuality, however, are the descriptions of encounters that Gomez queers by blending sexual imagery with comparisons to mother-child relationships. Gilda's transformation of Julius, for example, although superficially heterosexual, transgresses boundaries in numerous ways. At the start of the scene, Gomez portrays her protagonist with an abundance of maternal imagery: Gilda is "enjoying the softness of his skin, smiling at the freckles that marked his nose and cheeks. [. . .] She encircled him with her arms, kissing his eyes and nose" (191). The dynamic soon crosses over into the sexual, however.[9] Giving Julius a kiss "both passionate and chaste" (192), Gilda slices his neck, drains blood, and then "bit[es] her own tongue, and kissed him hard, breaking the skin inside his lip. She thrust the tongue into his mouth" (192). In doing so, she breaks his symbolic hymen—the skin inside his lip (a rhetorical double for the labia). As Rody notes, the novel "maternalizes the convention of the vampire's bite, recasting the scene of vampire-making as one of childbirth" (81). It also feminizes the male partner and masculinizes the female partner according to typical conceptions of sex and the missionary model, thus "queering" heterosexual pairings as well. When Gilda looks for signs of protest from Julius "[e]ach time she took him closer to the edge of life, [. . .] he only opened wider for her" (192), reinforcing his symbolic feminization. Rody asserts that these vampiric transformations that evoke both childbirth and sex suggest that "all varieties of love become interchangeable, and none is stigmatized" (98). I would push this interpretation even further: Gomez's project addresses not only love but also the specific physical, sexual roles allowed to women and men in contemporary society.

The scene returns to maternal imagery when Gilda slices the skin under her breast and Julius sucks "insistently" (192), suggestive of breast-feeding. Searching his inner thoughts, Gilda feels deluged by "the sense of well-being only a child can feel when lying in the arms of its parent" (192). She sends a telepathic message to Bird: "*We've finally delivered a brother for me*" (194, emphasis in original). Notably, she construes him as a brother and not a son, which might imply a hierarchy of power—and, for a woman, unending maternal responsibility—rather than an equitable relationship.

This same attempt at creating equality between lovers by imposing and then inverting maternal imagery applies as well to Gomez's portrayal of the relationship between Gilda and Bird. At the end of their first sexual encounter, both are cast as newborns, "their faces red and shining, their eyes unfocused and black, the sound of their bodies slick with wetness, tight with life" (140). The blood shared in this sexual exchange of fluids resembles the fluids covering an infant after labor. Reading "[t]he sucking of blood, transformed into suckling, [as] reflect[ing] a revision of our cultural horror of mother-love" (Johnson 78), I would argue that both characters *and neither character* is cast as mother: both get symbolically rebirthed into a new type of relationship with each other where each has given birth to the other but also to the self.

In this particular instance, Gomez does not shy away from the representation of the Black woman's body and desire: metaphorical penetration of the mind is coupled with the physical caresses that move back and forth between maternal and sexual: "[Gilda] felt Bird probing her mind, knowing everything she knew[. . . .] The soft touch of Bird's hand on her brow felt, for a moment, as if it were her mother's. [. . . Another touch] sparking a tingle inside her thighs. [. . .] Bird kissed her forehead[. . . .] Bird kissed her cheek softly then moved to her ear" (138–39). In prior encounters, Bird served as Gilda's teacher and mentor and also as the mother figure who helped complete the vampiric transformation. Whereas in that first event Gilda drank from the incision beneath Bird's breast, on the latter occasion she is configured as the nursing mother. The roles have been blurred and confused. And just in case the reader happens to miss the point, the author makes it explicit. After this sharing of blood, mind, and body, Bird gives Gilda a sponge bath. "She lingered over her as she would a child. She whispered sweet words to her as she might a lover" (140). Gomez uses the vampire trope to continually stress the power and pleasure to be found in fluid relationships and roles rather than immobile, fixed dynamics.

Like Gomez, U.S. speculative fiction writer Octavia Butler uses the figure of the Black female vampire to wreak havoc on sexual norms. In *Fledgling*, she consistently challenges taboos and undermines common notions of sexual propriety for women of African descent through the characterization of Shori, an amnesiac who appears to be a young African American girl of ten or eleven years old. In reality, the protagonist is a fifty-three-year-old vampire. Because of her preadolescent appearance as well as the fact that her life expectancy is five centuries and she has not yet reached sexual maturity, she is considered a "child" by the unsuspecting humans who see her and by her own people, the Ina.

Besides generating compassion for Shori via her youth and amnesiatic state, Butler emphasizes the protagonist's restraint in taking blood from humans and various instances of consideration and kindness toward her "hosts." Shori does not literally represent the hybrid of machine and organism described by Donna Haraway in her cyborg manifesto, but Butler does intriguingly "[e]xplor[e] conceptions of bodily boundaries and social order" (Haraway, "Manifesto" 216) with the genetically hybrid human plus vampire in her final novel.[10] As in *The Gilda Stories*, the sharing of blood is represented as a mutualistic exchange between the taker and the giver of the life-sustaining fluid. Shori learns: "We protect and feed you, and you protect and feed us" (183). In return for the nourishment of blood, the Ina strengthen their human partners' immune systems with the venom in their saliva, allowing symbionts to live to between 170 and 200 years old and function with improved memory. Those who are alone in life, like Theodora, whose "natural" scent exudes loneliness, also receive the benefit of a communal existence in Shori's family. In rejection of the idea of vampire/soucouyant as a figure of alienation and fragmentation, Butler highlights the bonds of community in her novel.

However, Butler's novel is a less utopian appropriation of the Black female vampire figure than Gomez's, with a more ambiguous portrait of her protagonist's sexuality. The drawing of the blood—typically performed in bedrooms and secluded spots, and featuring an orgasmic sense of gratification on the part of the host—as well as the chemical transferred during an Ina's bite, which "pacifie[s] people and pleasure[s] them" (36) and suggests the tangible exchange of bodily fluids, clearly mark the bloodsucking act as sexual. However, unlike Gomez's representation of equality and exchange, Butler—as is the case in most of her fiction—plays with questions of power. She blurs the lines, for instance, between mere blood drinker and monstrous anthropophagic creature, causing anxiety to mount. Readers learn that although Shori needs only blood when she's healthy, she must consume "fresh meat" (a human victim if live animals are not in close proximity) "for healing injuries and illnesses, for sustaining growth spurts, and for carrying a child" (25). The empathy one might ordinarily feel for the sick, for the growing child, or for the pregnant woman (often viewed in most societies as the most vulnerable populations) is thereby conjoined with the disgust prompted by the prospect of cannibalism.

Furthermore, Butler compels readers to consider issues of domination when she reveals that the bond between each Ina and his or her compatible symbiont is not merely emotional but psychological and physiological, much like drug addiction: if the Ina does not continue to take blood, the symbiont experiences withdrawal and possibly death. The addiction and vulnerability *do* go both ways: Shori notices that she must take small

portions of Wright's blood regularly, feeling "a need for it that was something beyond hunger" (43). However, the chemical found in Ina saliva
also renders humans "highly suggestible" (79), intimating compulsory
participation, forced lack of awareness, and psychological enslavement.
Interestingly, Ina males are also subject to the physical addiction of
female venom: "They become addicted to the venom of one group of
sisters. That's what it means to be mated. Once they're addicted, they
aren't fertile with other females, and from time to time, they need their
females" (115). Butler reinforces notions of a more powerful female subject. The history and trajectories of slavery get transferred onto Butler's
speculative landscape, allowing her to subtly explore issues such as Black
women's "willing" participation in sexual liaisons with White masters
and men of influence in the pre-Emancipation Americas.

And thus, in a radical inversion, Shori's first interaction with Theodora resonates with disturbing rape imagery, despite the fact that Shori
is much younger, smaller, mentally disadvantaged (with a concussion,
psychological trauma, and amnesia), and essentially homeless and socio-
economically impoverished. The protagonist lies down next to the sleeping woman and uses her hand to cover her unsuspecting host's mouth. "I
held on to her with my other arm and both my legs as she began to struggle. Once I was sure of my hold on her, I bit into her neck. She struggled
wildly at first, tried to bite me, tried to scream. But after I had fed for a
few seconds, she stopped struggling. After a while, I whispered to her, 'Is
it good?' [and Theodora gave] a satisfied little sound" (31). The physicality of the scene is distressing, to say the least. The older woman eventually experiences a passionate desire for her vampiric mate, later stating,
"I want to be with you[. . . .] It's all I've wanted since you first came to
me. I don't truly understand my feelings for you, but they're stronger
than anything I've ever felt, stronger than anything I ever expected to
feel" (206). However, questions of choice and control are unmistakably
raised in this first encounter when Theodora starts to turn to face Shori
but then "obey[s]" the young woman's command of "No, stay as you are"
(31).

While by no means arguing for any positive aspects to Shori's actions
in this scene, I find Butler's choice of a young, Black female—an intersection of three of the least empowered populations in societies of the African diaspora—to be quite provocative. Although childlike in appearance
and without full access to her personal, cultural, and historical legacies
because of her amnesia—a metaphor for her position as African in the
Americas—she becomes a more than capable matriarch when the male

side of her Ina family is murdered. When she gets shot, she tells Wright: "'Don't buy steaks unless you want them for yourself. I'll hunt. [. . .] Build a shelter,' I said. 'Put me in it. Then go home. Come back Sunday morning before sunrise'" (53). In a series of five orders, she establishes herself as the authority, despite her tiny stature and apparent youth; she also inverts the racial and gender hierarchies that exist within U.S. society. At another point, when she orders "You will do it!" Wright draws back, "angry, wanting to dispute, yet knowing he would obey" (144).

The blending of the maternal and sexual as seen in *The Gilda Stories* permeates the narrative: Shori "adopts" her relatives' symbionts like a parent but must bite them and take their blood to ensure their survival. Butler again renders the sexual dynamic in disconcerting ways. Shori's first experience with Celia also resembles rape: "She gave a little scream, then frantically tried to push me away, tried to struggle free, tried to hit me . . . I had to use both my arms and my legs to hold her still" (117). Her first experience with Brook leaves the woman in tears (119).

Equally as alarming—and perhaps moreso to many readers—is how the sexualized vampirism plays out in Shori's relationship with Wright. When the twenty-three-year-old White man first picks her up on the side of the road, she bites him instinctively and then is drawn to the blood:

I ducked my head and licked away the blood[. . . .] He tensed, almost pulling his hand away. Then he stopped, seemed to relax. He let me take his hand between my own. I looked at him, saw him glancing at me, felt the car zigzag a little on the road.

He frowned and pulled away from me[. . . .] but I didn't let go. I licked at the blood[. . . .]

He made a noise, a kind of gasp. [. . .]

"What are you doing?" he demanded, watching me, not pulling away at all now, but looking as though he wanted to—or as though he thought he should want to. (17)

The entire scene—the ducking, the licking, Wright's loss of control of the automobile, the gasp—all suggest fellatio, clearly linking the vampiric act to an erogenous one. Eventually Wright pulls Shori onto his lap, accentuating her position as young child but also evocative of a sexualized act. The suggestion of pedophilia cannot be ignored, especially since, throughout the novel, adults—both human and Ina—are constantly picking Shori up or putting her on their laps: Wright does so repeatedly; we also witness it with Theodora and Daniel and hear about it of Joel (225). And Shori does not resist this infantilization in any way:

"I decided I liked it and wondered whether I would someday grow too big for them to be able to do it. I hoped not" (225). Although Wright later supposes that Shori is about eighteen or nineteen years old, his first perception of Shori is "What a lovely elfin *little girl*" (66, emphasis added)—no more than ten or eleven. The fact that Shori is truly fifty-three does not alleviate any of the reader's apprehensions, since the author continually reminds us of how small she is and of her childlike appearance. In other words, even if Butler had written Shori as one hundred years old, the body Wright embraces and has intercourse with is still that of an eleven-year-old. And Wright is fully aware of this fact; when he meets Shori's Ina father Iosif, who asks how old the human thinks Shori is, Wright guesses eighteen or nineteen, at which Iosif snipes, "That would make things legal at least" (70). He intuits that whatever Wright *claims* he believes, he has been hiding his lover from friends and family "lest someone think you were having an improper relationship with a child" (74). As a way of asserting pride in the Ina way of life, Iosif continues, "Once you're living with us, there will be no need to hide. And to us, there is nothing improper about your relationship" (74). Butler creates a fantasy landscape that sits beside our "real" world and allows characters to cross back and forth, but she continually fingers the "wound" she has created on the reader's consciousness.

Butler creates other scenes reminiscent of *The Gilda Stories* in their similar blurring of boundaries between parent, child, and lover. In one, Wright and the amnesiac Shori ponder what name she should go by. On one hand, Wright shows respect for the protagonist by asking if she would like him to choose a name for her; only after she states "Give me a name" does he do so (19). The scene initially resonates with the structures of patriarchy and not slavery; Shori obviously has alternatives, and the passage therefore reads as most suggestive of a woman taking a man's surname upon marriage. However, when Wright decides upon the name Renee because "[a] friend of mine told me it meant 'reborn.' That's sort of what's happened to you. You've been reborn into a new life'" (19), he typifies Father and Master—bestowing his patronym on the newborn—rather than his lover.

Butler further queers the categories by making Wright a symbolic mother as well—he must feed the "newborn" with liquid from his own body, intimating breastfeeding. In another blood/sex scene, Shori is lifted on Wright's lap while in the car. He kisses her and then passively waits for her penetration: "I bit him deeply and felt him spasm and go hard under me. [. . .] I took his blood quickly, rocking against him, then stayed for just a few minutes more, licking the wound to begin its heal-ing, comforting him, comforting myself" (102). Shori's being lifted onto Wright's lap, "rocking," and self-soothing point toward the ambivalence of the dynamic—is she sexual partner or a baby being pacified? When she comforts Wright, is she precocious child or protective parent? Butler continues to modify the categories, turning the reader's sense of perspec-tive upside down. She participates in a project quite similar to Gomez's—emphasizing the importance of fluid relationships and also definitions, especially for women of African descent in the Americas. However, the interactions that she represents, evocative of parent-child nurturing as well as erotically gratifying sex, trouble the question of true equality in love. They also problematize the possibility of Rody's assertion for *The Gilda Stories* that "all varieties of love [are] interchangeable, and none is stigmatized" (98).

Representations of homosexual encounters abound in *Fledgling*, but, unlike in Gomez's novel, there are a variety of responses, both positive and negative. The Ina culture, more accepting and visionary than many of its human counterparts in terms of views on sex, intimacy, and com-panionship, allows space for all types of gender configurations. It is the human symbionts—and especially the men—who demonstrate the most homophobia and rigidity about gender roles. On her first formal meet-ing with Shori, for example, Theodora looks at her "with a kind of hor-ror" (95). Shori wonders aloud whether the reaction is to her youth or her race; the woman replies, "You are a vampire[. . . .] you're supposed to be a tall, handsome, fully grown white man. Just my luck" (97). She, like most contemporary readers, has only been exposed to European, heterosexual models. When Wright first undresses Shori and notices her lack of developed breasts, he supposes, "I guess you really are a kid. Or maybe. . . . Are you sure you're female?'" (24). It is said without anxiety or malice, suggesting that he is open to this sexual option. However, when he finds out about Shori's relationship with Theodora, he bitterly jabs, "Swing both ways, do you?" Later that night, he shakes her awake, "filled with rage and confusion." His solution: to attempt to rape her—perhaps an attempt to induce sexual shame or to forcefully take the body he views as his and his alone. "He rolled onto me, pushing my legs apart, pushing them out of his way, then thrust hard into me. I bit him more deeply than I had intended and wrapped my arms and legs around him as I took his blood. He groaned, writhing against me, holding me, thrusting harder until I had taken all I needed of his blood, until he had all he needed of me" (91).

Shori's assertiveness, passion, and physical strength allow her to maintain control of her body and the dynamic, but Butler hints at the violence that so often accompanies acts that transgress social norms. Wright lashes out in his discomfort with anything outside the heteronormative monogamous bond: later in the novel, he punches a hole in a wall when he finds out that Shori wishes to adopt a male symbiont: "I was hoping you'd get all women—except me. I think I could deal with that[. . . .] I don't think I can do this, Shori. I can't share you" (163). Even though he knows that Shori needs another food source, he is unwilling to relinquish his position as "ruling" male with all of the sexual relationships within his purview. (How striking, then, that Butler writes sex with an adolescent into his code of acceptability.)

When Shori asks an African American symbiont, Martin, if he regrets the way his life has turned out, married to a human woman but the host to an Ina male, he explains that he was allowed to make his own decision to stay or to leave. "I did leave. They didn't stop me. William asked me to stay, but that made me run faster. The whole thing was too weird for me. Worse, I thought it sounded more like slavery than symbiosis. It scared the hell out of me" (210). He expresses less concern about queer "sex" than about losing his freedom—a telling statement for someone of African descent in the United States. He continues, "I stayed away for about ten months. I'd only been bitten three times in all, so I wasn't physically addicted. No pain, no sickness. But psychologically. . . . Well, I couldn't forget it. I wanted it like crazy. God, it was a relief" (210).

The vampire figure represents the violation of borders of all types: as she pursues the blood needed for her survival, she moves between vibrant life and final death, between a thriving society and spaces of alienation and isolation. She penetrates the boundary of the skin—that which most desire to be unassailable, incorruptible—and in doing so resembles the male sexual aggressor rather than the passive female. In the case of the soucouyant, there is the ambiguous realm between the power and wisdom of old age and the physical weakness and mental decline that this stage of life sometimes entails; there is also the margin between human and Other as she shifts out of and into her skin, as well as the space between land and sky and physically embodied being and flaming spirit as she takes flight. The fiction discussed in this chapter adds to these categories in that the writers who employ the Black female vampire figure successfully challenge the conventional myths of bloodsucker as perversely sexual, evil demon. These authors cross into and out of the established literary vampire genre, denying it as exclusively within the purview of European and White American males; they resist and reject the idea of non-normative sexual desire as deviant, the Black woman's body as a site of aberrant behaviors, and the nuclear, heterosexual, patriarchal family model as the only one able to provide stability, protection, contentment, and joy.

5 / Reconstructing a Nation of Strangers: Soucouyants in the Work of Tessa McWatt, David Chariandy, and Helen Oyeyemi

Myth is an unbreakable mirror that helps second-generational sons and daughters of any culture, not just Nigerian, access the fears, joys, humor and identity of their original country in a way that food, music and family sometimes can't[. . . .] They capture the mind, imagination and heart.

—HELEN OYEYEMI

As I discussed in Chapter 4, one of Nalo Hopkinson's primary goals in *Brown Girl in the Ring* is to employ soucouyant folklore to interrogate gender norms in contemporary society, particularly those surrounding motherhood. Another prominent theme of the novel is the exploration of definitions of national identity for the immigrant and other subaltern populations of Canada. For example, when Premier Uttley—ostensibly the voice and representative of all Canadian people—awakens from the surgery in which the heart of African Caribbean Gros-Jeanne has been placed in her body, the rhetoric is suggestive: the politician refers to the heart as a "foreign" body (168) and an "alien" organ (237). On a personal, individual level, this wording might seem appropriate: the heart is not the one with which she was born. On the sociopolitical stage, however, the language of the White Canadian leader regarding the heart she has received from a Black Trinidadian immigrant implies that only those born in Canada who occupy White racial identities will ever be acknowledged as "real" Canadian citizens; they do not belong to the "'truthful' visual knowledge [that] regulates and normalizes how Canada is seen— as white, not blackless, not black, not nonwhite, not native Canadian, but white" (McKittrick 96–97). And even though the healthy heart has been stolen in Hopkinson's novel—quite ironic, given the discourses associating non-White people with disease, dirtiness, and vice—and not willingly donated for the benefit of the woman and the larger body politic that she represents, Uttley feels "invaded in some way, taken over" when it is implanted (236). In a dream state, she orders it to stop resisting and assimilate: "You're here to help me. Just settle down and do your job" (236–37). Such language reinforces the colonial ideology of superior "metropole" and meager "periphery" from which the colonized must flee in order to achieve financial, if not social, success.

In this chapter, I look at several novels that use the figure of the sou-couyant to challenge designations of national subjects in the Global North as White, "natural," and possessing an inherent belonging. Tessa McWatt's *Out of My Skin* (1998) and David Chariandy's *Soucouyant* (2007), both of which are also set in Canada, are by writers of Caribbean descent. Helen Oyeyemi's *White Is for Witching* (2009), which is set in England, is penned by an author born in Nigeria. All three hint at the notion that the true vampiric figure in world history is not the foreigner who, like Hopkinson's Mami Gros-Jeanne or, a century earlier, Bram Stoker's Dracula, penetrates the heart of the "civilized" nation from the outlying margins of the (current or former) empire. Rather, the actual monster is the colonial or neocolonial nation that greedily sucks the life-blood of foreign lands and foreign people via economic, political, sexual, cultural, and ecological exploitation. In two of the works discussed here, a young girl of color must reconcile her identity as the adopted daughter of a White couple living in the "metropole"; in the third, a young man struggles to determine his place in a metropolitan society that denies the validity of the culture and experiences of his Caribbean-born parents. The three novels use the figure of the soucouyant and metaphors of vam-pirism to probe the formal definitions posited by the law and politicians when creating a public face of nationhood, simultaneously calling atten-tion to the contradictory ideas held by everyday people when consider-ing "real" or "valid" citizenship.

Tessa McWatt's *Out of My Skin* begins with an epigraph from Derek Walcott's "The Castaway," suggesting journeys gone wrong and the iso-lation that ensues. The lines "We end in earth, from earth began. / In our own entrails, genesis" also gesture toward a backward trajectory; the first line starts with the "end" and gestures toward death, then pro-ceeds to "began," while the final word of passage, "genesis," places the "beginning" at the end. Correspondingly, the section titles of McWatt's novel—Quarter, Half, Gibbous, and so forth—are phases of the moon, suggesting cycles rather than a linear timeline. The backward trajectory combined with a cyclical time scheme suggest counterclockwise motion and imply repetition rather than progression and events out of order. And indeed, the protagonist's emotional development has gone askew. At the same time, her pursuit of understanding her place in the world can never be complete or final; she cannot be magically transformed into a fixed (as in cured or static) being. The novel begins and ends with "Crescent," and the protagonist's psychological growth is aligned with the waxing and waning of the moon—an occurrence that is ongoing, never-ending, and distinctly female.

During a visit to her childhood home, this protagonist—Daphne Baird—trips and scrapes her palms. Symbolically significant for an inter-rogation of soucouyant imagery, her "skin was torn back like a pealed [sic] peach and blood dripped onto her wrist" (162). Her flesh strips away like that of the vampiric, skin-shedding figure from folklore. One familiar with the folk stories might ask: is she a predatory character who drains other individuals of their life force? Do her nocturnal activities suggest flight and movement? Will she have an outer appearance of fra-gility that contrasts with an inner Self that radiates strength and power? As readers make their way through the novel, they come to realize that Daphne has numerous layers of "skin" that must get peeled back before she can truly see who she is, how she is connected to her adoptive par-ents, Guyanese culture, the First Nations community, and the African diaspora. Additionally, her possibly mutable body should cause readers to question prevalent visualizations of the larger, more abstract political body: the body politic. Following David Goldberg's assertions about the politics and philosophy of racist cultures:

> the body comes to stand for the body politic, to symbolize soci-
> ety, to incorporate a vision of power. Porous and permeable though
> the boundaried "skin" of the body politic may in fact be, it is con-
> stituted always in terms of the bordered criteria of inclusion and
> exclusion, identities and separateness, (potential) members and
> inevitable non-members. (Goldberg 54)

Tessa McWatt creates a character who feels the push and pull of multiple affiliations. Daphne, born to a Guyanese woman who drowned herself shortly after her daughter's birth, was adopted by a White Canadian couple. Readers learn that through her childhood, Daphne grappled with her racial, ethnic, and national identity, and, at thirty, she is still torn. The author conveys this in obvious and subtle ways. The protago-nist is obsessed by Greek mythology—narratives from the alleged height of civilization—and not the local cultural traditions of her current time and place: either those of her White Canadian adoptive family, those of her Guyanese blood relations and biological ancestors, or those of other African Canadian subjects. The absence of the latter two corresponds to what Katherine McKittrick identifies as a centuries-long concealment of the bodies, histories, and geographies of people of color from the Canadian landscape, including

> the demolition of Africville in Nova Scotia and Hogan's Alley in Vancouver; threatening and administering black diaspora deportation; the renaming of Negro Creek Road to Moggie Road in Holland Township, Ontario; the silence around and concealment of Canada's largest unvisible slave burial ground [. . .]; racist immigration policies; the ploughing over of the black Durham Road Cemetery in southwestern Ontario; the relocation, and recent renaming, of Caribana; and the commonly held belief that black Canada is only recent and urban. (96)

McWatt's protagonist perceives her adoptive mother's European features as "sharp" and beautiful, while she describes her own as "sloppy" (158), suggesting internalized racism despite Canada's prominent public diversity campaigns. When she tentatively looks into mirrors, her observations reveal a disturbing alienation from self: "The first thing that always came into view was *the* nose" (4, emphasis added). She passively views "the," and not "her," nose as it seemingly invades the space of her face, appearing "large, wide, and fleshy, nostrils asymmetrical, one an imperfect oval, the other circular" (4). This hypercritical scrutiny further reveals internalized racism: wide noses are often read as a sign of African bloodline in racist discourses. Interestingly, Daphne *does* claim "*her* curly brunette bangs" (4, emphasis added)—possibly evidence of mixed racial identity. She continues her self-evaluation: "Her skin was brown, not a permanent, wealthy tan"—a sign of Whiteness—"but rather copper-coloured in the summer and sickly olive by February. She was small-boned *but* had a [. . .] bouncing, high-rumped gait. A trace of Africa" (4–5, emphasis added). Being petite fits into Western standards of beauty, which privilege diminutive women, but a prominent bottom makes her body disturbingly (to her) legible as a member of the African diaspora. Correspondingly, Daphne notes that her "girlish appearance" inspires "a pat on the head," not lust or passion (4–5). In the predominantly White circles in which she travels, her features are not associated with physical attractiveness—tellingly linked in her mind with inspiring sexual responses—or with adulthood. One might recall the colonial discourse attributing childhood to non-European subjects in order to establish these people's "natural" inferiority.[1] Daphne has fully absorbed the hegemonic ideals of the North American society in which she lives.

However, it could also be asserted that Daphne's perceived childlike demeanor is a sign of her stunted emotional and psychological growth as a member of the African diaspora in a racist culture; although she is *physically* a woman of thirty years old, Daphne still must mature as a subject who embraces all aspects of her identity. In response to the protagonist's naïve questions about race, the First Nations character Surefoot comments, "you seem like just a kid" (98). Additionally, Daphne suffers from trichotillomania—a disorder that involves obsessive-compulsive hair plucking. She has pulled out her pubic hair since puberty, viewing it as an "impurity" (21); only when all traces of hair have been removed does she view the area as "clean" (48). This behavior renders her body like a baby's or young child's; she is thus psychologically complicit in maintaining a type of physical stasis. Repeated scenes of masturbation also tie her to a perpetual state of immaturity: like a child, she seeks the "sedative of touch" (36). She is more inclined to self-stimulation than a mutually reciprocal adult sexual experience.

McWatt brings soucouyant imagery into the novel to highlight Daphne's position as an alienated subject in a mainstream Canadian social and cultural space as well as her estrangement from her Self. As the narrative opens, readers learn that Daphne is an avid birdwatcher and a voyeur, and both can be interpreted as abstracted connections to the soucouyant. The protagonist, like Mi-Jeanne and Ti-Jeanne at the beginning of Hopkinson's *Brown Girl in the Ring*, is preoccupied by the idea of flight; however, the flight Daphne hopes for is not empowering but escapist. She flees from Toronto to Montreal in order to escape a boyfriend and find "something else into which she could dissolve" (27), in essence wishing to bolt from a concrete sense of individualized and recognizable Self. To avoid a dinner that a male friend offers to cook for her, she says she's busy doing research on "birds . . . bird . . . movement, migration, habits, stuff like that" (91). And during the debates about the First Nations Oka Conflict, she wishes to depart from her body as well as society's problems: "She would swirl above the day's events as if in a dream[. . . .] above the room, unable to come down" (41). This last act strongly resembles the flight of the soucouyant, but its emphasis on absconding from the "real world" and connections to other people is not a positive configuration. The protagonist's constant desire to "disappear" is distinctly alienating and disempowering—not only for her but also for a larger community in need of more members for strength and solidarity. Daphne furthers notions of people of color in Canada as "'not here' and 'here' simultaneously: they are [. . .] concealed in a landscape of systemic blacklessness" (McKittrick 93).

Like the soucouyant, McWatt's protagonist invades homes—albeit symbolically—with her voyeuristic gaze. She violates taboos by penetrating the private sphere—especially as a female watcher—and remarks that observing these "unvarnished moment[s]" in people's lives makes her feel "[s]omewhat nourished" (2). She satiates an emotional thirst instead of the traditional vampiric bloodlust and thus is rendered distinct from a purely demonic and predatory character: she is much more clearly represented as the alienated victim, especially as the author casts her as seeking to make some sort of connection—to "reach across the crack to touch the other side" of the windows into which she peers (2). Her voyeurism reads as a clear extension of her racial discomfort, signaling her perception—but also her reality—as someone outside the physical windows as well as metaphorically outside Canadian mainstream culture as an African diasporic subject.

Again, however, McWatt does not completely excuse her character from responsibility in her situation. Daniel, Daphne's boss at the copy store, accuses her of being "Like a fly on a wall: [. . .] [a]lways watching but not doing anything" (140). The protagonist's gazing is actually incredibly active but Daniel's comment accurately describes Daphne's sociopolitical apathy and lack of involvement in the world around her. In another instance she flips past headlines about a First Nations protest, the international news, the business section, and even the list of new movies in order to read the obituaries (31); she is completely alienated from local, national, and world communities—the entire world of the living. Like the soucouyant, she is the isolated figure at the edge of the village, the one who seems somewhat sinister because of her lack of engagement in the community.

More tangible soucouyant imagery comes with McWatt's explicit references to "old hyge"—another name for the skin-shedding, vampiric old woman from Caribbean folklore. When Daphne initially phones her aunt Sheila, the only biological relative listed in her adoption file, she hears a Caribbean-accented voice in her head that taunts and hisses, "*old hyge 'gon suck ya blood out*" (62–63, emphasis in the original). Severed from her Guyanese cultural heritage, she has no idea what old hyge is, but the words and imagery are clearly frightening. Readers come to recognize the voice as unreliable, perhaps signaling Daphne's warped mental constructions of what it means to be Caribbean. Emblematic of her conflicting feelings, right before the phone conversation the character wonders, "Would her aunt have flapping, warm folds of skin Daphne could curl into?" (49) While the manta ray illustrated on the title pages of the text and featured later in the narrative might be the first image to jump to mind here, the close proximity of the old hyge allusion cannot be ignored. Readers are given the possibility of a distinctively comforting and protective soucouyant—an old woman with loose, removable skin who will embrace and nurture rather than drain and abuse.

McWatt presents another soucouyant figure in the First Nations character of Surefoot, who is not of Caribbean ancestry. For McWatt, the association functions to unite communities by experience rather than by bloodline or racial heritage. Therefore, when Daphne watches her friend's skin peeling off, readers can move beyond the literal act of picking a scab to consider the implications of linking an indigenous character to circum-Caribbean folk legends: a richer, more diverse network is revealed.

> [T]he crust that had formed over the wound was dry and dark brown. She began to pick away at the scab. A few small pieces flew off into the air. Then she raised and bent the wounded arm so the elbow was at eye-level and calmly, purposefully, tore off the dried blood and skin until the scab was almost gone; underneath the revealed pink flesh, blood welled up to pour again. Each fragment of old skin was tossed onto the pavement of the bridge. Daphne was repulsed. (149)

The protagonist's repulsion yet compulsion to watch corresponds to Kristeva's discussion of the abject. As it is for the soucouyant, a boundary is dissolved when the skin that is supposed to contain the blood, flesh, and bones of the body is stripped away. As Kristeva posits, the most enthralling-yet-distressing boundary crossings are often stimulated by an anxiety of what lies within the self. Daphne suddenly recognizes what she and Surefoot share: as people of color in a majority White society, very much like the soucouyant "[t]hey were creatures that made sense only in the imagination, that had to be invented like the improbable animals formed by clouds in a childhood game. Animals that floated against all odds. That belonged nowhere else" (149). The conventional soucouyant's alienation is not simply self-created and self-determined; it is reinforced and dictated by the whims and desires of the surrounding society, whether in the Caribbean, Canada, the United States, or Europe. It is the same at each node in the network of soucouyant stories, and exposing this intricate web of tales lays bare an important set of dynamics that typically disempower women of all ages, class backgrounds, and geo-graphical locations.

In David Chariandy's *Soucouyant: A Novel of Forgetting*, the soucouy-ant figure takes on layers upon layers of meaning as the story unravels. This novel, too, suggests the "multidirectionality, multidimensionality, and multitemporality" of Irad Malkin's distributed network (19)—a sys-tem that does not privilege any particular geographical space, political community, site of knowledge production, or route of cultural exchange. A full literal description of the folk character is not revealed until more than halfway through Chariandy's book (135), and the soucouyant thus comes to function as a postmodern symbol of constantly shifting mean-ings, ambiguous truths, and identities that might be described by some as fluid but by others as unstable. The author draws a complex set of asso-ciations and implications in his narrative and, in so doing, rather than maintaining the traditional imagery of the soucouyant as a demonic woman who is to be condemned for her uncontrolled and uncontrollable mobility, her predatory nature, and her alienation from the community, posits the U.S. military and, in turn, Canadian dominant culture as the truly monstrous forces. Chariandy also insinuates that just as mythical as Caribbean tales of the night-flying, skin-shedding vampire-woman are ideas of a Canadian national identity that is cumulative, plural, and possessing "the historical depth of [. . . global cultural] memories" from which its citizens originate (A. D. Smith 180).

Rather late in the book, the protagonist—a nameless man born and raised in Canada by an Afro-Trinidadian mother and Indo-Trinidadian father—learns that his maternal grandmother once labored in the sex industry on the island of Trinidad, primarily catering to U.S. soldiers on the military base occupied by the States during World War II. This woman is, initially, the reader's clearest example of a symbolic soucouy-ant. As a prostitute, she is ostracized by the rest of her community. She roams the town at night and drains men of their money and their bodily fluids. As a child, her daughter Adele—who is the narrator's mother—sees her mother as a something like a disembodied skin: at one point she views the working woman's dress as "a sloughed form on the floor" (186); at another, she metonymizes it and the dress/skin "flies toward her as if borne upon storm-winds" (191). Adele also witnesses a suicide attempt that resembles the soucouyant's bloody act of peeling off her skin: she sees her mother "standing naked in the galvanized tub that they use for baths, [. . .] still holding a pair of scissors to the ragged wounds on her wrists" (186). Much like the U.S. soldiers who disparagingly identify this woman as "Nobody" and "[s]ome whore from Carenage," but never by her name, Adele denies her mother's humanity when she perceives her first as the dress and then as "this creature" from whom she feels "the need to get away" (192). Her mother gets humiliatingly splashed by the soldiers with a mixture of water, oil, and tar—the latter of which, readers should note, is used to destroy women accused of being soucouyants in traditional versions of the tale—and thus she again gets rendered as the monstrous vampire figure. The parallel is accentuated when Adele flicks on a lighter that has been given to her by one of the soldiers and her mother goes up in flames, comparable to the ball of fire in which folklore's soucouyants travel from victim to victim.

Significantly, however, Adele's mother has no supernatural powers; she survives the incident but is horribly disfigured. Years later, she becomes a shocking creature for the narrator when he recalls his childhood visit to her home, and he literally calls her a monster: "She was a monster. Someone with a hide, red-cracked eyes, and blistered hands" (116). Chariandy carefully builds on this depiction, slowly revealing that what is truly monstrous is her physical isolation: "[she] was careful not to brush too closely near, or bring her attention too forcefully towards me. That gesture of consideration somehow the most terrible thing of all" (116). This self-imposed remoteness evokes a great deal of compassion for the individual woman but also, by extension, for conventional soucouyants whose reasons for seclusion are never fully explained.

The calypso "Rum and Coca-Cola" by Lord Invader, popular in the World War II–era 1940s and cited in the text by Chariandy, speaks of "Both mother and daughter, / Working for the Yankee Dollar" (179), suggesting that it will not be long before Adele is forced to follow in her mother's footsteps as a prostitute. The truly vampiric force, therefore, is *not* the woman who sells her body to support her daughter and herself but the military-industrial complex of the colonizer (Great Britain) and the newest colonial power (the United States) that drained (bled) sugar from the Caribbean throughout the eighteenth and nineteenth centuries, sapped (bled) oil from Trinidad in the 1930s, and cast the Black and South Asian people in Chaguaramas out of their homes when the military base was built, depleting (bleeding) them of their ability to sustain themselves on their land. Even if they had been adequately compensated for their homes, these exiles had no skills to support themselves in the sites to which they were sent: "Agricultural skills passed on for generations were suddenly useless. Extended kinship links were broken, and surviving families were plunged into new forms of poverty without trusted networks of support" (Chariandy 179). Sex work is one of the only options to which Adele's mother can turn in order to survive, which eventually brings the vampiric imagery into even greater focus: the U.S. military bleeds this woman of her pride and eventually of her mental stability and will to live.[2] On a morning before the fire when Adele witnesses her mother's face and body horrifically battered by a client, readers might recall that according to legend, villagers who see the flaming ball at night are supposed to swing at it with a stick in order to bruise and mark the body of the soucouyant and reveal her identity to the community. Rather than rendering Adele's mother as a figure of evil monstrosity, this incident evokes the reader's sympathy for the brutality she must endure at the hands of the U.S. neocolonizers. She "begins living *outside of herself*" (185, emphasis added)—much like the soucouyant exists outside its old-woman skin at night—and then attempts to commit suicide. She is a distinctly tragic figure, not a frightening or inherently evil one. Most notably, when she catches afire, the flame is described as "a miraculous aura" (193), evoking the idea of spiritual transcendence instead of terror. Adele, too, is accidentally set ablaze during the Chaguaramas accident, and the flames align her with a redeemed soucouyant identity as well: the blaze is represented as a "halo" around her head and shoulders (193), and the positive religious connotations of the word undo stereotypical demonization and conjurations of hellfire. Such a recuperative reading is encouraged by the scene in which Roger and Adele go to see the horror film *Nosferatu* in the early years of their marriage. Rather than feeling scared, Adele is "gripped" by the portrait of the vampire: "Is the expression on the creature's face. [. . .] Is not the frightfulness. Is the sorrow. Such horrid sorrow" (74).

Less obvious than the protagonist's grandmother, Adele also functions as a soucouyant figure in the novel. A key can be found in the epigraph of the book, which comes from traditional soucouyant folklore. It reads: "Old skin, 'kin, 'kin, / You na know me." The soucouyant screeches this line to her skin if it has been salted or peppered during her nocturnal flight without it, and this seasoning prevents her from being able to put it back on. Skin shies away from flesh and bone. The shrieked line most obviously highlights disruptions within the Self: the skin—the outside—refuses to reconnect with its insides; it does not recognize, or "know," that from which it has been separated. More subtle, perhaps, is the way the line suggests disruptions between Self and family: the abbreviation of "skin" to "kin"—"*Old skin, 'kin, 'kin, / You na know me*"—intimates family members who "dis-recognize" the speaker.

In the present time of the novel, Adele suffers from dementia. Her mental illness causes disruptions of the Self in that it prevents her "inside"—her mind—from comprehending her "outside" experiences, making her a symbolic soucouyant. The illness also means that her "kin" can "na know" her: just as she does not recognize her own husband and children at times, they cannot recognize the vibrant woman they once knew—or the woman they *thought* they knew. Forgetfulness makes Adele a figure who is longed for by her son, "even so frightening a mother as she had become" (33), despite the fact that physically she is immediately present.

The notion of absent presence comes through in Chariandy's depiction of the narrator as well. In a 2007 interview with Kit Dobson, the author stated that the reference to the soucouyant in his title is primarily designed as a cultural reference:

> I wanted my title to suggest that the protagonist of the novel, a second-generation Caribbean immigrant based in Canada, was engaging with a cultural legacy that seemed, at least on the surface, to be attached to a very different space, a legacy that seemed, at times, to be remote, otherworldly, and spectral, and yet hauntingly present at the same time. (811)

For the narrator, too, then, one part of the body—his Caribbean sense of self, inherited from and taught by both mother and father—has been separated from the other—the Canadian sense of self, since Canada is the only country in which he has ever lived. Trinidadian culture and Caribbean identity are ghostly, and sometimes ghastly, in this North American environ. He searches for the figurative soucouyant through his mother's stories and oblique references, but the folk character is always just beyond his reach—a fact accentuated by Adele's mental illness: "Mother never explained any of this to me. [. . .] [S]cenes and secrets were spilling out of her involuntarily[. . . .] but she never explained or deciphered. She never put the stories together. She never could or wanted to do so" (136). At one point, even after repeated tellings of a time in her youth when she thought she crossed a soucouyant's path, Adele denies her son access to this particular story, as well as to her longer life-story, his roots as a person of African descent, and his Caribbean cultural heritage:

> "Mother?"
> "Yes, child?"
> "Did you really see a soucouyant?"

"Oh dear," she said, still smiling. "Whatever you think you want with some old nigger-story?" (194)

By identifying the tale as "old," Adele establishes it as a relic of the past, with no connections to the narrator's present time *or* present place. In a sense, she attempts to fracture and fragment the soucouyant network that her own anecdotes help establish. While her son seeks connections (though not always wholeheartedly), she—a first-generation Black immigrant—cuts ties. Her denigrating reference to the folktale as "nigger-story" further severs attachments. Interestingly, the split is chiefly based upon socioeconomic status; in Trinidadian English, the adjectival phrase "old nigger" primarily alludes to class more than race and thus can be applied to any racial or ethnic group—folk stories and folk culture being more closely (and disapprovingly) associated with the plantation working class. For the Canadian-born narrator, however, and for most non-Trinidadian readers, there is a greater likelihood that the phrase would be interpreted as a racial slur. As a result, the statement leaves the narrator in an even more conflicted space as the child of an interracial marriage raised in Eurocentric Canadian culture. When he turns to "official" sources for information, he is faced with tourist images of a Caribbean pleasure isle—a constructed myth, much like the soucouyant: "My history is a travel guidebook. My history is a creature nobody really believes in. My history is a foreign word" (137). Adele sagely notes: books "does always tell the biggest stories" (175)—in Trinidadian English the word "stories" can mean fictions or, alternately, lies.

The postmodern narrative does not allow the reader to locate an ostensible source of Adele's dementia: however, it seems just as likely that the racist landscape in which she found herself as a new migrant to Canada was equally as significant a trauma in sparking her mental illness as the childhood incident in which she and her mother caught on fire. For example, after a vacation to Niagara Falls early in her married life, Adele and her husband, Roger, return to their apartment and find it egregiously vandalized, with feces left on the bed and painted on the walls in the form of a message: "GO BACK" (77). The landlord, likely complicit in the violation since no locks have been broken, has previously warned them: "You don't know how lucky you people are to be here. I don't know anyone so stupid to have niggers in their place!" (76). Adele experiences some of her first psychological breakdowns in this "home." Strikingly, she initially moved to Canada because of the Canadian government's enticements in the early 1960s, offering landed status to single

Caribbean women willing to work for one year as domestics (47–48). By 1970, because of rapidly increasing numbers of Canadian women working outside the home, White middle-class families' demands for domestics skyrocketed; to meet this need, the Canadian government changed its policy regarding foreign domestics in 1973. Immigrants who entered Canada to serve as domestics could arrive on work permits or visas, were not required to have more than an eighth-grade education, had to be "single and without dependents," and were obligated to remain with the same employer for two years—at which point return to the Caribbean was mandatory. Between July 1975 and June 1976, approximately 45 percent of all the women participating in Canada's foreign domestic program were from the Caribbean, as opposed to 0.3 percent from all Asian nations combined (Crawford 105).

The "pull" of the government's advertisements conflicts with the "push" of racism, creating a "two-ness" in Adele—one linkable to the two-ness of a soucouyant's identity: frail old woman by day versus powerful vampiric demon by night; outer carapace, or sheddable skin, versus core inner self. The narrator identifies his mother's love for lemon meringue pie as emblematic of this divergence: she desires the "velvet sweet and sharpness at once. A two-ness" (53), but he does not know about her first experience with the dessert: eyeing the "fluffy sweetness as exotic as snow" in a restaurant window (49), she enters the establishment only to be greeted by "the dead weight of disapproval"; giggles; a sexual proposition; and, finally, the owner notifying her that "no coloureds or prostitutes" are allowed to eat there (50). Adele becomes mentally unhinged, easily read in conjunction with McKittrick's insight of how the displacement of blackness from the historical, cultural landscape "unhinges black people from Canada, [. . .] reducing black specificities to an all-encompassing elsewhere" (99). The real demon here is Canadian racism, and the myth of a contentedly multicultural nation is revealed to be as much of a fantasy as the soucouyant.

In Canada, Adele and her family live an isolated existence. Folklorist Gérard Besson's description of a typical soucouyant residence—a shack "at the end of the village road" (31)—becomes, in Chariandy's hands, an old, run-down house "in a cul-de-sac once used as a dump for real-estate developers" (9). In the latter case, the alienation is clearly the result of bigotry on the part of real estate agents and community members: while the family is reassured that they are getting a home in "a *good* part of Scarborough"—the unspoken synonyms for "good" here are "residential" and "non-urban" and, in a more oblique code, "White" and "middle class"—they must literally cross the railroad tracks to get anywhere and are shunned by their neighbors. In this way, the entire family takes on the soucouyant identity. They are rendered horrific while eating Trinidadian foods: when they partake in a meal of roti, for example, the food is depicted as "like swaddled children for ogres" (40), connecting the family to gruesome ingestion but also, per- haps more tellingly, revealing the narrator's absorption of hegemonic ideas. Like Daphne from *Out of My Skin*, he functions as an ambivalent figure of internalized racial fears and anxieties. When he prepares an ostensibly "authentic" Canadian dish called "saucy wieners," he seems aware of the fiction of a singular White Canadian identity: "I learned [the recipe] from a roommate who was born out west. He was a pretty great cook. A talent for improvising and making do. He said this was an authentic white Canadian recipe, but I never believed him. I've tried it before, but I couldn't ever match his success. There was always some- thing missing" (93). The narrator's continued lack of success in prepar- ing this meal provides clues to the reader about his perceived failure in achieving a genuine Canadian subjectivity. He sees himself in terms of deficiency instead of as adding something rich, positive, and unique to the Canadian experience. The unspeakable "something [always] miss- ing" would appear to be Whiteness. Chariandy's narrative proposes that the narrator must learn to recognize and speak what U.S. writer Toni Morrison calls "unspeakable things unspoken"—the realities of race in a White-dominated society. He must combat the premise that his identity as a "true" Canadian stands as an impossibility and chal- lenge the White Canadians who view him as a foreign Other primarily because of the color of his skin. He is a conventional soucouyant figure in their eyes—one who invades the national homespace, one who is frightening and must be kept out, one whose dark outer skin slips and slides, marking an unnatural departure from the "normal" white body, grounded in Canadian landscape.

Notably Meera, his mother's health aide, also constructs him as a vampiric figure. She critiques him as being too "needy" (118) after he performs cunnilingus on her: both the act and the accusation suggest his draining of her body—physically in one case, emotionally in the other. She continues on: "Do you realize that you're eternally sad? [. . .] It drains you. It sucks your life" (119). This analysis suggests that he is essentially sucking his own life force away.

The narrator's father, Roger, is also cast in soucouyant-like terms when his skin literally peels off of his body. The trait is not self-determined, however; it is caused by the brutal labor he performs in a Canadian furniture factory: it "rip[s] the skin from his hands" (74). The fact that he dies in a workplace accident that slashes open his neck, the site of the conventional vampire's bite, repeats the suggestion that Canadians—in this case, Roger's employers—are the actual vampiric figures. When the lawyers and foremen attempt to cheat the family out of Roger's death benefits, they are metaphorically sucking them dry of their financial rights and stability.

It is Adele's symbolic vampirism, however, that gets highlighted throughout most of the novel. Her overexertions at brushing her teeth cause her gums to bleed, and her "lurid drool of blood" invokes images of a bloodsucking creature (129). As an old woman, she wears a wig that often slips forward on her head. The incident reminds her son of soucouyants removing their skins: "[H]er hairline slips. Her scalp comes off at the back. [. . .] I look upon her skull as if for the first time. The glistening pink skin infected with purple and brown. The corrugations and whorls like an organ exposed to the air. A brain obscenely naked and pulsing with life" (122). In her senility, she is also obsessed by her fingernail clippings, which she wanders around the house trying to retrieve (118). This action resembles the soucouyant's stooping to pick up grains of rice—tiny and white like the clippings—but also suggests the creature's attempts to reunify with her "shed" skin. The fact that Adele becomes increasingly soucouyant-like as she ages and her illness intensifies allows the reader to make connections to the conventional folk legend: the elderly and the mentally ill are often demonized, just like the soucouyant, in contemporary society, and traditional soucouyant imagery clearly ostracizes old women in particular.

More abstractly, though, Chariandy conveys that Canada's racist environment has led Adele to want to shed her black skin. When she immigrates, she becomes a monstrous oddity, alienated and isolated like the soucouyant. White Canadians stare at this woman with brown skin, which becomes "just too much, too heavy" (49). Like the soucouyant, she evokes sexuality out of control according to the stereotypical image of the Black female jezebel, especially when she is propositioned in a restaurant and yet the owner asks *her* to leave his "family" establishment. She desires to escape—to attain a liberty that, interestingly, she eventually achieves with her dementia. Because of her severe memory loss, she becomes "free from [her] past" (8), taking mental flight instead of fleeing in a literal, physical sense. Without memories, she becomes a "new being" (40), "transforming into something else" (121). Meera, her home health aide, gives the name "sundowning" to episodes when Adele fades out of consciousness of the people and events around her. This word implies nocturnal roamings where her inside—her mind—leaves its "skin" or bodily outside casing. By employing the soucouyant figure in a nontraditional way, then, Chariandy is also able to reconfigure dementia as a disease that has potentially positive ramifications.

In ways more threatening to the society in which she lives, Adele's dementia means that she might harm someone. Her son realizes that she has the potential to stab and kill him in a moment of not recognizing him; she picks up a knife and he conjures the image of a penetration that can draw blood, "red oil leaking from [his] young man's body" (43). It would seem to be a truly Oedipal moment, given that the incident of misrecognition is immediately followed by a playful scene where Adele dances with the protagonist, but a warm embrace turns into a fiery kiss and then public masturbation. This sexuality out of control, both for its incestuous nature *and* its public display that is neither procreative nor male focused, marks the character as grotesque in conventional terms: she falls outside the patriarchal order. Like the soucouyant, who eerily sheds her skin, transforms into a ball of fire, takes flight, and ingests human blood, Adele violates the codes that dictate "the proper things to do with one's body" (12). On one occasion, she goes out in public wearing only a bra, pantyhose, several sets of panties, and a pair of shoes. When she forgets where the bathroom is, she begins urinating in potted plants (18). The narrator has already informed the reader that his mother neglects social laws, such as when she "'borrow[s]' things" from shops and neighbors' garages (18). Like the soucouyant, she rejects the concept of "private property" (18) and the boundaries of the Individual valued by European constructs of Self and social order.

Adele is established as even further outside the Law of the Father—Lacan's symbolic order—when she begins "to forget the laws of language" (12). In trying to greet a neighbor one day, she chirps, "Good . . . peanuts!" and "Goodbutterbread!" instead of "Good morning" (108). Chariandy supports this subversion of linguistic rules, however, in his implicit critique of the role of language in establishing a hegemonic imperative. Earlier in their history together, Adele and Roger must "practice speaking 'Canadian'" in order to find a decent apartment (75), suggesting the homogenizing influences that prevail in their country of residence, despite its promises of being a diverse and open society. And during his elementary school days, the protagonist is assumed to lack intelligence because of his Trinidadian accent. A frustrated speech teacher writes him off as not interested in "improving [him]self" (102), revealing the nationalist, anti-immigrant ideology embedded in the educational system.

Chariandy posits that the truly insidious nature of the Canadian nationalist project is the way it gets members of various communities to turn on themselves and each other. Like the soucouyant, who encourages her neighbors to suspect and police each other's behavior, the desire to belong to the Canadian body politic makes various characters point fingers and accuse those who resist the established norms. Meera, of Trinidadian heritage like the narrator and also a bicultural, biracial Canadian subject, experiences the double-consciousness so aptly described by W.E.B. Du Bois in a U.S. context in *The Souls of Black Folk*. She hates steelpan music and avoids "dangerous proximities" to the narrator and his brother—two dark-skinned boys (158)—as if she fears social and even physical contagion from being associated with them. She, like the narrator, and hopefully the readers of the novel, must recognize the myth that the only "real" Canadians are White Canadians. They must get beyond the telling incident that Chariandy provides regarding a Heritage Day parade in the narrator's neighborhood—and this is *despite* the fact that Canada was the first nation in the world to adopt multiculturalism as an official government policy in 1971. The parade is advertised as existing in recognition of "'people of multicultural backgrounds' and 'not just Canadians'"(60, emphasis added)—as if "Canadians" cannot and do not hail from a variety of cultures. Notably, the costumed Whites in this scene pose as pioneers rather than immigrants from other countries. They rewrite History, and historical memory gets reconstructed to exclude particular populations. As Michelle Reid explains,

Canadians often define their nation by its lack of dramatic history on which to found collective memories and myths; instead the country was "[b]rokered into existence by rational men with a rational plan" (Shainblum and Dupuis 8). In contrast to the violent confrontations between settlers and Natives crucial to American frontier myths, Canadian settlers supposedly achieved a less violent and more "legal" dispossession of Native groups. Consequently, the prioritizing of geography over history can be considered part of Canada's national narratives. (431–32)

Despite the distinctions drawn between U.S. and Canadian national identity, however, readers can easily see similarities in the ways both

mainstream cultures render immigrants of color within their geopolitical borders as well as these people's descendants as inauthentic, "unnatural" citizens, invading the national landscape. Chariandy effectively
undermines the myths of Canadian "neutrality" and Canada as "safe-
haven"—an image McKittrick aptly identifies as "one of the key ways in
which the nation secures both its disconnection from blackness and its
seeming exoneration from difficult histories" (119).

A similar employment of the soucouyant figure to interrogate national
history and cultural myths, as well as the need for women of color to
escape their surroundings in communities that constrain their physical
movement, social roles, thoughts, and imaginations, occurs in the novel
Soledad (2001) by Dominican American writer Angie Cruz. The title character struggles with her racial, cultural, and national identity, wrestling
with her absorption of mainstream definitions of "American" as White,
nonaccented, upper-middle class, and European cultured. I'd like to focus,
however, on the character of Olivia, Soledad's mother. Although I have not
found explicit references to the soucouyant figure in folklore and literature from the Spanish-speaking Caribbean, flight, fire, and the shedding
of the outer skin come together in Olivia's story. She, like Adele's mother,
labored as a sex worker to U.S. and European tourists while living in the
Dominican Republic. Like Chariandy, Cruz renders these White men as
hideously draining the stamina and pride of Caribbean women, as well
as of the economic resources of the island. The sociopolitical and legal
analysis of Jacqui Alexander would implicate the Dominican government
as well: "the [Bahamian] state relies upon tourism as its primary economic
strategy, and it, in turn, rests on women's bodies, women's sexual labor,
and the economic productivity of women's service work in this sector to
propel the economic viability of the nation" (87).

Like Adele, Olivia suffers from a breakdown of her mental capacity—
although hers takes the form of a trance-like state and is only temporary.
On one night during her recuperation, she sheds the "skin" of her clothing and stands naked by her apartment window. Then, "She is standing
on the corner of the fire escape, leaning back on the brick wall, with her
arms spread open as if she's about to fly. Her eyes are closed. The sun has
set, the full moon is out, it hits her face, her breast and thighs. Olivia
is smiling, glowing in the moonlight like a firefly" (45). Glowing like a
small ball of fire, anticipating flight, and standing exposed in a crowded
New York City neighborhood (albeit several stories up from the ground
floor), she flouts social norms. She has "flown" from her everyday life and
"sanity," escaping into her dreams and refusing to participate in reality.

Interestingly, when one reads about the incident from Olivia's perspective, the focus is on a dream in which she gives birth to a full-grown child: *"And like a bird she perches up on the fire escape and asks me to follow her. I undress, to be naked like her. [. . .] Then with a soft voice she says, Mami, flying is not so hard. You just need to find the space for your wings"* (46). Although unsuccessful, Olivia promises the child that she will make another attempt. Strikingly, the encouragement to fly free is passed from child to mother instead of the typical translation from mother to daughter. Too much the product of cultural and generational expectations for women to be moored to the domestic space and everlasting motherhood, Olivia finds hope and inspiration in young women of the future.[3]

Turning back briefly to *Soucouyant: A Novel of Forgetting*, in many ways, memory serves as the most frightening soucouyant figure of all: it pierces the minds of the characters as if with fangs when they don't wish to remember certain painful occurrences. The narrator of *Soucouyant* states: "Occasionally, a memory lances me with anxiety and dread. [. . .] Revulsion builds in my stomach" (82). Memories penetrate and have the power to drain subjects of happiness, contentment, and the denial that allows them to endure traumatic circumstances. However, memory is also necessary to preserve a type of coherence of the Self and a richness of national identity that includes a diversity of experiences.

Like Chariandy, Helen Oyeyemi raises the question of how memory and forgetting are related to the creation of a national identity in her 2009 novel *White Is for Witching*. On an individual level, protagonist Eliot Silver fears that his twin sister, Miranda, nicknamed Miri, won't "forget *or* recover" from their mother's unexpected death (106, emphasis added), suggesting, as in *Soucouyant*, the importance of but also an ambivalence toward disremembering for the emotional and mental stability of all subjects who have experienced trauma. However, it is Eliot's earlier, panicked assertions that "We have to *remember* [their mother Lily] or she'll be gone," conjoined with the threat that Miri must stay awake "or Lily will die" (6, emphasis added), that might be said to *contribute* to Miri's sense of trauma and ongoing psychological battles. Miranda does fall asleep, Lily does die while on photo assignment in Haiti, and Miri becomes stuck in the past. Not only does she keep Lily's watch set six hours behind (Haitian time), she finds herself jolted back in time on two occasions to the World War II bombing of her Dover home. Thus, when at one point she claims that she is "not sure what time it [is]" (82), the reader is uncertain if she is talking about hour or day, month, year, or era. And when she swallows watch batteries near the conclusion of the novel, she essentially stops time and joins mother, grandmother, and great-grandmother in corporeal death as well as an apparent stasis of consciousness, their spirits locked in the house. Women's bodies are the ones implicated as the sites of trauma, battle, attempted resistance, and memory.

On a national scale, despite the participation of African Caribbean and African continental soldiers in the British World War II effort, characters like Anna Good—the twins' maternal grandmother—and the Anglo-British cousins of Ore—Miri's college lover—express virulent racism. In *White Is for Witching* as well as in *Soucouyant*, writers of the African diaspora convey how forgetfulness has been strategically employed to aid the dominant population in maintaining its position of power and privilege. And as Jane Bryce argues in her article on representations of twins in recent Nigerian women's literature, the doubled figure often signifies how "the text of contemporary social reality is haunted by traces of a repressed past" (59).

Oyeyemi emphasizes her twins' Whiteness and intimates their social, political, and cultural advantages throughout the text. Not only are they racially White, but in physical appearance they are exceptionally pale and unable to tan (97, 111). Allusions to Whiteness in literature abound in the novel, further emphasizing the favoritism for this color in Western culture. Part 1 is titled "Curiouser" and part 2 is "and curiouser," referring to Alice's adventures down the white rabbit's hole in Lewis Carroll's fiction. Eliot reads about Ahab's maniacal pursuit of the white whale in Herman Melville's *Moby Dick* (86), hinting at a more symbolic obsession with Whiteness.[4] The character Ore recalls C. S. Lewis's Narnia Chronicles and makes specific reference to the White Witch (143)—not as a symbol of purity but rather the sinister, Hitlerian desire to master an ostensibly pure empire.

Oyeyemi also infuses the color imagery with strong gender implications in the opening lines of the narrative, which allude to the Snow White fairy tale. Miri is "in the ground" and "her ears are filled with earth," suggesting someone dead and buried, but since "her heart thrums hard" and a piece of apple is stuck in her throat, it would appear that she is merely entranced (1). Miri's white skin parallels the fairy-tale damsel's "skin as white as snow"—a feature ingrained in the minds of readers around the world as the epitome of beauty. One comes to understand how often-repeated accounts, from fairy tales like "Snow White," to folk stories like those about the soucouyant, to patriotic songs and narratives about national belonging, can inspire and guide their audiences but also constrain and oppress them.

And "Snow White" references proliferate throughout the book. Besides frequently employed references to apples and choking on apples, the repeated allusions to mirrors seem to correspond to Snow White's stepmother's obsession with her magic mirror. Several characters are or become mirror images for each other: Eliot and Miri, Emma and Miri, Anna and the house, Miri and Lily, Jennifer, and Anna. Miranda's bedroom is nicknamed the Psychomantium—a dark, mirrored room set up for communication with the spiritual realm. In ancient Greece, reflective objects and surfaces such as water, glass, and blood were believed to be conduits for voices from the other realm and were placed in psychomantiums to encourage apparitions and visions; Oyeyemi simultaneously uses these substances as a riff off Stoker's *Dracula*. It therefore seems to be no accident that Oyeyemi gives her protagonists the surname Silver, a highly reflective metal: each Silver has the potential to channel the ghosts of those who have gone before. Further, when the ghost of Anna (although the identity of the actual attacker is left ambiguous in the novel) assaults a Kosovan immigrant, she states that her name is the same back and forth, "the same word in a mirror" (105).

White Is for Witching is a fragmented, multivoiced narrative, leading several book reviewers to comment on the difficulty of the reading experience. This textual ambiguity resembles Miranda's (and Eliot's) confused and often chaotic mental state; form echoes content and the reader is often left feeling similarly muddled and bewildered. Near the start of the novel, Miri has just returned from a five-month stay at a psychiatric facility and continues to struggle with numerous psychological conditions, including pica (an eating disorder that involves craving and ingesting nonfood substances), anorexia, trichotillomania (23), and insomnia (71). The eating disorders might be categorized as perversities of consumption, much in the same way one would identify the vampiric consumption of blood. In a September 2009 *New York Times* book review, Andrew Ervin asserted that British and U.S. readers were differently affected by the altered titles of British and U.S. publications: "The novel was published in Britain as 'Pie-kah' (the pronunciation of Miri's affliction), a less sensational title that grounds the narrative in the girl's sad psychic state rather than in its supernatural elements." I would argue, however, that the references to pica are more crucially tied to references to soucouyant figures, Dracula, and nationalism throughout the text.

In terms of a British domestic discourse, Miri's pica suggests a complex layering of racial, ethnic and political ideology. The disorder leads her to consume boxes and boxes of chalk, plastic spoons and "a blue plastic spatula she had been working on for two months" (70), soil (153), bits of onyx (47), and, it is implied, her grandmother's blood (67). The red of the blood, white of the chalk, and blue of the plastic reflect the colors of the Union Jack, indicating an unconscious nationalistic bent to her choices—and perhaps also Paul Gilroy's provocative title, *There Ain't No Black in the Union Jack*—but not until near the end of the novel does the significance of the chalk become fully clear. As Miri and Ore walk along the Dover coast, "Miranda sat on a heap of rock and tapped it. 'Chalk,' she said" (208). It is as if by eating chalk she has been attempting to consume Whiteness and ingest the tangible land of England itself. It should be noted that Eliot, too, seems obsessed by consuming Whiteness: he and his friends continually drink milk from glass bottles that can be heard clanking in their schoolbags.

England here is not a space of diversity, encompassing difference; Dover's famous white cliffs, packed with the chalk Miranda eats, become representative of a nation impenetrable to outsiders, though held out to them as an irresistible gem—what the staunchly anticolonial Antiguan writer Jamaica Kincaid calls "a special jewel [. . . that] only special people got to wear [. . . and those] people who got to wear England were English people" ("On Seeing England for the First Time" 365). Kincaid specifically constructs Dover's white cliffs as emblematic of English people's sense of geographical, cultural, and racial exclusivity, a feeling of elitism against which she rails in her essay:

> The moment I wished every sentence, everything I knew, that began with England would end with "and then it all died, we don't know how, it just all died" was when I saw the white cliffs of Dover. I had sung hymns and recited poems that were about a longing to see the white cliffs of Dover again. [. . .] The white cliffs of Dover, when finally I saw them, were cliffs, but they were not white; you would only call them that if the word "white" meant something special to you. (374–75)

One of the poems Kincaid's statement suggests is Alice Duer Miller's 1940 "The White Cliffs," which begins:

I have loved England, dearly and deeply,
Since that first morning, shining and pure,
The white cliffs of Dover, I saw rising steeply
Out of the sea that once made her secure.

The poem's persona is a traveler for a mere week, and yet

when they pointed "The white cliffs of Dover,"
Startled I found there were tears on my cheek.

Miller links the cliffs—an arresting physical border between Britain and Europe, and the rest of the world—with feelings of estrangement: the poem's speaker is White, but she is from the United States and eventually comes to realize that "Only the English are really her own." Later in the twentieth century, however, this alienation was more disconcertingly experienced by formerly colonized subjects of African descent who could explicitly correlate it to skin color and an increasingly vituperative racism. In 2009, singer Vera Lynn sued the ultraconservative British National Party (BNP) for its unauthorized use of her rendition of the popular World War II–era song "(There'll Be Bluebirds Over) The White Cliffs of Dover," which expressed hope for a time when peace would again reign over Britain's shores. The BNP had used the song on a CD allegedly designed to generate money to support anti-immigration campaigns.[5] In *White Is for Witching*, Dover functions as the principal site of the battle for England's physical, cultural, and racial shores. Miranda recalls learning about Dover as "the key to England[. . . .] Key to a locked gate, throughout both world wars, and even before. It's still fighting" (100). Even Ore's racist cousins, who identify Dover as "a fucking mess" because of the influx of refugees and their conflicts with the locals, seem awed by the xenophobic violence there: "some Kosovan brer and his landlady got stoned. On the actual doorstep of the landlady's house! That's dark, man" (188).

Whereas novels like Stoker's *Dracula* portray the entry of eastern European figures and other foreigners into England as a horrifying penetration of British geographical borders and literal bodies, Oyeyemi reverses the trope to emphasize the gruesome nature of White British xenophobia. Anna Good Silver, Miranda's great-grandmother, represents a key combatant in this battle. She fights it on and through the bodies of her female descendants, much in the way the male heroes of Stoker's novel fight the vampire over, on, and through the bodies of Lucy and Mina—the women in their lives—and the male figures of Britain's imperial project fought to uphold notions of British racial superiority via the carefully protected bodies of the women of the empire. As Felicity Nussbaum argues in *Torrid Zones: Maternity, Sexuality, and Empire in Eighteenth-Century English Narratives* (1995), "a particular kind of national imperative to control women's sexuality and fecundity emerged when the increasing demands of trade and colonization required a large, able-bodied citizenry, and [. . .] women's reproductive labor was harnessed to that task" (1).

Anna Good is completely complicit in this process, as are many of Britain's citizens, continuing into the era of the world wars. Anna's husband, Andrew, draws political cartoons, the largest and most visually potent of which warns against revealing secrets to foreign enemies by chattering in public spaces:

> Two sweet-faced teenage girls talked avidly on a bus, while behind them, two men grinned with their teeth and leaned closer to the girls, closer, closer, more as if they were about to devour the girls than eavesdrop on their conversation. One man was a fat solider covered in swastikas, the other was slit-eyed, uniformed, with a moustache that fell to his knees. You don't have to be that close to someone to listen in on their conversation. *You don't have to be licking the person's neck.* (64, emphasis added)

The revulsion of vampirism, the terror of miscegenation, and the dread of invasion all get collapsed in the illustration: not only must British women keep their wagging tongues quiet, but British men must beware the evil foreign characters—always physically distinctive and highly visible—seeking to consume their women's blood, corrupt their sexual purity, and taint the blood of future generations.

Losses incurred during World War II make Anna exclaim "Blackies, Germans, killers, dirty" (109) for the rest of her life. And in death, Anna's desire to protect her family gets contorted into a stifling domestic imprisonment. Her consciousness merges with the voice of the house, and the two struggle to preserve an impenetrable border, the description of which resonates with hypernationalist rhetoric: "We are on the inside, and we have to stay together, and we absolutely cannot have anyone else. It's Luc [the twins' father and Lily's husband, who significantly hails from France, not Britain] that keeps letting people in" (109). Similar to Edgar Allan Poe's "The Fall of the House of Usher," to which Oyeyemi also alludes, purity of bloodline is maintained by a close confinement to the house.[6]

After Miranda timidly proclaims her love for Nigerian British Ore, Anna, in an apparently collapsed consciousness with the House, states, "We saw who she meant. The squashed nose, the pillow lips, [. . .] the reek of fluids from the seam between her legs. The skin. The skin." (179). The "reek of fluids" suggests menstruation, and presents this presence of blood—and by extension the women's bodies that produce it—as shameful and dirty. The phrase also corresponds to the pervasive hypersexualization of women of African descent in literature (more extensively discussed in Chapter 2). Anna's repetition of "The skin. The skin" indicates the source of her anxiety—not a lesbian liaison but an interracial one. It is this black skin she haunts Ore into believing is peeling off during her visit to the family's home:

> The towel the girl in the mirror was drying herself with—I frowned and looked at my towel. Where it had touched me it was striped with black liquid, as dense as paint
> (don't scream)
> There were shreds of hard skin in it. [. . .]
> "The black's coming off," someone outside the bathroom door commented. Then
> they whistled "Rule Britannia!" and laughed. (198)

While it has become almost cliché that people need to remember the past in order to avoid repeating traumatic scenes from history and create better futures, Chariandy and Oyeyemi complicate the issue. When the character of the House in Oyeyemi's novel conveys information about mental illness in earlier ancestors, it says to Miri: "It is useful, instructive, comforting to know that you are not alone in your history. So I have done you good / and now, / some harm" (22). The pica disorder also runs in Miranda's maternal ancestors: Lily ate ladybugs, Jennifer gnawed on tree branches, Anna chewed on acorns and pebbles. Most gruesome, though, are the acts of the unnamed woman who drank her own blood and ate her own flesh (22)—this self-consumption is subtly mirrored in Jennifer's "bit[ing] at her fingers" (78). While knowledge of the past can provide a sense of grounding, connections, and family ties, the sense of legacy indicated by the House seems utterly inescapable—good for those who wish to carry on an assumed birthright of power and privilege but terrifying for those who wish to step outside the path of fate—especially when the inheritance is bound up in pain and tragedy.

In a similar vein, Ore—given up for adoption by her Nigerian birth mother and raised by a White English couple—claims to be "glad I don't remember anything" from her first year of life before being put into care (138). She imagines physical abuse and pain because of her birth mother's postnatal depression, but the emotional pain of abandonment is left unspoken. Ore also attempts to distance herself from a Nigerian cultural heritage and community. She especially resents attempts by other Black people to draw her into an African identity. In this way, she fits the North American model of second-generation immigrant—born and raised in the land of the parents' immigration—who resists what Dwayne Plaza calls a "transnational lifestyle," which means embracing the land and culture of origin while integrating with the White mainstream cultural and social life (Plaza 213). Instead of embracing the soucouyant's "transaesthetic" delight in movement and mobility, Ore prefers to remain rooted to a singular cultural space—she chooses complete assimilation. When approached on campus to join the Nigeria Society mailing list, for instance, she frowns, declines, and is tempted to toss the flyer on the floor (139). She expresses ambivalence over the Nigerian name her birth mother gave her, preferring the English name Rose instead: "Rose Lind is easily filed, she is a delight, she is Shakespearean, sort of" (138). The reference to Shakespeare invokes the history of British colonialism and the conditioning of colonized subjects to believe themselves English even though they would not be accepted as such within the geographical bounds of the British isles: the British colonial agenda employed the Bard's body of work to create a national identity that could unite the vast expanses of the British Empire. The "sort of," however, is crucial; it reveals the character's awareness that despite her attempts to blend in and belong to the dominant culture, there is an unspoken/unspeakable something that prevents her complete national and cultural adoption. The tangled nature of the narrative and ensuing textual ambiguity can hence be interpreted as a metaphor for feelings of displacement from the national script; the reader's confusion parallels Ore's and that of all others—especially the non-White, and the non-British born—who feel disillusionment and "unbelonging."[7]

Ore also initially resents and challenges the comments encouraging an "us" versus "them" cultural and racial solidarity that are made by Sade, the Nigerian cook and housekeeper at the bed and breakfast owned by the twins' father. Sade cynically inquires, "I'm sorry[. . . .] You are a maid of Kent, are you not?" (195). Whether a reference to the fourteenth-century Joan, Countess of Kent, who came to be known as "the fair maid of Kent," or to the sixteenth-century Elizabeth Barton, who experienced epileptic seizures as religious prophesies, leading to her being called "the holy maid of Kent," the image is distinctly tied to English nationalism: Joan was the first English Princess of Wales, and Barton was involved in a critical moment of England's reframing itself as a Protestant nation: as a Catholic nun, she spoke vehemently again Henry VIII's divorce of Catherine of Aragon and remarriage to Anne Boleyn. Sade questions Ore's choice to remain grounded (as in beached, not as in well supported) rather than taking flight in "bound motion" and embracing a multilayered, flexible identity.

What Oyeyemi proposes is not an either-or model, which solidifies rigid national boundaries fixed in exclusive racial identities, but rather a both-and conception of identity: "it's OK to be Nigerian and English at the same time" (Sethi n.p.), just as it's possible to be Black and English at the same time. Mainstream culture participates in a process that suggests that national identity is set, permanent, unchangeable; however, "Ideological constructions of race and nation must be continually produced and reproduced, adjusted and readjusted, in order to sustain the illusion that they are natural, factual, divine, or biological" (Hudson 129).

Oyeyemi employs notions of illusion, hallucination, magic, and the supernatural to call attention to the ways that multiple cultural outlets contribute to the hegemonic discourse: movies, fairy tales, political speeches, billboards, schoolbooks. She notes that as a child growing up in England, she did not realize that people who looked like her could be the protagonists in literature: "You can read a lot of books and the main characters are white people—especially in the classics—and after a while you forget that you're not white, almost, because it's this big pervasive culture" (Sethi n.p.). In *White Is for Witching*, the box of books that Sade brings with her is filled with the "classics"—"Dickens and the Brontës even" (84)—evidence of the cultural and racial education she has had as a member of the former British Empire. However, she—unlike Ore—embraces her Nigerian heritage. She drinks Malta, prepares other Nigerian foods, acknowledges the voices from the Other Side, and watches Nigerian melodramas on TV.

As in *Soucouyant*, the skin-shedding, bloodsucking figure in *White Is for Witching* is a shifting, layered signifier. Miranda appears as a vampiric figure throughout Oyeyemi's novel. Readers can infer that when GrandAnna smeared her own blood on the twins' lips, Miri ingested it although Eliot "wiped it off" (67). While lying beside her new lover, Miri sniffs "the other girl's body, turning the beginning of a bite into a kiss whenever Ore stirred, laying a trail of glossy red lip prints" (177). These red stains, suggestive of, yet unspecified as, lipstick also imply a trail of blood. Earlier in the novel, Eliot notes that "Miri didn't use lipstick, she used something in a little pot that was applied with a fingertip. [...] The red on her mouth was so strong; maybe it was just the early morning but I'd never seen a red as startling, as odd. Maybe she'd bitten her lip" (57). The unknown "something" in a little pot and the reference to the early morning hours both hint at vampires but also the soucouyant figure who, recently back from nightly excursions to drain the blood of her victims, must retrieve her skin out of a pot or mortar. Similarly, while the lines "Miranda had needed Ore open. Her head had spun with the desire to taste" seem to resonate with sexual desire, bloodlust can be read just beneath the surface. At the last moment, Miri snaps into full consciousness,

> Then came the recoil—
> would I really?
> and she'd bitten her own wrist. (177)

Later, in the Dean's Office, she writes herself a reminder: "*Ore is not food. I think I am a monster*" (177). And at the end of the novel, while looking at herself in a mirror, she sees blood on her face and feels the evidence of fangs:

> There [... were] two slick punctures in her lips. A pain as if her mouth had been stapled. She looked in the mirror and blood was drying on her chin. When she opened her mouth her teeth lifted, then sliced her bottom lip again. She couldn't see the teeth, only the cuts they made. But she felt the teeth. Her features couldn't accommodate the length of them.
>   What am I? (219)

Miranda's psychological illnesses—also readable as her haunting—implicate her in the mysterious attacks on immigrants taking place in Dover, a set of stabbings that penetrate victims and drain them of their blood, much like a vampire. Furthermore, she can't handle the sun; when the curtains stand wide open one morning, "It was more sun than Miranda could tolerate" (155). She construes herself as the undead: she believes she died in the mental health facility, though Ore tries to convince her otherwise (168). And like a soucouyant, her insides depart from her outer Self on occasion—her memory lapse from the stay in the clinic, for instance, is described as a time in which "she'd left herself" (24). All she recalls is "the sensation of travel" (25). Additionally, she expresses a desire to peel the skin of her face away from her skull at one point (90). When her father kisses her, "She felt the kiss on her actual skull, the skin of her scalp crinkling between his lips as they broke through" (37), insinuating a skinless body.

Near the book's conclusion, Ore has a dream vision of splitting Miranda open and finding "another girl" inside, who wails at being released: "'No, no, why did you do this? Put me back in.' She gathered the halves of her shed skin and tried to fit them back together" (213). In response to Ore's questions, the girl states that she is Miranda while the "rubbery skin" is "the goodlady"—another name for Anna Good Silver. Despite Ore's demands that she resist, the girl sews herself back into the skin. Here, Oyeyemi turns the soucouyant convention on its head. Rather than describing an inner demon protected by the disguise of frail outer skin, the skin is what confines, constricts, and controls Miranda. Anna's yearning to have all her female offspring safeguarded within the house, along with her insistence on the superiority of all things white—from skin to clothing—eventually stifles Miri's potential to be a new kind of British citizen. She gets buried by and beneath the House, an act that Ore identifies from the very beginning of the novel as "the only way to fight the soucouyant" (1).

The soucouyant legend that Oyeyemi explicitly provides to readers specifies that the creature consumes the souls, and not the blood, of her victims (137). It would seem that Miranda's behavior follows suit. As her relationship with Ore develops, she seems to drain and absorb the young Black woman's life essence into herself. The image provides clues as to how the folk story and nationalist narratives are joined together: in the same way that Ore initially wishes to completely reject her Nigerian sense of self in favor of a "true" English identity, she shows signs of "disappearing" (171) and shrinking away to nothingness during her relationship with Miranda. When she and Miri kiss, it seems as if the latter is about to suck the air from her lungs: "I kissed [Miranda], and she kissed me back and we were like that until we gasped for air" (155). The sucking and draining become more unequivocal later in the text: "As we kissed I became aware of something leaving me. It left me in a solid stream, heavy as rope. It left from a hurt in my side, and it went into Miranda, into the same place in her" (198).

This image of blurred or merging identities is important, especially when one considers Ore's hypothesis that the danger of the soucouyant lies not only in her potential as a predator but also in her ability to transform her victims into replicas of herself: "I wanted to write about [the soucouyant . . .]. Something that explores the meaning of the old woman whose only interaction with other people was consumption. The soucouyant who is not content with her self. She is a double danger—there is the danger of meeting her, and the danger of becoming her" (144). This creation of replicas has clear connections to aspects of the colonial enterprise, which conditioned White British women of all classes to think of themselves as mothers of the nation rather than as sisters in a feminist struggle that might cross bounds of race and class. Thus, whether possessed by the ghost presences of her female ancestors or experiencing a split personality disorder, Miri believes that "We are the goodlady[. . . .] The house and I" (202). She unifies with and becomes indistinguishable from generations of heterosexual White women rather than bonding most powerfully with her Black female lover. By the end of the novel, she notes that Anna, Jennifer, Lily, and she "looked the same now, all four of them. It was tiresome to see herself repeated so exactly" (219).

Ore resists this conflation, which in her mind represents the core of abjection in its dissolution of borders: "I told myself that no matter what Miranda said, the soucouyant was the old lady. That was the rule. It was the young girl that defeated the soucouyant. The two did not enter the story in each other's bodies; the two did not share one body, such a thing was a great violation. Of what? I didn't know" (203). For most of the semester that they spend together, this "violation" has been significantly occurring on Ore's Black body and not Miri's White one. Ore has "been eating and eating" but continually loses weight, no matter how much she consumes (183–84). By the time she visits Miranda at the Barton Road house, she seems to have absorbed her lover's anorexia: she is "careful not to let any food or water touch my lips—I tilted my glass and swallowed air" (199). At one point, Ore tells Miri that the latter is "burning up" (159), and later she feels "heat rising from [Miri's] skin" (200). Both scenes evoke the image of the soucouyant as ball of fire as well as all-consuming force. Ore's skin is also noticeably hot, however, suggesting the hazy borders between the two women (159). She must extricate herself from the net in which she is encased in her last vision: "knotted at the top, [. . .] a huge white bag" (214). Sade instructs her to "Stand up and it will unravel" (214), but she must stand on her own. This independence manifests in her departure from the House, leaving Miri behind. The separation renders Miri distraught, "crying because something stood between her and another girl and said, no" (216). This ambiguous "something" can readily be interpreted as the distinct borders of the body and of the Self.

It should be noted how Oyeyemi stresses the Whiteness of the net that entraps Ore. She sees through "white squares"; there are "Tens of feet of white cotton bunched around" her; when she sits in the white bag she feels "so safe," but when she listens to the Nigerian housekeeper and breaks free, "the net fell around me with such sudden weight that I nearly lost my footing" (214). The intermingling of her identity with Miri's is an obvious burden for the young woman; in addition, her aspirations to the Whiteness epitomized by Miranda's pallid skin and believed by many to be necessary for true British subjecthood are also undermined. The bag thus represents the overwhelming, ensnaring presence of a British normative ideology. Oyeyemi denotes the situation as especially complex for people of color, whose appearance prevents full acceptance in the racist society in which they live. It is almost as if they must shed their skins, like soucouyants, in order to achieve not only formal rights and privileges but also their own psychological peace. Quite significant, then, is the detail that Agim, the young Kosovan immigrant who is attacked in a series of assaults on "foreigners," eventually commits suicide by swallowing bleach—a chemical agent used for whitening.

When initially considering the soucouyant legend, Ore feels some sympathy for the figure, viewing it in terms of lonesomeness rather than as a manifestation of pure evil. She questions her folklore book's representation of the soucouyant as "unnatural," thinking, "As always, the soucouyant seemed more lonely than bad" (137). However, at other times Ore insists that the soucouyant is a "monster" who "deserve[s] to die" (155) and, in doing so, voices conventional social mores. Although—or perhaps because—she herself is emblematic of the figure of unwanted seclusion because of her racial difference in a country that privileges Whiteness, Ore finally rejects the folkloric figure as demonic Other. Miri, on the other hand—also a figure of unasked for solitude because of her psychological disorders and/or Anna's/the House's attempts to alienate her from society—contests these mores; she interprets the soucouyant figure as an empowering one who "gets away" from hegemonic prescriptions of heteronormative romance, marriage, and childbearing and rearing, and the traditional fairy-tale scripts where girls must be "'happy' and 'good'" (153)—ostensibly meaning obedient, humble, and passive. Tellingly, Miri is the character who ends up dead. With this conclusion, Oyeyemi suggests that iconoclasts cannot survive in contemporary England—a nation tied too closely to the past. And in the "real life" of the early twenty-first century, it is women of African descent who remain disfigured: they are "marked by blackness rooted in a legacy of a racial past and their bodies continues [sic] to bear these psychic and corporeal scars in dominant visual culture" (Fleetwood 145). The next chapter further considers issues of Black women's invisibility and racial hypervisibility in the context of the soucouyant's sheddable skin.

6 / Shedding Skin and Sucking Blood: Playing with Notions of Racial Intransigence

*To live in the skin of a black woman is to live permanently in a night
without stars[. . . .] A dense night that weighs on us like a burden. That's
why we want to get rid of it, to distance ourselves from it without looking
back. We want to run away from our black woman's skin like one shuns
the night and its demons. Thus, we abandon our own people; we kill our
children; and we flee even from our own shadow.*
— MARIE-CÉLIE AGNANT, *THE BOOK OF EMMA*

*Blood. The old people say it is the carrier of ancestral memories, and our
future's promise.*
— CELU AMBERSTONE, "REFUGEES"

In conventional vampire tales, part of the anxiety over the vampiric bite concerns the contamination of the blood of the victim, whether this corruption occurs inside the victim's body or outside of it, in the body of the vampire. Even in contemporary scientific discourse—where blood, with its white blood cells and antibodies, is viewed as the human body's best defense against germs and other invading elements—the narrative of a closed circulatory system rejecting "foreign bodies" promotes these feelings of anxiety. Up to the late 1930s in the United States, the American Red Cross refused to accept blood donations by African Americans. The organization desegregated their blood supply shortly after the war but reportedly permitted chapters in the U.S. South to continue segregating blood through the 1960s.[1]

As was discussed in Chapter 2, horror shifts from the eighteenth century, when Gothic narratives focused on anxieties about debased aristocracy, to the nineteenth century, when ideologies of race led to a predominance of images of monstrously racialized—and often feminized—bodies: bodies that were seen as sites of depravity, threatening corporeal corruption. Popular culture scholar Judith Halberstam neglects the gender aspect when she notes: "[W]ith the rise of bourgeois culture, aristocratic heritage became less and less of an index of essential national identity, [and] the construction of national unity increasingly depended upon the category of race and class. Therefore, the blood of nobility now became the blood of the native" (16). However, her emphasis on the significance of the blood and its relationship to conceptions of "pure" British identity are crucial to understanding the layers of unease generated by traditional European vampire narratives. The anthropologist Aisha Khan argues: "When they are the raison d'être, ideologies of mixing work both in tandem with and at cross purposes with ideologies of purity (and at times, authenticity) as the essential core of the individual, the nation, and the community" (4). And as William Hughes explains in *Beyond Dracula*, "The nation, the race, the family are all structured metaphorically and/or metonymically in terms of blood relations, the individual functioning as a blood-bearing synecdoche of the greater unity in which he—and his blood—circulate" (139). Terms such as "hybrid" were long endowed with negative associations, and this angst-inducing mixing was definitely at stake in representations of the soucouyant. In T. B. Jackson's 1904 *Book of Trinidad*, for instance, the "Soucouyan" is described as a "species of diabolic hybrid" (115), with the blending of two kinds being linked to the devil.

The importance of discrete systems of blood also arises in various African and diasporic cultures; in Guyana, for example, *kenna* forbids certain families from consuming particular meats. Since each family's blood is considered distinct from every other family's, the meat that nourishes one set of relations might be "blood poison" to another (Abrahams and Szwed 153). Vampires throw these notions into disarray by drinking the undrinkable and mixing the blood of Other and Self within their bodies. They not only contaminate the flesh in their symbolically sexual bite; they contaminate blood, upsetting racial (and national) certainty by creating a "creature" in whom genotype might not match phenotype. One's skin becomes an even more unreliable marker of "true" racial identity. An issue that arises is how fidelity to family—to one's blood—contradicts affiliations and allegiances provided by the skin—the physical markers of race that so often haunt Caribbean and other American societies. As Sidney Mintz remarks about the disparate cultures of Jamaica, Puerto Rico, and Haiti, there is typically an "obsessive preoccupation" with complexion owing to social perceptions about skin color and its role in denoting or corroborating one's status in the social hierarchy (52). The presumption of *embranquecimento*, the desired "whitening, or the gradual progression toward European appearance and cultural practices," prevails in many Latin American cultures, such as Brazil, Costa Rica, Argentina, and Colombia (Khan 3). And therefore, even though "race" has been scientifically disproven as a fixed or valid method of human categorization and revealed as a social construction, it continues to be quite real in many people's minds and integral to their experiences.

In this chapter, I analyze several African-diasporic texts that employ the soucouyant figure to interrogate the workings of race and racism in the Americas. The "horror" tales examined here trouble narrow conceptions of race and gender, typically when they dispute the idea of the "corruption" of allegedly "pure" bloodlines by an impure (configured racially, nationally, and sexually) woman of African descent. The rhetorical power of the "one-drop rule" guarantees that the figure of the vampire conjures nightmares about race and miscegenation. Judith E. Johnson comments that "having a drop of non-Caucasian blood immediately transforms ordinary humans into members of an alien and only semi-human race," making the vampire narrative perfect for probing racial issues (76). The stories under review in this chapter, however, reveal that although the contagion of the blood is frightening, it is not the only source of apprehension. Much textual disquiet surfaces around the concept of the soucouyant's sheddable skin. Skin ostensibly carries the clearest signs of racial identity and evidence of racial belonging (or nonbelonging), and a removable skin suggests that fixed racial identities are, in fact, quite unstable.

In contemporary U.S. culture, Halberstam links skin and blood as she analyzes the character of Buffalo Bill from the horror film *Silence of the Lambs*: "Skin, in this morbid scene, represents the monstrosity of surfaces and as Buffalo Bill dresses up in his suit [of flayed women's skins] and prances in front of the mirror, he becomes a layered body, a body of many surfaces laid one upon the other. Depth and essence dissolve in this mirror dance and identity and humanity become skin deep" (1). Where Halberstam's interpretation takes a more postmodern approach, focusing on issues of identity that may apply to any subject, I see the issue of skin in the soucouyant tales as critically tied to notions of racial identity. From the first moments of enslavement, figures like the soucouyant are invented and re-visioned by African Americas populations to philosophize about the impossible predicament of their humanity in plantation society: the skin-shedding vampire-woman, with her dense and shifting meanings, confronts the issue of what it means to have a skin—and what it might mean to be able to remove it—in a culture that always already denigrates blackness. As demonic figures, and figures of the "undead," soucouyants and other vampires are closely aligned with the "socially dead": enslaved peoples who lack power, voice, and mobility in the social landscape, whose bodies get destroyed by plantation labor and then punished because they are no longer useful to plantation capitalism. Even in contemporary times, the idea of a skin that can be removed at its owner's whim—besides being exceptionally grisly and harkening back to the ruthless punishments of the slavery era—threatens the mainstream discourse on race: that it is permanent; that it is an observable or legible (and thus a "fixed") text; that it is determined by social perception and not influenced at all by a subject's choice to belong to one group or another or multiple groups at the same time. (See figure 8.)

The body has long been conceived in certain circles as bounded and fully contained by the skin: even though the skin is porous, investments in fixed and stable borders cause it to be seen as inviolable, with nothing penetrating in or exiting out. Katherine McKittrick's work on reconstructing geographies and Black women's cartographies is useful here:

If we imagine that traditional geographies are upheld by their three-dimensionality, as well as a corresponding language of insides and outsides, borders and belongings, and inclusions and exclusions, we can expose domination as a visible spatial project that organizes, names, and sees social differences (such as black femininity) and determines *where* social order happens. (xiv)

Ideas of stasis and rootedness run amuck, as the Western concept of geography has traditionally been employed as "not only anchor[ing . . . our] feet to the ground, it seemingly calibrates and normalizes where, and therefore who, we are" (xi). The conventional soucouyant figure flies—literally—in the face of this ideology: she also generates trepidation around the notion of the impenetrable geography of the body. She penetrates others through her bloodsucking bite, but she also suggests the flimsiness of her own boundaries of the Self. The sloughing off of the skin is beheld with horror and revulsion.

In an early twentieth-century essay on superstitions in Trinidad, L. O. Iniss reports: "Any old woman who is grumpy and unsociable in a village, and further has the white of her eyes red, is generally suspected of being a 'Soucouyan.' The red eye is held to be an infallible sign. It may be that the violent contortions necessary to *peel* themselves is [*sic*] the cause of their bloodshot eyes" (116). Identity is read off of and onto the physical body—a type of written text with unmistakable "signs" that are believed to have one and only one interpretation. As discussed in Chapter 3, when

FIGURE 8. Gevonne Kresge's charcoal sketch of a soucouyant, standing outside a window and shedding her skin (2012).

Haitian writer Edwidge Danticat publishes "Nineteen Thirty-Seven"
nearly a century later, she represents this tendency to read Black women's
bodies as vampiric scripts: the "proof" of the female cellmates' identities as
life-sucking creatures able to cast off their skins is their wrinkled appearance, which the villagers believe results from their repeated removal and
reapplication of their skins. As the women starve to death during their
unjustified captivity and their skins sag even more, prison guards become
increasingly certain that the inmates are demonic and have the power to
escape their outer membranes and the prison each evening.

The trouble with reading skin as an invariable sign of its wearer's identity, however, can be detected early in Haiti's history, with terms like *gens
de couleur*, or "free colored," in the eighteenth and nineteenth centuries.
The single phrase did not (and could not) reflect a single, unified collective in terms of complexion or social, economic, or political class. Some
members of the group were African born and then freed after many years
of enslavement, while others were a third or fourth generation distant
from bondage and culturally and psychologically disconnected from

their enslaved ancestors. Some *gens de couleur* had begun generating a good deal of wealth but could claim no political power; some had been educated in France while others were illiterate; some were dark, while others were light. As time went by, light skin became inextricably tied to wealth, social connections, political power, and all types of privilege; dark skin signaled poverty and the lack of social and physical mobility, and color class stratification was firmly set into place.

While *light* skin was privileged, however, "unnaturally" *white* skin was denigrated. In 1990, Haitian colonel Jean-Claude Delbeau published a book that explicitly made the connection between the Haitian social and cultural obsession with skin color and folk figures who could flay their own skins. As Joan Dayan describes in *Haiti, History, and the Gods* (1995):

> He lists the names for different shades—distinctions that still remain important to Haitians—including white, mulatto, griffon, marabou, red-brown, brown, black, albino. Then, he moves from these physical attributes to legends: the san pwèl who shed their skin before committing their nightly atrocities, and the blacks who turn white. He recalls the story of a man turning white during the American occupation of Haiti: "An inhabitant of Marigot, known in his village as a very dark black, suddenly changed skin and became completely white. His terrified parents took him to Port-au-Prince where he was admitted to the general hospital. (265)

Dayan attributes the stories of skinless demons such as *baka, san pwèl,* and *lougawou* and the tales of inexplicably "whitened" people whose skin transformations frighten their relatives to an African-centered ideology. Influenced by literary texts such as Harriet Beecher Stowe's *Uncle Tom's Cabin* (1852), in which Topsy mentions that if she "could be skinned, and come white," she'd try to be good, and Toni Morrison's *Beloved* (1987), with its reference to the European slave traders as "men without skin," Dayan argues that "to be without skin is to be white," and, in the Haitian context, "to be white is to be a devil" (266). In other words, both sets of bodily alterations described by Delbeau link monstrosity to being completely whit*ened*. According to this line of thought, the soucouyant epitomizes the conqueror, the colonizer, the plantation owner.

Interestingly, although the white/removable skin is associated with frightening power, it is also the source of great vulnerability. A simple salting or peppering of the soucouyant's hidden outer covering can lead to her demise. This characteristic in the folklore might have corresponded in the past to the enslaveds' perceptions of their social superiors. "Surrounded by evidence of white omnipotence, yet witness to the frailty of this apparent omnipotence, the *Bossale* organized his life in terms of the deep differences that separated him from the Western master" (Casimir-Liautaud 37).

Jean Rhys's *Voyage in the Dark* (1934) is one text that ushers issues of Caribbean Whiteness into the twentieth century. Set in England in the 1910s, the novel relates the experiences of Anna Morgan, a young White woman who is "fifth generation born out there [in the Caribbean colonies], on my mother's side" (52). She therefore identifies herself as "a real West Indian" (55), but this puts her in a precarious social position with the chorus girls with whom she works, who "call her the Hottentot" (13), alluding to the hyperracialized, hypersexualized Venus Hottentot who was exhibited in nineteenth-century Europe. Anna's claim to a distinctly Caribbean identity also affronts her stepmother, Hester, who continually condemns her behavior and speech: "I tried to teach you to talk like a lady and behave like a lady and not like a nigger and of course I couldn't do it. Impossible[. . . .] That awful sing-song voice you had! Exactly like a nigger you talked—and still do" (65). Hester alludes here to suspicions that despite skin color, Anna's mother—and therefore Anna herself—was of mixed race. Ironically, one of Anna's deepest desires reveals a rejection of the shame that White Europeans try to force upon her: she wishes to pare away her white skin and become black—a way she envisions of resolving the cultural alienation and emotional isolation she feels. On one occasion, she recalls that during a childhood fever, "I wanted to be black, I always wanted to be black. [. . .] Being black is warm and gay, being white is cold and sad" (31).

The protagonist's desire to symbolically slough off the white outer casing in favor of a black essence is less about embracing the beauty or value of a dark complexion than yearning for cultural affiliation. It is evidence of Rhys's repeated attempts in her fiction to address the issue of belonging. Anna remembers:

Obeah zombies soucriants—lying in the dark frightened of the dark frightened of soucriants that fly in through the window and suck your blood—they fan you to sleep with their wings and then they suck your blood—you know them in the day-time—they look like people but their eyes are red and staring and they're soucriants at night—looking in the glass and thinking sometimes my eyes look like a soucriant's eyes. (163)

The imagery reflects the character's ambivalence: the wings that fan one to sleep suggest comfort, a gentle lulling as opposed to a fearsome violation. Furthermore, she identifies with the soucriant rather than rejecting her for her reddened eyes, which might suggest tears and sadness as easily as an escape from reality through drunkenness.

Toward the end of the novel, Anna dreams of taking flight and trying to reach her home in the West Indies: "I took huge, climbing, flying strides among confused figures. I was powerless and very tired, but I had to go on" (165). Throughout the course of the narrative, she has subverted racial stereotypes and geographical expectations as well as gender norms in her refusal to be happy, to be pleasant and pleasing, and via her sexual promiscuity; however, at the conclusion, she seems to be a soucouyant whose flame has been extinguished. Readers are left with the constant image of her being chilly in this British landscape, "as if someone had thrown cold water over me" (36), and unable to generate the fire of a Caribbean that she can only fantasize about when she remembers how the golden sunlight caused her to see "fire-colour" (43).

Regardless, in almost all of the texts evoking soucouyants that are written by contemporary authors, losing one's skin is not tied to demonic activity but rather freedom for women. *The Book of Night Women* (2009) provides another example. Marlon James creates a neo–slave narrative that explores the history of female involvement in a major insurrection in slave-era Jamaica. The story is based upon a late eighteenth-century, island-wide plot to murder all of the masters, destroy the plantations, and form villages of free Black people.[2] Graphic scenes of whippings and images of brutally flayed skins allow the novelist to convey the monstrosity of the owners, overseers, and the slave system itself; these passages also provide subtle references to the skin-removing soucouyant figure and the enslaved population's desire for the flight and freedom that she represents. The only explicit reference to the folk figure is a glancing one—the narrator compares a Maroon woman's ugliness to "Ol'Hige herself" (78)—but the pain of salted skin is indicated when slaves are bathed in a brine solution to prevent infection and inflict greater punishment. When the novel's protagonist, Lilith, receives one of these thrashings, the sensations experienced and thoughts running through her head echo with the imagery of soucouyant lore:

> [F]ire going off in her head. *Blood spraying* and *flesh tearing.* Lilith can't sleep, not 'cause the cuts from the whip *burnin' her,* but because *darkness burnin'* in her own heart. Ashanti *blood racing*

through her and she can't stop thinking about white people *shed-ding theirs. Even the two young children.* [. . .] She think of Mistress Roget getting tie to a tree and getting whip till she raw. She think of *dashing salt in her* gashes until the mistress smell like corned pork. (210, emphasis in original)

In her moment of victimization, Lilith thrills over the prospect of drawing blood from her oppressors; she craves to be powerful rather than powerless and is unequivocal in targeting children. Whereas conventional Ol' Hige stories demonize the old woman who imbibes children's blood in order to maintain her youth and extend her life, James constructs a character whose imagined acts are based on ideas of vengeance and retribution. His narrative sets the conflict up as one where the boundaries between Self and Other, community and foreign outsider, are distinct; this is not the typical scene of abjection where borderlines blur and categories appear to blend. Lilith as soucouyant acts on behalf of herself as well as other enslaved peoples; additionally, she strikes out against a specifically White plantation class. Her "Ashanti blood" is overtly configured in opposition to the European blood she wishes to see spilled.

Later in the novel, the soucouyant's facility with casting off her skin, her supernatural powers of flight, and her freedom are associated with Lilith and the other enslaved women who sneak out at night. Notably, these traits are depicted as intimately tied to women of African descent because of their dark complexions: "This is why we dark, cause in the night we disappear and become spirit. Skin gone and we become whatever we wish. We become who we be. In the dark with no skin I can write. And what write in darkness is free as free can be, even if it never come to light and go free for real" (427). In distinct opposition to the previously mentioned associations between whiteness and skinlessness, dark complexions in the shadowy night mean that "Skin gone." Dark coloring is embraced for its power to give the women figurative invisibility, a means to achieve freedom, and a flexible and self-determined identity. The skinless body is distinctly race*less*—without the outer carapace that holds the melanin, others cannot identify, label, or racially (and socially) contain the soucouyant figure.

In Euro/American racist discourse, "a racially liminal subject who represents a dissolution of the line between white self and black Other" (L. Young 113) becomes a threat to the notion of the inviolable white skin and incorruptible white blood. Mimi Sheller cites an 1899 travel narrative by Susan de Forest Day to demonstrate the disgust felt by many visitors to the region who witnessed the common crossing of sexual boundaries:

I say the children were black, but they had flaxen hair tied with pink ribbons[. . . .] But the flaxen hair had the telltale kink, which is the infallible sign of Negro blood, and their red-brown eyes, thick lips and slightly hooked Semitic noses, were sickening evidences of a mixture of races which cannot but result in demoralization. (quoted in Sheller, *Consuming the Caribbean* 132)

Many of these types of chronicles conveyed the belief that the observer could always perceive the "corruption" of blood: ostensibly, these transgressions could not be disguised or hidden from view and would always be visible in the skin or other physical features.

Caribbean racial classification systems proposed finely distinguished identities predicated upon finely distinguished shades of complexion. The taxonomies did not perseverate on notions of contamination, but they still obsessed over tracking the presence of African blood—no matter how minute an amount. Dayan explores this apprehension in her discussion of Médéric-Louis-Elie Moreau de Saint-Méry's 1797 writings on the people of Saint Domingue (later Hispañola), which featured 110 racial combinations, ranking from pure white (128 parts white blood) to pure black (128 parts African blood). The "scientific" precision reveals a preoccupation with blood and with race, as well as with the specter of darkness—both literal and metaphorical—that one might carry in one's veins. This fixation is crucial for our understanding of race and racial dynamics in contemporary societies all over the world but also for our comprehension of why vampire narratives, with their focus on "stolen" and contaminated blood, create so much uneasiness.

Belinda Edmondson observes that in contemporary Jamaica, "where the population is 90 percent black, the brown [light-complexioned] and non-Black members of society are featured so prominently in public spaces like the national newspaper, beauty contests, and tourism posters as to reflect a more ethnically diverse population than is actually the case" ("Public Spectacles" 7). In the Latin American context, Dolores Shapiro cites Skidmore's and Andrews's studies on the "pressure" to "whiten" or "stay light" in Brazilian society—an ideology intensified by commonplace associations between African origins and negative traits such as "laziness, bad manners, lack of enterprise, and lasciviousness" (829). And Dany Bébel-Gisler identifies a rigid color classification system in modern-day Guadeloupe, including terms like *mulâtre(sse)* and *métis(se)* ("mulatto")—most frequently used—*chabin(e)*, or "mulatto with light skin and fair hair"; *câpre(sse)*, the child of "a mulatto woman and a very dark black man"; *quarteron(ne)*, the child of "mulatto man and a white woman." There is also *"po chapé*, Creole for *peau-échappée*, or escaped skin. In this last example, having light skin is equated with escaping from being a slave" (240n19), although—more significantly for *The Things That Fly in the Night*—it also intimates the legacy of the sou- couyant and her connections to liberty.

In *The Book of Emma*, from which the epigraph of this chapter is taken, Marie-Célie Agnant employs the figure of the soucouyant to expose how the dynamics of skin, blood quantum, and racial ideology come together in the contemporary circum-Caribbean. Fifie and her twin sister, Grazie, are identified as *chabines:* their "faces had been sculpted in pure gold"; they were "the colour of fire. [. . .] Two *chabines* with eyes of molten gold" (141). Despite their beauty, the author initially aligns them with conventional demonic soucouyants. Images of the folk figure abound in the sisters' "skin full of sun, a flame of arrogance and contentment growing each day behind their pupils" (143). Emma's description of her mother's complexion as "that inside-out skin" (31) further accentuates the soucouyant connection: like the skin-shedder from folklore, Fifie is depicted as having an outer casing that can be detached and inverted when put back on.

In Agnant's fictional world, a removable white skin is not desirable; instead, it causes psychological distress for several generations of Afri- can Americas women: "You'll see, when you learn my mother's story, Fifie's story, you'll see; it's useless to fight against one's black skin; it's like attempting to change the colour of the ocean" (31). Fifie is at first vilified by the reader for internalizing the racist discourse to such a degree that she despises her daughter Emma for her dark coloring. Later in the narrative, however, Agnant revises her portrait of the twins to highlight their positions as lost rather than demonic. Fifie's inability to bond with Emma can be attributed to the fact that she was raped. The appearance of a minor character—a Dominican woman—who has had a psychological breakdown stimulated by the push-pull dynamics of Black womanhood reveals that Fifie's racial issues transcend her as an individual, as well as traversing barriers of nation and race. The Latin American woman explains: "My three sisters had light skin[. . . .] [M]e, I was the only *negrita*, the only one, the shame of my mother. Ah, if you knew how they scorned me!" (61) Besides being socially conditioned to cherish light complexions, Fifie and Grazie are exposed as not knowing how to cope with the pressures, expectations, and limitations of their white skins/white masks when these are coupled with their womanhood: "They floated about, weren't tied to any perch, weren't tied up to any dock. So, they offered that skin to all comers, that skin, an envelope without a soul" (150).

Aside from this background, the main setting of the novel is Montreal, where Emma is being held at a mental facility while awaiting trial for the murder of her daughter Lola. Flore, Emma's interpreter and eventual advocate, and the first-person narrator of the novel, also possesses "inside-out skin," suggesting that she, too, functions as a soucouyant figure. Emma describes her as having "straw-coloured hair and [. . .] eyes made to fool the night" (30). She accuses her: "When one comes into the world like that, with those eyes of yours and that inside-out skin, and all those mixed-up features, one foolishly assumes that one will be spared the effects of their [White people's] hate" (30–31). During the course of the narrative, Flore must come to recognize her internalized racism and embrace the multitude of complexions to be found in members of the diaspora. She admits to having often thought of herself as being "the perfect skin colour: just right, not too pale, not to [sic] dark. That is how they like us. 'Like honey,' some exclaim" (43). Being "too light" intimates illness and sickly pallor; being too dark is associated with ugliness, an absence of sophistication, and lack of civilized ways. Flore seeks to accentuate her light skin as much as possible; she admits to highlighting her hair with gold streaks "to bring out the sparkle" of her green "cat eyes" with pupils "made to fool the night" (43–44)—perhaps another reference to the soucouyant, moving about after dark.

Significantly, in most soucouyant lore and literature generated by people of African descent, neither the "spreading" of the vampiric condition nor the fear of contamination of the blood is an issue. From the time of earliest colonization in the Americas, having one's African blood mix with European blood would not have meant pollution or adulteration but rather could facilitate moving up the social—and often economic—ladder. This ideology shifted during nationalist and Black consciousness movements in the twentieth century, when racial blending was viewed negatively by many people in the diaspora, but other subjects—especially those who were not politically engaged—still clung tightly to beliefs in a racial hierarchy that could be ascended permanently by one's increasingly "whitened"—although never "pure"—mixed-race descendants as well as the practice of passing in the U.S. context.

Nella Larsen's 1929 novel *Passing* provides a well-known example: when Irene and Clare first survey each other in an exclusive Chicago restaurant, Irene feels alarm over the possibility of being exposed as a Black woman passing for White. Like the soucouyant, she has temporarily achieved power—hers is racial and social clout—by slipping out of the superficial identity that mainstream culture wishes to foist upon her (Blackness) and experiencing the freedom of her physical body, which literally reads as White. As critic Lauren Berlant notes, "The gaze of one woman [Clare] virtually embodies the other [Irene], calling her back from her absence-to-her-body, an absence politically inscribed by the legal necessity to be non-black while drinking iced tea at the Drayton Hotel in Chicago in 1927" (110). When Irene becomes self-conscious about her physical body, it is as if she is forced to re-don her cast-away skin.

In Jamaica Kincaid's *At the Bottom of the River* (1978), the reenvisioned soucouyant provides a powerful example of celebrated womanhood, but the message about shedding one's outer covering is more ambiguous. The text is full of transitions, particularly the narrator's transformation from child to adult. At one point, she wonders, "perhaps my life is as predictable as an insect's and I am in my pupa stage" (21), emphasizing her likeness to metamorphosing insects. Similar to the shape-shifters of Octavia Butler's *Patternmaster* series, whom Gregory Jerome Hampton asserts "consciously change the narratives written upon their bodies and by doing so bring into question the value and stability of bodily inscriptions" (xxiv), the skin-shedding characters of Kincaid's book resist a singular, steadfast identity.

In another chapter, *At the Bottom*'s narrator describes, in a surreal scene, how she and her mother transform into reptiles: "[My skin] had just blackened and cracked and fallen away and my new impregnable carapace had taken full hold" (56). Kincaid's images of insects breaking free from cocoons and molting reptiles project the notion of ridding oneself of metaphorical skins that have grown too tight and constrictive—whether these be familial or social roles, intimate relationships, or the physical traits associated with one's identity. One need only briefly consider Kincaid's *Annie John* (1983), *Lucy* (1990), *The Autobiography of My Mother* (1996), and *My Brother* (1997) to see the author wrestle with the line between love and resentment in the fraught and often constrictive relationships between mother and daughter. *A Small Place* (1989) advances comparable emotions in its political critique of Antiguan not-quite-so-postcolonial society. On a more subtle level, however—one, I would suggest, that only those familiar with Caribbean folk culture can access—Kincaid's images suggest the soucouyant, shedding the skin that restricts her by day to achieve freedom at night.

Kincaid's relationship to race has been interpreted in various ways, but perhaps the author's own words represent it best; in an interview published in 1989, she stated: "It's just too slight to cling to your skin color" (Cudjoe, "Jamaica Kincaid" 401). It is as if the skin were as insubstantial and impermanent as clothing: as if it could be slipped on and off. In the introduction to *Talk Stories*, Kincaid discusses the process of trying to peel away the conventional markers of femininity and "blackness" when she first arrived in the United States: "I had cut off my hair to a short boy-like length and I had bleached it from its natural black color to blond; I had shaved off my eyebrows completely and painted in lines with gold-color eye makeup" (6). She chooses a look that might be identified as "unnatural"—perhaps as unnatural as a skinless being flying through the night sky—and throws off the "skin" of conformity. She notes that while people of all races gawked at her, young African Americans in particular "would stare at me and laugh at me and then say something insulting" (7). The assumption, perhaps, was not that she was trying to discard a skin that was readable as Kincaid-the-Respectable, Kincaid-the-daughter-of-Annie-Drew, but specifically attempting to put on a skin that was legible as "white" (as bleached hair and gold brows would likely have been interpreted during the Black Power Movement).

Because Kincaid had been raised in a society where she was the racial majority, her perceptions of race were quite different from the African American subjects she encountered in New York. Skin color was only one of many features by which people were judged. She asserts:

> I had grown up in a place where many people were young and black and men and women, and I had been stared at and laughed at, and insulting things had been said to me: I was too tall, I was too thin, I was very smart; my clothes had never fit properly there, I was flat-chested; my hair would not stay in place. And so when the young black men and women [in the United States] would stare at me and make fun of me, I was used to it, I did not feel threatened by it at all, it was familiar. (7)

Like Xuela Richardson, her protagonist from *The Autobiography of My Mother* (1996), who "refuse[s] to belong to a race" (226), Kincaid refused to be locked into traditional conceptualizations of cultural identity.

When, during the same time period, she was wondering to a friend how she could possibly have been denied a job at the magazine *Mademoiselle*, he responded, "[D]idn't [you] know that they never hired black girls? And I thought, But how was I to know that I was a black girl? I never pass myself in a corridor and say, I am a black girl. I never see myself coming toward me as I come round a bend and say, There is that black girl coming toward me. How was I really to know such a thing?" ("Putting" 100). Kincaid presents skin (color) as a hindrance to progress in U.S. society, but she also points out that it does not preoccupy her vision of herself. She suggests that Du Bois's concept of double consciousness is not a universal outlook but limited to the experiences of those raised as minorities.

Kincaid's rejection of conventional definitions can also be seen in her depictions of the female-gendered body, and she uses the soucouyant to accomplish this task. Just as the narrator of *At the Bottom of the River* crosses and recrosses the boundary between child and adult, symbolically erasing it, the line between "real" and "magical" evaporates in the scene that reveals an explicit reference to a soucouyant figure. Men see "a woman who has removed her skin and is on her way to drink the blood of her secret enemies. It is a woman who has left her skin in a corner of a house made of wood. It is a woman who is reasonable and admires honeybees in the hibiscus. It is a woman who, as a joke, brays like a donkey when he is thirsty" (6–7). This soucouyant appears not in the context of a nightmare or fantastic imagination but instead as a part of the everyday realities of these men. She is an ordinary woman, who appreciates the beauty of ordinary things in nature, like bees and flowers, and who does ordinary things like joke and banter with her neighbors. She is a threat only to her enemies, not to every living inhabitant of her community, and her "reasonable" nature suggests that her antagonism toward these enemies is well-founded. This collection of details disconnects the soucouyant from the realm of the purely supernatural and grounds her in understandable human emotions. Jana Evans Braziel concurs, explaining the way that Kincaid's narrative "rusefully, and even guilefully, confound[s] these borders—those of self-other or selves-others—deconstructing colonialist notions of subjectivity and objectivity. [. . .] Here matter and spirit are interpenetrating" (63). And thus while Kincaid has eliminated the demonic threat from her soucouyant, she has not eliminated the vampire's metaphorical fangs. This woman is not angelic and pure or a ghostly, immaterial being; she still has the potential to cause physical harm. In a time when a woman's social acceptance is not typically associated with strength—unless exhibited while fighting for her children or "her man"—Kincaid creates a soucouyant who is integrated into a community in all of the complicated ways that a woman can be. She is both "good" and "bad": quietly vengeful and laughing loudly, aesthetically sensitive and prone to reason.

In the more realistic genre of memoir, Philadelphia writer Lorene Cary also refers to soucouyants and their ability to provisionally abandon their skins. The writer opens *Black Ice* (1992) with three epigraphs, the last of which reads: "Skin, skin, ya na know me?" The line is found repeatedly in stories from around the diaspora: Herskovits and Herskovits, for example, cite "'Kin, 'kin, you no know me? / 'Kin, 'kin, you no hear what you mistress say? / 'Kin, 'kin, come off, come off!" (*Trinidad Village* 254). Zora Neale Hurston's "De Witch Woman" features a hag crying out, "Skin, oh skin, old skin, don't you know me?" (64). David Chariandy's epigraph reads "Old skin, 'kin, 'kin, / You na know me," and, as Nalo Hopkinson states about the title of her short story collection: "when the soucouyant can't get back into her skin [. . .] she says to the skin, 'Kin-kin, you don't know me?'" (Johnston 207). With this allusion to the soucouyant, Cary claims the folk figure as an important yet subtle trope for the story; noticeably, however, it is the soucouyant in a moment of crisis—her skin will not stay on her body—and not in a moment of power or predation.

At the formerly all-White, all-male environs of St. Paul's boarding school in New Hampshire, the teenaged narrator of *Black Ice* tells herself her Barbadian great-grandfather's "old stories" for comfort. In one of these tales, a man almost gets lured out of his house by the voice of a woman who claims to need an escort home.

> We never said exactly what was outside the door, but I had no doubt that it was a witch, some vengeful, rapacious spirit. *I imagined that the spirits were always women*, like the one who slipped out of her skin at night and flew around in the darkness. She left her skin draped over a chair by the window, as easily as others leave their lingerie. When her husband realized what was happening, he went to an old woman in the village and asked how he could keep his wife home with him, *where she belonged.* (130, emphasis added)

A Caribbean cultural heritage and memories of loved ones provide emotional support for the young Lorene, but they also condition her with patriarchal ideals. She has already internalized messages about the evils of wandering women-spirits, readily applicable to the behavior of roving women who do not stay at home where they "belong." In addition to conjuring up images of belonging and fitting in, the phrase "where she belonged" simultaneously identifies the homespace as the only place women should be. Lorene, like the old woman in the tale who is sought for her wisdom but also therefore complicit in preventing the soucouyant's future flights, conforms to social mores in her initial refusal to question the need of husbands to keep wives bound to the home.

When confronted by recollections of the actual women in her family, however, the narrator begins to recognize how the spaces and roles in which these women are assumed to fit can be stifling. The soucouyant subtly transforms into a figure of kinesis and freedom:

[A]s surely as they worked and worried to get a man and then build a home . . . so too did they seem eager to fly away. I had no doubt that *if they could have*, my mother and her sisters and my grand-mother would have left their skins draped like pantyhose over their unsatisfactory furniture and floated up above us all: the men who never failed to oppress them; the children who'd ruined their beau-tiful bodies; and the boxy little houses fit to bursting with the left-over smells of their cooking and the smoke from their cigarettes, curling up and hanging just above our heads like ambition. (131, emphasis added)

Lorene discerns the unmet needs and unsatisfied desires of her female relatives; in contrast to the notion of women who are happy to be ever-giving, regret surrounds these women as they perform their female duties. To follow the metaphor of the soucouyant, these women long, if not to take blood, surely not simply to give it. Significantly, the children described in the passage, although loved, have ruined their mothers' bodies, not made them whole and fulfilled. And to counter the notion of the home as site of belonging, the narrator perceives the stability sig-nified by the squat "boxy little houses"—at one time struggled for—as binding and restrictive: women, smoke, and cooking smells all yearn to burst free.

Determined not to be caught in the same trap of enforced domesticity, the narrator eventually concludes, "Pap was wrong. His stories taught me fear and shame and secrecy" (236). Rather than permanently silenc-ing and rejecting this identity, as those who taught her the tales might expect, she fully embraces it. In a veiled reference, she models herself on the soucouyant: "I shushed the greedy girl within. Starved for some special notice, she stood inside my skin jumping up and down" (216).

Like the soucouyant, Lorene seems able to divest herself of her skin; she is greedy and hungry, but for attention rather than blood. Cary builds upon the image further at the text's conclusion:

St. Paul's would keep me inside my black skin, that fine, fine membrane that was meant to hold in my blood, not bind up my soul. The stories show me the way out. I must tell my daughter that. I must do it so she'll know. Then I can go to my own room where the window is open to the black night and fly out at dark to rub against the open sky. . . . I must leave my mother and father. I must leave my husband and daughter sleeping. They will come, too, if they want. The night can carry us all. . . . Others are there already, calling, welcoming. At dawn I will alight on my sill. I can slip into my smooth black skin. It will welcome me. . . . The skin will grow wrinkled as the nights come and go, but my husband will not salt it. My skin will know me, and I will not have to fear my skin. (237)

Like the mother in "Nineteen Thirty-Seven," the adult Lorene will bestow the legacy of proud flight upon her daughter. Rather than participate in Ottley's view of a cursed "long line of ancestral soucouyants," she celebrates this heritage to be passed onto future generations. Mother and daughter will join a community of soucouyants, "there already, calling, welcoming." Cary effectively neutralizes the idea of the soucouyant as a completely alien and isolated force; her soucouyant is one of many, not one against many. This image has profound implications for women's collective agency. While one person alone might be afraid to act or unable to effect substantial changes in her environment, individuals joined together can empower themselves and each other, moving together toward social transformation.

Many citizens of the Americas would identify racism as a disabling social ill that requires healing; unlike most of the other literary examples cited in this book, the passage from Cary's memoirs explicitly incorporates notions of race. The narrator's description of her "fine, fine membrane" conveys the fragile delicacy of her black skin—her racial identity as well as the organ itself—and its solidly admirable qualities. At the same time that she praises it, however, she expresses the desire to find a "way out" of this covering that potentially binds her soul. Like Kincaid's narrator from *At the Bottom of the River*, whose skin had "blackened and cracked and fallen away" while her "new impregnable carapace had taken full hold," the physical body—particularly the black[ened] body—appears as an obstacle to the achievement of true liberty.

What does it mean to want to leave the "blackness" behind? The answer is not the same for all writers. Kincaid's narrator revels in the "impregnable" form that remains once her "blackened" skin falls away, giving rise to troubling racial considerations. The text suggests that black skin is pregnable and synonymous with vulnerability and weakness. By extension, Kincaid's image proposes that safety and its associated comforts and happiness are incompatible with being a subject of African descent. Cary comments on this belief as held by the new African American students from predominantly Black neighborhoods who visit the exclusive St. Paul School: "I could see fear in their eyes as surely as John must have seen it in mine [when I first came to the formerly all-White school]. . . . What did it mean to be black in America if it did not mean handicap, shame, or denial?" (229). She further laments the tragic ways in which the Black community has internalized and subsequently perpetuates society's suggestions of Black inferiority: "[W]hile black intellectuals debate the impact of the 1960s on black self-image, people on my street still say a baby looks like a monkey if she's too dark" (233–34).

Therefore, when Cary refers to St. Paul's keeping her inside her black skin, she is critiquing the racial interactions of the larger U.S., circum-Caribbean, and other African diasporic societies as well. Just as she refuses to be bound to the domestic space, she also rejects being confined by dominant notions of Blackness. Mostly overtly, she repudiates the constrictive racial stereotypes—tokenism and exoticism not to be overlooked—of the privileged White students (and teachers) who read her solely through her black skin. She employs the tale of the soucouyant for strength and inspiration to move beyond this superficial focus on color: "I was given [the story] to plait into my story, to use, to give me the strength to take off my skin and stand naked and unafraid in the night, to touch other souls in the night" (237). In contrast to Kincaid's narrator, who relishes the loss of skin because it allows her a new invulnerable surface, Cary values the loss of her outer casing because it allows her certain intimacy; she suggests that only through this heightened vulnerability, emphasized in her nakedness, can true understanding be achieved. Cary thus transforms the bloodsucking activities of the soucouyant into a powerful act of connection between souls.

One could not interpret Cary's desire to escape her black skin as a rejection of her racial identity and cultural heritage or an acceptance of notions of Black inferiority (and, by default, White superiority); she always returns to it at dawn, slipping into its smooth blackness, and it welcomes her. The site of reconnection is clearly a positive one. In distinct contrast, the main character in Nalo Hopkinson's short story "A Habit of Waste" from the collection *Skin Folk* (2001) is never able to achieve this level of comfort in her skin; she literally discards her physical shell with its conventionally "Black" features in order to fit European standards of beauty.

Cynthia—the daughter of African Trinidad immigrants living in Canada—saves up for five years to purchase a slim, white body with "flippy blond hair" (187). She is astonished one day to see a woman "wearing the body I used to have! [. . .] same full, tarty-looking lips; same fat thighs, [. . .] same outsize ass" (183). She is disgusted by the woman's choice to let her hair go natural; she is confused by her obvious pride in her appearance and by the confidence of her gait. The protagonist also notices a particular "glow" to the woman's skin. Soucouyant imagery is apparent through many of the stories in the collection, and "Waste" is no exception; additionally, rather than depict a demonic, skin-shedding blood drinker, Hopkinson casts the woman who has taken up the black outer covering and now glows with racial and gender pride—much like the traditional soucouyant glows when she travels as a globe of flame—in an extremely positive light. Interestingly, Cynthia's racial self-hatred, distress over her body image, and Eurocentric assumptions and stereotypes shift over the course of the story so that when she is attacked by a mugger and bites down on his hand, drawing blood, she, too, is rendered as an empowered soucouyant character rather than a predatory vampire. Monstrosity in this piece of speculative fiction, as in so many of the other texts explored in *The Things That Fly in the Night*, lies in the hands of the larger dominant culture—the one that perpetuates certain images of beauty and success. Hopkinson takes her epigraph for the story from a work written by her father, Slade Hopkinson, who condemns "the latitudes of ex-colonised"—places where "degradation [is] still unmollified" and "mayhem [is] committed on the personality, / and everywhere the wrecked or scuttled mind" (183).

In much of her fictional and critical writing, Toni Morrison has mourned the waning of oral forms, such as folktales, in contemporary African American culture: "We don't live in places where we can hear those stories anymore; parents don't sit around and tell their children those classical, mythological archetypal stories that we heard years ago" ("Rootedness" 340). She attempts to revive some of these myths in her fiction: the flying

Africans in *Song of Solomon;* revamped Aesop's fables in the *Who's Got Game?* children's picture books; the Police-heads in *Love:*

> *People in Up Beach, where I'm from, used to tell about some crea-*
> *tures called Police-heads—dirty things with big hats who shoot up*
> *out of the ocean to harm loose women and eat disobedient children.*
> [. . .] *Like that woman who furrowed in the sand with her neighbor's*
> *husband and the very next day suffered a stroke at the cannery.* (5,
> emphasis in original)

Like the soucouyant, the abject figure of the Police-head is exclusively female; she reveals fear of the female body hovering on the border between life and death. Outwardly, however, she serves as a coercive social force for the entire community—a force meant to remedy and prevent certain behaviors. Much more explicit in Morrison's text than in the soucouyant folklore is the way that the stories are meant to control *female* unruliness. The adulterous husband is not struck down by the Police-heads: only the woman who "furrow[s] in the sand" with him. The narrator, L, initially opines, "you'd think women up to no good and mule-headed children wouldn't need further warning, because they knew there was no escape: fast as lightning, nighttime or day, Police-heads could blast up out of the waves to punish wayward women or swallow the misbehaving young" (6). Men who are "up to no good," stubbornly persistent in breaking the rules—the ones they themselves have created—"wayward," or "misbehaving" need have no fear. By the end of the section, however, L's conservative voice shifts to acknowledge the ways that the tale is "trash," a "story made up to scare wicked females and correct unruly children" (10). She, like Morrison, craves "Something better. Like a story that shows how brazen women can take a good man down" (10). Her words set up the rest of the novel as a type of revisionary narrative: one, like the contemporary soucouyant stories, meant to empower women rather than demonize them or configure them as resigned victims.

In *Paradise,* Morrison incorporates vampire imagery with a delicate touch. Consolata's distress after being abandoned by her lover, Deacon Morgan, leads her to turn to isolation, sleep, and alcohol. Noting that her cot in the Convent's cellar is "belowground" (221) and her sleeping patterns are irregular, the narrator suggests a "sluglike existence" (221), but Connie simultaneously evokes the conventional vampire: "in a space tight enough for a coffin," she is "devoted to the dark" (221). She has long "lost the ability to bear light" (242). She is also "long removed from appetites" for food or human contact (221) and participates in "raising the dead" (242) when she supernaturally resurrects the body of Deacon and Soane's son, Scout, and repeatedly revives Mary Magna. The phrasing carries Judeo-Christian connotations but also resounds with imagery of vampires creating legions of the "undead" or "living dead."

As a nine-year-old child, Consolata was taken from Brazil by six U.S. nuns, the Sisters Devoted to Indian and Colored People. Sister Mary Magna is captivated by Connie—a young girl with green eyes and "tea-colored hair" (223), traits that contemporary readers might associate only with Europeans or light-complexioned Latin American subjects, but Morrison firmly establishes these as part of the diversity of features found in the African diaspora. Connie has "untamable hair" (301) and "smoky, sundown skin" (223) that is lighter than Deacon's "darker than the darkness" coloring (229) but still approaches the range of evening and nighttime shades. More important, perhaps, she feels deep nostalgia for the Black Brazilian community of her youth when she witnesses a celebration of the all-Black residents of the newly established town of Ruby:

> As Consolata watched that reckless joy, she [. . . . had] a memory of just such skin and just such men, dancing with women in the streets to music beating like an infuriated heart, torsos still, hips making small circles above legs moving so rapidly it was fruitless to decipher how such ease as possible. [. . .] And although [these people] were living here in a hamlet, not in a loud city full of glittering black people, Consolata knew she knew them. (226)

As an outsider to the bloodlines of the nine original families or the fifteen "New Fathers," as a non-"8-rock" subject whose racial mixture is evident in her eye and hair color, and as a woman "uncontrolled" by father, son, brother, husband, or priest, Connie represents a threat to Ruby's male establishment. As critic Sue-Ellen Case describes of anxieties over vampires, racial purity, and inheritance in the U.S. and European Golden Ages: "Blood, in the dominant discourse which was writing racial laws along with [. . . the Golden Age] tragedies, is geneaology, the blood right to money; and blood/money is the realm of racial purity and pure heterosexuality" (385). *Paradise* explores these issues in an all-Black, staunchly middle-class town. Instead of revising conventional laws and rules, however, the Black men of Ruby merely replicate the hegemony.

The historic relationship between European, West African, and New World traditions feeds into all of Morrison's mythmaking. A relational, archipelagic logic appears in her use of the Black female vampire—it is not exclusive to the States or Europe but extends outward in a circum-Caribbean, U.S., Canadian, and larger Americas network. Connected by histories of colonial exploitation, brutality, confinement to spaces based on one's "race," and the continuing need to wrestle with issues that find their source in colonial racial formation, people feature the Black vampire-woman as a way to probe these concepts. In this way, Connie's potential for corruption—whether that "pollution" occurs in the altered minds and natures of Ruby's submissive townswomen or in the "pure" black blood that the older generation has struggled to maintain—echoes the threat of the soucouyant and peaks during her affair with Deacon.

Morrison depicts Connie's infatuation with Deek as possessing "an edible quality" (228). When their rendezvous become irregular, her dulled sense of "hunger" gets sharpened (236). She sees the end of their relationship as "her big mistake": during a postcoital conversation, she bites his lip, draws and licks the blood, and hums with pleasure. "He'd sucked air sharply. Said, 'Don't ever do that again.' But his eyes, first startled, then revolted, had said the rest of what she should have known right away. Clover, cinnamon, soft old linen—who would chance pears and a wall of prisoner wine with a woman bent on eating him like a meal?" (239). While cannibalism might come to mind with the language of "eating" and a "meal," it is Connie's drawing and consuming of blood that repulses Deacon. For thirty years, she and the White nuns lived on the cusp of the town without incident. While Ruby's patriotic veterans of World War II, who served in Europe, Guam, and Inchon (17), might have considered her a foreigner who pierced the borders of the nation, she had not invaded the town limits. After the affair with Deek, however, she becomes a tellingly fanged "snake" that must get "beat out" of the townsmen's created Eden (17). She has not simply engaged in the sexual exchange of bodily fluids but of blood—that archetypal fluid representing not just Deacon's life force but his familial line of inheritance and legacy, his race, and the racial purity—that is, superiority—that he and his neighbors claim as founders and residents of Ruby. In this penetration of the skin and consumption of blood, Connie acts according to Donna Haraway's descriptions of the literary vampire: she disrupts and transforms distinct racial categories through "passages of substance"; she "drinks and infuses blood in a paradigmatic act of infecting whatever poses as pure" and in this way "promises and threatens racial and sexual mixing" (*Modest Witness* 214).

Morrison critiques the obsession with purity and the process by which the community maintains its bloodlines by alluding to the fact that an incestuous pool of genes might have caused the illnesses of Jeff and Sweetie's children: Jeff Fleetwood and his father, Arnold, participate in the massacre of the Convent women because "well, they'd been wanting to blame somebody for Sweetie's children for a long time. Maybe it was the midwife's fault, maybe it was the government's fault, but the midwife could only be disemployed and the government was not accountable. [. . . Nothing could] keep them from finding fault anywhere but in their own blood" (277). Where Haraway asks, "Why should our bodies end at the skin [. . .]?" ("Manifesto" 220), considering the flexibility of definitions of self that allow for the blending of the human consciousness with a technological one—of organism with machine—Morrison creates in Connie a wish for a different type of blending of identities: one grounded in the flexibility of racial and nationalistic categories but equally as demanding of flexibility. In the days that follow the "big mistake," Consolata prays, "Dear Lord, I didn't want to eat him. I just wanted to go home" (240). She has transferred the lessons of her Catholic upbringing to her circumstances as an isolated alien in the United States: instead of seeking an eternal home in Heaven through the body and blood of Communion, she seeks not the national home of Brazil but a racial home of the diaspora through the body and blood of Deacon Morgan. The "loud city full of glittering black people" is not available to her, however, and the men of Ruby hunt her down, penetrating her allegedly wicked and satanic space in order to wipe out Connie and the community of women who have found safety, healing, and peace there. The women all realize, through Connie's words, the value of *themselves*, especially selves balanced in physical body and spiritual being:

> My child body, hurt and soil, leaps into the arms of a woman [Mary Magna] who teach me my body is nothing my spirit everything. I agreed her until I met another. My flesh is so hungry for itself it ate him. [. . . The spirit] is true, like bones, It is good, like bones. One sweet, one bitter. [. . .] Hear me, listen. Never break them in two. (263)

By the end of the novel, the image of Connie with "blood near her lips" (289) might initially recall the image of the predatory vampire, but Morrison goes to great lengths to shift the monstrous traits to the nine men. They are the predators who have infiltrated and polluted the sacred space by shedding blood. Consolata, on the other hand, is imbued with a mystical beauty. She does not look directly at the hunters but rather smiles at something "high above the heads of the men"—quite suggestive of the pose of an iconic saint. The blood on her face, which has come from cradling and trying to resurrect the woman shot in the foyer, "takes [Deek's] breath away." He looks into Connie's eyes and recognizes "what has been drained from them and from himself as well." The true vampiric force—the one that has sapped the "green springtime" (301), the innocence, from Consolata's eyes—encompasses the contortions made to perpetuate the original forefathers' search for safety, prosperity, holiness, and pride in their achievements and racialized selves. Deacon recognizes that these contortions have turned him into "the kind of man who set himself up to judge, rout and even destroy the needy, the defenseless, the different" (302)—all traits, ironically, of the stereotypical vampire.

Other scholars have connected the vampire figure to Morrison's writing. Carl Plasa, for example, reads Beloved as a succubus who drains Paul D of his semen, specifically evoking African American folklore and the "shape-shifting witches who 'ride' their terrified victims in the night" (74). Plasa also attributes a vampiric identity to Beloved in that she saps Sethe of her physical strength and actual bodily mass, and "feeds off" various characters' memories and psychological vitality. Like the nephews of schoolteacher who suck Sethe's milk against her will, Beloved "sucks Sethe dry" (78) when she returns from the dead and appears to take a great deal of pleasure in doing so.

Plasa links vampirism to the institution of slavery as well. Likewise, Cedric Gael Bryant asserts that Beloved specifically appropriates Stoker's Dracula "to Gothicize the horrors of slavery" (546)—he links the uninvited entry of schoolteacher and the slave hunters into the woodshed to the violation of conventional vampires, even though it is Sethe who slices through her crawling already? baby's neck. Bryant suggests that the true monsters are the White men who perpetuate a system of enslavement and an ideology that omits people of African descent from eighteenth- and nineteenth-century definitions of humanity.

As I discussed in Chapter 5, Octavia Butler "queers" sexuality in the novel Fledgling; she simultaneously encourages readers to consider the social meanings of skin. Even though Butler uses conventional vampire tropes and not specific references to the molting Old Hag or soucouyant—skin gets intricately tied to blood and ideas of "racial" purity. Her vampire narrative functions as another crucial node in the circum-Caribbean network of soucouyant stories: the Black female protagonist occupies "the demonic ground" left open by the absent Sycorax and renders it a site of anticolonial resistance.

When protagonist Shori Matthews initially awakens from a coma-like state at the start of the narrative, one of the first things she notices is her skin: "My skin was scarred, badly scarred over every part of my body that I could see. The scars were broad, creased, shiny patches of mottled red-brown skin" (10). In this scene of symbolic rebirth, one skin begins to grow after another has been destroyed—significantly by a group of "pureblood" vampires among the ultra-pale Ina who despise the protagonist for her melanin-rich complexion, one clear sign of her physical difference from them, as well as for her "mixed" blood—she is the result of a genetic experiment bonding Ina and human DNA. In the original description, however, the reader knows none of this; regardless, attention is immediately brought to the skin, and throughout the novel Butler clearly identifies the complexion of each character, not merely for the reader's imaginative process but to allude to issues of social class, power, individual dynamics, and historical conflict.

Joel Harrison, for example, is identified as "as dark skinned as I was and [with] hair like mine" (160); Linda Higuera is "a nervous, muscular brown woman, at least six feet tall" (166); Martin is "a man so brown he was almost black" (166); Shori's Ina father, Iosif, is "blond and [. . .] as white as the pages of Wright's books" (67); Joan and Margaret Braithwaite, Ina females, are described as "very pale women" with hair "twisted and pinned up neatly on their heads. One was brown-haired— the first brown-haired Ina I'd seen" (216). The author never resorts to easy racial labels: Shori starts to protest at one point that she is "brown, not black" (37); Wright Hamlin is not "white" but rather "a young man, pale-skinned, brown-haired, broad, and tall" (13). The wording might initially suggest that Ina do not distinguish humans by race or process all the social and cultural baggage of these categories; rather, they only note the color of one's skin in a sequence of traits like height and weight. Later in the novel, however, when one Ina insists that "Ina weren't rac- ists" because Ina "looked for congenial human symbionts wherever they happened to be, without regard for anything but personal appeal" (154), the statement rings false: attacks have been made on Shori as the only brown-skinned Ina, and the scientists who could replicate their genetic experiment have been massacred. The reason that race does not matter among the Ina is not because they lack prejudice but instead because all human symbionts are under Ina control, without equal social status in Ina communities.

Butler employs the pallor of the skin found in much conventional vampire literature to signify the creatures' identity as "the living dead," but she uses the feature to comment on racial dynamics in contemporary human society. A "tall, ultrapale, lean, wiry people," the Ina have been discriminated against in many of the communities in which they've lived; as a hypervisible Other, many were driven out of their homes or even killed by suspicious neighbors (136). Their experience thus parallels that of many racial "minorities" in the United States and around the world. Still, many of the Ina are outraged by Shori's presence because *she* is visibly Other: Her complexion makes clear that she is of African descent, and her small size reveals to the Ina that she is half human. She represents the inferiority that many Ina attribute to humans, who "breed and breed and breed[. . . .] Their lives are brief, and without us, riddled with disease and violence" (298). The elitist Ina animalize humans in much the same way White Americans and Europeans constructed—and still construct, if one thinks of mainstream discourse about a racialized urban core and inner-city poverty—African peoples. And issues of blood quantum and anxieties over miscegenation become explicit when Shori discovers that the Ina who opposed the genetic experiments by which she was created "thought mixing human genes with ours [Ina] would weaken us" (231).

The racial implications of Butler's novel become even more overt when Shori interviews Victor Colon, one of the mercenaries hired to murder her and her family. He reveals that his employers repeatedly called Shori "dirty little nigger bitch" and "Goddamn mongrel cub" (179). Colon states: "Ina mixed with some human or maybe human mixed with a little Ina. That's not supposed to happen. Not ever. Couldn't let you and you . . . your kind . . . your family . . . breed" (179). The issue of "pure" versus "impure" when it comes to evaluating blood and race arises, but blood as a constantly shifting metaphor is quickly brought to the surface when Victor apologizes for letting the slurs slip through his mouth: "[My sister's] kids are darker than you, and *they're my blood*, too. I would kick the crap out of anyone who called them what I called you" (180, emphasis added).

While some of the Ina look upon Shori with distaste and go to radical ends to ensure the purity of their kind, others, like Daniel Gordon and his family, are eager to join with Shori and her sisters because of her African coloring. In contrast to scenes in the work of Jamaica Kincaid, Lorene Cary, and Marie-Célie Agnant, a dark complexion in Butler's novel becomes a supremely desirable attribute. There is no wish to cast off this outer covering; it is necessary for the protagonist's individual survival, the survival of her symbiont family, and the survival of the Ina species overall. Margaret Braithwaite concurs: "Child, do you understand your uniqueness, your great value? [. . .] You are a treasure" (220).

Notably, Shori's amnesia and returning memory serve as another way to identify her as a member of the African diaspora: Butler constructs this identity as more than just melanin and the color of the skin. Thinking about the massacre of her family, Shori wonders:

> What about my mothers and sisters, my father and brothers? What about my memory?
>
> They were all gone. The person I had been was gone. I couldn't bring anyone back, not even myself. I could only learn what I could about the Ina, about my families. I would restore what could be restored. The Matthews family could begin again. The Petrescu family could not. (316)

These lines resonate with the experiences of Africans in the Americas—people subject to the cultural devastation of the slave trade as well as its physical brutalities. Shori also feels extremely uncomfortable when she realizes she must use her Ina powers to wipe out the memories of the special operations team sent to destroy her and her families (208). This discomfort is logical not only given her personal experience with amnesia and the ensuing turmoil but also given her position as a member of the African diaspora whose ancestors were forced to disremember cultural practices, religious beliefs, languages, and personal pasts. Butler suggests there is no return to "origins"—the legacy is one of loss, although also one of promise. The same might be said of the protagonist's name, taken from the designation for an East African nightingale. It gets temporarily "lost" during Shori's amnesia but eventually connects her to her African American birth mother.

When the Ina Council of Judgment finds the Silk family guilty of massacring Shori's family and attempting to murder her, the chosen punishment forces them to live out the legacy of destroyed family that they initially visited upon the protagonist. Interestingly, it also evokes the racialized discourse of bloodline. Because the sentence is "the dissolution of the Silk family" (305), the five single sons are to be adopted by five different families in five different countries, breaking apart bonds of proximity, parental influence, affection, and lineage—the "bloodline" that they struggled so hard to keep pure and pass on as the inheritance of future generations. Butler effectively poses the question of what would have happened if the slave master's family could be pulled apart in the same way that enslaved families were.

Butler also complicates categories of race by creating a protagonist who is "biracial"—both in terms of her Ina and human parentage and because of her "White" father and Black mother. The Ina are a white-skinned monoracial group before Shori is created by her eldermothers; even those who live on the continent of Africa do not have brown complexions. Shori is identified as a "celebrity" because of her engineered features—"People traveled from South America, Europe, Asia, and Africa to see you and to understand what our mothers had done" (84)—a somewhat alarming image in its resemblance to scenes of White Europeans flocking to see the Venus Hottentot; nevertheless, in this speculative world, brown skin and mixed blood are to be celebrated, not repulsed.

Even though Preston Gordon is one of Shori's supporters, he advises her: "You, more than anyone, must show that you can follow our ways. You must not give the people who have decided to be your enemies any advantage. You must seem more Ina that [sic] they" (272). Butler points to the contemporary racial discourse that, while changing and becoming more progressive in places like official documents, is often still imagined by many as a series of discrete categories. In other words, Preston intimates that Shori will not be allowed to act as an individual making her own way in the world; she must prove her belonging, her worthiness, and her authenticity to one singular group.

While Butler seems to urge readers to recognize the falseness of this binary construction of Ina *or* human—and by extension, White *or* non-White—sometimes the lesson falls flat. For example, it is clear that the Ina Katharine, an antagonist, holds views with which readers should not agree. During the trial, she taunts Shori: "you are neither Ina nor human. Your scent, your reactions, your facial expressions, your body language—none of it is right. You say your symbiont has just died. If that were so, you would be prostrate. You would not be able to sit here telling lies and arguing. True Ina know the pain of losing a symbiont. We are Ina. You are nothing!" (278) Rather than allowing the protagonist to claim both sides of her identity, Katharine denies her either—she identifies her as "nothing." However, at the end of novel, Shori must live as Ina and disguise her true identity from the human world. She cannot be "both-and"; for practicality's sake, she must be "either/or."

One of the most disturbing ways that Shori fits in with her Ina relatives is in her conception of her symbionts as her property. She says to Celia: "I inherited you [. . .] from my father's family. You're mine" (130);

she also tells Joel, "You're mine" (290); she gets annoyed with the Gordon men for "scaring *my* symbionts" (150, emphasis added). In each case, the implications are disconcerting: "be mine" is a phrase associated with true love, and Shori is trying to reassure Celia that she won't abandon her, but slavery, paternalistic ownership, and objectification are clearly evoked. Shori later confesses that "having [symbionts] scares me" (211), which suggests her discomfort with her role, and Joan Braithwaite explains a relationship that is more biologically and emotionally mutualistic than the economics of slavery: "We need our symbionts more than most of them know. We need not only their blood, but physical contact with them and emotional reassurance from them. Companionship. [. . .] We either weave ourselves a family of symbionts, or we die" (276). In this way, Butler continuously leaves the reader off balance, unable to find a clearly marked path and easy resolution. By destabilizing conventional boundaries, she encourages readers to question their validity. As many Butler scholars have noted (Wolmark, Sands, and others), the author typically worked to subvert clear-cut lines between human and alien, self and other.

In the early 1990s, Judith E. Johnson proposed about the surge in vampire writing by women:

Given all these various subtextual aspects of vampire stories, it becomes clearer why women writers have begun challenging the genre. If part of the current social project with which we are all (feminists and non-feminists alike) grappling is the redefinition of social structures to eliminate abuses of power based on race, sex, and unequal access to resources, the vampire novel, whose central metaphor contains our anxieties about these very issues, is a natural field for revisionary effort. (77)

Although racial metaphors are mentioned, Johnson focuses primarily on issues of sexuality, family, and mutual exchanges versus violent invasions; how much richer the discussion gets when one considers the vast number of new vampire stories written by people of the African diaspora, grappling with this part of their identity along with numerous others.[3]

I wonder, however, where the soucouyant's desire to abandon her outer membrane leaves those of us who cannot abandon our material skins. Similarly, the idea of a genetic experiment resulting in the privileging of brown complexions sounds fabulously empowering for subjects who have felt ostracized, disparaged, or scorned because of their non-white coloring, but the fetishization of brown skin is another stumbling block, as is the reality of adoption agencies and fertility clinics bombarded by requests for White, blue-eyed children. Current discourse in race theory identifies race as a social construction, but constructed or not, the category still functions as a prime determinant of social interactions. Therefore, in many of the narratives examined for this book, the intersection of the fantastic myth, speculative fiction, and real-life situations provides room for maneuvering around previously confining classifications, but it also creates the space for the trap of metaphor without substance. In other words, the soucouyant figure and other Black female vampires hold tremendous subversive potential for women of the African diaspora, but they do not, and cannot, provide answers to all questions of gender, sexuality, race, and class.

Conclusions

*Our salvation lies in our capacity to create new and more inclusive
mythologies, to move beyond the homeland myths of origin.*
—PATRICIA MOHAMMED

As I began writing these concluding remarks, I had the opportunity
to reread "The Goophered Grapevine," a short story by U.S. African
American writer Charles Chesnutt, first published in the collection *The
Conjure Woman* in 1899. The character of Aunt Peggy is described as a
woman who "rides folks" at night: a detail I did not recall when I first
read the narrative in my undergraduate American Literature survey
course. Besides being fascinating to me now as yet another example of
the soucouyant figure in African Americas cultures, I am struck by the
fact that rather than the conventional evil woman who is ostracized by
her neighbors, Peggy is portrayed by Chesnutt as a respected member
of her community. As a renowned conjure woman, she is consulted by
the racist White slave owner of the story as well as the people of African
descent who live on nearby plantations. Her freewoman's status seems
as integrally related to her social status as her uncanny abilities; and her
capacity to fly through the night works easily as a metaphor to reinforce
the impression of her physical and legal freedoms—her participation in
the local economy as an active, voluntarily mobile subject rather than a
piece of property. Thus, nearly a century before novels like Hopkinson's
Brown Girl in the Ring, Butler's *Fledgling*, and Oyeyemi's *White Is for
Witching*, readers get an inkling of the potential of a Black woman to
take control of her life and fate and not be condemned for that act; we see
an early example of what Katherine McKittrick describes as a site of both
"place and placelessness in tension," held there by both "imagination *and*
materiality" (106, emphasis added).

Positive instances like Chesnutt's are rare, however, until near the end of the twentieth century. More typically, those suspected and/or accused of being soucouyants are ostracized by their communities and sometimes physically attacked. For example, in the 1881 log of his experiences in British Guiana, the Reverend Charles Dance records some Guyanese communities' belief in bloodsucking "Witches, or Old Hags," who can remove their skins. He discerns that the superstition has real, physical consequences for old women, including being whipped with calabash switches or pelted with mud when the community's children suddenly fall ill: "The staunch defender of the old women of a certain village was the missionary residing there. The dames who [. . .] were fortunate enough to hobble to his house were safe, for the time, from the approaching *witch hunt*; for the whole sisterhood came in, at such times, for a share of the abuse" (Abrahams and Szwed 151). Throughout the African Americas, the consistent brutality of slavery—what folklorist J. D. Elder calls the "absolutism of plantation regulation" (*Song Games* 29)—and the equally oppressive authoritarianism of colonialism in the Caribbean make it clear why folktales that reject the grounded/immobile physical body and vilify flagrant individualism initially held such prominence and were sustained across many locations and eras. One can see the function of the soucouyant metaphor in conceptualizing an existing reality but also, as language theorists George Lakoff and Mark Johnson propose, evidence of "the power of metaphor to *create* a reality" (144, emphasis added): the metaphorical associations are not simply "a matter of mere language" but also "a means of structuring our conceptual system and the kinds of everyday activities"—like whipping old women or pelting them with mud—"we perform" (145).

Dance's account simultaneously reveals a contrast between the folk beliefs of the community and the Western beliefs of the Christian missionaries (including Dance)—beliefs that the Europeans interpreted as (inferior) superstition and ignorance in conflict with (superior) knowledge of "facts." However, if one considers the stories from the perspective of the community instead of from the perspective of the British narrator, faith in the supernatural—what historian Lawrence Levine calls "slave magic"—actually situates African Americas peoples in a position of power. There are beings, like the soucouyant, about whom White people do not know, cannot control, and cannot emulate.

Lacing my study of the soucouyant and other Black vampire figures as found in formal literature with the stories of everyday women that emerge from testimonies like Dance's can be difficult to justify in certain circles. I agree with the anthropologist Sidney Mintz, however, when he argues that casual tales from individuals allow "us to see how [one person's] experience and the wider world lie next to each other in the consciousness of the narrator. [. . .] If we are fortunate, it may help us get a notion of history that we can only rarely produce for ourselves" (17). How valuable it would be, for instance, to have firsthand testimony from Marie-Joseph Angélique, an enslaved woman in eighteenth-century Montreal, who allegedly burned down most of the city in an attempt to escape her captivity in April 1734. I posit Angélique as soucouyant figure par excellence. Historians have shown that enslaved people in New France were typically separated and worked alone in private residences instead of in groups; Angélique thus reflects the soucouyant's position of isolation and alienation from her community. The Code Noir cast slaves as "immovable property," to be "severely punished, or killed, for moving [by theft, revolt, or escape]" (McKittrick 112), indicating forbidden flight—flight that Angélique does take, much like the soucouyant, when she runs away during the commotion caused by the fire. That she allegedly flees with her White lover—an illegal union—loosely suggests the "perverse" sexuality and parasitic nature associated with the bloodsucking soucouyant and women of African descent; like the conventional soucouyant, she is physically and publicly tortured when captured. The burning of her corpse after she was hanged evokes images of the soucouyant's body ablaze in the night. Angélique's behavior, like the soucouyant's, can be interpreted as one of stunning resistance and rebellion; her fate simultaneously reveals the White community's insistence upon Black female criminality. She undergoes the "spectacular punishment of someone and something that is said not to exist" (McKittrick 117)—someone and something that engenders a great deal of fear. Following McKittrick's readings, I see Marie-Joseph Angélique as a Black woman with the potential for "reworking traditional geographies; [replacing] the politics of boundaries, nationhood, and race [. . .] with experiential and material diaspora geographies." Her story allows us to "insist that the [Americas'] nation-space is simultaneously occupied by and implicated in different forms of blackness" (104).

Thus, in this book, I identify the female figure of the bloodsucking, skin-shedding soucouyant as a central trope of literature of the Caribbean and the larger Caribbean diaspora but one that extends to other African-diasporic communities with no apparent Caribbean ties. We find a vast complex of narratives that has no geographical center but still might be called a network of the circum-Caribbean imaginary because of the female subject at the center: she corresponds strikingly with Sycorax—magical, voiceless, and thus potentially misunderstood, and of African descent—and highlights her past role and future prom- ise as a guiding cultural force instead of the conventional Caliban of much twentieth-century Caribbean writing. Published on the cusp of the twenty-first century, Margaret Cezair-Thompson's *The True His- tory of Paradise* (1999) reveals one such reference during a conversation between two Jamaican citizens:

> "I remember that play. We read it in fourth form. What was the name of that guy, the savage? Caliban, right? It was his island."
> Jean nods. (283)

And similarly, while Elizabeth Nunez revises and reclaims Caliban in *Prospero's Daughter* by transforming him into the articulate Carlos Codrington, his mother remains a negative figure and, if not completely silent, then a stifling force when she blackmails the adolescent Ariana—a remodeled Ariel figure. Thus when Peter Gardner, the Prospero char- acter, plunges off a cliff at the end of the novel, allowing his daughter, Virginia/Miranda, Carlos/Caliban, and Ariana/Ariel to attain a certain amount of freedom, Nunez successfully encourages readers to question the motives of the colonizers—in Shakespeare's play as well as in his- tory—but her book still leaves working-class Caribbean women of color symbolically voiceless. Ariana is the only major character not to have her own section in the narrative, and as a blue-eyed, white-skinned woman, Miss Sylvia/Nunez's Sycorax is given the social privilege of her race, complexion, and class.

The soucouyant, like Shakespeare's physically absent yet haunt- ingly present witch mother, inhabits what Sylvia Wynter identifies as "demonic"—yet productive—"ground" as she embodies a discourse *out- side* the established, masculinist speech of the colonial and postcolonial eras. And Sycorax is an even more theoretically empowering figure than Wynter's proposed "Caliban's Woman"—not only because age suggests wisdom but because age allows her to escape from the strictures of sex conjoined with reproduction and maternal duties and the presumed het- erosexuality that accompanies these obligations.

Although some readers might argue that Jewelle Gomez's Gilda, for example—a vampiric character who always remains firmly ensconced in her skin—bears no resemblance to the soucouyant in traditional stories, I also read these narratives together because of the indistinguishable roots/routes of African cultures during the transatlantic slave trade and subsequent migrations, back and forth along multiple paths: intricate passageways between places, ideological spaces, times. The network of references to the soucouyant and other Black female vampires is significant throughout African Americas literature, and even in recent work by an African British writer of Nigerian—not Caribbean—heritage, for its ability to reflect the processes of change *and* retention—what Herskovits and Herskovits called "the mechanisms of readaptation and reinterpretation" (*Trinidad Village* vi)—in all societies where people holding different customs and beliefs come into contact. The results are soucouyant, Old Hag, and vampire narratives that are not in complete resonance with African or European traditions or with each other.

Folklore, an incredibly mobile genre, travels easily across regional, national, and geographical boundaries as well as those of age, socioeconomic class, occupation, ethnicity, and language. Tales get redirected and remodeled to perform new purposes. My purpose is to analyze the features that remain consistent and persistent, as well as those that shift and get cast off like the soucouyant's skin. Thus, while the soucouyant as a folk character might be defined as an "in-betweener" who traverses numerous physical and social boundaries, much like the figures in Roger Abrahams's collection of (non-vampire) folktales from the African Americas, her position is never, like theirs, one of moral ambiguity or ethical flexibility. She does not cause commotions and "*patterned disordering*" (emphasis added) that evoke the audience's "pleasure of getting the action going through some kind of boundary-breaking revelation." She does not allow one to conclude that "the principle of vitality seems more important than that of right and wrong" (Abrahams, *Afro-American Folktales* 23). While the conventional soucouyant might reveal a fascination with a life on the margins of the community, she is simultaneously repulsive: she is a figure of abjection, with all of her behaviors clearly marked as horrifying, thanatophic, and worthy of severe punishment.

The pervasive incidence of the soucouyant figure in a variety of genres—calypso, legends, folk stories, novels, and poetry—as well as its figurative uses in writings from across the diaspora reveal threatening Black femininity: at times condemned and at times celebrated. In a sense, I have essentially collated an archive of Caribbean/diasporic and African/diasporic allegorical tales about womanhood, sexuality, mobility, Blackness, and subalternity. The conventional soucouyant story condemns old women who might embrace the possible freedoms that come with age (widowhood, physically and financially independent children, retirement from demanding labor, whether outside or inside the home); more recent versions applaud her ability to claim new spaces, dominate old ones, be flexible and mobile, satisfy and please her Self instead of only the relations to whom she feels beholden. And while la diablesse tales, with the seductiveness of the folk figure, more explicitly tantalize and quell audiences' zeal for examples of female sexual and antimaternal behavior, the soucouyant tales, with the soucouyant's piercing of her victim's body, read more clearly as a reference to sexual penetration, making the figure more immediately perilous and powerful than being lured away from family, community, and life by the vision of a beautiful woman.

The soucouyant figure, like most vampires, occupies a position of great potency in her ability to breach seemingly impenetrable borders, from locked doors and windows, to the gravitational pull of the earth, to the skin of her victims. However, in many ways, her greatest potential lies in her ability to shed her skin in a cosmos built upon arbitrary but rigid boundaries between races, genders, classes, and nations. She is unbound by these parameters.

"A project on Black female vampires? How fascinating! What are you looking at besides . . . " I winced in preparation: "*Queen of the Damned?*"

Dared I say it? I had not seen *Queen of the Damned*. Or read the book. I had not even read *Interview with a Vampire*.

"My project mainly explores representations of the vampire figure within literature of the African diaspora."

"Huh?"

"Writing by Black people from around the world."

"Oh."

Over the decade during which I conducted research for and wrote *The Things That Fly in the Night*, this conversation happened too many times for me to count. So when thinking about the overall implications of my book and the kinds of concluding remarks I might make, I decided to tackle the text that I had avoided over the years of labor on the project: the above-mentioned film, based on two novels from Anne Rice's Vampire Chronicles series: *The Vampire Lestat* (1985) and *Queen of the Damned* (1988).

Cultural critic Judith E. Johnson asserts that all vampire narratives involve "questions of social justice, power, exploitation, race, and class, as well as the more obvious gender conflict" (75). The tricky matter, however, is whether authors always acknowledge these inequities of power in ways that encourage readers to pursue these lines of inquiry. The situation is especially fraught when non-White subjects employ bodies of color in their creative works. Mimi Sheller outlines some of the difficulties of body, voice, and representation: "Feminist theorizations of embodiment offer a critique of the universal 'disembodied' (white male) subject who animates Western philosophies of freedom through the disavowal and abjection of grotesquely 'embodied' others (women and racialized others)" ("Work That Body" 346). What does one do with narratives about black bodies—particularly Black women's bodies—that can penetrate and control the bodies of others? That can slip out of the physical encapsulation of their skin? The issue of freedom is frequently at stake, but the consequences of seeking various forms of liberation come across quite differently, depending on the subjectivity of the writer.

Despite my hesitations against foregrounding narratives by authors from U.S. dominant culture in the last chapter of this book, I realized that the selected works provided an important platform for me to reiterate my argument: we are over one decade into the twenty-first century, and yet women of African descent are still relegated to the social, political, and artistic margins, or they are rendered by mainstream media in exceedingly stereotypical ways—even in narratives that purport to place them front and center. And thus, unlike the recent proliferation of texts by authors of the African diaspora that feature Black female vampires in ways that urge for complexity, mobility, sexual expressiveness, and cultural empowerment, the vampire stories generated by Western dominant cultures continue to depict Black women in ways that perpetuate notions of them as either nonexistent or sexually grasping, as well as physically, psychologically, and spiritually menacing.

In the video commentary accompanying the 2002 Warner Brothers DVD release of *Queen of the Damned*, film director Michael Rymer, producer Jorge Saralegui, and score composer Richard Gibbs describe their desire to rectify the absence of Black women on the silver screen by choosing a brown-skinned actor for the role of Akasha, the Egyptian queen of the movie's title. Although Anne Rice originally depicted *her* Queen Akasha as very pale in the novel, R&B singer Aaliyah (1979–2001) was selected to play the title role: the filmmakers believed this to be an important historical reflection of the realities of the African continent. However, as film scholar Dale Hudson observes, "Akasha's racial identity is reduced to visual style rather than a narrative focus of the film" (148)— once again, we remain at the level of skin, and phenotypes, rather than history or culture. Furthermore, the choice has distinct sexual implications in that many of the movie's scenes end up replicating disturbing images of the hypersexualized Black jezebel, which has been discussed throughout *The Things That Fly in the Night*.

Describing Queen Akasha to the newly created vampire Lestat as "the mother of all vampires," Maurius attributes great power to Akasha, as well as identifying her as the possessor of the "purest blood." The language echoes with ideas of Africa as the cradle of life. Interestingly, however, this Black woman's blood, some of which flows in the veins of every vampire in the contemporary setting of the film, ends up being a corrupting and destructive force rather than a life-giving one: Akasha has—and unreservedly uses—the ability to incinerate every vampire in her proximity because of this shared blood.

Further, Maurius explains that Akasha and her king, Enkil, "nearly drank this world dry when they ruled over Egypt." Both king and queen are represented as acutely dangerous to human beings, but Akasha is cast as definitely worse: Maurius warns that "She has no respect for anything except for the taste of blood—human and immortal alike." Since drinking blood is easily connected to sexual avarice, as in the case of the soucouyant who "did suck she own husban'" and then, "when she was not satisfied with what she got from him, [...] went elsewhere at night" (Herskovits and Herskovits, *Trinidad Village* 253), Maurius's line furthers the stereotype of the oversexed—and sexually treacherous—woman of African descent. Later in the film, she leaves a wake of corpses around a pool and on the beach. Her desire to live with Lestat "in the light," while potentially empowering for her as a Black woman, particularly in a relationship with a White man, ends up being a menace to all viewers: living unafraid, in the light versus the dark, entails dominating humans, whom she considers merely as food.

And while Enkil's greed diminished and he eventually lost his will to drink, Akasha's voracity seems limitless; she loses her thirst only when she loses her mate, suggesting a dependence on the male figure. When she is reawakened by Lestat, she rips out the king's throat, taking his blood and absorbing his power. She becomes "the most powerful" vampire, but her dominion is generated out of violence and murder and is derived from a male source.

Although the filmmakers anticipated creating a character for whom viewers could feel sympathy, the racialized narrative is hard to dismiss. In the contemporary time of the narrative, Akasha uses her highly sexualized brown body—replete with minimal clothing, a hip-swaying, stalking stride, and serpentine dance movements—to lure a blond male vampire toward her in the coven/nightclub before ripping his heart out and sinking her teeth into it. Whereas in the novel she only bites Lestat and begins their exchange of blood, in the film they share a rose-petal bath and a scene in a red-veiled bed, making the transfer of fluids explicitly sensual and sexual.

When Akasha pierces Lestat's chest—a clear image of female penetration—and then kisses him on the mouth with bloody lips, the scene lies in stark contrast to the interactions between Lestat and Jesse, his young White love interest. In the first instance, Jesse offers herself to Lestat by scratching her breast. Not only is the nipple unexposed, but the meager scratch barely lances the skin, bringing minimal blood to the surface. She is a "cleaner," purer candidate for his affections. Near the film's climax, Akasha orders Lestat to kill Jesse. He bites her in a moment of subterfuge, but, after Akasha's destruction, when Jesse must drink Lestat's blood to make her an immortal, the consumption takes place off-screen, and no blood is shown on Jesse's mouth. Again, the visualization of White woman as wholesome contrasts with that of Black woman as sexually perverse.

Additionally, Akasha is rendered as a Black woman who is destructive to conventional notions of family, while Maharet, her White counterpart, comes to represent family values, maternal sacrifice, and an accentuated Whiteness. During the scene of Akasha's annihilation, her skin *literally* darkens to black. She changes into a metallic black-colored statue, which disintegrates into swirling ash and sand. In another striking contrast, Maharet, who sacrifices herself by drinking the last drop of Akasha's blood, also turns into a statue but one made of a white-colored stone. These intersections of race, color, and complexion, of gender and sexuality, of blood, skin, and vampirism have powerful implications in contemporary society, where the mainstream media rarely challenge the associations between brown-skinned women of African descent and corruptive sexuality.

The trope of the soucouyant holds much potential for finding a way out of these seemingly inextricable correlations. Even though many people in today's society think only of Akasha when they hear the phrase "Black female vampire," there are myriad narratives that tackle these issues that are raised by the entire vampire genre. Thus, although critic Ingrid Thaler acknowledges the film version of *Queen of the Damned*, Octavia Butler's *Fledgling*, and Jewelle Gomez's *The Gilda Stories*, because she is not aware of the rich tradition of circum-Caribbean vampire lore she misses an opportunity for further analysis of the ways that the Black Atlantic imaginary revises and reworks conventional (European) fiction.

In her groundbreaking work on the evolution of posthuman ideology, Katherine Hayles characterizes our current era as one that privileges informational patterns, thought, and consciousness over bodily, material instantiations. For subjects of the African diaspora, however, the reality of experiences in the contemporary Americas reveals the physical body to be inescapable. Critic Gregory Jerome Hampton argues that African diasporic science fiction and fantasy writers—and Octavia Butler in particular—allow readers to think of the Body outside traditional definitions of the term; much mainstream vampire literature, however, still encourages the opposite: it foregrounds the material form, especially when it comes to Black women's bodies. These bodies come to be seen in simplistic ways—as highly sexualized; as consorts and physical mates; as physical and emotional vessels for others. Traditional soucouyant tales expose the anxiety generated by women who can escape the physical carapace of the skin, as well as the grounded body enclosed by the domestic space. Recent adaptations of these folk stories typically transform this apprehension into hope and inspiration: they present soucouyants and other Black female vampires as having bodies that extend "far beyond the flesh and bone" (Hampton xii): bodies that can transgress the physical but are not afraid to return to it; bodies that can unhinge fixed and confining markers of identity, such as gender, class, and race; bodies that encompass consciousness, desire, agency, and will. To close, I'd like to reprint a poem written by one of my graduate students, Crystal Boson, in the spring of 2011 after she completed my course on the vampire tradition in literature of the African diaspora. She provides an example of the next generation of writers and scholars to see potential in the trope of the soucouyant.

The Sorceress

skin, 'kin, 'kin
each night i will pull
you outside to the in
before i will jar you away
skin, 'kin, 'kin
so if they do salt you
the bad small white

grains will whisk off
skin, 'kin, 'kin
sit pretty all night
stretch you out in the morn
they don' know me

Notes

Introduction

1. For ease and simplicity, I will most often use the spelling/word "soucouyant" in this book to apply to the skin-shedding, blood-ingesting, female folk figure instead of listing the entire range of spellings (soucriant, sukugnan, etc.) and group of related terms (Ol' Hige/Higue, hag, volant, loogaroo, etc.).

2. For a comparable discussion of the mythic, castrating *vagina dentata*, see Phyllis Roth's assertion that in Bram Stoker's *Dracula* "it is not surprising that the central anxiety of the novel is the fear of the devouring woman" (419).

3. See also Lawrence Levine's historical study of how folk beliefs among enslaved populations in the United States served to invert conventionally depicted hierarchies of White and Black: "[In tales of the supernatural,] whites were neither omnipotent [n]or omniscient; there were things they did not know, forces they could not control, areas in which slaves could act with more knowledge and authority than their masters, ways in which the powers of the whites could be muted if not thwarted entirely" (73–74).

4. One exception to the rule can be found in a story that Gérard Besson shared with me in a 2014 telephone conversation; in it, a man is delighted to accompany two "ladies of the evening," even though they happen to be soucouyants. He ends up getting abandoned, naked, in a tall tree when dawn approaches.

5. Trinidadian linguist Maureen Warner-Lewis also mentions the *obayfo* from Akan lore (although with slightly altered spelling), which she links to the Trinidadian soucouyant because of its skin-shedding abilities. However, Warner-Lewis traces the term "soucouyant" to the Fula/Soninke words *sukunyadyo* (male) and *sukunya* (female), both of which mean "man-eating witch" (177). Novelist Maryse Condé's glossary to *I, Tituba, Black Witch of Salem* proposes that the word *soukougnan* literally means "bloodsucker" and comes from "the African language of the Tukulör people, where it designates a spirit that attacks humans and drinks their blood like a vampire"

(186). Others assert that the word is a French or patois derivation of the English verb "to suck"; Besson cites folk collector Ursula Raymond, who argued that the word is derived from "the French 'soupcon,' 'soupconner,' 'soupconnant,' that is, the suspecting of a person to be a witch" (Besson 1989, 32). The myriad possibilities reveal the difficulty of pinpointing sources.

6. For the application of this concept in linguistics, see the work of Peter Roberts, who suggests that although West African *and* separate British parallels can be attributed to many elements of Caribbean speech, "it is virtually impossible to demonstrate a direct line of descent of any feature" (125), and David Sutcliffe, who describes how certain elements of traditional culture and language can remain "very localized and resistant to outside influences" while others spread extensively, appropriated when they fit (35).

7. Belinda Edmondson's "Race, Privilege, and the Politics of (Re)Writing History" dissects how Shakespeare's Caliban and Jean Rhys's rewriting of Charlotte Brontë's Bertha serve as "the two gendered symbols of Caribbean independence and invisibility," with the Black woman's presence notably absent (184). For more on how the names Prospero, Caliban, Ariel, and Miranda have come to function as "interpretive touchstones" in postcolonial writing, see Thomas Cartelli, "After *The Tempest*: Shakespeare, Postcoloniality, and Michelle Cliff's New, New World Miranda," *Contemporary Literature* 36.1 (Spring 1995): 82–102.

8. The connection between vampiric bloodsucking and sexuality has been laid forth in many articles, notably those by Phyllis Roth, Carol Senf, Christopher Craft, Ernest Jones, C. F. Bentley, and Dale Hudson. Michael Rowe's argument is somewhat different: he suggests that the link between the vampire, "'the grave . . . mud and dirt and slime' was 'a metaphor for societal perception of sex as dirty and degrading and base'" (quoted in Bosky 218).

9. See, for example, "Her Husband's Ghost" in James Haskins's *The Headless Haunt*; Reverend Charles Dance's 1881 account, which mentions using an "an odd number of grains of Indian corn, which she is bound to pick up and reckon before she can put on her skin; but as she can pick them up only in pairs, [. . .] the last odd one troubles her, and so she has to throw them down again" (quoted in Abrahams and Szwed 151); and the Herskovitses' *Trinidad Village*, which relates how soucouyants approach their neighbors each morning, meekly requesting either salt or matches (253).

10. Authors, respectively, of "Der Vampyre" (1748); "Die Braut von Korinth" ["The Bride of Corinth"] (1797); "The Giaour" (1813); "Christabel" (1816); "Lamia" (1819); *The Vampyre* (1819); "The Vampire of the Carpathian Mountains" (1846), "The Pale Lady" (1848), and *The Return of Lord Ruthven the Vampire* (1851); *Carmilla* (1872); *Dracula* (1897); the Vampire Chronicles (beginning in 1976 with *Interview with the Vampire*); the Count Saint-Germain series (first installment published in 1978; twentieth novel in 2007); the *Twilight* saga, including *The Short Second Life of Bree Tanner* (2003–10).

11. Accessed April 2011.

12. Ingrid Thaler also contests the concept of "white genres and black traditions" (3), arguing against separate genealogies of "White literature" and "Black literature."

13. Examples of cultural gestures can be found in Jean Rhys's *Wide Sargasso Sea* (1966): 116; Samuel Selvon's *Ways of Sunlight* (1957): 14; Olive Senior's "Lily, Lily" in *Arrival of the Snake Woman and Other Stories* (1989): 123; Elizabeth Nunez's *Beyond the Limbo Silence* (1998): 16 and *Bruised Hibiscus* (2000): 15; Kwadwo Kamau's

Flickering Shadows (1996): 85; Ramabai Espinet's "In the Minor Key" (2003) in *Stories from Blue Latitudes* (2006): 106; Thomas Glave's *Words to Our Now: Imagination and Dissent* (2005): 44; and Rabindranath Maharaj's *A Perfect Pledge* (2005): 222.

1 / Conventional Versions

1. One must also determine by contextual clues if references to "loup-garous," lagahoos, ligahoos, nigahoos, etc., correspond to the soucouyant myth or to the body of tales about shape-shifting werewolves (male or female). See Melville Herskovits's *Life in a Haitian Valley* (1937) and his notes from diaries kept during a 1939 field trip to Trinidad: "If a woman's newborns die one after the other, people say infants are being taken by 'Niga-oo,' ol' hag, or sukiyan (everyone calls it by another name)" (*Trinidad Field Trip*, Box 15, Folder 88: "Trinidad Notes—Book II—Toco" 121).

2. Refer to L. O. Iniss's essay, "Folk Lore and Popular Superstition," in T. B. Jackson's 1904 *Book of Trinidad*, for a nonfiction example of how a European education is rendered incompatible with—and superior to—folk knowledge. Iniss describes folk figures such as the "Soucouyan" using distinctive allusions to Shakespeare and ancient Greek philosophy: soucouyants fly "like Macbeth's witches" (115) and he carefully "add[s] just here, as old Herodotus used to do: 'This I have never seen myself, but I was told so'" (116).

3. In the explanatory footnote, the creature is initially described as follows: "*Soucounyan. Volant* or *soukounyan*, the latter word originating in Africa, designates a human being transformed into a ball of fire" (239n15). It is unclear here whether Leonora's idea expressed in Creole, Bébel-Gisler's applied sentence structure for the publication in French, or Andrea Leskes's translation into English renders the transformation from an active one—with the soucouyant transforming herself—into a passive one, where she is "transformed" by some unnamed force, seemingly out of her control. The following paragraph, however, reassigns agency to the "people, most often elderly women, [who] *have the power* to slip out of their skins, transform themselves into a ball of fire, and suck blood from their victims" (emphasis added).

4. The conclusions of the Grimms' "Little Snow-White," "The Goose Girl," and "Cinderella," respectively.

5. Virginia Hamilton retells this tale as the title story in *The People Could Fly: American Black Folktales* (1985).

6. The association between vampirism and sexuality is well established in literary criticism. Maurice Richardson, C. F. Bentley, Christopher Craft, Phyllis Roth, and Carol Senf all make unique contributions to this dialogue.

7. Douen (pronounced <dwen>): creatures that appear to community members as children or little people with their feet on backward; they are said to lure unsuspecting victims—especially children—into the woods. Papa Bois (<bwah>): the guardian of forests and the natural world. La diablesse (<lah-jah-BLESS>): an extremely beautiful woman with one human leg and one goat or cow leg beneath her gown; she tempts men to their doom, or sometimes to madness, with her sexual allure.

8. Triple Kay, featuring Jeff Joe, "Fly (Soucouyant)" (2010), http://www.youtube.com/watch?v=61Mw4fhVFG8 (accessed May 24, 2012).

9. Grammacks, "Soucouyant." http://www.youtube.com/watch?v=u6GTyNv46j8 (accessed May 24, 2012).

10. Scrunter, "Soucouyant," track 13, *The Very Best of Scrunter* (September 2008, Charlies Records/VP Records).

11. The author acknowledges Besson's *Folklore and Legends of Trinidad and Tobago* for her background material.

12. According to Douglas's author's note from the 2012 edition of *Diamond Sky*, Jack Stewart is actually one of Douglas's pen names.

2 / Nineteenth-Century Connections

1. See the introduction for a discussion of the African *obayfo/obayifo* cited in the works of Maureen Warner-Lewis, Dudley Wright, and Margarite Fernández Olmos and Lizabeth Paravisini-Gebert.

2. For a more complete history of conventional vampire literature, see the work of Nina Auerbach, particularly *Our Vampires, Ourselves* (1995) and the supplementary material to the Norton Critical Edition of *Dracula*, coedited with David Skal.

3. Rudyard Kipling's poem "The Vampire," inspired by a Philip Burne Jones painting, was also published in 1897.

4. See, for example, Maria Edgworth's *Belinda* (1801); William Makepeace Thackeray's *Vanity Fair* (1848)—especially the Caribbean character of Rhoda Swartz, the "rich woolly-haired mulatto from St. Kitts" (14); and Wilkie Collins's *Armadale* (1866), set partly in Barbados and Trinidad. For a discussion of British and American fiction on the subject, see Jennifer DeVere Brody's *Impossible Purities: Blackness, Femininity, and Victorian Culture* (1998).

5. For a discussion of Count Dracula as the threat of interracial sexual competitions, see Margaret L. Carter, "The Vampire as Alien in Contemporary Fiction."

6. The following list—by no means comprehensive—reveals the steady flow of materials to the British reading audience throughout the nineteenth century: Mungo Park, *Travels in the Interior Districts of Africa* details his journeys that took place between 1795 and 1797; James Kingston Tuckey, *Narrative of an Expedition to Explore the River Zaire, Usually Called the Congo, in South Africa, in 1816* (pub. 1818); Alexander Gordon Laing, *Travels in the Timannee, Kooranko, and Soolima Countries, in Western Africa* (pub. 1825); Hugh Clapperton, *Into the Interior of Africa* describes his second expedition, 1825-27; Richard Lemon Lander's two-volume *Records of Captain Clapperton's Last Expedition to Africa* (pub. 1830); Richard Francis Burton, *First Footsteps in East Africa*, recording the events of an 1854 expedition; James Augustus Grant, *A Walk Across Africa; or, Domestic Scenes from my Nile Journal* (pub. 1864); John Hanning Speke, *Journal of the Discovery of the Source of the Nile* (also pub. 1864); Henry Morton Stanley's numerous publications, including *How I Found Livingstone; Travels, Adventures, and Discoveries in Central Africa* (pub. 1874) and *Through the Dark Continent, in Two Volumes* (1878). David Livingstone's reputation had gained near mythic status by the time of his death in 1873.

7. Hare's story was recorded by Charles C. Harper in 1907 and can be found on numerous Internet sites, but I have used Anthony Masters's reprinting of the text in *The Natural History of the Vampire* (1972) for my analysis.

8. E-mail correspondence of October 29, 2011.

9. See Malchow, Zanger, Mulvey-Roberts, Bram Dijkstra, Joe Valente, and Auerbach and Skal for readings of *Dracula* as emblematic of English anxieties over Jews in the nineteenth century.

10. Christopher Craft cites Ernest Jones's *On the Nightmare* (London, 1931) as one of the first critical texts that explicitly equates blood with semen.

11. I am indebted to Joo Ok Kim for pointing out this passage.

12. Hughes cites A. White, *Efficiency and Empire* (1901), in E. J. Evans, ed. *Social Policy, 1830–1914* (London: Routledge and Kegan Paul, 1978), 224, and G. R. Searle, *The Quest for National Efficiency* (Oxford: Basil Blackwell, 1971), 60–61 (*Beyond Dracula* 199n81).

3 / Draining Life Rather than Giving It

1. Hopkinson makes numerous references to Canada's role in world imperial history when she describes Toronto's collapse. The conjoining of the soucouyant legend with critiques of North American and British nationalism is explored in greater detail in Chapter 5.

2. For a more extensive discussion of blindness and other aspects of Hopkinson's first novel, see my "A Feminist Reading of Soucouyants in Nalo Hopkinson's *Brown Girl in the Ring* and *Skin Folk*," *Mosaic: A Journal for the Interdisciplinary Study of Literature* 37.3 (September 2004): 33–50.

3. See Chapter 2 for a more elaborate discussion.

4. Numerous texts, from slave narratives such as *The History of Mary Prince* (1831) and Harriet Jacobs's *Incidents in the Life of a Slave Girl* (1860) to the late twentieth-century collection *All the Women Are White, All the Blacks Are Men, But Some of Us Are Brave* (1982), address this issue.

5. See the work of Caribbean historians Hilary Beckles and Verene Shepherd and the influential "Mama's Baby, Papa's Maybe" essay by Hortense Spillers for additional analysis.

6. The Haitian Kreyol word for "mama."

4 / "Queering" the Norm

1. Although some Caribbeanists argue that the term "queer" suggests the dominance of a First World or Global North perspective, I use the word here for its destabilizing potential to carry a plethora of meanings, all of which stand in opposition to the dominant culture. For further elaboration, see the work of Richard Dyer.

2. Chapter 6 contains further analysis of the shedding of the skin.

3. For more discussion of ways that Caribbean folklore can not only entertain children but also validate traditions and compel behavioral conformity, see the work of J. D. Elder (*Song Games from Trinidad and Tobago*), Alan Dundes, Lawrence Levine, and the introduction of this book.

4. For a more statistical approach, see M. Jacqui Alexander's study of violence against women in the Bahamas in the 1970s, 1980s, and 1990s: "Most acts of incest were committed against girls under ten years old. Female victims of incest outnumbered male victims by a ratio of almost ten to one" (70). Girls as young as three years old were clinically diagnosed with STDs. "All together these data shattered the myth of the sanctity, safety, and comfort of the matrimonial home" (71).

5. Keeling defines "common sense" as that which is commonly held/believed, not that which is logical or obvious.

6. For studies on Caribbean women in same-sex relationships, see Marks (Curaçao); Lorde (Carriacou and Grenada); Silvera, *Silenced Talks* (Jamaica/Canada); Wekker, "Mati-ism" and "One Finger" (Suriname); Alexander, "Not Just (Any) *Body*" (Trinidad and Tobago and the Bahamas); and Tinsley (pan-Caribbean).

7. See *The Daughter's Return* for Rody's discussion of how Gomez reworks the slave narrative genre by representing enslavement as a type of "prehistory," with the escape, and not any experience from being enslaved, serving as the determining historical moment in the character's life.

8. See Rody's book for further analysis of this idea: "Far from turning people into monsters, then, these undead work to humanize the human race" (79). She argues that Gomez counters traditional vampire lore with its emphasis on European male sexual predation by depicting her "idealized vision of mutually nurturing lesbian communalism" (79).

9. Jana Evans Braziel calls the combination of both maternal and erotic desires "transdesires" (73) in her examination of Jamaica Kincaid's *At the Bottom of the River* (1983).

10. See Haraway's description of Octavia Butler and several other fiction writers as "theorists for cyborgs" ("Manifesto" 216).

5 / Reconstructing a Nation of Strangers

1. For analysis of the trope of colonized people's childlike dependence on their colonizers, see Ashis Nandy's *The Intimate Enemy* (1983).

2. See M. Jacqui Alexander's work on the exploitation of women in the post-Independence Bahamas for further insight. Alexander notes: "there is a contradictory and ironic state reliance on women who work as prostitutes [. . .], whom state managers outlaw, and therefore wish to be kept hidden. Everyone knows and talks about prostitution [. . .] with American soldiers. [. . .] State managers rely almost insidiously, therefore, upon the (tacit) acquiescence of her somewhat fixed location between the boundaries of (im)morality and (il)legality to maintain and consolidate the silence" (95).

3. See Chapter 3 for a more in-depth discussion of the soucouyant's implications for social constructions of maternity.

4. See the first section of Toni Morrison's essay "Unspeakable Things Unspoken."

5. "Dame Vera Lynn Takes on BNP over White Cliffs of Dover," *Daily Telegraph*, February 18, 2009, http://www.telegraph.co.uk/news/politics/4687730/Dame-Vera-Lynn-takes-on-BNP-over-White-Cliffs-of-Dover.html (accessed July 27, 2014).

6. For scholarship connecting vampirism to Poe's writing, see Moretti, Dayan's *Fables of the Mind*, and McDonald. Besides "Usher," Oyeyemi mentions Poe's "Ligeia." It should be noted that Poe's "Berenice" also features an eerie preoccupation with premature burials and teeth. Oyeyemi cites more conventional vampire narratives as well: the film *Nosferatu* (142), Keats's "Lamia" (92), Le Fanu's *Carmilla* (149).

7. *The Unbelonging*, by Joan Riley (1987), focuses on the racial identity struggles of a young African Jamaican woman in England.

6 / Shedding Skin and Sucking Blood

1. See the work of historian Elise Lemire for further study of the U.S. obsession with blood, including social and legal laws against interracial relationships that were propagated as biological rules, such as the notion that intraracial reproduction was instinctual.

2. For a more detailed discussion of rebel plots in Jamaica, see Chapter 2.

3. See also Halberstam's discussion of the "postmodern Gothic," in which contemporary readers and movie watchers are alerted to the suspicious nature of "monster hunters, monster makers, and above all, discourses invested in purity and innocence. The monster always represents the disruption of categories, the destruction of boundaries, and the presence of impurities and so we need monsters and we need to recognize and celebrate our own monstrosities" (27).

Works Cited

Abrahams, Roger D. *Afro-American Folktales: Stories from Black Traditions in the New World.* New York: Pantheon Books, 1985.

———. *Deep the Water, Shallow the Shore: Three Essays on Shantying in the West Indies.* Austin: U of Texas P for the American Folklore Society, 1974.

Abrahams, Roger D., and John F. Szwed, eds. *After Africa: Extracts from British Travel Accounts and Journals of the Seventeenth, Eighteenth, and Nineteenth Centuries Concerning the Slaves, Their Manners, and Customs in the British West Indies.* New Haven: Yale UP, 1983.

Agnant, Marie-Célie. *The Book of Emma.* Trans. Zilpha Ellis. Toronto: Insomniac Press, 2006.

Alexander, M. Jacqui. "Erotic Autonomy as a Politics of Decolonization: An Anatomy of Feminist and State Practices in the Bahamas Tourist Economy." *Feminist Genealogies, Colonial Legacies, Democratic Futures.* New York: Routledge, 1997. 63–100.

———. "Not Just (Any) *Body* Can Be a Citizen: The Politics of Law, Sexuality and Postcoloniality in Trinidad and Tobago and the Bahamas." *Feminist Review* 48 (1994): 5–23.

Anthony, Michael. *Folk Tales and Fantasies.* Port of Spain: Columbus Publishers, 1976.

Arata, Stephen D. "The Occidental Tourist: *Dracula* and the Anxiety of Reverse Colonization." *Victorian Studies* (Summer 1990). Reprinted in *Dracula: A Norton Critical Edition.* Ed. Nina Auerbach and David J. Skal. New York: W. W. Norton, 1997. 462–70.

Auerbach, Nina. "*Dracula:* A Vampire of Our Own." *Bloom's Modern Critical Interpretations: Bram Stoker's "Dracula."* Ed. Harold Bloom. Philadelphia: Chelsea House Publishers, 2003. 191–228.

———. *Our Vampires, Ourselves.* Chicago: U of Chicago P, 1995.

Auerbach, Nina, and David J. Skal, eds. *Dracula: A Norton Critical Edition.* New York: W. W. Norton, 1997.

Bacchilega, Cristina. "Reflections on Recent English-Language Fairy-Tale Fiction by Women: Extrapolating from Nalo Hopkinson's *Skin Folk.*" *Fabula* 47.3–4 (2006): 201–10.

Bacchus, Rosaliene. "The Ole Higue." *Guyana Journal* (July 2008). http://www.guyanajournal.com/Ole_Higue.html. Accessed August 27, 2009.

Backus, Margot Gayle. *The Gothic Family Romance: Heterosexuality, Child Sacrifice, and the Anglo-Irish Colonial Order.* Durham, NC: Duke UP, 1999.

Baker, Ronald L. "Lady Lil and Pisspot Pete." *Journal of American Folklore* 100.396 (April–June 1987): 191–99.

Barnes, Natasha. *Cultural Conundrums: Gender, Race, Nation, and the Making of Caribbean Cultural Politics.* Ann Arbor: U of Michigan P, 2006.

Barrow, Christine. *And I Remember Many Things: Folklore of the Caribbean.* Kingston, Jamaica: Ian Randle Publishers, 1992.

Bébel-Gisler, Dany. *Leonora: The Buried Story of Guadeloupe.* Trans. Andrea Leskes. Charlottesville: Caraf Books/UP of Virginia, 1994.

Beckles, Hilary McD. *Centering Woman: Gender Discourses in Caribbean Slave Society.* Princeton, NJ: Markus Wiener Publishers, 1998.

———. *Natural Rebels: A Social History of Enslaved Black Women in Barbados.* New Brunswick, NJ: Rutgers UP, 1989.

Beckles, Hilary McD, and Verene Shepherd, eds. *Caribbean Slave Society and Economy: A Student Reader.* New York: The New Press, 1993.

Beckwith, Martha Warren. *Black Roadways: A Study of Jamaican Folk Life.* Chapel Hill: U of North Carolina P, 1929.

———. *Jamaica Folk-Lore.* New York: American Folk-lore Society. Vol. 21, 1928.

Bell, Sir Henry Hesketh J. *Obeah: Witchcraft in the West Indies.* London: Sampson Low, Marston, Searle, and Rivington, 1889.

Bentley, C. F. "The Monster in the Bedroom: Sexual Symbolism in Bram Stoker's *Dracula,*" *Literature and Psychology* 22 (1972): 27–34.

Berenstein, Rhona. *Attack of the Leading Ladies: Gender, Sexuality and Spectatorship in Classic Horror Cinema.* New York: Columbia UP, 1996.

Berlant, Lauren. "National Brands/National Body: *Imitation of Life.*" *Comparative American Identities: Race, Sex, and Nationality in the Modern Text. Essays from the English Institute.* Ed. Hortense Spillers. New York: Routledge, 1991. 110–40.

Besson, Gérard. *Folklore and Legends of Trinidad & Tobago.* Port of Spain, Trinidad: Paria Publishing, 1989.

———. *Folklore and Legends of Trinidad and Tobago.* Expanded 2nd ed. Port of Spain: Paria Publishing, 2001.

———. Telephone conversation with the author. February 25, 2014.

Bhabha, Homi K. "Of Mimicry and Man: The Ambivalence of Colonial Discourse." *October* 28 (1984): 125–33.

"Boby, John (b1774)." *Re-framing Disability: Portraits from the Royal College of Physicians* [exhibition]. http://www.rcplondon.ac.uk/museum-and-garden/whats/re-framing-disability/john-boby-b1774. Accessed August 3, 2011.

Bogle, Donald. *Toms, Coons, Mulattos, Mammies and Bucks: An Interpretative History of Blacks in American Films*. New York: Continuum, 1993.

Bosky, Bernadette Lynn. "Making the Implicit, Explicit: Vampire Erotica and Pornography." Heldreth and Pharr, 217–33.

Brand, Dionne. *Bread Out of Stone: Recollections, Sex, Recognitions, Race, Dreaming, Politics*. Toronto: Coach House Press, 1994.

———. *In Another Place, Not Here*. New York: Grove Press, 1997.

———. *No Language Is Neutral*. Toronto: Coach House Press, 1990.

———. *Sans Souci and Other Stories*. Ithaca, NY: Firebrand Books, 1989.

Brantlinger, Patrick. "Victorians and Africans: The Genealogy of the Myth of the Dark Continent." *Critical Inquiry* 12.1 (1985): 166–203.

Brathwaite, Edward Kamau. "Caribbean Man in Space and Time: A Bibliographical and Conceptual Approach." Mona, Jamaica: Savacou Publications, 1974.

———. *Contradictory Omens: Cultural Diversity and Integration in the Caribbean*. Mona, Jamaica: Savacou Publications, 1974.

Braziel, Jana Evans. "*Jablesse*, Obeah, and Caribbean Cosmogonies in *At the Bottom of the River*." *Caribbean Genesis: Jamaica Kincaid and the Writing of New Worlds*. New York: State U of New York P, 2009. 53–78.

Brinks, Ellen, and Lee Talley. "Unfamiliar Ties: Lesbian Constructions of Home and Family in Jeanette Winterson's *Oranges Are Not the Only Fruit* and Jewelle Gomez's *The Gilda Stories*." *Homemaking: Women Writers and the Politics and Poetics of Home*. Ed. Catherine Wiley and Fiona R. Barnes. New York: Garland, 1996. 145–74.

Brody, Jennifer DeVere. *Impossible Purities: Blackness, Femininity, and Victorian Culture*. Durham, NC: Duke UP, 1998.

Brontë, Charlotte. *Jane Eyre*. 1847. Ed. Q. D. Leavis. New York: Penguin Classics, 1985.

Brooks, Daphne A. *Bodies in Dissent: Spectacular Performances of Race and Freedom, 1850–1910*. Durham, NC: Duke UP, 2006.

Brown, Toni. "Immunity." *Night Bites: Vampire Stories by Women*. Ed. Victoria A. Brownsworth and Judith M. Redding. Seattle: Seal Press, 1996. 71–79.

Bryant, Cedric Gael. "'The Soul Has Bandaged Moments': Reading the African American Gothic in Wright's 'Big Boy Leaves Home,' Morrison's *Beloved*, and Gomez's *Gilda*." *African American Review* 39.4 (2005): 541–53.

Bryce, Jane. "'Half and Half Children': Third-Generation Women Writers and the New Nigerian Novel." *Research in African Literatures* 39.2 (Summer 2008): 49–67. Accessed through Project MUSE, May 31, 2011.

Burford, Barbara. "Dreaming the Sky Down." 1988. *What Did Miss Darrington See? An Anthology of Feminist Supernatural Fiction.* Ed. Jessica Amanda Salmonson. New York: The Feminist Press at CUNY, 1989. 90–100.

Butler, Octavia. *Fledgling.* New York: Seven Stories Press, 2005.

Carter, Margaret L. "The Vampire as Alien in Contemporary Fiction." Gordon and Hollinger. 27–44.

Carvalho-Neto, Paulo de. *The Concept of Folklore.* Trans. Jacques M. P. Wilson. Coral Gables: U of Miami P, 1971.

Cary, Lorene. *Black Ice.* New York: Vintage Books, 1992.

Case, Sue-Ellen. "Tracking the Vampire." *Writing the Body: Female Embodiment and Feminist Theory.* Ed. Katie Conboy, Nadia Medina, and Sarah Stanbury. New York: Columbia UP, 1997. 380–400.

Casimir-Liautaud, Jean. "Haitian Social Structure in the Nineteenth Century." *Working Papers in Haitian Society and Culture.* Ed. Sidney W. Mintz. New Haven: Antilles Research Program, Yale University, 1975. 35–49.

Cassidy, Frederic Gomes, and Robert Brock Le Page, eds. *Dictionary of Jamaican English.* Mona, Jamaica: U of the West Indies P, 2002.

Carroll, Denolyn. "Rev. of Skin Folk, by Nalo Hopkinson." *Black Issues Book Review* 4.1 (January/February 2002): 56.

Césaire, Aimé. *Discourse on Colonialism.* 1955. Trans. Joan Pinkham. New York: Monthly Review Press, 1972.

Cezair-Thompson, Margaret. *The True History of Paradise.* New York: Random House, 1999.

Chariandy, David. *Soucouyant: A Novel of Forgetting.* Vancouver: Arsenal Pulp Press, 2007.

Cliff, Michelle. *No Telephone to Heaven.* New York: Vintage International, 1989.

Cobham, Rhonda. "'Mwen na rien, Msieu': Jamaica Kincaid and the Problem of Creole Gnosis." *Callaloo* 25.3 (Summer 2002): 868–84. Accessed via JSTOR, June 8, 2013.

Cofer, Judith Ortiz. *Silent Dancing: A Partial Remembrance of a Puerto Rican Childhood.* Houston: Arte Publico Press, 1990.

Comhaire-Sylvain, Suzanne. "Creole Tales from Haiti." *Journal of American Folklore* 50.197 (July–September 1937): 207–95. Accessed via JSTOR, March 25, 2004.

Comissiong, Lynette. *Mind Me Good Now! A Caribbean Folktale.* Toronto: Annick Press, 1997.

Condé, Maryse. *Crossing the Mangrove.* 1989. Trans. Richard Philcox. New York: Anchor Books, 1995.

———. *I, Tituba, Black Witch of Salem.* Trans. Richard Philcox. Charlottesville: UP of Virginia, 1992.

Cooper, Carolyn. *Noises in the Blood: Orality, Gender, and the "Vulgar" Body of Jamaican Popular Culture.* Durham, NC: Duke UP, 1993.

Cornell, Drucilla. "Beyond Traditional Isms? Passing as a Liberal." American Literature Section. MLA Convention. New York, December 28, 1992.

Craft, Christopher. "'Kiss Me with Those Red Lips': Gender and Inversion in Bram Stoker's *Dracula*." 1984. Auerbach and Skal. 444–59.

Crawford, Charmaine. "Sending Love in a Barrel: The Making of Transnational Caribbean Families in Canada." *Canadian Woman Studies* 22.3/4 (Spring/Summer 2003): 104–9.

Croley, Laura Sagolla. "The Rhetoric of Reform in Stoker's Dracula: Depravity, Decline, and the Fin-de-Siècle 'Residuum.'" *Criticism* 37.1 (1995): 85–108.

Cruz, Angie. *Soledad: A Novel.* New York: Simon and Schuster, 2001.

Cudjoe, Selwyn R. Introduction to *Caribbean Women Writers: Essays from the First International Conference.* Ed. Selwyn R. Cudjoe. Wellesley, MA: Calaloux Publications, 1990. 5–48.

———. "Jamaica Kincaid and the Modernist Project: An Interview." *Callaloo: A Journal of African Diaspora Arts & Letters* 12 (Spring 1989): 396–411.

Dance, Daryl Cumber, ed. *Folklore from Contemporary Jamaicans.* Knoxville: U of Tennessee P, 1985.

Danticat, Edwidge. *Breath, Eyes, Memory.* New York: Vintage Books, 1994.

———. *The Farming of Bones.* New York: Penguin, 1999.

———. "Nineteen Thirty-Seven." *Krik? Krak!* New York: Vintage Books, 1996. 31–49.

Davis, Angela Y. *Blues Legacies and Black Feminism: Gertrude "Ma" Rainey, Bessie Smith, and Billie Holiday.* New York: Vintage, 1999.

Dayan, Joan. "Codes of Law and Bodies of Color." *New Literary History* 26.2 (1995): 283–308.

———. *Fables of the Mind: An Inquiry into Poe's Fiction.* New York: Oxford UP, 1987.

———. *Haiti, History, and the Gods.* Berkeley: U of California P, 1995.

———. "Vodoun, or the Voice of the Gods." Olmos and Paravisini-Gebert. 13–36.

Diawara, Manthia. "Black Spectatorship: Problems of Identification and Resistance." *Screen* 29.4 (1988): 66–76.

Dijkstra, Bram. "Dracula's Backlash." Auerbach and Skal. 460–61.

Dobson, Kit. Interview with David Chariandy. "Spirits of Elsewhere Past: A Dialogue on *Soucouyant*." *Callaloo* 30.3 (Summer 2007): 808–17.

Doerksen, Teri Ann. "Deadly Kisses: Vampirism, Colonialism, and the Gendering of Horror." Holte. 137–44.

Dorson, Richard M. *Folklore and Folklife: An Introduction.* Chicago: U of Chicago P, 1972.

———. *Folktales Told Around the World.* Chicago: U of Chicago P, 1975.

Douglas, Ken, and Jack Stewart. *Diamond Sky: A New Millennium Thriller.* Portland: Bootleg Press, 2003.

Douglas, Marcia. *Madame Fate.* New York: Soho, 1999.

Dove, Rita. Foreword to *Jonah's Gourd Vine.* By Zora Neale Hurston. 1934. New York: HarperPerennial Modern Classics, 2008. vii–xv.

Dumas, Alexander, and Paul Bocage. "The Pale Lady." 1848. *Vampire Omnibus*. Ed. Peter Haining. London: Orion Books, 1995.

Dundes, Alan. *The Study of Folklore*. New York: Prentice Hall College Division, 1965.

Durrell, Lawrence. *The Black Book*. 1938. The Traveller's Companion Series. Paris: Olympia Press, 1959.

Dyer, Richard. "Dracula and Desire." *Sight and Sound* 3.1 (January 1993): 8–12.

Edmondson, Belinda. "Public Spectacles: Caribbean Women and the Politics of Public Performance." *Small Axe* 7.1 (March 2003): 1–16.

———. "Race, Privilege, and the Politics of (Re)Writing History: An Analysis of the Novels of Michelle Cliff." *Callaloo* 16.1 (Winter 1993): 180–91. Accessed via JSTOR, August 2, 2013.

Edwards, Bryan. *The History, Civil and Commercial, of the British Colonies in the West Indies*. 2 vols. Dublin: Luke White, 1793. Electronic resource accessed September 14, 2011 through *Eighteenth Century Collections Online*. Gale Cengage Learning.

Elder, J. D. *Folk Song and Folk Life in Charlotteville*. Paper prepared for Twenty-first Conference of the International Folk Music Council, Kingston, Jamaica. August 27–September 3, 1971. Printed by Universal Printing Products, Port of Spain, Trinidad, 1972.

———. *From Congo Drum to Steelband: A Socio-Historical Account of the Emergence and Evolution of the Trinidad Steel Orchestra*. St. Augustine, Trinidad: U of the West Indies P, 1969.

———. "I Recall . . . : Growing Up in Tobago." *Brown Girl in the Ring: An Anthology of Song Games from the Eastern Caribbean*. Ed. Alan Lomax, J. D. Elder, and Bess Lomax Hawes. New York: Pantheon Books, 1997.

———. *Song Games from Trinidad and Tobago*. 1964. First edition, *Song Games of Trinidad and Tobago*. Delaware, Ohio: Cooperative Recreation Service, 1961.

Ervin, Andrew. "Miri's Hunger."/"White Is for Witching by Helen Oyeyemi." *New York Times Book Review* 114.37 (September 13, 2009): 24.

Espinet, Ramabai. "In the Minor Key." *Stories from Blue Latitudes: Caribbean Women Writers At Home and Abroad*. Ed. Elizabeth Nunez and Jennifer Sparrow. Seattle: Seal Press, 2006. 104–11.

Fleetwood, Nicole R. *Troubling Vision: Performance, Visuality, and Blackness*. Chicago: U of Chicago P, 2011.

Froude, James Anthony. *The English in the West Indies; or, The Bow of Ulysses*. London: Longmans, Green, and Co., 1888.

Gadsby, Meredith M. *Sucking Salt: Caribbean Women Writers, Migration, and Survival*. Columbia: U of Missouri P, 2006.

Gelder, Ken. *Reading the Vampire*. New York: Routledge, 1994.

Gilman, Sander L. *Difference and Pathology: Stereotypes of Sexuality, Race, and Madness*. Ithaca, NY: Cornell UP, 1985.

Glave, Thomas. *Words to Our Now: Imagination and Dissent.* Minneapolis: U Minnesota P, 2005.

Glissant, Édouard. *Caribbean Discourse.* Trans. J. Michael Dash. Charlottesville: U of Virginia Press, 1999.

———. *Le discourse antillais.* Paris: Gallimard, 1997.

Goldberg, David Theo. *Racist Culture: Philosophy and the Politics of Meaning.* Oxford: Blackwell, 1993.

Gomez, Jewelle. "Black Women Heroes: Here's Reality, Where's the Fiction?" *Black Scholar* 17:2 (1986): 8–13.

———. *The Gilda Stories.* Ithaca, NY: Firebrand Books, 1991.

———. "Lye Throwers and Lovely Renegades: The Road from Bitch to Hero for Black Women in Speculative Fictions." *Forty-Three Septembers.* Ithaca, NY: Firebrand Books, 1993. 109–28.

———. "Recasting the Mythology: Writing Vampire Fiction." Gordon and Hollinger. 85–92.

Gonzalez, Anson. "Tabiz." *The Oxford Book of Caribbean Verse.* Ed. Steward Brown and Mark A. McWatt. Oxford: Oxford UP, 2005. 157–58.

Gordon, Joan, and Veronica Hollinger, eds. *Blood Read: The Vampire as Metaphor in Contemporary Culture.* Philadelphia: U of Pennsylvania P, 1997.

Green, Celia A. "'A Civil Inconvenience'? The Vexed Question of Slave Marriage in the British West Indies. *Law and History Review* 25.1 (2007): 1–59. http://www.historycooperative.org/journals/lhr/25.1/green.html. Accessed September 8, 2011.

Halberstam, Judith. *Skin Shows: Gothic Horror and the Technology of Monsters.* Durham, NC: Duke UP, 1995.

Hall, Lynda. "Passion(ate) Plays 'Wherever We Found Space': Lorde and Gomez Queer(y)ing Boundaries and Acting In." *Callaloo* 23.1 (2000): 394–421.

Hamilton, Virginia. *The Dark Way: Stories from the Spirit World.* New York: Harcourt Brace Jovanovich, 1990.

———. *Her Stories: African American Folktales, Fairy Tales, and True Tales.* New York: Blue Sky Press/Scholastic, 1995.

———. *The People Could Fly: American Black Folktales.* New York: Alfred A. Knopf, 1985.

———. *Wee Winnie Witch's Skinny: An Original African American Scare Tale.* New York: Blue Sky Press/Scholastic, 2004.

Hammack, Brenda. Introduction to *The Blood of the Vampire,* by Florence Marryat. Kansas City: Valancourt Books, 2009. v–xix.

Hammer, Patricia J. "Bloodmakers Made of Blood: Quechua Ethnophysiology of Menstruation." *Regulating Menstruation: Beliefs, Practices, Interpretations.* Ed. Etienne van de Walle and Elisha P. Renne. Chicago: U of Chicago P, 2001. 241–53.

Hampton, Gregory Jerome. *Changing Bodies in the Fiction of Octavia Butler: Slaves, Aliens, and Vampires.* Lanham, MD: Lexington-Rowman, 2010.

Haraway, Donna. "A Manifesto for Cyborgs: Science, Technology, and Socialist Feminism in the 1980s." 1985. *Feminism/Postmodernism*. Ed. Linda J. Nicholson. New York: Routledge, 1990. 190–233.

———. *Modest_Witness@Second_Millennium: FemaleMan©_Meets_Onco-Mouse*™. New York: Routledge, 1997.

Harse, Katie. "*Dracula*'s Reflection: *The Jewel of Seven Stars*." Holte. 23–29.

Haskins, James. *The Headless Haunt and Other African-American Ghost Stories*. New York: HarperCollins, 1994.

Hausman, Gerald. *Duppy Talk: West Indian Tales of Mystery and Magic*. New York: Simon & Schuster Books for Young Readers, 1994.

Hayles, N. Katherine. *How We Became Posthuman: Virtual Bodies in Cybernetics, Literature, and Informatics*. Chicago: U of Chicago P, 1999.

Heath, Roy. "The Function of Myth." *Caribbean Essays: An Anthology*. Ed. Andrew Salkey. London: Evans Bros, 1973. 86–94.

Heldreth, Leonard G., and Mary Pharr, eds. *The Blood Is the Life: Vampires in Literature*. Bowling Green, OH: Bowling Green State University Popular Press, 1999.

Herskovits, Melville J. *Life in a Haitian Valley*. New York: Alfred A. Knopf, 1937.

———. *Trinidad Field Trip*. Boxes 15–16, Melville J. and Frances Herskovits Papers, Schomburg Center for Research in Black Culture. Manuscripts, Archives, and Special Collections. New York.

Herskovits, Melville J., and Frances S. Herskovits. *Suriname Folk-Lore*. New York: Columbia UP, 1936.

———. *Trinidad Village*. New York: Alfred A. Knopf, 1947.

Hochschild, Adam. "Against All Odds." *Mother Jones* (January/February 2004). http://www.motherjones.com/politics/2004/01/against-all-odds. Accessed August 10, 2013.

Holte, James Craig. "*Blade*: A Return to Revulsion." *Journal of Dracula Studies* 3 (2001): 27–32.

———, ed. *The Fantastic Vampire: Studies in the Children of the Night. Selected Essays from the Eighteenth International Conference on the Fantastic in the Arts*. Westport, CT: Greenwood Press, 2002.

hooks, bell. *Black Looks: Race and Representation*. Boston: South End Press, 1992.

Hopkinson, Nalo. *Brown Girl in the Ring*. New York: Warner Books, 1998.

———. *The New Moon's Arms*. New York: Warner Books, 2007.

———. *Skin Folk*. New York: Warner Books, 2001.

Hoving, Isabel. *In Praise of New Travelers: Reading Caribbean Migrant Women's Writing*. Stanford: Stanford UP, 2001.

Hudson, Dale. "Vampires of Color and the Performance of Multicultural Whiteness." *The Persistence of Whiteness: Race and Contemporary Hollywood Cinema*. Ed. Daniel Bernardi. New York: Routledge, 2007. 127–56.

Hughes, Langston, and Arna Bontemps, eds. *Book of Negro Folklore*. New York: Dodd, Mead & Co., 1958.

Hughes, William. *Beyond Dracula: Bram Stoker's Fiction and Its Cultural Context.* New York: St. Martin's Press, 2000.

Hughes, William, and Andrew Smith, eds. *Bram Stoker: History, Psychoanalysis and the Gothic.* New York: St. Martin's Press, 1998.

Hunt, Margaret. "Racism, Imperialism, and the Traveler's Gaze in Eighteenth-Century England." *Journal of British Studies* 32.4 (October 1993): 333–57.

Hurston, Zora Neale. "De Witch Woman." *Every Tongue Got to Confess: Negro Folk-tales from the Gulf States.* Ed. Carla Kaplan. New York: Perennial/HarperCollins, 2002. 63–64.

———. *Jonah's Gourd Vine.* 1934. New York: HarperPerennial Modern Classics, 2008.

Iniss, L. O. "Folk Lore and Popular Superstition." *The Book of Trinidad.* Ed. T. B. Jackson. Port of Spain, Trinidad: Muir, Marshall and Co., 1904. 111–24.

Isichei, Elizabeth. "Introduction: Truth from Below." *Voices of the Poor in Africa.* Rochester: U of Rochester P, 2002. 1–21.

Jackson, T. B., ed. *The Book of Trinidad.* Port of Spain: Muir, Marshall and Co., 1904.

James, Cynthia. "Searching for Anansi: From Orature to Literature in the West Indian Children's Folk Tradition—Jamaican and Trinidadian Trends." 2004. http://www.sacbf.org.za/2004%20papers/Cynthia%20James.rtf. Accessed June 15, 2005.

James, Marlon. *The Book of Night Women.* New York: Riverhead Books, 2009.

Jesús, Melinda de. "Of Monsters and Mothers: Filipina American Identity and Maternal Legacies in Lynda J. Barry's *One Hundred Demons.*" *Meridians* 5.1 (2004): 1–26.

John, Marie-Elena. *Unburnable.* New York: Amistad/HarperCollins, 2006.

Johnson, Judith E. "Women and Vampires: Nightmare or Utopia?" *Kenyon Review* 15.1 (Winter 1993): 72–80.

Johnston, Nancy. "'Happy That It's Here': An Interview with Nalo Hopkinson." *Queer Universes: Sexualities in Science Fiction.* Ed. Wendy Gay Pearson, Veronica Hollinger, and Joan Gordon. Liverpool: Liverpool UP, 2010. 200–214.

Jones, Ernest. *On the Nightmare.* London: Hogarth Press, 1931.

Jones, Grace. Interview. 1986. Published April 29, 2012, by VOGUESPIRIT. www.youtube.com/watch?v=y5ouP4F_Zgk. Accessed June 13, 2012.

Jones, Miriam. "*The Gilda Stories*: Revealing the Monsters at the Margins." Gordon and Hollinger. 151–67.

Jordanova, Ludmilla. *Sexual Visions: Images of Gender in Science and Medicine Between the Eighteenth and Twentieth Centuries.* New York: Harvester Wheatsheaf, 1989.

Joseph, Lynn. *A Wave in Her Pocket: Stories from Trinidad.* New York: Clarion, 1991.

Kamau, Kwadwo Agymah. *Flickering Shadows.* Minneapolis: Coffee House Press, 1996.

Keeling, Kara. *The Witch's Flight: The Cinematic, the Black Femme, and the Image of Common Sense*. Durham, NC: Duke UP, 2007.

Khan, Aisha. *Callaloo Nation: Metaphors of Race and Religious Identity Among South Asians in Trinidad*. Durham, NC: Duke UP, 2004.

Kincaid, Jamaica. *Annie John*. New York: Farrar, Straus and Giroux, 1983.

———. *At the Bottom of the River*. New York: Vintage Books, 1978.

———. *The Autobiography of My Mother*. New York: Farrar, Straus and Giroux, 1996.

———. Introduction. *Talk Stories*. New York: Farrar, Straus and Giroux, 2001. 3–14.

———. *Lucy: A Novel*. New York: Farrar, Straus and Giroux, 1990.

———. *My Brother*. New York: Farrar, Straus and Giroux, 1997.

———. "On Seeing England for the First Time." http://www.hamiltonunique.com/wp-content/uploads/2013/08/OnSeeingEngland-Kincaid.pdf. Accessed August 2, 2014.

———. "Putting Myself Together." *The New Yorker* (February 20, 1995): 93–101.

Kristeva, Julia. *The Powers of Horror: An Essay on Abjection*. Trans. Leon S. Roudiez. New York: Columbia UP, 1982.

Labat, Jean-Baptiste. *Nouveaux voyages aux Isles d'Amerique*. Paris: G. Cavelier, 1722.

Lahens, Yanick. "The Survivors." *Aunt Résia and the Spirits and Other Stories*. 1994. Trans. Betty Wilson. Charlottesville: U of Virginia P, 2010. 16–39.

Lainé, Daniel. *African Gods: Contemporary Rituals and Beliefs—Photographs by Daniel Lainé*. Paris: Flammarion, 2007.

Lakoff, George, and Mark Johnson. *Metaphors We Live By*. Chicago: U of Chicago P, 1980.

Lee, Janet, and Jennifer Sasser-Coen. *Blood Stories: Menarche and the Politics of the Female Body in Contemporary U.S. Society*. New York: Routledge, 1996.

Le Fanu, Sheridan. *Carmilla*, from *In a Glass Darkly*. 1872. New York: Oxford UP, 1993. 243–319.

Lemire, Elise. *"Miscegenation": Making Race in America*. Philadelphia: U of Pennsylvania P, 2009.

Lévi-Strauss, Claude. "The Structural Study of Myth." 1955. *Structuralism in Myth*. Ed. Robert A. Segal. New York: Garland, 1996.

Levine, Lawrence W. *Black Culture and Black Consciousness: Afro-American Folk Thought from Slavery to Freedom*. New York: Oxford UP, 1978.

Lisser, Herbert de. *The White Witch of Rosehall*. 1929. Oxford: Macmillan Education, 1982.

Lomax, Alan, J. D. Elder, and Bess Lomax Hawes. *Brown Girl in the Ring: An Anthology of Song Games from the Eastern Caribbean*. New York: Pantheon Books, 1997.

Long, Edward. *The History of Jamaica: Or, General Survey of the Antient and Modern State of That Island*. London: Printed for T. Lowndes, 1774.

Lorde, Audre. *Zami: A New Spelling of My Name.* Trumansburg, NY: Crossing Press, 1982.

Longinović, Tomislav. *Vampire Nation: Violence as Cultural Imaginary.* Durham, NC: Duke UP, 2011.

Lott, Tommy L. "A No-Theory Theory of Contemporary Black Cinema." *Black American Literature Forum* 25.2 (Summer 1991): 221–36.

Lubiano, Wahneema. "Black Nationalism and Black Common Sense: Policing Ourselves and Others." *The House That Race Built: Black Americans, U.S. Terrain.* Ed. Wahneema Lubiano. New York: Pantheon Books, 1997. 232–52.

Macfie, Sian. "'They Suck Us Dry': A Study of Late Nineteenth-Century Projections of Vampiric Women." *Subjectivity and Literature from the Romantics to the Present Day.* Ed. Philip Shaw and Peter Stockwell. New York: Pinter Publishers, 1991. 58–67.

Madhavan, Sangeetha, and Aisse Diarra. "The Blood That Links: Menstrual Regulation Among the Bamana of Mali." *Regulating Menstruation: Beliefs, Practices, Interpretations.* Ed. Etienne van de Walle and Elisha P. Renne. Chicago: U of Chicago P, 2001. 172–86.

Maharaj, Rabindranath. *A Perfect Pledge.* New York: Farrar, Straus and Giroux, 2005.

Malchow, H. L. *Gothic Images of Race in Nineteenth-Century Britain.* Stanford: Stanford UP, 1996.

Malkin, Irad. *A Small Greek World: Networks in the Ancient Mediterranean.* New York: Oxford UP, 2011.

Marks, A. F. *Male and Female and the Afro-Curaçaoan Household.* The Hague: Nijhoff, 1976.

Marryat, Florence. *The Blood of the Vampire.* 1897. Kansas City: Valancourt Books, 2009.

Masters, Anthony. *The Natural History of the Vampire.* New York: G. P. Putnam's Sons, 1972.

McClintock, Anne. *Imperial Leather: Race, Gender, and Sexuality in the Colonial Conquest.* New York: Routledge, 1995.

McDonald, Beth E. *The Vampire as Numinous Experience: Spiritual Journeys with the Undead in British and American Literature.* Jefferson, NC: McFarland, 2004.

McKissack, Patricia C. *The Dark-Thirty: Southern Tales of the Supernatural.* New York: Alfred A. Knopf, 1992.

McKittrick, Katherine. *Demonic Grounds: Black Women and the Cartographies of Struggle.* Minneapolis: U of Minnesota P, 2006.

McNally, Raymond T. "Bram Stoker and Irish Gothic." Holte. 11–21.

McWatt, Tessa. *Out of My Skin.* Toronto: Riverbank Press, 1998.

Medovoi, Leerom. "Theorizing Historicity, or the Many Meanings of *Blacula.*" *Screen* 39.1 (Spring 1998): 1–21.

Mehta, Brinda. *Diasporic Dis(locations): Indo-Caribbean Women Writers Negotiate the "Kala Pani."* Kingston, Jamaica: University of the West Indies Press, 2004.

———. "The Shaman Woman, Resistance, and the Powers of Transformation: A Tribute to Ma Cia in Simone Schwarz-Bart's *The Bridge of Beyond.*" Olmos and Paravisini-Gebert. 231–47.

Melton, J. Gordon. *The Vampire Book: The Encyclopedia of the Undead.* 3rd ed. Canton, MI: Visible Ink Press, 2011.

Mercer, Kobena, ed. *Black Film; British Cinema.* London: Institute of Contemporary Arts, 1988.

Miller, Elizabeth. "Shapeshifting *Dracula:* The Abridged Edition of 1901." Holte. 3–9.

Mintz, Sidney W. *Three Ancient Colonies: Caribbean Themes and Variations.* Cambridge, MA: Harvard UP, 2010.

Mintz, Sidney W., and Richard Price. *The Birth of African-American Culture: An Anthropological Perspective.* Boston: Beacon Press, 1992.

Mittelhölzer, Edgar. *A Morning in Trinidad.* Garden City, NY: Doubleday, 1950.

Mohammed, Patricia. "Morality and the Imagination—Mythopoetics of Gender and Culture in the Caribbean: The Trilogy." *South Asian Diaspora* 1.1 (March 2009): 63–84.

———. "Reflections on the Women's Movement in Trinidad: Calypsos, Changes and Sexual Violence." *Feminist Review* 38 (Summer 1991): 33–47. Accessed via JSTOR, September 19, 2013.

Mootoo, Shani. *Cereus Blooms at Night.* New York: Perennial, 2001.

———. "Out on Main Street." *Out on Main Street & Other Stories.* Vancouver: Press Gang Publishers, 1993. 45–57.

Moretti, Franco. "'[A Capital Dracula]' from *Signs Taken for Wonders.*" Auerbach and Skal. 431–44.

Morrison, Toni. *Beloved.* New York: Plume, 1988.

———. *Love.* New York: Alfred A. Knopf, 2003.

———. *Paradise.* New York: Alfred A. Knopf, 1998.

———. "Rootedness: The Ancestor as Foundation." *Black Women Writers (1950–1980).* Ed. Mari Evans. Garden City, NY: Anchor Press, 1984. 339–45.

———. *Song of Solomon.* 1977. New York: Vintage International, 2004.

———. "Unspeakable Things Unspoken: The Afro-American Presence in American Literature." *Michigan Quarterly Review* 28.1 (1989): 1–34.

Mulrain, George MacDonald. *Theology in Folk Culture: The Theological Significance of Haitian Folk Religion.* New York: Verlag Peter Lang, 1984.

Mulvey-Roberts, Marie. "Dracula and the Doctors." *Bram Stoker: History, Psychoanalysis and the Gothic.* Ed. William Hughes and Andrew Smith. London: MacMillan, 1998. 78–95.

Nandy, Ashis. *The Intimate Enemy: Loss and Recovery of Self Under Colonialism.* Oxford: Oxford UP, 1983.

Narain, Denise deCaires. "The Body of the Woman in the Body of the Text: The Novels of Erna Brodber." *Caribbean Women Writers: Fiction in English.* Ed. Mary Condé and Thorunn Lonsdale. New York: St. Martin's Press, 1999. 97–116.

Neal, Mark Anthony. *Soul Babies: Black Popular Culture and the Post-Soul Aesthetic.* New York: Routledge, 2002.

Nerad, Julie Cary. "Slippery Language and False Dilemmas: The Passing Novels of Child, Howells, and Harper." *American Literature* 75.4 (December 2003): 813–41.

Nordberg, Heidi L. "Blood Spirit/Blood Bodies: The Viral in the Vampire Chronicles of Anne Rice and Chelsea Quinn Yarbro." Holte. 111–21.

Nunez, Elizabeth. *Beyond the Limbo Silence.* Seattle: Seal Press, 1998.

———. *Bruised Hibiscus.* New York: Ballantine Books, 2000.

———. *Prospero's Daughter.* New York: Ballantine Books, 2006.

Nussbaum, Felicity. *Torrid Zones: Maternity, Sexuality, and Empire in Eighteenth-Century English Narratives.* Baltimore: Johns Hopkins UP, 1995.

Nyberg, Suzanna. "Men in Love: The Fantasizing of Bram Stoker and Edvard Munch." Holte. 45–55.

Okorafor-Mbachu, Nnedi. "Me and My Shadow: A Remarkable First Novel from a Young Brit Haunts the Mind and Soul." *Black Issues Book Review* (November–December 2005): 50–51. Accessed via Academic Search Premier, May 31, 2011.

Olmos, Margarite Fernández, and Lizabeth Paravisini-Gebert, eds. *Sacred Possessions: Vodou, Santería, Obeah, and the Caribbean.* New Brunswick, NJ: Rutgers UP, 1997.

Ottley, C. R. *Tall Tales of Trinidad and Tobago.* Port of Spain: Victory Commercial Printers, 1977.

Oyeyemi, Helen. *White Is for Witching: A Novel.* New York: Penguin Group, 2009.

Paquet, Sandra Pouchet, Patricia J. Saunders, and Stephen Stuempfle, eds. *Music. Memory. Resistance: Calypso and the Caribbean Literary Imagination.* Kingston, Jamaica: Ian Randle Publishers, 2007.

Parsons, Elsie Clews. *Folk-Lore of the Antilles, French and English.* Vol. 2. New York: American Folk-Lore Society, 1936.

———. *Folk-Lore of the Antilles, French and English.* Vol. 3. New York: American Folk-Lore Society, 1943.

———. *Folk-Tales of Andros Island, Bahamas.* New York: American Folk-Lore Society/G. E. Stechert & Co./New Era Printing, 1918.

Patai, Raphael. "Lilith." *Journal of American Folklore* 77.306 (October–December 1964): 295–314.

Pearse, Andrew, ed. "Mitto Sampson on Calypso Legends of the Nineteenth Century." *Caribbean Quarterly* 4.3/4 (March 1956; June 1956): 250–62. Accessed via JSTOR, May 1, 2012.

Penzler, Otto, ed. *The Vampire Archives: The Most Complete Volume of Vampire Tales Ever Published*. New York: Vintage Crime/Black Lizard, 2009.

Phillpotts, Eden. *In Sugar-Cane Land*. London: McClure, 1890.

Plasa, Carl, ed. *Columbia Critical Guides: Toni Morrison, Beloved*. Icon Critical Guides Series. New York: Columbia UP, 1998.

Plaza, Dwaine. "The Construction of a Segmented Hybrid Identity Among One-and-a-Half-Generation and Second-Generation Indo-Caribbean and African Caribbean Canadians." *Identity* 6.3 (July 1, 2006): 207–29.

Poe, Edgar Allan. "Berenice." *Great Short Works of Edgar Allan Poe*. Ed. G. R. Thompson. New York: Perennial Classic, 1970. 152–61.

———. "Ligeia." *Great Short Works of Edgar Allan Poe*. Ed. G. R. Thompson. New York: Perennial Classic, 1970. 175–93.

Pollard, Velma. *Anansesem: A Collection of Caribbean Folk Tales, Legends, and Poems for Juniors*. Kingston, Jamaica: Longman Jamaica, 1985.

———. "The World of Spirits in the Work of Some Caribbean Writers in the Diaspora." *Changing English: Studies in Culture and Education* 17.1 (March 2010): 27–34.

Potocki, Jan. *The Saragossa Manuscript*. Edited and with preface by Roger Caillois. Translated from the French by Elisabeth Abbott. New York: Avon Books, 1960.

Price, Richard and Sally Price, eds. *John Gabriel Stedman's Narrative of a Five Years' Expedition Against the Revolted Negroes of Surinam, in Guiana, on the Wild Coast of South America, from the Year 1772 to 1777: Transcribed from the Original 1790 Manuscript*. Baltimore: Johns Hopkins UP, 1988.

Priest, Jack. *Night Witch*. Portland: Bootleg Press, 2003.

Propp, Vladimir. *Morphology of the Folk Tale*. 1928. Trans. Laurence Scott. Austin: U of Texas P, 1968.

Punter, David. *Postcolonial Imaginings: Fictions of a New World Order*. Edinburgh: Edinburgh UP, 2000.

Ramsawack, Al. *Flamme Belle: A Caribbean Folk Tale*. Port of Spain, Trinidad and Tobago: Lyrehc, 1978.

Reid, Michelle. "Urban Space and Canadian Identity in Charles de Lint's *Svaha*." *Science Fiction Studies* 33.3 (November 2006): 421–37.

Renne, Elisha P., and Etienne van de Walle. Introduction. *Regulating Menstruation: Beliefs, Practices, Interpretations*. Ed. van de Walle and Renne. Chicago: U of Chicago P, 2001. xiii–xxxvii.

Rhyme, Nancy, ed. *Slave Ghost Stories: Tales of Hags, Hants, Ghosts, & Diamondback Rattlers*. Orangeburg, SC: Sandlapper Publishing, 2002.

Rhys, Jean. *Voyage in the Dark*. 1934. New York: W. W. Norton, 1968.

———. *Wide Sargasso Sea*. 1966. New York: W. W. Norton, 1982.

Richardson, Maurice. "The Psychoanalysis of Ghost Stories." *The Twentieth Century*. 1959. 419–31.

Richardson, Samuel. *Pamela; or, Virtue Rewarded*. 1740. Ed. Albert J. Rivero. New York: Cambridge UP, 2011.

Riley, Joan. *The Unbelonging*. London: Women's Press, 1987.

Ringgold, Faith. *Tar Beach*. New York: Crown Publishers, 1991.

Roach, Joseph. *Cities of the Dead: Circum-Atlantic Performance*. New York: Columbia UP, 1996.

Roberts, Bette. "The Mother Goddess in H. Rider Haggard's *She* and Anne Rice's *The Queen of the Damned*." Holte. 103–9.

Roberts, Peter A. *West Indians & Their Language*. New York: Cambridge UP, 1988.

Rody, Caroline. *The Daughter's Return: African-American and Caribbean Women's Fictions of History*. New York: Oxford UP, 2001.

Rohlehr, Gordon. *Calypso and Society in Pre-Independence Trinidad*. Trinidad and Tobago: Gordon Rohlehr, 1990.

Rose, Jeane. "'A Girl Like That Will Give You AIDS!': Vampirism as AIDS Metaphor in *Killing Zoe*." Holte. 145–50.

Roth, Phyllis A. "Suddenly Sexual Women in Bram Stoker's *Dracula*." 1977. Auerbach and Skal. 411–21.

Rowe, Karen E. "Feminism and Fairy Tales." *Folk and Fairy Tales*. Ed. Martin Hallett and Barbara Karasek. Lewiston, NY: Broadview Press, 1991. 346–67.

Rymer, Michael, dir. *Queen of the Damned*. Screenplay by Scott Abbott and Michael Petroni. Warner Bros Home Video, 2002.

Said, Edward. *Culture and Imperialism*. New York: Knopf, 1993.

Sappington, Rodney, and Tyler Stallings, eds. *Uncontrollable Bodies: Testimonies of Identity and Culture*. Seattle: Bay Press, 1994.

Saxon, Lyle, Edward Dreyer, and Robert Tallant, eds. *Gumbo Ya-Ya: Folk Tales of Louisiana*. 1945. Gretna, LA: Pelican Publishing, 1998.

Schaffer, Talia. "'A Wild Desire Took Me': The Homoerotic History of Dracula." 1994. Auerbach and Skal. 470–82.

Schopp, Andrew. "Narrative Control and Subjectivity: Dismantling Safety in TM's *Beloved*." *Understanding Toni Morrison's Beloved and Sula: Selected Essays and Criticisms of the Works by the Nobel Prize–Winning Author*. Ed. Solomon O. Iyasere and Marla W. Iyasere. Troy, NY: Whitston Publishing, 2000. 204–30.

Schwarz-Bart, Simone. *The Bridge of Beyond*. Trans. Barbara Bray. Portsmouth, NH: Heinemann, 1982. French original: *Pluie et vent sur Télumée Miracle*. Paris: Editions du Seuil, 1972.

Sedgwick, Eve. *Between Men: English Literature and Male Homosocial Desire*. New York: Columbia UP, 1985.

Selvon, Samuel. "Johnson and the Cascadura." *Ways of Sunlight*. 1957. London: MacGibbon & Kee, 1961.

Senf, Carol A. "Daughters of Lilith: Women Vampires in Popular Literature." Heldreth and Pharr. 199–216.

———. "Dracula: The Unseen Face in the Mirror." 1979. Auerbach and Skal. 421–31.

Senior, Olive. "Lily, Lily." *Arrival of the Snake Woman and Other Stories.* Burnt Mill, Harlow: Longman Group UK, 1989. 112–45.

Sethi, Anita. "'I didn't know I was writing a novel'—Helen Oyeyemi." *Nigeriaworld All About Nigeria* (January 10, 2005). http://naijanet.com/news/source/2005/jan/10/1001.html. Accessed May 31, 2011.

Shapiro, Dolores J. "Blood, Oil, Honey, and Water: Symbolism in Spirit Possession Sects in Northeastern Brazil." *American Ethnologist* 22.4 (November 1995): 828–47.

Sheller, Mimi. *Consuming the Caribbean: From Arawaks to Zombies.* New York: Routledge, 2003.

———. "Work That Body: Sexual Citizenship and Embodied Freedom." *Constructing Vernacular Culture in the Trans-Caribbean.* Ed. Holger Henke and Karl-Heinz Magister. New York: Lexington Books/Rowman & Littlefield, 2008. 345–76.

Silver, Alain, and James Ursini. *The Vampire Film: From "Nosferatu" to "Bram Stoker's Dracula."* New York: Limelight Editions, 1994.

Silvera, Makeda. *Piece of My Heart: A Lesbian of Colour Anthology.* Toronto: Sister Vision Press, 1991.

———. *Silenced Talks with Working-Class Caribbean Women About Their Lives and Struggles as Domestic Workers in Canada.* Toronto: Sister Vision Press, 1992.

Smith, Anthony D. "Towards a Global Culture?" *Global Culture: Nationalism, Globalization and Modernity.* Ed. Mike Featherstone. London: Sage, 1990. 171–91.

Smith, Sidonie. *A Poetics of Women's Autobiography: Marginality and the Fictions of Self-Representation.* Bloomington: Indiana UP, 1987.

Spillers, Hortense. "Mama's Baby, Papa's Maybe: An American Grammar Book." *Diacritics* 17.2 (1987): 64–81.

Stallings, Tyler. "Introduction." Sappington and Stallings. 15–17.

Stedman, Capt. John Gabriel. *Narrative of a Five Years' Expedition Against the Revolted Negroes of Surinam, in Guiana, on the Wild Coast of South America, from the Year 1772 to 1777: Transcribed from the Original 1790 Manuscript.* 1796. Ed. Richard Price and Sally Price. Baltimore: Johns Hopkins UP, 1988.

Stetson, Erlene. "Studying Slavery: Some Literary and Pedagogical Considerations on the Black Female Slave." *All the Women Are White, All the Blacks Are Men, but Some of Us Are Brave: Black Women's Studies.* Old Westbury, NY: Feminist Press, 1982. 61–84.

Stevenson, John Allen. "A Vampire in the Mirror: The Sexuality of Dracula." *PMLA* 103.2 (March 1988): 130–49.

Stevenson, Robert Louis, and Fanny Van de Grift Stevenson. *More New Arabian Nights: The Dynamiter.* New York: Henry Holt, 1885.

Stoker, Bram. *Dracula*. 1897. *Norton Critical Edition*. Ed. Nina Auerbach and David J. Skal. New York: W. W. Norton, 1997.

———. *The Mystery of the Sea*. London: W. Heinemann, 1902.

Sturgess, Charlotte. "Dionne Brand: Writing the Margins." *Caribbean Women Writers: Fiction in English*. Ed. Mary Condé and Thorunn Lonsdale. New York: St. Martin's Press, 1999. 202–16.

Sutcliffe, David. *British Black English*. Oxford: Blackwell, 1982.

Thackeray, William Makepeace. *Vanity Fair: A Novel Without a Hero*. 1848. New York: Signet Classics/New American Library, 1962.

Thaler, Ingrid. *Black Atlantic Speculative Fictions: Octavia E. Butler, Jewelle Gomez, and Nalo Hopkinson*. New York: Routledge/Taylor & Francis Group, 2010.

Thomas, Deborah. *Modern Blackness: Nationalism, Globalization, and the Politics of Culture in Jamaica*. Durham, NC: Duke UP, 2004.

Thurer, Shari L. *The Myths of Motherhood: How Culture Reinvents the Good Mother*. New York: Penguin, 1995.

Timothy, Helen Pyne. "Adolescent Rebellion and Gender Relations in *At the Bottom of the River* and *Annie John*." *Caribbean Women Writers: Essays from the First International Conference*. Ed. Selwyn R. Cudjoe. Wellesley, MA: Calaloux Publications, 1990. 233–42.

Tinsley, Omise'eke Natasha. *Thiefing Sugar: Eroticism Between Women in Caribbean Literature*. Durham, NC: Duke UP, 2010.

Tucker, Terry. *Bermuda and the Supernatural: Superstitions and Beliefs from 17th–20th Centuries*. Bermuda: Island Press, 1983.

Upton, Nick, with Paul Keens-Douglas. "Vampires, Devilbirds and Spirits: Tales of the Calypso Isles" [video]. *The Nature World*. Port of Spain: British Broadcasting Company and the National Geographic Society, 1994.

Valente, Joseph. *Dracula's Crypt: Bram Stoker, Irishness, and the Question of Blood*. Urbana: U of Illinois P, 2002.

Walcott, Derek. *Ti-Jean and His Brothers*. *"Dream on Monkey Mountain" and Other Plays*. New York: Farrar, Straus and Giroux, 1986. 81–166.

Wall, Geoffrey. "'Different from Writing': Dracula in 1897." *Literature and History* 10.1 (1984): 15–23.

Waltje, Jörg. *Blood Obsession: Vampires, Serial Murder, and the Popular Imagination*. New York: Peter Lang, 2005.

Warner-Lewis, Maureen. *Guinea's Other Suns: The African Dynamic in Trinidad Culture*. Dover, MA: The Majority Press, 1991.

Weissman, Judith. "Women and Vampires: Dracula as a Victorian Novel." *Midwest Quarterly: A Journal of Contemporary Thought* 18 (1977): 392–405.

Wekker, Gloria. "Mati-ism and Black Lesbianism: Two Ideal Typical Constructions of Female Homosexuality in Black Communities of the Diaspora." 1993. Reprinted in *Journal of Lesbian Studies: Classics in Lesbian Studies*, part 1, vol. 1, no. 1 (1996): 11–24.

———. "One Finger Does Not Drink Okra Soup: Afro-Surinamese Women and Critical Agency." *Feminist Genealogies, Colonial Legacies, Democratic Futures*. Ed. M. Jacqui Alexander and Chandra Talpade Mohanty. New York: Routledge, 1997. 330–52.

White, Luise. *Speaking with Vampires: Rumor and History in Colonial Africa.* Berkeley: U of California P, 2000.

Williamson, Milly. *The Lure of the Vampire: Gender, Fiction and Fandom from Bram Stoker to Buffy*. New York: Wallflower Press, 2005.

Wisker, Gina. "Crossing Liminal Spaces: Teaching the Postcolonial Gothic." *Pedagogy* 7.3 (Fall 2007): 401–25. Accessed via Project Muse, August 21, 2012.

Wolff, Christian. "An Interview with Nalo Hopkinson." *MaComère* 4 (2001): 26–36.

Wolkstein, Diane. *The Magic Orange Tree and Other Haitian Folktales*. New York: Knopf, 1978.

Wright, Dudley. *The Book of Vampires*. New York: Causeway Books, 1973.

Wynter, Sylvia. "Afterword: Beyond Miranda's Meanings: Un/silencing the 'Demonic Ground' of Caliban's 'Woman.'" *Out of the Kumbla: Caribbean Women and Literature*. Ed. Carole Boyce Davies and Elaine Savory Fido. Trenton, NJ: Africa World Press, 1990. 355–72.

Young, Lola. *Fear of the Dark: "Race," Gender and Sexuality in the Cinema*. New York: Routledge, 1996.

Young, Robert J. C. *Colonial Desire: Hybridity in Theory, Culture and Race*. New York: Routledge, 1995.

Zaleski, Jeff, and Peter Canon. "Rev. of 'Greedy Choke Puppy,' by Nalo Hopkinson." *Publishers Weekly* 248.42 (2001): 51.

Zanger, Jules. "Metaphor into Metonymy: The Vampire Next Door." Gordon and Hollinger. 17–26.

Zimmerman, Bonnie. "Daughters of Darkness: Lesbian Vampires." *Jump Cut: A Review of Contemporary Media* 24–25 (1981): 23–24. http://www.ejump-cut.org/archive/onlinessays/JC24-25folder/LesbianVampires.html. Accessed July 31, 2014.

Zimra, Clarisse. "Righting the Calabash: Writing History in the Female Francophone Narrative." *Out of the Kumbla: Caribbean Women and Literature*. Ed. Carole Boyce Davies and Elaine Savory Fido. Trenton, NJ: Africa World Press, 1990. 143–59.

Zoboi, Ibi Aanu. "Old Flesh Song." *Dark Matter: Reading the Bones*. Book 2. New York: Warner/Aspect, 2004.

Zobel, Joseph. *Black Shack Alley*. 1950. Trans. Keith Q. Warner. Boulder, CO: Three Continents/Lynne Rienner Publishers, 1997.

Index

About the Author

Giselle Liza Anatol received her doctoral degree from the University of Pennsylvania, with a dissertation exploring representations of motherhood in Caribbean women's writing. As an associate professor of English at the University of Kansas, she currently teaches classes on Caribbean and African American literature, including a Major Authors course on Toni Morrison's fiction, and classes on literature for children and young adults. In the spring of 2011, she published *Bringing Light to Twilight: Perspectives on the Pop Culture Phenomenon*, an edited collection featuring essays from an international array of scholars. The vampire theme thus crosses over from Anatol's study of Caribbean and African diasporic literature to her work on writing for young people. Anatol has also edited two volumes of essays on J. K. Rowling's Harry Potter series—*Reading Harry Potter: Critical Essays* (2003) and *Reading Harry Potter Again: New Critical Essays* (2009)—and published numerous articles on the works of authors such as Jamaica Kincaid, Audre Lorde, Nalo Hopkinson, Derek Walcott, and Langston Hughes.